MW01122597

SILENT
NIGHT

Tara,

Welcome to Haven City.

Emma K. C. Couetta

SILENT NIGHT

Copyright © 2019 by Emma Couette

All rights reserved. This book or any portion thereof
may not be reproduced or used in any manner
whatsoever
without the express written permission of the
publisher
except for the use of brief quotations in a book review.

Printed in the United States of America

First Printing, 2019

ISBN 9781088957585

Imprint: Independently published

emmacouetteauthor.com

THE GUILD TRILOGY
BOOK ONE

SILENT
NIGHT

EMMA K. C. COUETTE

To the girl I used to be, dreaming of this moment.
You did it!
And to all those still hoping.
You can do it too. I know it.

CHAPTER ONE

Haven City, 05/2110

The stupidity of humanity never ceases to amaze me. They all must have a death wish. Well, I'll consider myself a genie, but they'll have to get in line. I already have my target for today—Lincoln McColl—and these morons have been giving me his information all morning.

Nobody suspects a thing when a young woman comes up to them in tattered clothes, crying her eyes out, saying she's from out of town, her parents just died, and she's looking for her Uncle Lincoln.

Do you know Lincoln McColl? Where does he live? Does he have a job? What time will he be home?

It works like a charm, and before I know it, I have all the information I need. People are suckers for a crying girl, even in a city like this. One day, it'll get them killed, but today is not that day. I can't say the same for Lincoln. If luck is on my side, he'll be dead by midnight and if not... Let's just say I won't be pleased. Things might get messy. You never know what the day will bring you.

I don't mind messy; it's more fun than clean. Don't get me wrong—I'm not a violent person, but I never said I was honest either. I lie to get by. I do whatever it takes, and if that means killing for a living, I'll take it over dying any day.

I continue down the street, keeping my head down and hood up. I've found the information I need, enough with catching people's attention. It's time to blend into the shadows again. I love the shadows. They're dark and mysterious, full of danger, just like me. Some people say assassins are demons from hell, spawns of Satan. I disagree.

I am a child of darkness, one with the night.

I take a right at the next street corner, following the directions given to me by a middle-aged man.

What did he say his name was again?

Bernard or something like that. His briefcase had read "Whitman."

Well, Mr. Whitman, you better hope these directions are right or you'll be next.

I walk five blocks down William Street, heading away from the heart of Haven City. The bustle of downtown shops and office buildings gives way to homes and gardens cloaked in despair. The sidewalks are cracked, the gardens full of weeds. Sometimes, I wonder what the city looked like in its glory, before the Assassin's Guild tainted its streets with malice. The rest of the time, I revel in the horror of what we've done.

I hang a left at Richard Avenue, the road sign bent and faded. According to Whitman's directions, this is the right street and Lincoln's house is the only two-story red brick, number 358.

I count the house numbers as I go, keeping an eye out for the red brick, as well as any Resistance agents I could have fun with. Sadly, I reach the house a few minutes later with nobody in sight.

This is it: a dilapidated brick building with a front porch and dying window box flowers.

Quaint.

Beside the door, the numbers three, five, and eight hang in gold-painted metal.

Satisfied, I turn around and head back down the street. I'll enter the house through the backyard.

At the corner of Richard, I turn right and head toward George Street, which runs parallel. I count the houses in my head as I walk down George, until I reach a brick bungalow that should back onto Lincoln's property.

I don't check to see if anyone is looking before I make my way across the front lawn. It's better to act like you belong and get seen, than to look like you shouldn't be there. I should know. I've learned from experience and have bluffed my way through situations on more than one occasion, though not in recent months. I've never been caught. That's why I'm one of the best, though it's not the only reason.

When I reach the back gate, I hop it with ease and stroll to the back fence. I climb over it, landing like a cat in Lincoln's flower bed.

Tulips. How nice.

I straighten and head towards the back porch.

The back door is locked, but no matter. I reach into my hair and pull out two bobby pins. I shove both into the lock and, after a couple of expert twists, the bolt slides over with a click. Smiling, I replace the pins in my hair and turn the knob. The door swings open without a sound and I slip inside, shutting it behind me with a soft thud.

The interior of the house is unimpressive with its fake wooden floors, dull paint choices, and minimal decoration. The kitchen is cluttered with dishes, though there isn't much food in the cupboards or fridge.

There are a few pictures on the mantelpiece in the living room. One is of a brown-haired, blue-eyed man of average height, presumably Lincoln. The other is of the same man with a blonde woman at his side. She must be his wife, though by the look of the kitchen, I guess she's been gone for a while.

There's nothing else of interest on the main floor, so after checking for a basement and finding no sign of one, I head upstairs. The fifth stair creaks. I make a note of that for later. The landing leads to a hallway and I creep down it, counting my steps and checking for any more loose floorboards. I'm disappointed when I find none.

Squeaky floorboards always make for an interesting story, always point the finger in my direction after a murder. A house full of creaks and groans makes it impossible for an assassin to go undetected, unless of course, that assassin is me.

There are four doors in the upstairs hall. One leads to a nasty-looking bathroom. I linger long enough to catch a glimpse of myself in the cracked and grungy mirror. My hair is growing too long for my liking and the black is showing through the blue in my bangs again.

I sigh and then scold myself.

Now is not the time.

I leave the bathroom behind. The other three rooms upstairs must be bedrooms and I have to inspect each one before I go.

I open the first door on my right. Boxes and old furniture fill the small space. In the corner sits an old metal box I recognize only from stories I've been told. Nobody in Haven has watched television since before the war. It strikes me as odd that Lincoln would have one.

I poke my nose into a few of the cardboard boxes. There isn't anything of value in them. One is full of miscellaneous items: markers, cutlery, and keys. It's strange. Two others are crammed full of newspapers, dating back forty years. Then, four more boxes overflowing with women's clothes, shoes, and jewelry. They must be his wife's belongings. I pick up a necklace with a name engraved in it: *Margaret*. That would make them Lincoln and Margaret McColl.

How lovely.

I drop the necklace into the box and leave the room. I won't find anything here.

The next room is a guest room. It's sparsely furnished with only a nightstand and a bed. It's painted a dark grey.

Very depressing.

I suppose this is the room Lincoln would've offered to his "niece."

Too bad she isn't real.
I move on.

The last room at the end of the hall is Lincoln's, but for a master bedroom, it's rather disappointing. The single bed is pushed up against one wall, opposite the two windows. There is no closet, only a chest of drawers, and clothes litter the floor, enough that I can't tell whether it's hardwood or carpet.

In the far corner is a desk and I navigate around the piles of clothes to reach it, careful not to disturb them, though I doubt Lincoln would be able to tell the difference. I bet his wife wouldn't approve of this mess. Again, I wonder how long she's been gone, but I'm not paid to wonder. I'm paid to get results. I turn my mind back to the task at hand.

The desk is a paper war zone. Sheets are torn in half, scribbled over, and a whole pile lies shredded. A lot of the papers bear his name.

What are you trying to hide, Lincoln? Don't you know nothing gets past us?

I guess I won't be collecting much evidence tonight, though I check the desk drawers for anything he might have left intact. The first three are empty, but the last one is locked.

Bingo.

I pull out my bobby pins again and have the drawer open in seconds. Inside is a white envelope. It lays unmarked save for the plain red seal.

Interesting.

6

I know without a doubt that this is what I need.

Satisfied, I replace the envelope and lock the drawer again. I'll retrieve the envelope tonight after I'm done. I walk out of the room without leaving a single trace of my presence behind.

I return to the storage room and unlock the window, making sure it opens. This will be my entry point tonight. There is no way Lincoln will notice it's unlocked and he has no reason to check it. If he does lock it again for some reason, I know I can pick the lock on the back door. No matter how hard he tries to keep me out, I'm getting in tonight.

I go back downstairs and lock the back door before heading out the front. I walk down the front steps like I own the place, ready to spout my niece story if need be, but the street is empty.

Too bad.

With a resigned sigh, I flip up my hood and start down the street. It's time to head home and give my report. The Charger will be eager to learn what I have found.

CHAPTER TWO

The streets in the south end of Haven City are quiet; some would say dead. I say silence is sometimes louder than noise, but no one else understands. I hear the silence like a slow beating drum when I advance on my victims, drowning out their heartbeat until it stops.

Silence presses in on people in their weakest moments, its sound rendering them deaf to what they want to hear, but I've long since learned how to push back, to mold that silence into something I can use. I've made silence my own, so now when I walk down these streets, the quiet cacophony of them does not deter me. I saunter towards the lion's den.

People stay clear of this side of Haven. Some remember the rebels who once owned these streets, but all fear the assassins the rebels left behind. The war was not kind to this city and neither are we. People can sense our presence. They see it in the abandoned bungalows with ripped curtains and unkempt lawns. They see it in the buildings turned to rubble, red staining the dusty remains. They feel it in the silence, in the emptiness. Nothing thrives here except for the destruction we create. No one has confirmed the suspicion that the dreaded Assassin's Guild calls these streets home, but they aren't willing to take that chance.

The truth is, the assassins don't live *on* the streets but *beneath* them, in a warren of passageways, caves, and caverns. The houses of the south end are only used as access points to our lair, though some hold no connection at all. The Charger is the only assassin who knows the location of every entrance and exit. Most assassins are given one or two. I know of twenty, but that's one of the perks of being in the higher ranks.

I go several streets out of my way, down dead-end alleyways, through overgrown backyards, and under bridges to shake off any possible pursuers. Even an assassin can't be too careful, especially in a city crawling with Resistance agents, despite our efforts to pare them down.

Eventually, I come to the abandoned house that is my usual entrance, a small brick bungalow on a corner lot.

As it should be, the door is unlocked, and I push it open. I listen for the sounds of any trespassers: scavengers, city outsiders, or other assassins. I hear no one and head down to the basement.

The basement is finished, but neglected, and I walk through it to the back bedroom. I cross the room and step into the closet. In the corner, under a pile of clothes, lies a trapdoor. I crouch down and pull it open with one hand;

it's lighter than it looks. Nothing but darkness lies beyond it. I listen once again for company and hear nothing.

It's safe.

Holding onto the trapdoor with one hand, I step into the hole, my foot landing on a ladder rung. I drop the other foot down and descend into the gloom, pulling the door behind me. When the door shuts, it cuts off all light, but I am not afraid. Only weak people fear the dark.

The shaft I climb down is about five meters deep and I land on the ground a few moments later. Though it is dark, I know I'm in a tunnel. I brought a lantern with me the first time and memorized every feature. I haven't brought a light since.

I head down the tunnel a hundred paces before light spills into the space. A single light bulb hangs from the dirt ceiling, illuminating a door and a buttoned panel beside it. I type in the code and enter the elevator. Darkness once again reigns as I descend.

The elevator journey is only two and a half minutes, but it seems like forever before the box slows down and hits the ground with a muffled bang. The doors open automatically and I step out. Another lonely bulb illuminates a second tunnel. I continue down it without a backward glance.

This is where the journey becomes dangerous, not for me, but for any non-assassin who is lucky enough to make it this far. I count my steps as I go. After ten, the tunnel widens and in twenty more, it opens up into a huge cavern, though you can't tell in the dark. Anybody who shouldn't be here would continue straight and walk right off of a cliff, free falling into an underground lake full of jagged rocks. I keep to the left, following a ledge hugging the cavern wall. The tunnel continues fifty paces later.

Five minutes after that, the tunnel turns sharply to the right and I can see again. Every few feet along the ceiling is a light bulb, all the way to the end of the tunnel where a ladder carved into the wall ascends upward into a dark shaft. I ascend and reach up to push open the trapdoor, just enough to see through.

I peer into the hallway above. No one is in sight. I listen for footsteps heading my way but hear nothing.

Satisfied, I push the heavy door up the rest of the way and slide it over gently so the tile doesn't scrape against the floor and announce my presence. I climb out of the shaft into the bright hall and slide the trapdoor back into place. Nobody would ever guess the tile is an entrance to our lair; even I can't find it once it's been replaced, which is why it's only an entry point, not an exit.

I dust myself off and look around. I'm back into the Guild proper, though there's no one to be seen. I don't let that bother me as I continue on my way.

I navigate the hallways and dark corridors of the Assassin's Guild with the ease of someone who's memorized every inch of the place. I could get anywhere in my sleep. Soon, I hear the familiar noises of the Guild: yelling, small conversations, and the satisfying clack of

11

weapons meeting as I pass by one of the countless training rooms.

I allow myself a small sigh. This is home, but now is not the time to lose myself in the charms of the place. I have a mission to complete.

I go a little out of my way in order to bypass the Grand Cavern, our wide open gathering place where we can do anything and everything we want. It's at the centre of the underground compound and you can see all the training rooms from its floor, as all of them have glass walls facing the cavern. I usually spend time there after missions, but I'm not done yet. The Charger is waiting for my report.

I walk faster, eager to get it over with. Like many of the assassins, I don't enjoy spending time with the Charger. He is King of us all and has murdered more people than we could ever dream of. His soul is as dark as they come and he's the only common thing we all fear. None of us would ever dare cross him, which is why I don't want to be late.

Ten minutes later, after a route that sends me doubling back several times, I head down a hall cloaked in darkness. Only thirty assassins, out of the hundreds living here, actually know where the Charger's office is. I'm included in the few who receive missions from him personally and am required to report back to him face to face. The others receive envelopes shoved under the doors of their quarters, depicting the details of their missions, and they send back written reports.

I dreaded the written reports in the past, but now I often wish I could go back to them. The Charger gives me chills and after being in his presence, I can't shake off the feeling of dread for hours, but I fare better than others. Agent Ten wouldn't speak or leave his room for a whole week after he met the Charger. Three years later, and now Agent Six, he still shuts himself in his room for five hours after he gives his report.

Some people are so weak.

I reach the end of the hall then. Two assassins in black stand on either side of the Charger's door. Their job is such a joke; as if the King of Assassins needs bodyguards. He could probably kill any intruder with his eyes closed and both hands tied behind his back. Yet, the guards still stop me and ask me my name and business. I suppress the urge to pull a knife and gut them.

I keep my expression neutral as I say, "Don't be a fool. You know who I am, and you also know how quickly I can make you disappear. So, I suggest you drop the act and let me in. The Charger doesn't like to be kept waiting."

Threats in the Assassin's Guild aren't usually alarming, as we are all skilled killers. However, I'm more known among the citizens of Haven City and every assassin is aware I'm almost as lethal as the Charger. The guards don't test me further and let me through.

I knock on the door and a dark voice says, "Come in."

I push the door open and step into the Charger's office. A single lamp illuminates the space and the Charger sits behind a tall oak desk opposite the door, almost blending into the shadows with his black fatigues and dark skin.

The room around him seems to breathe and I try not to think about the stack of skulls shelved on the left wall where the light can't reach. I try not to think about the eyes watching me from the darkness or about the blood-red carpet beneath my boots. It used to be white, once upon a time.

The Charger smiles as I enter, all teeth and no eyes, like neither are aware of the other's agenda. There is warmth in that smile, but it's an inferno, something to keep an eye on, lest it swallow you whole. Every time I see that smile, I understand why the people named him Black Death.

He smiles his evil smile and says, "Hello, Silent Night. I've been expecting you."

CHAPTER THREE

I try to keep the trembling out of my voice as I answer. "I came as soon as I could."

"Of course," he drawls, leaning back in his chair. His height is not at all diminished by the act. "What did you find?"

I take a deep breath to calm my racing heart and say, "I found his security lacking for a start. He will be an easy target. I already have an entrance and escape route."

He nods and crosses his arms, showing off the various tattoos painting his dark skin. A black snake coils around his right forearm and his left hand is covered in unknown symbols. Some say he has a tally of his kills on his back, but I don't believe it. There wouldn't be enough room.

"What of evidence?" he asks.

I force a smile. "The desk was covered in shredded paper, a poorly-constructed distraction. I found an envelope locked in a desk drawer. It was sealed, but had nothing written on it."

The Charger's black eyes gleam. "Excellent, you have performed well."

I bow my head. "Thank you."

He is quiet for a minute and I stand there, waiting patiently. You do not leave a meeting with the Charger before he dismisses you, not if you value your life. Many assassins learn that the hard way.

Finally, he speaks again. "There's one more thing. I have a mission for you this afternoon. I would send someone else, seeing as you're working on another assignment, but this job requires your *special* skills."

I beam a little inside. "Certainly," I reply. "What is the task?"

"I need someone followed. We have a traitor in our midst. She's been giving information to the enemy. That does not sit well with me, as you can imagine."

We have another traitor?

There have been countless of them in our history, at least a dozen in my time here. They all died gruesome deaths. I don't understand how anyone could still consider it worth the risk.

"It does not sit well with me either," I say. "Who is the suspect?"

"Agent Eleven," he replies and I nod. I know her as Rachel. To the Charger, she is just another nameless face in the crowd. She's not famous enough to warrant a public name like me, but she *is* skilled enough to hold the eleventh spot on the assassin list.

"She has a scheduled outing today at one o'clock," the Charger continues. "See where she goes and with whom

16

she speaks. Report back to me as soon as you both return. I want this dealt with before it gets out of hand."

"Of course, I'll see it is done."

"Good. I expect the Lincoln report tomorrow at nine." I nod and he says, "You may go."

I bow and take my leave.

I say nothing to the guards as I walk past them, not trusting my voice after my brief encounter with the Charger. I'm not pleased about this other mission either, because it means speaking with him twice in one day. I try to shake off my unease as I make my way to the Grand Cavern to cool down before my next excursion. It's noon, so I have an hour.

The sounds of shouting and cursing grow louder the closer I get. I smile.

Oh, the sounds of home.

The Cavern is bustling when I arrive. Assassins are sparring over territorial issues, bragging about their latest exploits, and swapping black market products.

The Charger heads Haven City's black market as well as its assassins, though the Resistance believes the black market to be a separate enemy, one to vanquish in their spare time.

Idiots.

I talk to no one as I make my way through the crowd to my usual spot, snagging a lunch tray off an occupied table on my way. Today is chicken, fries, and water. My spot is in the far corner of the enormous room where a grey boulder sits in the shadow of the mezzanine above. It's quiet and dark there; I love the privacy it offers.

I sit down on the rock and observe the other assassins milling around the room as I nibble on a fry. Some of them gathered around one table are talking and laughing, but I see through the façade. None of them are true friends.

Assassins don't have the compassion for friendship. We'll laugh at your jokes one day and stab you in the back with a fork the next, if it suits us. We're all bloodthirsty and cutthroat. We're all after the coveted Agent One spot and we'll do whatever it takes to get there, even if it means leaving our so-called "friends" in unmarked graves behind us.

The Charger encourages ruthlessness and there is no punishment for maiming or killing a fellow assassin. If they were stupid enough to trust you, they deserve what they got. I've killed plenty of my own in order to get where I am now, but I also work hard and execute missions with unparalleled precision. You don't get to be Agent Two by sitting on your butt all day.

I spend the majority of my lunch scanning the room for Rachel and I don't take my eyes off of her once I find her. I finish eating just as she does and mirror her as she stands up. She heads to the doors at the far side of the Cavern and I follow her, weaving my way through the crowd without anyone so much as glancing in my direction. I smile.

Silent as death itself.

I trace her through the halls of the Guild as she makes her way towards an unknown exit. She looks back once to see if she's being followed, but I have already melted into the shadows.

This is going to be fun.

Finally, she heads down a staircase and I know we're nearing a secret path. Sure enough, she ducks under the stairs at the bottom and, a minute later when I take a look, she's disappeared. I wait another minute before I follow her through the trapdoor. I descend a ladder into a tunnel lit with bulbs every few feet and watch her shadow turn a corner. I trail after her.

I manage to avoid the enemy traps as we make our way through the underground and I'm still in one piece when we emerge into the outside world via a second trapdoor. We come out into a barn and I wait in the corner as she scans the field outside for any signs of life. When she's sure it's safe, she slips out the door. It's too bad the real danger—me—was inside with her and not far behind now.

As I would have done, she takes a difficult, roundabout route through the city outskirts to shake off any pursuers, but she doesn't do a thorough job and I have no trouble keeping up. She checks behind her often, but never catches me before I duck into an empty doorway or dark alley. When we get closer to downtown Haven, it becomes much easier to hide amongst the bustle of people, but a lot harder to keep track of her. Try as she might, she doesn't lose me.

After an hour of pointless detours and seeing the same empty grocers and faded dollar stores multiple times, she approaches a dilapidated office building. Vinyl siding hangs from its walls in places and the steel roof is rusted. I watch from across the street as she ascends the steps and disappears inside.

This is it. It's time to see what our little traitor has been up to.

I stalk up to the building and slip inside. It doesn't take me long to locate Rachel again and resume the chase. She goes up one flight of stairs and stops in the middle of a long hall. I duck behind a nearby garbage bin and stand stock still as I peer around it.

Her eyes flick up and down the hall, but don't land on me. After one more glance, she goes up to a door on the right and knocks on it—three taps. From my spot, I can just make out the name scrawled across the door: Avery. Rachel stands with her hands behind her back, shifting from foot to foot as she waits.

A few moments later, the door opens and a man that must be Avery walks out. He's a hulking man with dark skin and hair, dressed in a light grey suit. The suit makes him seem small and I get the sense that he does not enjoy being confined to it.

"Rachel?" he says. "What brings you here?"

"I have news," she replies, "but nothing I'll discuss out here in the open." Her voice is tight.

"Surely this place is secure enough," Avery says.

She takes a deep breath. "Fine," she replies through gritted teeth. After yet another fruitless glance around the hall, she walks up to Avery and rises on her tiptoes to whisper in his ear.

His eyes go wide. "Are you sure?"

"Positive," she assures him.

"Well then, you're right. We better continue this discussion behind closed doors. Come in, come in." He ushers her inside the office and his eyes search the hall before he pulls the door closed.

Interesting.

The Charger will be pleased to hear what I have found.

Rachel is in Avery's office for half an hour. Then, it takes her another hour to return to the trapdoor in the barn. She doesn't go anywhere else, but she seems nervous, constantly checking behind her. Not once does she see me. I trail her all the way back into the Guild to the staircase and then I turn down another hall as she goes up the stairs.

A job well done, if I do say so myself.

I pull my pocket watch out of my coat: three thirty. I still have hours before I leave to dispatch McColl and I decide to train until dinner, after I report back to the Charger. For the second time today, I head toward his office in the darkened hall.

I should get a medal for this.

I'm stopped at the door by the guards again, new ones this time. The shift changed at noon. Again, I am asked my name and business. I scowl at the guards.

"I am *so* not in the mood for this," I say as I make to push past them. One of them grabs my arm and throws me back. I stumble, but remain on my feet, letting out a growl of annoyance.

"I *said*, state your name and business," the violent one repeats, though he knows very well who I am. I know who he is too. He's Agent Four, also known as Anane, also known as a pain in my ass.

"Get out of my way, Anane."

"Or what," he challenges, "you'll gut me?" He smirks and I ignore every urge to punch him right in his chiselled jaw. Such arrogance does not deserve such beauty.

Instead, I smile. "No," I reply, "I'll skin you alive." He shrugs and I scowl. "Don't think that I won't."

"Whatever," he says, brushing his black hair out of his eyes. "Your threats don't scare me, Two. We both know who would win if it came down to a fight."

"I'm glad you've accepted your fate."

He bristles–that isn't what he meant–but before he can retort, I push past him and into the office.

Jerk.

He's still upset a girl nine years his junior has surpassed him. Well, he can get used to it; I'm not going anywhere.

"Hello again," the Charger says, and the same chill from before runs down my spine. "What took you so long?"

He has more lights on this time and I can see every detail of the room. Hollow eyes watch me from their perch and my skin crawls.

I avert my gaze from his trophy skulls and say, "She led me all over the city, trying to shake off any pursuers, which of course didn't deter me in the least. However, it took us an hour to reach her destination."

"I see, and what was that destination?"

"A three-story office building on Charles Avenue, number 1253."

"Very good. Who did she see?"

"She didn't call him by name, but Avery was written on his door. I can't be sure if it's a first name, last name, or an alias."

"First name and alias," the Charger says.

I fight to keep my shock from showing. "You know him?"

He nods. "All too well, I'm afraid. We go back a long way, Avery and I. I know him well enough to be certain the office you speak of will be vacant in an hour or so, without any sign he was ever there. He's probably packing up now. Still, I shall send someone to apprehend him if they can. When you go, send Agents Three and Four in, would you?"

"Of course."

"Did you hear anything the two said?"

I shake my head. "Rachel refused to tell him anything out in the open, but when he persuaded her, she was cautious enough to whisper it in his ear. Whatever she said convinced him that the conversation should be held in the office."

"Naturally," he sighs. "Anything else?"

"Nothing of value," I reply. "She was there for thirty minutes and then she led me around Haven for another hour before returning."

"Very well," he says. "We didn't learn much, but at least the traitor has been confirmed."

"How shall we deal with her?"

"The usual way," he replies. "You know where to bring her."

I nod and he dismisses me.

I give Anane a push on my way out. "The Charger would like to see the both of you," I say. Then I disappear down the hall in search of Rachel.

So much for training.

It only takes me ten minutes to locate Rachel's room. All assassins are required to keep their number posted on the chalkboard hanging from their doorknob. When we move up or down a rank, we have to erase the number and write a new one. We're given a new list every other Sunday. The top ten spots don't change often. I've been Agent Two for six months. Hai has been Agent One for seven years. It's the numbers past thirty that are always shifting.

I knock on Rachel's door and she answers it after a minute, opening it an inch and peering out.

Fool.

If I wanted her dead, all I have to do is stick a sword through the gap right into her skull. Lucky for her, the Charger doesn't want her dead, not by my hand anyway.

"Who are you and what do you want?" she asks, irritated.

"Agent Two," I reply and her eyes go wide. "The Charger wants you to come with me."

Her expression goes from shock to panic in less than a second. She turns and slams the door behind her, but my knife is already wedged in the gap. I discard the broken blade and fling the door open.

I dodge the first and second blow she deals me with her sword and block the third with my own sword that I somehow manage to draw between opening the door and needing to use it. Our duel begins in earnest and she fights me off, but I'm far more disciplined than she is. I could do this in my sleep.

I catch her off guard with a swipe at her face. While she spits out blood, I draw my gun with my free hand and shoot her in the foot. She drops like a stone, screaming. She doesn't try to fight back as I lean over her.

"Stupid girl," I say. "You know better than to fight me. Don't you know who I am?"

"Yes," she gasps through the pain. "You're a *brat*."

"Wrong answer," I chide and slam the pommel of my sword into her head.

She is much easier to deal with unconscious, I'll give her that. While she's under, I remove all the weapons from her person: two guns, three daggers, a vial of belladonna, and the sword she still clutches in her hand. Then I peel off her coat, roll her over, and snap cuffs around her wrists and ankles. Blood trickles from her shot foot. I tear a strip off the blanket from her bed and bind the wound. We wouldn't want her dying before the show.

I grab one of her own knives next and cut her hair. Several bobby pins fall to the floor with the brown locks. Then I sit on the bed as I wait for her to come to. It shouldn't be long; I didn't hit her that hard.

Sure enough, she coughs a minute later and tries to sit up. That's when she notices the handcuffs and the hair on the floor.

"What did you do?" she gasps.

"What I had to. You shouldn't have betrayed us, Eleven."

"I... I don't know what you're talking about," she stammers.

"No? Well, I'm sure Avery does; do you want us to bring him in for questioning?"

She stiffens at his name. "No," she whispers. "I was *sure* I hadn't been followed."

I laugh. "I know, you tried so hard, but I'm one of the best. Didn't they tell you?"

"It was *you*?"

"Of course. I am the executioner, am I not? Now, enough questions. It's time to go."

I grab her by the back of her shirt and drag her out the door, her body supported by her heels and my arm. She squirms and kicks, but my grip is iron. Still, she tries to escape her fate. She knows what is coming. She's seen it happen enough times to fear it.

26

I head toward the Grand Cavern, passing countless rooms full of assassins as I go. They take one look at my charge and smile like feral animals before joining my trek.

Soon, I am being followed by an entourage of bloodthirsty assassins. You can feel the bloodlust in the air, so thick you can almost reach out and touch it. Rachel cannot hold back her tears now. The other assassins smile at her weakness.

I keep my expression neutral as I march through the entrance to the Grand Cavern. All eyes turn to face me and the room grows hushed. I drag Rachel to the centre of the room where the tables give way to wide open space. The assassins gather hungrily around us.

"Traitor!" one shouts.

Another echoes him and it soon becomes a chant.

"Trai-tor! Trai-tor! Trai-tor!"

I come to a stop and the room goes quiet again in anticipation. Without taking my eyes off of the crowd, I unlock Rachel's shackles. They fall to the ground with a clank that resounds in the silence.

The energy in the room builds to a crescendo. I drop Rachel's shirt collar and run. Still, I have to fight my way through the crowd as they rush towards the traitor, wanting to be the first to tear her to pieces.

CHAPTER FOUR

Hours later, I'm sitting on the edge of my bed in the dark. The only light is from the occasional sparks flying off the blade I'm sharpening. I scrape it against the whetstone methodically, letting myself get lost in the familiar motion. I can still hear the snarls of the crowd and Agent Eleven's screams. I shudder and drop the knife into the growing pile beside me.

I reach for my gun next. Readying my weapons for tonight has brought me back to normal, has pushed any guilt away. I find sharpening blades and cleaning guns to be soothing. I tell myself to forget Eleven. There's no use mourning a traitor.

Sighing, I stand up and strap on my weapons. It's ten thirty, time to get this show on the road.

My swords go in twin shoulder sheaths, creating an X across my back. Two long daggers find homes in my boots. My guns go in holsters, one on each hip, locked and loaded. A handful of throwing knives dangle from my belt with a few more in my coat and a dagger up each sleeve. I grab a few vials of poison off of my dresser as an extra precaution and slip them into an outside pocket.

I'm ready.

I leave my room, locking the door behind me. I shove the key into my coat and head down the hall. My boots don't make a sound, my presence unnoticed in the dark. They don't call me Silent Night for nothing.

As I make my way to a secret exit, my thoughts turn back to the traitor. I heard from the other assassins that she killed five of us before being struck down; it's impressive, seeing as I stripped her of her weapons and shot her in the foot, but even traitors don't give up. They fight until their last breath, hoping to leave whatever mark they can.

In addition to the lives she ended, we lost twenty others; those who participate usually turn on each other in their thirst for blood. I killed a couple myself, but it was only to carve a path out of the crowd, self-defence so to speak. I always keep a level head during the massacre and never much enjoyed being an animal like the rest, which is why the Charger appointed me as the executioner. I apprehend the traitors and drag them to their demise, taking great pride in my position.

I emerge from the tunnels into a basement much like the one I entered through this morning, but across the street. I listen for company before slipping out of the bedroom. Upstairs, I linger at the window, scanning the street outside through the tattered curtains. Nothing moves in the black beyond the house, so I take my leave, down the front steps and across the lawn to the street. It's eleven o'clock.

• • •

It takes me thirty minutes to reach the house that backs onto Lincoln's. I strut across the lawn, then hop the gate and back fence when I come to them. Unfortunately, I land in a rosebush this time and I hiss in annoyance as the thorns prick me.

Sucking on my cut thumb, I brush the dirt off of my clothes and walk towards the house. It won't be hard to reach the second-story window; all I have to do is climb onto the back porch roof.

I stretch my arms and legs and pull on my easy grip gloves. Then, I put up my hood and, wrapping one hand around the post holding up the porch, hoist myself up. My legs curl around the wood and I start climbing.

A few seconds later, I pull myself onto the roof without a sound. I'm not even breathing heavy. This whole mission is effortless. Why couldn't a lower-ranking assassin have done it?

I creep past Lincoln's bedroom window to the storage room. Then I pull the window open and throw one leg over the sill. The room is dark and my every breath seems to echo in the silence.

The moment my second foot touches the floor and I pull the rest of my body through, I know something is wrong. My skin prickles as my blood goes cold. I grab for a knife, but then something slams into my head.

• • •

The first thing I do when I come to is reach for my knife again, but whoever knocked me out was clever enough to handcuff my hands around the back of a bedpost. I scowl and look up, into the terrified eyes of none other than Lincoln McColl. I recognize him from the picture on the downstairs mantel.

"Well, well," I drawl. "I didn't think you would have it in you. You should be quite proud of yourself. Not many people can say they've caught the legendary Silent Night. In fact, you're the first."

"For someone in chains, you're incredibly arrogant," he replies.

I shrug. "It's part of my charm."

"I could kill you at any second."

"Yes, but you probably won't."

"And what makes you say that?"

I give him a look. "If you wanted me dead, Lincoln, we wouldn't be having this conversation. So tell me, what *do* you want from me?"

He huffs a laugh. "Clever girl," he says. "You're right. I don't want you dead. I need to tell you something."

I raise an eyebrow. "Why me?"

"You're the only one who would care."

"What makes you say that?"

"You'll understand when you read the letter."

"What…"

He holds up an envelope, the same envelope I found in his desk drawer this morning.

My eyes widen. "How did you…?"

"What else would your master want from me? I've been waiting for him to send someone since I found the damned thing two weeks ago. As soon as I came home this afternoon and found that window unlocked, I knew today was the day. I spent the evening preparing, knowing I would only have one chance at this."

"One chance at what?" I demand to know. "What is going on here?" My voice is raised, but I don't care. I might be at his mercy, but I'm not afraid to die. If he doesn't kill me, the Charger will. Getting caught by your target is a death sentence.

"One chance to give you the letter," Lincoln replies.

"I was going to take it anyway," I protest, "why go to all of this trouble? If you're trying to save your life, I can tell you it's futile."

"No, I know that no matter what I say or do, you're still going to kill me. I've accepted that." His eyes are sad. "What I can't accept, is the way Haven City is falling to pieces. I can't accept the Master Assassin's cruelty and I know you won't accept it either, once you learn the truth. So give this to your master," he finishes, holding up the envelope, "and take *this* for yourself."

He reaches into his pocket and pulls out a second envelope. "This is an exact copy."

"Why me?" I ask again.

"Because I know you, Ms. Ballinger, and you won't stand for what's written in this letter."

Anger flares inside of me and I'm out of my chains in seconds. I shoot to my feet and, before he can blink, my knife is against his throat.

Fool to think chains could hold me, a complete and utter fool.

Escaping handcuffs is the first thing they teach at the Guild and I've been waiting for the right time to reveal his mistake.

"Who told you my name?" I ask him, fighting to keep a semblance of calm.

He shakes his head.

I press the knife down harder. *"Who told you my name?"* I growl.

"No one. I... I knew your m-mother," he stutters.

"Liar!"

"No! I swear it's the truth."

I pull the blade back a bit. "Explain yourself."

"There's nothing else, I just knew her and I thought..."

"You thought *what*?" I snarl. "You thought that because she was my mother, because *she* was a nice person that *I* would be too? You thought I would help you?"

Tears pool in Lincoln's eyes. "What... What happened to that cute little girl who used to help her mother plant tulips in the front garden?"

I stiffen at the memory his words resurface.

He knows too much.

"She died a long time ago," I reply. Then I slit his throat.

Lincoln crashes to the ground with nothing but a wet gurgle escaping his lips. I write my name on the wall with the blood dripping from my fingers: Silent Night. I wipe what's left on the window curtains.

I pry the two envelopes out of Lincoln's stiffening hands and stuff them in my coat. Then I sheathe my knife and without another glance at Lincoln, I leave the bedroom behind. I head downstairs and out the front door, checking my watch once more before disappearing into the night: twelve o'clock.

• • •

I wasn't always called Silent Night. I had a real name once, one people have long since forgotten. When I first joined the Guild, I was referred to simply as Agent. You don't get a cool name until the people fear you enough to give you one, so I worked hard to build my reputation.

I became known as an assassin who killed without sound, someone you never knew was coming, until it was much too late. People swapped stories of my murders, though they each had different names for me at first, names like Dead Quiet, Dark Silence, and Invisible Death.

Then someone came up with Silent Night and it stuck.

I've been told it was once the title of a song, a song about hope and happiness and salvation. Now, whenever people hear it, they shudder, knowing I bring despair and sorrow and damnation. Silent Night is the perfect name and I've called myself nothing else since. Even *I* had almost forgotten my true name, until that bastard McColl brought it up.

Silent Night is a perfect match. You never hear or see me coming. I'm silent as a wraith, dark as night. The only sign of my presence is my name scrawled across the walls in my victims' blood.

• • •

I wake up at dawn the next day and assess the damage. There is a bump on my head from whatever was used to knock me out and bruising around my wrists from the cuffs. No one will see the bump, but the bruises will be harder to hide, even though I always wear long sleeves. Wrists are almost guaranteed to be exposed when you stretch your arm out, which I will have to do when I hand that wretched envelope to the Charger, the envelope whose oh-so-important contents led to my capture.

I don't know what Lincoln was playing at, but I'm not about to join his little game. Still, I slipped the copy of the envelope under my mattress last night while the original stayed stuffed in the pocket of my coat. I'll have to give it to the Charger in a few hours when I give my report. Until then, I must put all my effort into making it look like I wasn't caught last night; otherwise this report will be my last. The Charger will kill me on sight, even though I still succeeded in my mission.

I wash my face and hands first and then work with concealer creams, slowly trying to mask the purplish bruises around my wrists. When I'm satisfied they look as close as they can to my skin colour, I dig in my closet for a coat with the longest sleeves I can find. Then I down a couple of pain pills for my headache.

What in the Guild did he hit me with?

I ignore my own question and focus on my next course of action. I need to go to breakfast and come up with a good cover story. I have to be ready for anything.

I arm myself with six daggers and a vial of poison as assurance. If it comes to it, I'll kill myself, rather than let the Charger torture me to death. I'd do anything other than put myself at his mercy.

After breakfast and a nerve-wracking wait, I find myself, once again, standing outside the Charger's office. The guards let me in without a hassle this time and I step into the office just as the clock behind his desk chimes nine. Right on time.

"Silent Night," the Charger says, "it pleases me to see your lovely face again. I trust you had no trouble last night?"

"None at all," I lie. "Mr. McColl was sleeping like a baby. Now he's experiencing a much deeper sleep." I smile my own evil assassin smile and he returns it.

"Excellent," he replies. "I knew you would not fail me. Now, the envelope if you please. You did get it, didn't you?"

"Of course, I would hardly be standing here if I hadn't."

"Smart girl."

I reach inside my coat for the envelope and hold it out to him. I forget how to breathe as I wait for him to notice the bruising, wait for him to notice that the creams don't quite match the tone of my skin, but he grabs the envelope without even glancing at my wrists and I let myself relax.

He studies the envelope. "You were right," he mutters. "There's no return address and you haven't broken the seal." He looks up at me. "Good girl."

"I wouldn't dream of tampering with it," I assure him. "My life means too much to me."

"Of course," he replies. "We wouldn't want the executioner to become the victim now would we?"

I try not to let my fear show. "No, that would be...unfortunate."

He laughs. "You are a true assassin, Silent Night. I don't know why you're still Agent Two."

My heart skips a beat.

Did he just compliment me?

"I..." I stammer. "What do you mean?"

He smiles, a genuine smile this time. "I mean that you're one kill away from securing that top spot: Hai himself."

"Agent One?" I can hardly breathe. "What are you saying?"

The Charger leans back in his chair. "Oh, I'm not saying anything, but if he were to be found dead tomorrow, well, I wouldn't be too terribly upset." He grins and I return it.

"Right, and if I were to become Agent One tomorrow, I wouldn't be terribly upset either."

"You've got it."

"May I ask the reason for this sudden indifference?"

He shrugs. "I may or may not have grown tired of him. I may or may not think he doesn't have what it takes. Strength of mind and body is what I value, Silent Night, and you may or may not have a lot of it."

"Thank you, I think."

He smiles. "You may go now and remember: I may or may not be counting on you."

I walk out of the office smiling from ear to ear. I have my next mission, kill Hai and rise to the top like I've wanted to do for years. I will be one of the youngest assassins to reach Agent One, second only to the legendary Kuen.

I'm only eighteen and Hai is thirty, but I should have no trouble overpowering him. The older assassins grow lazy and make mistakes.

I admire the Charger's strategy in asking me to take out Hai. He's not supposed to send us on missions to kill each other, unless we're dealing with a rogue assassin, but this is something I've been planning for a while now anyway. Hai is as good as dead.

• • •

That night, as I'm preparing for my next assassination, one that will secure for me everything I've ever wanted, everything I've spent my entire life working towards, my thoughts drift toward the unopened envelope under my mattress. I can't help but wonder what's in it. Lincoln had been so adamant I read it.

Why me though? How am I any different than the other assassins? What did Lincoln know?

The more I consider it, the more I want to find out. I *need* to know what's inside. I promise myself that whatever it is, it won't change my course, but it'll put my mind at rest. I tell myself I'm not doing it for Lincoln. I'm doing it to satisfy my own curiosity.

I walk over to my bed and lift up the mattress, pulling the envelope out from under it with my free hand. I tear it open, taking care not to rip the contents.

I start reading and my heart drops into my stomach. It isn't a letter at all. It's a list of assassins and their kills. I see my name countless times as I flip through the pages. It doesn't take me long to figure out that these are just the assassinations they've solved.

The list doesn't strike me as something important for the Charger to have. He *knows* who killed who. He assigned the missions to us.

What possible purpose could Lincoln have had for giving me a copy?

I don't understand, so I study the list closer.

Robert Jameson, farmer. Assassinated by Agent Thirty One, pitchfork to the stomach.

Alani Clarke, teacher. Assassinated by Agent Four, dagger to the throat.

Donte and Amiya Solarin, Resistance agents. Assassinated by Pyro. Killed in the fire that took their house.

Richard Cole, baker. Assassinated by Agent Twelve...

I stop reading when my shaking hands blur the words beyond recognition. My heart thunders in my chest like a war drum.

This isn't just a list of victims and killers. This is also a list of who the victims *were*. They weren't all Resistance members.

Half of the names on the pages once belonged to innocent civilians who had nothing to do with the silent but deadly war between the Guild and the Resistance.

Why would he make us kill innocents? How many did I contribute to?

I try to relax my hands as I read through the papers, finding innocent name after innocent name beside the elegant script that wrote Silent Night.

Kate Hill: gardener.

Trevor Quance: shopkeep.

Mark Brown: carpenter.

The list goes on and I recognize every name.

My heart is a leaden weight in the pit of my stomach.

I was told they were all working for the Resistance, that they posed a threat to the Guild.

This is wrong. I did not sign up for this.

The deal was that we kill Resistance members in exchange for food and shelter, nothing more. We...we have a code. *I* have a code.

Don't I?

I flip to the last page and something jumps out at me. My heart drops to my *toes*.

The name Ismae Ballinger is written beside Black Death.

My whole world stops.

The Charger killed my mother.

CHAPTER FIVE

I can't breathe. My body has gone numb from the shock.

The Charger killed my mother.

All these years... All these years he led me to believe the Resistance had done it. I killed them because of that belief. I killed them to avenge my mother, so I could sleep at night.

But they didn't do it.

Angry tears fall onto the page, drowning the elegant scrawl.

The Charger killed my mother and has been using my fabricated ire as a weapon. The Charger is my real enemy and I have been *helping* him...

I crumple the letter in my fist, my muscles burning with the instinct to kill.

Not now, I chide myself, *you need to remain calm.*

I unfurl my fingers and drop the letter on my bed. Then I smooth it out, refold it, and slide it back in the envelope, which I shove in my pocket.

I grab extra weapons from the closet, shove them in a rucksack with a few other trinkets, and leave my room.

I'm not killing Hai tonight. In fact, I'm not killing anyone else for the Guild so long as I live. The Charger has done nothing but lie to me for the past thirteen years and I am done doing his bidding. I want to end him, but I know going to him now would be foolish. I need a clear head and, as much as I don't want to admit it, I'm going to need help.

It's time to seek out the Resistance and offer them aid in taking down the Assassin's Guild for good.

I take a deep breath.

Are you sure you want to do this?

My eyes darken.

Someone has to pay for what happened to my mother. I'll do what it takes, even if I have to dance with my mortal enemies.

• • •

I stay in one of the abandoned houses that serve as my entrances and exits to the Guild that night. I head out at dawn. I move on autopilot, not really aware of my surroundings. Around me, Haven City is stirring—its citizens shuffling to work, children preparing for school if they have the funds to attend—but I am not mentally here to witness it.

Still, I manage to stay hidden as I make my way across Haven to the office building where Avery met with Rachel.

Rachel.

It hits me then what I am doing. I'm going to betray the Guild, all of our closely-guarded secrets, everything we've worked for...

No. There is no we. I am no longer their willing pawn.

I need to find the Resistance before whoever the Charger sent finds me. I'm sure my absence has been noted by now. Hai is still alive and kicking. I failed my mission.

I move faster. I don't relish the idea of being tortured by the Charger once he learns of my treachery. Silent Night, his perfectly trained assassin turned traitor.

When I reach the office building on Charles Avenue, I walk up to it and enter like I own the place. I don't bother to hide as I make my way down the halls. I don't have time for that.

My heart falls when I come to the door that should have Avery's name on it and find it clear.

I kick the door in and turn in a slow circle as I take in the room. It's empty. No furniture, no garbage, nothing but the wooden floors and white walls. The Charger was right; Avery vanished without a trace.

Curse him.

At least I won't leave a trail behind either. I sigh and slip out the open window. I'll find nothing here.

• • •

I pace Haven furiously as I try to think of another way to contact the Resistance. The streets are growing crowded with the morning rush and I slip down an alley to avoid the hassle. I pass by a huddle of the homeless and throw my hood up to distance myself.

Nothing to see here; nothing to take.

I turn my thoughts back to the task at hand, kicking through piles of garbage as I walk. Avery was the only lead I had. I know of no other Resistance members. We're forbidden to have any sort of contact with them, for obvious reasons. The only members I've met are the ones I've killed, and then, well they're usually not alive long enough to chat. Except... Except Lincoln.

An idea hits me then and I start running towards Haven's east end. Lincoln wouldn't have given me that list without leaving a clue behind and, if he didn't, then I have to hope the Resistance is watching his house. I don't care if I have to be captured, as long as it gets me into the Resistance.

• • •

I enter his house from the front this time, after scanning the street for onlookers. I don't see anybody, but that means nothing. I can't be the only one who can move undetected.

I don't bother searching the main floor, knowing he would never leave anything of importance down there. I head straight upstairs, bypassing the guest room and storage room. I don't look in the storage room to see if his body has been discovered yet and hold my breath until I reach the master bedroom so I don't breathe in the acrid scent of death.

The master looks the same as it did the last time I saw it, clothes covering the floor and paper covering the desk, which I head over to. I check all the drawers and find the bottom one locked again.

Bingo.

He gave me the envelope. There is no longer any reason to lock the drawer, unless he put something else inside it.

It doesn't take me long to pick the lock with my bobby pins and I open the drawer to reveal a black envelope this time. I rip it open. Inside is a letter addressed to me from Lincoln.

Silent Night,

If you are reading this, you made the right decision and so did I. I knew you wouldn't stand for the kind of atrocities the Charger has made you commit. You are no doubt seeking the Resistance now and I can help you with that. The second page of this letter will direct you to our hideout. I trust you will treat this information with care. Thank you for reading the list and understanding. You have chosen the right side.

Sincerely,
Lincoln McColl

I turn the page and find the directions he mentioned. I'm surprised at where their operations are located: directly across the city from the Assassin's Guild. The entrance I am given is an abandoned warehouse in the north end.

Interesting.

I waste no time. The clock is ticking and I could have hours or mere minutes before the assassin—or possible assassins—catch up to me.

I sprint downstairs and out the back door. I hop the neighbour's fence this time and continue on through backyards until I reach the street corner. I take a left and slow to a walk. I don't want to look suspicious, though I suppose the black cloak isn't a great start.

Oops.

• • •

Half an hour later, I'm only three blocks away from the warehouse. I expect to encounter scouts, but maybe the Resistance is just as confident in its secrecy as we are. I quicken my pace as I near my destination.

Not too much longer now.

Then I hear it, the sound of footsteps behind me.

I bite back a curse of frustration. I don't have the time or patience for this. I make a split-second decision. I toss my rucksack to the side and then, throwing caution to the wind, I break into a full sprint, streaking past the buildings on the street. I hear a muffled curse behind me and the sound of footsteps coming faster.

I don't look back as I weave in between buildings, down alleys, and across fields of pavement. I lead my pursuer in a high speed, high stakes chase across the north end of the city.

I figure it'll only take a few sharp turns to lose him, but he sticks with me and I'm beginning to tire. I near a corner and see a second cloaked figure out of the corner of my eye coming down the left road.

Shit.

I veer to the right and pick up my speed as the two – men? – race after me. Without slowing down, I pull out my gun, aim behind me, and fire. I hear yells of fear and, as I fire off a second and third shot, a squeal of pain.

Bingo.

One down, one to go, assuming it was a kill shot.

You can never assume, I chide myself.

I risk a backwards glance. They're both still coming at full speed, one of them holding a hand tight to their arm.

An arm shot? Is that all I can manage?

I scowl and shoot again. The injured man goes down.

Success.

I turn my gaze forward again and assess my options. Trying to lose him isn't working; I have to attempt another approach.

Is there a place nearby where I can take a stand?

I scan my surroundings. Nothing but apartment buildings and empty pavement fields.

I hang sharp lefts at the next two consecutive intersections and head back the way we came. It's time to try something a little unconventional, not to mention dangerous, but danger is my middle name.

I turn left down a side street and head east. Two more blocks to go and I can put my plan into action. Not a moment too soon either. I don't know how much longer I can keep my pace, but my pursuer must be tiring too.

Finally, I come to Milne Street. I veer right and am soon running parallel to the North River, though heading south. I look ahead as my escape route comes into sight: the iron bridge, an intimidating metal monstrosity, four feet wide and spanning the thirty feet across the river. At least, it used to be. I've heard the stories.

The bridge has deteriorated over the years and now there's a single strip of metal running over the rushing water. It's about as wide as a train rail and people have slipped and fallen just inching across it on a dare. I'll be sprinting. My hope is that I'll make it across and my pursuer won't be that lucky.

One hundred metres until the turn.

I risk a glance behind me. I'm separated from my tail by a gap of about forty metres. I wait for the right moment before I head for the river shore, making a beeline for the bridge. I hear a curse behind me as I do so.

"Really, Two?" A ragged, dry voice shouts out. It's a voice I know.

Anane.

I don't let that detail distract me as I pick up the pace.

Fifty metres to go.

A glance; Anane is still behind me. A sharp wind picks up as I near the river, pulling at my coat and blowing hair into my eyes. I resist the urge to brush it away.

Almost there.

Thirty metres between us.

Twenty metres to go. Full speed now.

My first foot lands on the bridge.

Steady.

I focus on nothing else but the shore ahead of me. I let my feet do the work. If I look down, I will fall.

I can still hear Anane behind me, about ten metres now.

Somewhere beneath me, the water rushes past, carrying refuse and Guild knows what else through and eventually out of the city. I've been in it once and that was enough for me. It took me weeks to feel clean again.

My boots touch firm soil and I realize I've reached the other side of the bridge.

Please.

A few seconds later, I hear, "Shit!" Then a scream sounds, followed by a splash.

I grin.

Enjoy your dip, Four.

I slow down to a jog as I come back onto the road. I've never run so fast in all my life. I turn left at the first intersection I come to and stop to catch my breath. My legs and lungs burn, but I laugh at my victory. Then the laugh turns into a cough and I can't breathe for a moment.

How long did I run for?

It had to have been at least twenty minutes without stopping, but what can I say? I'm one of the best.

Perhaps Four will need to be replaced. I know Three will. That gunshot was a death wound; no one can survive a bullet to the head. Anane might've survived his fall, but it'll cost him precious time he doesn't have and he'll lose me. The Charger won't be too happy with him. I have a feeling his death is not far away.

I clear my throat and start jogging again, disappearing into the city without a trace.

• • •

It's around noon before I make it back to the side of the city where the warehouse is located. I retrieve my rucksack from the alley I flung it into and slow down to a walk, not wanting to appear confrontational in case they are watching.

Can't be far now.

Sure enough, a few minutes later, I find myself in front of a two-story, decrepit warehouse. The metal walls are rusted and warped. The second floor windows have cracked and foggy glass. One is missing its entire pane, plastic put up in its stead. It ripples in the breeze.

Fancy.

I wasn't aware the Resistance was a dump.

I analyze the building for a minute, deciding on a course of action.

The front door would be the best.

I have to make the right first impression or I'm screwed. It's going to be hard enough to gain their trust, best not to slip in through a second-story window.

I take a deep breath and approach the door. The thing is twice my height and a tad bit intimidating. This entire venture is intimidating. I'm only going to join my enemy, people I've hated and killed for over a decade. No biggie. No *pressure*. It's not like they'd kill me or anything.

I grab the door handle before I lose my nerve.

Here goes nothing.

I ease open the door, giving myself plenty of time to back out. I peer into the crack, but the sliver of light reveals nothing. I hesitate but then stop myself. I am Silent Night and I am *not* afraid of the dark. I *am* the dark and all shadows bow to *me*.

I fling the door open wide enough for me to get through and step inside. I hear the sound of a gun being cocked and drop to the ground. When the shot rings out, the bullet zips over me and out the open door. I swear and roll to my feet.

I resist the urge to draw my own gun and raise my hands above me in surrender. "Please," I say, choking on the word. "I come in peace."

I can't see my attackers. They are concealed in the darkness of the warehouse's second-story mezzanine. They don't answer me. Another shot goes off instead, but I've already ducked behind a pillar in their moment of silence, not willing to take any chances.

"I'm not here to kill anyone," I try again. "Please, I need to speak to your...um...leader."

Again, there is no response.

"Come *on*," I say, "can't you at least give me the benefit of the doubt?"

"Never," says a voice to my left.

Close. Much too close.

I whirl and come face to face with a dagger.

A man stares me down. "You're an assassin, we would never dream of underestimating you."

I feel a presence behind me then and realize I'm cornered. I reach for a knife, but something slams into the back of my head before I can get a grip.

CHAPTER SIX

When I wake, it doesn't take me long to realize one important fact: I am in a dungeon. The place is cold, dark, and damp. The ground beneath me is rough stone and the wall of bars across from me is a dead giveaway. I swear, loud and colourful, breaking a hole through the endless silence around me. I am in deep shit.

This is what happens when you betray your people, Silent Night, a voice in my head chides me. *You never should have left.*

Quiet, I snap. They *betrayed* me.

I couldn't have stayed there any longer without killing someone and I already have enough blood on my hands. I sigh. I just have to go with the flow and hope the Resistance doesn't kill me before I have the chance to plead my case.

• • •

I've been huddled in the corner of the cell for a good hour before I hear footsteps. I stand up and reach for a knife, only to realize I have none. They must have stripped me of my weapons after they knocked me out, the bastards. They even found the vial of poison. I look up and see a young man standing on the other side of the bars.

He's tall, though he looks to be about my age. Straggly brown locks frame his face and blue eyes stare me down.

"What do you want?" I ask.

He crosses his arms. "You said you wanted to talk to our leader. I've come to take you to him." He doesn't seem happy about it.

"They sent *one* of you to escort me?"

He shrugs. "You're just one girl."

"Just one girl," I scoff. "You... You have no idea who you're dealing with, do you?"

"Not in the slightest. I suppose you wouldn't care to share?"

"And give you the advantage? Never. You'll have to wait and see."

He rolls his eyes. "Whatever, Assassin," he says. "I'm going to unlock this door now and you're going to let me tie your hands. You try anything funny and I'll kill you. Got it?"

"Sure," I reply, "but if anyone's doing any killing today, it'll be me."

He pulls a pistol out of his coat. "Listen closely, Assassin," he says. "You're not the only one who knows how to use one of these and I won't lose any sleep over shooting you in the head. Is that clear?"

I sigh in exasperation. "Clear as crystal, now would you get on with it?"

He returns his gun to his coat and produces a large key ring. He also grabs a long piece of rope.

He unlocks the door and pushes it open. I resist the urge to knock him over and run. Even I wouldn't manage to make it far.

"Turn around," he says and I obey, though it's against my better judgment. He proceeds to tie my wrists together behind my back with the rope, tight. I admire the effort, but it wouldn't take much for me to escape it.

"Now stand in front of me."

I do as he says, walking out of the cell and around him without making eye contact.

"Now walk. You start into a run and I'll shoot you. Understand?"

"Yeah," I mutter.

"Let's go then."

I start walking; he follows close behind.

As soon as we exit the dungeon, the guy pulls a blindfold out of his coat and ties it around my eyes. Apparently, they don't want me familiarizing myself with the place. Unlucky for them, I was trained to find my way without sight; every turn we make is catalogued in my memory.

So, when he finally takes my blindfold off in front of a metal door at the end of a corridor, I know we took three lefts, a right, staircase with ten steps, left, staircase with fifteen steps, two rights, a long hallway, stairway down three steps, and a final left. I also know I could get to the dungeon in about seven minutes, not that I would want to go back there.

The guy turns to me and says, "The people you want to impress are through that door. If you value your life, be honest and don't do anything stupid."

"Fine, but what do you care?"

"I don't," he replies. "I'm just trying to be nice." He sneers at me.

I roll my eyes. "Whatever, can we go in now?"

"Sure," he says, grabbing me by the arm and opening the door with his free hand.

I start to protest, but then the door swings open and I see eleven people sitting around a long table. Four guards stand on either side of it. I swallow. Nineteen pairs of eyes fall on us as the guy drags me through the door.

"Thank you, Ajax," the man sitting at the head of the table says. He addresses the guy who brought me in.

Ajax? That's a stupid name if I ever heard one.

The man's voice is warm and gentle, but it turns cold and harsh as he looks at me and says, "Have a seat, Assassin." He gestures to the empty chair in front of me, across the table from him.

I don't move right away. Ajax takes this as an invitation to rough me up a bit. He pulls the chair out quickly and pushes me into it with enough force to jar my bones. I'm going to have bruises tomorrow. I give him a death glare and, to his credit, he doesn't flinch.

I scowl and turn to face the man who spoke. Ajax takes up a position behind my chair. He must be some kind of guard, which would mean nine people in the way of my escape, assuming the others wouldn't attempt to engage. It won't be enough to stop me if I try.

"So, Assassin, you said you wanted to speak to our leader," the man across from me says. "Here I am. Now talk."

I choke. "*You're* the leader of the Resistance?"

The golden-haired man facing me looks young, hardly old enough to be in charge of anything, but upon closer study, I notice the worry lines in his face and forehead, a silvery sheen to his buzz cut in some places. His appearance may hide his age, but his eyes do not. This man is tired. This man has seen a lot. If I had to guess, I'd put him at late thirties, early forties.

"I didn't say you could ask questions," he replies. "Why are you here?"

"I came to find you, the Resistance. I want to help…"

"Liar," he snaps. "Did your master send you? What is he after?"

"I'm telling the truth and he is *not* my master anymore. He is *dead* to me."

Oh, how I wish he was dead.

The head man laughs. "And we're supposed to believe that?"

"I don't expect you to, but someone said I could come here and I intend to do what they asked of me." Not strictly true. I came for revenge and revenge only.

The head man raises an eyebrow. "Who sent you?"

"A man, his name was Lincoln McColl."

"Lincoln?" the head man questions.

"Was," another echoes. "She said was."

"What is the meaning of this?" the head man demands to know.

I snap.

"Would you people just listen and let me talk for a minute?" I want so desperately to slam my fist on the table, but I can't. "I'll tell you what you want to know, but I can't if you're constantly asking questions!"

"Shut your mouth, girl," the head man rebukes me. "I don't trust you."

"I could kill all of you right now, but I choose not to. How's that for trust?"

Some of them look at me in fear; the guards finger their guns, but the head man does not react.

"What is your name, Assassin?" he asks.

I stiffen a bit. Keeping your true identity a secret is one of the most sacred rules of the Guild. "I..."

"Answer that simple question and I'll let you speak."

You don't belong to the Guild anymore. If you're going rogue, you might as well break a few rules.

I take a deep breath. "They call me Silent Night."

Behind me, I hear Ajax suck in a breath.

Scared now, boy?

"My God," one of the men gasps.

"I never would've guessed," the head man replies. "How old are you?"

"Eighteen."

He raises an eyebrow. "I would've expected Haven's most renowned assassin to be a bit—oh, how should I put it—older."

I scowl. "Age has nothing to do with talent and hard work."

"I'd hardly call killing a talent."

"Yes, well, if you have a problem with my previous vocation, I don't think we'll be able to work together."

"Work together?" he scoffs. "How so?"

I lean toward him. "I've come here to offer my services. I hear your organization desires the destruction of a certain Assassin's Guild. I may or may not be able to help you."

A grin appears on the man's face. "Do tell, Assassin, do tell."

I explain my situation. I tell them about my capture and conversation with Lincoln, my complete betrayal when reading the information from the envelope, and the letter that led me to their hideout. They demand to see both documents. I go to reach for my pocket before I remember my bound hands.

"I can't reach them with my tied hands," I tell them.

"Wait," Ajax says from behind me. "I pulled a couple of envelopes out of her coat when we searched her yesterday."

The head man looks at him sharply. "Where did you put them?"

"In the bag with the rest of her confiscated belongings."

There is a fuss over that and somebody at the table is sent to fetch the documents. It takes the man almost ten minutes to retrieve them, and the group spends another five minutes perusing them and talking under their breaths to each other. Finally, the head man looks up.

"You did not question the contents of this list?" he asks me.

"What do you mean?"

"Well, I'm sure you considered the possibility the information was fabricated, didn't you, Assassin?"

"I thought about it, yes, but there was no one I trusted enough at the Guild to ask. If the letter was truth and I was found asking interesting questions, well… I would be pushing daisies instead of having this conversation. I couldn't risk it."

"But you decided to risk your safety on the contents of this single letter?"

I nod. "I figured I would be safer taking my chances with you than with the Master Assassin."

It kills me to say it, but it's the truth.

"If it *was* fabricated," I go on, "I'm not sure what could be gained from it."

He raises an eyebrow. "Other than this exact alliance you have suggested?"

"No offence, but the Resistance isn't smart enough to cook up something like this and you were all surprised at my story. I've fooled enough people to know an act when I see one, and that wasn't it. You guys knew as much as I did, and besides, if it was a forgery, you wouldn't have asked me that question. You wouldn't want my mind to start turning."

"Fair enough," he replies, "and you are right. As far as any of us know, this is real. I just wanted to see if you were sharp enough to consider all possibilities."

My eyes scowl, but I force a smile. "Oh, I assure you, I am as sharp as they come."

"I am not sure where Lincoln could've found such a list, but that will be a matter for later discussion. Where is he now, Assassin?"

"He's dead, and I prefer Silent Night."

"I'll call you what I like. How did he die?"

"I killed him. That was before my, uh, eyes were opened, so to speak."

"I see," he drawls. "Well, I thank you for the information you have given us. We will think about your offer."

I sit up straighter. "What do you mean?"

"You're a dangerous assassin. I'm not about to let you into our inner circle just so you can start planning an attack on the Guild. We can't be sure of your true motives, not until we trust you. For all we know, *you* could've fabricated this list and your entire story."

"But—"

He holds up a hand. "Save it. You will remain at the base under constant watch. If you raise our suspicions or we find out you're conspiring against us, we will take the necessary measures to protect the well-being of our organization. Do you understand?"

My blood boils, but I nod. "How will I know when you have decided to trust me and what am I supposed to do until then?"

"We'll call on you," he replies. "In the meantime, educate yourself and continue your training. Prove your worth to us and then we might talk about this attack."

I bite my tongue to keep from screaming obscenities. This is not in the plan. Silent Night does *not* sit and wait.

"Ajax," the head man addresses the guy behind my chair. "You will be the assassin's escort. She does not breathe without you knowing and I expect you to be smart about the kind of information you share with her."

Him, my escort? Assassins below.

"Yes, sir," Ajax replies. "I understand."

"Good. Take her to room 2413. It is up to you how you proceed from there."

"Yes, sir."

"All dismissed."

Everyone stands up, the guards following them into the hall.

When they are gone, Ajax steps into my line of sight and says, "Get up. It's time to go."

I give him a sad face. "This must really suck for you, having to babysit the assassin."

"I *said* get up. We're on a tight schedule."

"Fine, don't get your cloak in a twist."

I stand up, a bit awkwardly with my hands still tied. Speaking of which, my fingers are starting to go numb.

"Hey, do you think you could untie my hands? I'm losing my circulation."

He gives me a questioning look. "I thought assassins are trained not to feel pain?"

"We are, but it's still uncomfortable."

"Well, then you can stay like that for a while longer. Let's go."

He opens the door, and with a resigned sigh, I follow him out.

It takes us about fifteen minutes to reach room 2413. We have to enter the more populated section of the base to get to it and we receive an interesting mix of stares and glares as Ajax drags me along by the arm. No one stops us and no one says anything; they just watch.

Room 2413 is in an empty hall, mercifully, and Ajax pushes open the nondescript wooden door to reveal an equally bland room. A bed stands in the centre of it, with a nightstand on one side and a door presumably leading to a closet across from it. There's a mirror on the far wall and I quickly avert my gaze from the woman in the glass.

"What is this?" I ask Ajax.

"Your bedroom," he replies.

"This is it? Where's the bathroom?"

"It's down the hall a little ways," he says, pointing.

I look at him in horror. "You mean I have to share with someone else?"

"Normally, you'd be sharing with eleven others, but since you're a deadly assassin, we've opted for a vacant hall with extra guard security at either end. You'll still have to make the trek though."

"That's..." I trail off, not knowing what I want to say exactly. It's preposterous. Back at the Guild, the top twenty assassins had attached bathrooms; I haven't had to leave my room for basic necessities in years.

"I'm sorry it's not up to your standards, princess," Ajax drawls, "but we're being more than hospitable, considering who you are. I could bring you back to the dungeons, if you'd like."

I glare at him. "No, this will be fine, thank you." The words burn on my tongue.

He raises an eyebrow. "Really?"

"Yes, now stop pestering me."

"You don't have the right to give me orders."

I resist the urge to give him a swift kick in the shins. "Whatever," I reply. "Now could you leave me alone?"

He crosses his arms. "Nope, sorry. Jenson said you are not to leave my sight, and unlucky for you, I've got work to do. We're here so you can get changed and we can get to it."

"Changed? Why?"

"You can't go parading around in your assassin attire if you want to fit in here. Did you see how many looks we got?"

"Maybe that had more to do with my bound wrists and how you were dragging me around than it did with my outfit," I counter.

"Well, your outfit didn't help matters. There should be suitable clothes in the closet. Now, are you going to get it over with or are you going to waste my time arguing about it?"

I sigh. It seems I'm not getting out of this. "Fine, but you'll have to untie my hands."

He scowls.

"What? I suppose *you* could get dressed with your hands behind your back?"

"You try anything, Assassin…"

"Yeah, yeah, you'll kill me. I got it."

He pulls a knife out of his coat and slices the rope in one quick motion. I feel the whisper of metal against my skin and resist the urge to flinch.

"There," he says as the rope falls to the ground. "Now get on with it."

I rub my chafed wrists gingerly and step inside the room. He closes the door behind me. I lean against the wood and let out a breath.

What in the Guild have I gotten myself into?

Waiting was not in the plan, fitting in with the Resistance members was not in the plan, and taking orders from an arrogant jerk was *definitely* not in the plan. Ugh. I've screwed up immensely.

"Hurry up," Ajax barks.

"Oh, give me a break," I mutter.

I trudge over to the closet and slide open the doors. I nearly faint. Ten identical outfits stare at me from their hangers. Ten.

Assassins below, how can anyone live like this?

Ten outfits, that's it, and what's worse is that there isn't a single black one. They're all grey.

I can't work like this.

It's almost too much. I want to cry, but I'm an assassin, so I don't. Instead, I bite my lip, peel off my dirty assassin attire, and pull an outfit from the rack. I leave my old clothes in a heap on the stone floor and, cringing the whole time, force myself into the Resistance uniform.

Then I join Ajax out in the hall, without looking in the mirror. Seeing how hideous I look *will* make me cry.

"Took you long enough," he grumbles.

"Wouldn't *you* know?" I retort.

"Whatever, Assassin, let's go."

"Where are we going?"

"Normally, I'd go out scouting at this time of day, but since I don't trust you, I'll give you a tour of the base. One of the first steps to fitting in would be to know your way around probably."

"Yeah and the second would be for you to stop referring to me as Assassin."

He crosses his arms. "What do you want me to call you then? I don't suppose you'll tell me your name?"

I shrug. "Just call me Silent Night, everyone else does."

"But that's not your name," he argues. "It's an assassin title. I thought you wanted to fit in?"

"Ugh." I throw my hands up in the air. "Guild, you're annoying. Call me anything you want, so long as it's not Assassin."

He arches an eyebrow. "Is that so? You're alright with Shirley or Bernadette then?"

I give him my best death glare. "You are walking on razor thin ice there, boy."

To my surprise, he laughs—deep, heartfelt chuckles.

"What? Why are you laughing?"

"You're trying to intimidate me, over a name..." He runs a hand through his scraggly brown hair. "You know what, Assassin? I think we started off on the wrong foot. What do you say we try again?"

I shrug. "I guess it's worth a shot."

He holds out his hand and says, "Hi, the name's Ajax."

I look at his hand suspiciously for a second—thinking it must be some sort of joke—before I take it. "Nice to meet you," I reply, trying to be pleasant. "Call me Indigo."

We shake hands and I swear Ajax smiles.

CHAPTER SEVEN

It takes us about an hour to make our way around the base. I haven't spoken to anyone else yet, but the new clothing minimizes the stares. I never thought I'd say this, but my black clothes were actually doing more harm than good.

People wave to Ajax and smile at him as we pass by. He must be well-liked. It makes me wonder what rank he holds, and what infraction he committed to be tasked with watching me.

Ajax shows me where the training rooms are, and gives me a tour of the sleeping quarters and the hospital. We don't pass a single exit, either door or window, and I know that detail is intentional. The base itself has become my prison cell, but I suppose it's better than being down in the dungeon.

Ajax talks to me a little as we walk, but I get the feeling he's a quiet guy, it's not just me. Finally, he turns to me and says, "One last stop."

"And what is that?"

"The cafeteria; I'm starving."

The cafeteria is an interesting place. Wild is the first word that comes to mind. It's definitely loud. People are everywhere: sitting at tables with attached benches that crowd the circular space, leaning against the counter on the left wall as they wait in line for food, and standing in groups in the available floor space. They all seem to be talking at once.

"Is it always like this?" I ask Ajax as we walk through the doors.

"Pretty much, yeah," he replies. "What, you didn't have anything like this at...where you came from?"

"It's okay to say, Assassin's Guild," I tell him. "It's not like it's a bad word, and no, we did, it was just...different."

"How so?" he asks, leading me toward the lineup.

"Well, for starters, it's not exactly a room. It's an enormous underground cavern and it's loud, but it's so loud it becomes more of a background noise, you know? Plus, it's bigger so the sound doesn't seem as much."

"Interesting."

"Also, there's a hell of a lot more cursing."

He smiles at that. "Us Resistance folks are a little more sophisticated then, I take it?"

"Quite," I reply. "I don't see any gambling, pick-pocketing, or fist fights. It's unnatural. Not to mention that most of the assassins wouldn't even know the meaning of the word sophisticated."

He smiles wider. He looks as if he's about to say something, but then we reach the front of the line.

He hands me a tray. "What will it be?"

"What do you have?"

"A little bit of everything."

I follow his gaze and try to stop my jaw from hitting the floor. The counter is full of a variety of dishes: assorted vegetables, fish, meat, poultry, bread, soup, salads, and foods I don't even have names for. I've never seen so much food all in one place. They even have an entire container of peas, my favourite vegetable I rarely saw at the Guild.

"Guild," I breathe. "Where do you get it all?"

"What?"

"The food, where does it come from? I've never seen so much variety."

He narrows his eyes. "That's strange, I'd expect you people to have tons the way you raid the city trains every second week."

I frown. "What?"

"The food trains that come in from the farms, they're attacked by assassins at least every other week. None of the Resistance Agents guarding the cars return unscathed and not a single scrap of food is left behind when it's all said and done."

"We... We don't raid trains."

"That's what you think. Tell me, what do you really know about the organization you were a part of? Because as far as I can see, you don't know much of anything."

I don't answer and my appetite has lessened, but I spoon some peas and chicken onto my plate anyway. He

71

grabs a bowl of soup and some bread, and starts weaving through the tables with me close behind.

He stops at a table near the far side of the room. A boy and a girl are already present, sitting across the table from one another. The boy is a brunette with long light curls and the girl's hair is dark brown and braided, hanging over one shoulder. Her skin is only a couple shades lighter than her hair; she and I would be day and night standing next to each other. The two are wearing grey uniforms like mine. Theirs look like they fit better.

They look up as Ajax and I arrive, two pairs of brown eyes studying me.

"Hey, Jax my man, where you been all morning?" It's the boy who speaks and his excited sentence trails off as he eyes me beside Ajax.

The girl looks at me curiously.

"Jax man, who's the new chick?" The boy asks.

"She's a new recruit," Ajax lies. "I've been showing her around. She calls herself Indigo."

"Huh," the boy says, "is that so?" He turns his gaze to me. "Well, hello gorgeous."

I raise an eyebrow a fraction.

"The name's Sebastian, but you can call me Bast." He flashes me a grin and holds out his hand.

The girl brushes his hand away and says, "Actually, everyone calls him Bast, so we don't have to put up with his whining. He's quite full of himself." She smiles at me and holds out her own hand. "I'm Blake."

I take her hand and shake it. "Nice to meet you."

"You too, Indigo. We could use another crew member. Have a seat." She pats the space beside her on the bench and I sit down. Ajax takes the seat beside Sebastian.

"Wait right there, Blake," Sebastian says. "Who said she could waltz right in and nail a spot in our elite squad? We should see what she's made of first."

"Mmm, that's right," she muses. "How could I forget?"

"What?" I ask.

"Don't mind them," Ajax assures me as he digs into his soup. "They're just teasing."

Yet—judging from the grin Sebastian flashes me—it would be safer to assume they're doing anything but.

• • •

Around one o'clock in the afternoon, Ajax, Blake, and Bast take me to one of the many training rooms. Apparently, they want to test my skills. I'm not exactly sure what they mean by that, but I'm certain it'll be a far cry from what I've experienced at the Guild. Still, instinct tells me to proceed with caution.

The three lead me to a room on the second floor of the underground base. The whole venture is entirely Blake and Bast's idea; Ajax spent most of lunch trying to talk them out of it. He was adamant it was a bad idea, and as soon as I step foot in the room, I know why.

The room is one hundred feet by fifty feet with rubber mats positioned here and there on the floor. Covering the far wall are racks on racks of assorted weapons: hunting knives, throwing knives, daggers, all sizes of swords, crossbows, longbows, spears, single and double bladed axes, pistols, machine guns, and so on. The collection is extensive.

I resist the urge to grin.

Yes, Ajax, you were right; this is not the place to let an assassin loose.

"So, what do you think?" Bast asks, turning in a small circle.

Ajax eyes me as I answer. I go for the safe approach. "It's epic," I reply. "I've never seen so many weapons in one place." This is a lie. The collection in the Guild weapons store is four times the size, but Mr. Watchdog Ajax here doesn't need to know that.

"Yeah? Well, we're pretty proud of our collection," Bast says, smiling wide.

"Do you know how to use all of them?" I ask, searching for information I can use later.

"Personally, no, but we all specialize in one or the other, every type of weapon accounted for even if it's just one person who knows how to wield it."

"What's *your* specialty?"

"Me? Well, I consider myself an expert with any kind of bow you can name, but specifically the crossbow," he replies with a sly smile that I return.

"Is that so? You think I could see you in action?"

Blake rolls her eyes. "Quit stroking his ego, his head's big enough as it is."

"Oh, come on, Blakey," Bast says, "don't you want to see me work my magic?"

She gives him an unimpressed look.

"I'll take that as a yes. To the crossbows!"

I trail behind Bast as he practically skips over to the weapon wall. Ajax joins me. He's taking his watchdog job pretty seriously. Blake groans before tagging along.

We weave our way through the mats and people sparring on them with the various weapons. None of them are nearly as good as they should be to take down the assassins. They could best some of the younger ones, but it's the more experienced ones who are the problem. Namely, the Charger.

We reach the far wall and Bast stops in front of a rack full of crossbows and bolts. "Here we are," he says, "the best weapons in the building. Decisions, decisions..." He taps his foot on the floor as he studies the bows, thumb and pointer finger resting on his chin.

"For the love of God," Blake mutters, "just pick one."

"Patience friend, these things take time."

"How about that one?" I point to a bow hanging three rows up—a delicate, yet powerful-looking beauty. Its wood is a rich mahogany colour with a lacquered finish, even though the best bows are made of ash or yew. The metal limb is black steel, strong.

Bast smiles at me. "Very nice; you have an eye for weapons."

Ajax shoots me a look and I shrug, smiling.

Is that such a crime? my eyes ask.

His eyes narrow, but he says nothing and turns to Bast as he lifts the chosen crossbow off of the rack. He grabs a handful of matching bolts and the three of us—Ajax, Blake, and I—follow him to the target area of the training room.

Bast also grabbed a hook, and he uses it now to cock the string back as he loads the bolt into the bow. I notice his muscles as he pulls it into position, his foot against the stirrup, and his back and arms straining. Well, not straining exactly. It takes him no time at all to cock the weapon. His muscles are substantial.

Bast hefts the crossbow up to eye level and peers at the target. He breathes in, out, and pulls the trigger.

A muted gunshot sound echoes through the room, followed by a thud. I look at the target: dead centre and his crossbow doesn't even have a scope.

"Wow," I breathe, "that was extraordinary," and it was. I've never seen someone shoot a crossbow like that; he hardly had to think about it. He is someone I need to watch out for.

Dangerous.

He lowers the bow and grins at me. "It *was* pretty cool, eh?" He leans over again to reload and Blake rolls her eyes.

"Oh, please," Blake huffs. "It's not as if he can do it with his eyes closed."

I raise an eyebrow. "And *you* can?"

She blushes slightly, a hint of red brightening her dark cheeks. "No, but can anyone?"

"We'll see. Can I give it a go?" I ask Bast, holding my hand out for the weapon.

Bast starts to hand it over, but then he catches the death glare Ajax is shooting his way.

What? Bast's eyes ask.

Absolutely not, Ajax's reply.

"Actually," Bast says, "you probably shouldn't." He looks sad and confused at the same time, but tries to hide it. "Crossbows can be dangerous if you've never used one before. I think it would be best if—"

"No, *Ajax* thinks it would be best if I didn't," I retort. "I saw your exchange. Don't let him put words in your mouth."

Bast looks surprised and a bit taken aback.

I shoot Ajax a look. "Why can't I give it a shot?"

"You know perfectly well why," he says, fighting to keep his voice neutral.

"Are you going to stop me?" I ask.

Before he can react, I grab the crossbow from Bast's hand and aim it at the target. It's lucky he already loaded it or I would've wasted precious seconds. I close my eyes and pull the trigger.

I hear the thud that means I hit the target and open my eyes as I lower the bow. I turn back to the others. My eyes meet Ajax's.

If looks could kill…

But then his angered eyes turn to eyes of shock. I follow his gaze to the target and see my crossbow bolt stuck in it. My heart falls. It's in the bull's eye, but not the dead centre.

I missed.

"No way!" Bast exclaims. "A bull's eye? I've got to be seeing things. Your eyes were closed. You did it so fast there is no way..."

"Our little Indigo here is *very* special," Ajax says, interrupting him. His tone suggests that the little Indigo will also be very dead if I don't put the weapon down. His hand drifts to the gun at his hip. I set the crossbow on the floor without taking my eyes off of him.

Bast picks the weapon up and says, "Well done, friend, you'll be a nice addition to the squad."

I smile weakly, still nervous from my brief rebellion.

"Bast," Ajax says, "why don't you put that thing away and grab a few staves. We can start Indigo's training with them. Let's see how she does with two against one."

"All right," Bast replies. "I'll be right back." He walks off, whistling a catchy tune.

How on earth can anyone be so constantly cheerful?

• • •

Ajax gets me to spar with the other two for at least an hour. Thankfully, staves are more my forte than crossbows, but I would prefer a gun or knife. It's obvious why he chose the staves though, much less dangerous. He can pretty much guarantee that Bast and Blake will leave the matches with mere bruises. He doesn't know the staff was one of the first weapons I trained with and that I know exactly where to hit to break a limb, knock a person out, or even kill.

I stick to bruising though, whacking the two continually and running circles around their staves until they're dizzy. I'll wake up in the morning with less than a quarter of the bruises they'll have. They barely think the motion before I'm ducking and dodging the blow while planning my own.

I resist the urge to laugh. *This* is how I like to spend my time, not being led around on tours for hours on end. Of course, I still feel like a prisoner with Ajax watching my every move, but I'm the happiest I've been since I walked into the place.

Eventually, though, Ajax tells us to take a break and orders me to hand the wooden stick over. I sigh, but do what I'm told. I join Bast and Blake on one of the benches that sit against the walls. Blake hands me a bottle of water. Ajax stands guard in front of us. I wonder if he acts this way all of the time or if it's just because of me and, if so, do Bast and Blake notice?

We're sitting for about five minutes when the doors fly open and a tall girl about my age bustles in and looks around. I dismiss her quickly, but then she says, "Where's the assassin? Where's Silent Night?"

I look up sharply at the mention of my name and so does Ajax.

Who told?

She spots me then and says, "Ah, you must be her. Father said you were here at the Resistance. I didn't believe him."

Blake gives her a confused look. "What are you talking about? She's not an assassin. She's a new recruit; Indigo is her name. Maybe you should look somewhere else."

"Maybe *you* shouldn't question me," the girl retorts.

Blake hangs her head.

79

"You've been deceived," the girl goes on. "This is Silent Night."

This. As if I am some kind of inanimate object.

I sigh and cross my arms. "Well, I guess the cat is out of the bag now, and you are?"

"Natalie Sophia Roseanne," she says.

"That's quite a mouthful," I reply. "I'm surprised you can remember it all."

Beside me, Bast chokes on his water.

"At least I give out my real name," she retorts. "Silent Night at the Resistance, it's simply preposterous. My father is in the council room with Jenson as we speak, reminding him of what we stand for."

It takes me a moment to remember who Jenson is, but then the face of the leader pops into my mind and I realize what she means. Her father is trying to get rid of me.

The girl—Natalie—shakes her head. "An assassin walking among us..."

"She's here for a reason, Natalie," Ajax says, speaking for the first time.

"And you think that makes it okay?" she asks him, crossing her arms. "I would think you of all people would agree with me, Ajax. We're both very loyal to this cause." She tucks her hair behind her ear and...

Oh Guild, is she batting her eyelashes at him?

I'm going to be sick.

"Jenson said you've been assigned as her escort," she goes on, "but I can get my father to change Jenson's mind. You shouldn't have to consort with the likes of her." She glances at me.

"Thank you, Natalie," Ajax replies, "but that won't be necessary. I intend to do my job."

She goes to protest, but I interrupt her. "Ajax is right, Roseanne," I say. "Jenson isn't kicking me out anytime soon. I'm the person who's going to get you people in and out of the Assassin's Guild alive. I'm the one who's going to help you kill the Master Assassin. So maybe you should run along now and tell your father not to waste his breath."

She looks at me blankly for a minute before saying, "We'll see about that." Then she whirls around, sandy blonde locks flying, and flounces out of the room.

I have a feeling she's about to be proven wrong and when that happens, I will have made my first enemy here.

"Well," I say as the door closes behind her and I turn to the others, "I suppose you have questions."

Blake face is ashen and all the cheerfulness has left Bast's expression.

"What was she talking about, Indigo?" Bast asks. "Are you really...?"

"Silent Night? In the flesh." I resist the urge to grin as they both shift away from me.

"Seriously?" Bast breathes.

"Why would I lie about that?"

"Are you like the stories say you are?"

"That depends on what the stories say."

"They paint you as a ruthless criminal," Blake spits out, "a bloody, violent, merciless *killer*."

Someone isn't too fond of my exploits.

"*That* is a perfect description of the Master Assassin, not me," I reply. "I wouldn't exactly describe myself as merciless. Have I killed people? Yes. Will I kill again? Most likely. I'm not going to sugar-coat it, but I will not be compared to the sadistic monster that is the Master Assassin."

"But you're his right hand assassin, are you not?" Blake argues.

"Maybe I was, but those days are over. I betrayed him to come here and help you people."

"Why?" Bast asks.

"He betrayed me, so I decided to return the favour; an eye for an eye. He lied about who we were killing and he murdered someone close to me." I shudder as I relive the memory of seeing my mother's name next to his. "I came here to help you because if I get you people into the Guild, you can help me take revenge on the traitor."

Blake eyes me warily. "And Jenson trusts you?"

"Not exactly," I admit. "I'm supposed to be gaining his trust over the next few weeks and proving my worth."

"Hmmmm..." she muses. "What do you think, Jax? Do you trust her?" She looks over at him.

"It's not about whether I trust her or not," he replies. "I've been assigned as her escort, so she'll be with us at least until Jenson decides she's worth his time."

"Um, hello?" I say. "Do you mind not talking about me like I'm not here?"

"Sorry," Blake says, putting a hand to her head, "this is just...overwhelming." She looks at Bast and Ajax. "Are we really letting an assassin into our squad?"

"Not just any assassin, Blake," Bast adds. "She's the legendary Silent Night. This is *so* cool. No wonder she nearly bested me with the crossbow."

"*Cool*? You *do* realize she's killed countless people, including several of our agents?"

"Yeah, but...well, we've killed some of them too," he argues. "We liked her all right before we knew. Why should we let Natalie of all people change our minds?"

I smile. I do believe I like this guy.

"Fine," Blake says, turning back to me. "You could be telling the truth, so I'll give you a chance, but once it's gone, it's gone."

"Thank you," I tell her. It doesn't hurt as much this time.

"All right," Ajax says, "now that that's dealt with, you guys need to go do your usual training." He eyes Bast and Blake.

Bast sighs. "Do we have to?"

"Get going," Ajax barks, but his tone has changed. It's more relaxed now. I guess lying to his friends was more stressful than it looked.

Bast and Blake head off and I ask, "What about us?"

"You'll spar with me now, and it's not going to be as easy as it was earlier." He smiles at me.

I guess he's willing to be nicer now that the others know the truth, now that I've stepped out of the shadows, going against my very nature. I hope it's worth it.

• • •

83

Later, after dinner and some lessons, the others leave us to go to their rooms and Ajax escorts me to room 2413. The four of us had a lot of laughs, the tension from my identity reveal diminishing throughout the afternoon and evening. Bast asked a stream of questions about my life before. I answered him as best I could. Blake was quiet, but I figure that's the way she is. Ajax has been a lot friendlier and I even caught him smiling a few more times, which was odd to me.

Ajax stops in front of my door, putting his hands in his pockets. I'm about to go inside when he speaks.

"So, what do you think of Blake?"

"She's all right."

"All right? I thought you two would've been hitting it off by now."

I shrug. "Girls aren't my thing."

"That's not what I meant; the both of you could use a girlfriend—a friend that's a girl."

"I know what you meant," I retort, "and I'll say it again: girls aren't my thing. They involve too much gossip, pretty dresses, and general unnecessary drama." I think for a second and continue. "Actually, it's the whole 'friend' concept that's not my thing."

He scrunches an eyebrow. "What, so you're saying you didn't have friends at–at the Assassin's Guild?"

I snort. "Guild no; friends were just a good way to get yourself killed."

He crosses his arms. "And how do you figure that?"

"Well, let's see," I start, ticking things off on my fingers as I go. "When you get a friend, you start to trust them, and

EMMA COUETTE

when you trust someone, you let your guard down. Next thing you know, they're stabbing you in the back and—in my line of work—it's not a metaphorical knife. Assassins don't make good friends, not when life is a constant do-or-die competition to be number one."

He sighs. "Well, we're not out to get each other here. We watch each other's backs and work together to reach our goals. Maybe you could make friends now. It's okay to let your guard down. You're safe."

"I don't think so. I still have a ways to go before I can agree I'm safe, but we'll see what happens."

"You know, Silent," he says, "I think you're going to like it here."

"What makes you say that?"

He shrugs. "I don't know, just a hunch."

"Yeah?"

"Yeah." He smiles. "Well, anyway, goodnight. I'll see you tomorrow."

"Night," I reply.

He closes the door behind me and slides the bolt across, sealing me in. I wait until I hear his footsteps carrying him away.

Then I spin around and slam my fist into the wall.

Well, almost.

I stop my hand a centimetre from the cement. It quivers for a second before I drop it to the side and uncurl my fingers.

Assassin's below, all this smiling and fitting in and making friends... It will be the death of me. It's a miracle I

85

haven't slit anyone's throat, even with my lack of weapons, but it wasn't hard to remedy that.

I reach into my pocket and pull out the butter knife I squirrelled away during dinner. Then I shove it under the mattress and sit down on the bed.

Just stick to the plan, I tell myself. *Gain their trust, worm your way into the upper ranks, and get them to help you kill the Charger. Then, you can become the new Master Assassin and pick off the Resistance members one by one.*

Simple. All I have to do is survive this nightmare.

CHAPTER EIGHT

I've barely woken up the next morning when I hear a knock on my door. I don't answer it. It's too early to be up; I can feel it in my bones.

I groan and roll over. "Go away," I mumble.

The knock sounds again. I ignore it.

There is a pause and then a boy's voice calls from the other side of the door.

"I'm coming in, Silent, you better pray you're decent."

I open one eye.

Who dares to address me this way?

I'm about to tell them exactly what they can do when the door swings open. I sit bolt upright in bed.

"What in the Guild...?" I gasp. A boy stands in the doorway, watching me.

I jump out of bed and grab for the dagger sitting on the edge of the night table but...

It isn't there.

"*What* is going on?" I shout.

The boy steps into the room further and I see that he's more of a man. His brown hair and grey-blue eyes are familiar.

"Silent!" he says sharply. "It's me, Ajax. You're at the Resistance. You're safe. Calm down."

Oh.

Oh.

Everything comes back to me in a flurry of memory: leaving the Guild, getting shot at, waking up in a dungeon, and being led around the Resistance by this guy.

Ajax, I remind myself. *Right.*

I sit down on the edge of the bed.

Ajax eyes me warily. "Are you...?"

"I'm fine. Forgot where I was for a second. You startled me."

"Sorry about that," he says, running a hand through his hair, "but I did knock several times with no reply. I can't wait forever."

"So it's fine for you to let yourself into my room?"

"Technically, the room does not belong to you and yes, it's fine. I have to make sure you're not developing dangerous weapons in secret or trying to end your life."

"As if I have the materials to make any sort of weapon," I scoff, "and assassins live to end the lives of others. Why on earth would we kill ourselves?"

"I don't know," he admits, "but do you blame me for considering it?"

"No, I would've done the same. Never underestimate the enemy." I pause. "So, to what do I owe the pleasure of your presence?"

"The day's begun," he replies. "Breakfast is in ten minutes and after that, we have to hit the training rooms."

I rub my eyes. "This early?"

"It's seven o'clock, Silent," he replies, "I'd hardly call that early. Rise and shine."

"Seven o'clock," I repeat. "Are you insane?"

"What time do you usually get up?

"Whenever I see fit," I reply. "As long as my missions were done on time, I had free reign."

"Must be nice," he mutters.

"It was." I yawn.

"Well, you're not at the Guild anymore so get yourself dressed. I want to get down to the cafeteria before all the pancakes are eaten."

"Will Bast and Blake be there?"

"Yes, they'll be at breakfast, but they have their own schedule to attend to now that it's Monday. Now enough questions. Go get dressed."

"Must I wear that awful uniform? Don't you have anything in colour? Crimson perhaps? Oh, black would be nice."

He gives me a look. "First of all, black isn't a colour. Second of all, no. Now get on with it."

He leaves the room and shuts the door. I walk over to the closet and grab another one of the ridiculous, identical grey uniforms. I shudder, but put it on. I contemplate bringing my butter knife, but I decide I should be safe without it.

I open the door and step into the hall. Ajax shuts it behind me and starts walking away. I follow with a resigned sigh.

"How much longer am I going to have to tag along behind you all day?"

"Until I trust you."

"Which will be when?"

"When you stop asking so many curious questions," he replies coolly.

I give him an indignant look and stay silent until we reach the cafeteria.

The room is much quieter than it was during lunch or dinner yesterday. Everyone is sitting at the tables, some with their heads on their hands, dangerously close to getting syrup in their hair. I wince as one girl slips and does just that.

"Everyone have a long night or something?"

"Night shifts," Ajax explains. "Some people have to go back out in the morning."

"At the Guild, we sometimes go days without sleep, but we're always alert. These people would be dead long before they noticed the threat," I point out.

"I'm sorry we're not up to your standards," he snaps, "but we're a little short staffed with the way you people value life." He stalks off to the line.

"That's not what I..." I start, but he's already gone. "Meant," I finish lamely. I sigh again—I've been doing a lot of that lately—and take my place in line, two spots behind Ajax.

EMMA COUETTE

Ajax is already at the table chatting it up with the other two when I slide onto the bench beside Blake.

Bast looks up from the joke he was telling Ajax and says, "Morning, Midnight."

"What?" I say.

"I'm trying out new names on you," he replies. "I need something to call you."

"I'd rather you just call me Silent Night."

"Yeah, but it has to be cooler and less, I don't know, scary. You *are* trying to fit in."

I frown. Why does everybody keep telling me that?

"Right," I reply, "but I wasn't aware that required a new identity."

"You were perfectly fine telling us your name was Indigo yesterday," Blake points out.

"Am I being interrogated?"

"Not yet," Bast says with a grin.

"She doesn't need a new identity, guys," Ajax argues, "just a new perspective on life."

"How do you mean?" I ask.

"Well, everything you say is, 'Oh the Guild has this,' or 'The Guild would never do that,' and so on."

"And?"

"And I thought they betrayed you? Why would you waste breath talking about them? Stop looking at the world as a Guild assassin, because like it or not, those days for you are over. Look at it from your own perspective; be your own person."

91

Bast and Blake look at him like he's grown a second head.

"Whoa, man," Bast says, "you feeling okay? You're acting too philosophical for seven in the morning. Here, have some pancakes." Bast spears a few pieces with his fork and holds it out to Ajax as if feeding food to a baby.

Ajax brushes the fork away. "Cut it out. I'm fine."

"If you say so," Bast replies, shoving the forkful into his own mouth, "but you better keep alert just in case."

"Bast," Blake sighs, "you know how I feel about talking with your mouth full."

Bast sticks his tongue out at her. "Bite me."

I crack a smile and then shake my head. These people are having a weird effect on me.

Before we can start up another conversation, the cafeteria doors bang open and a horde of...children come running in. Their screaming laughter fills the space.

Several older agents file in after them, gently nudging them and giving orders to form a line in front of the counter.

It is such an odd sight, all the children dressed in grey. At the Guild, the orphans were kept separate from the fully trained assassins, so they wouldn't get in the way. I try not to let my mind wander, try not to think about what those first few years at the Guild had been like.

"Uh oh," Bast says, following my gaze, "the hellions have arrived."

Blake swats at him. "As if you're any better." She's smiling at the news and it lights up her face.

We continue eating in silence, but Blake can't seem to take her eyes off the children, as if guarding them from afar. Then I hear the sound of padding feet coming our way.

"Bwake!" someone cries out and I resist the urge to jump in my seat.

Blake puts down her fork as a small, dark-haired child comes barrelling at her. He crashes into her waiting arms and she lifts him up into her lap, tousling his hair.

"How is Simon today?" she asks him.

"Gooood," he says, giving her a gap-toothed smile.

She beams at him and I hear more footsteps.

A moment later, an older blonde girl and another dark-haired boy stop at the table. The girl puts her hands on her hips.

"Si-uh-mon," she chides, "you can't be running off like that. Remember what Sarah said?"

Simon just giggles.

"Hello, Lydia, Charles," Blake says to the older children. "What's for breakfast this morning?"

"Pancakes," the boy who must be Charles says.

"They're probably getting cold," Lydia adds.

Damn, the girl has fire for an eight year old.

Then I remember what I was like at that age and decide to cut her some slack.

Charles eyes Lydia and says, "We should probably go. Come on, Simon."

Simon sighs loudly, but nods.

Blake tousles his hair once more before setting him down on the floor and he laughs.

"Bye, Bwake," he says with a little wave.

"Bye, Simon," she says, then to the other two, "you kids behave yourselves."

Lydia takes Simon's hand and they head off to the other side of the room where the adults have secured five tables for the group.

I look over at Blake. There is a profound sadness in her eyes as she watches them go, but then she turns back to us and it's gone.

Bast whistles. "Lydia is going to be a handful when she's older."

Blake smiles. "You're one to talk."

"I'll have you know I'm the Simon of that group," he retorts.

"Do the children usually eat here?" I ask, interrupting the argument I can sense coming. "I didn't notice them at lunch or dinner yesterday."

"They typically only join us during breakfast, when it's quieter," Ajax answers, "but not every day."

"They seem to be in relatively good spirits, considering the state of this city."

"Some of them have never been outside," Blake says, "those that have Resistance parents, at least. Simon, Lydia, and Charles are orphans, family by chance."

"We found them on one of our patrols a couple years ago," Bast adds, "huddling in front of a burning garbage heap."

So the Guild isn't the only one in Haven who collects orphans, though I'm sure the ones here lead a much happier and safer life.

I wonder what could've happened if I'd run, if the Resistance had found me before the Guild all those years ago.

I clamp down on those thoughts.

Wondering can't change the past nor help the future.

"You seem really good with them," I tell Blake.

"Thanks," she says, smiling.

Maybe the two of us could get along after all.

We sit in silence for the next little while, eating our breakfast. We're almost done when Bast decides to resume his earlier questioning and asks me, "So, Night, how old are you?"

"Eighteen," I reply.

"Really? Eighteen and you're already a legend."

"A legendary killer," Blake reminds him.

I ignore her comment and ask, "How old are *you*?"

"Seventeen," Bast replies. "I know, I look young for my age. That's what hanging around these two geezers will do to you."

Ajax elbows him. "Don't you go belittling your elders, young man," he scolds him and I laugh despite myself.

"We're nineteen," Blake says, interrupting Bast's next words, "stop being so dramatic."

I roll my eyes at Bast. "That's not old at all."

"It depends on your perspective," he argues. "In this city, you're lucky to see your twenties. Look at you for example. People might call you old, having survived childhood, but you're young for what you've done. I mean, how many people have you killed?"

"*Bast,*" Blake gasps.

Ajax shoots him a look and then sneaks a glance at me.

I feel frigid. "You don't want to know," I say, suppressing the shiver that wants to shake itself out.

"Oh, come on," Bast goads. "Tell us. I can take it."

I turn my gaze on him; eyes like ice pierce his wide curious ones. "I said you *don't* want to know," I snap through clenched teeth, fingers curled tight around my fork. I stand up then, dropping the utensil. It clatters to the floor and a few people look up.

"Calm down," Bast says, "I didn't mean—"

"Shut up!" I clench my fists with the fingers that yearn to claw into Bast's throat.

Walk away, I tell myself. *Just walk away.*

So I do.

• • •

Ajax finds me in room 2413 sitting on the bed. My knees are pulled up to my chest and I'm trying *not* to visualize what it would feel like to shove my stolen butter knife down Bast's throat.

I'm failing.

Ajax eases the door open. "Hey," he says. "You okay?"

"Why should *you* care?" I snap.

"What, I'm not allowed to be nice?"

"No...it's just...never mind." I sigh.

96

He leans against the doorframe. "I don't exactly understand what happened back there, but I'm sure Bast didn't mean to hurt you."

"I'm not hurt."

"Okay... Then why...?"

"Look, can we just forget it?" I ask, looking up at him sharply. "I don't want to talk about it."

"Okay," he says again, skeptical. "Do you still want to train now? 'Cause we can..."

"I'm *fine*," I snap.

He holds his hands up in surrender. "All right, I was just checking. You don't need to be so confrontational."

"Whatever, now are we going or what?"

"Right, follow me."

• • •

He leads me to the same training room we visited yesterday. The place is mostly empty, two agents duelling with single blade axes in one corner of the room. Ajax tells me to pick a mat and goes over to the weapon wall.

The encounter with Bast is still chafing at me, but I can't help but feel a little excited at the prospect of training. It always calms my mind. I wonder what he will trust me with this time.

He returns with two wooden swords and my excitement fizzles out.

"A wooden sword? Are you serious?"

"Of course I'm serious. Were you expecting a real one?"

"Well, no," I reply. "Not really."

"Prove to me I can trust you with this and I'll see what I can do tomorrow."

I sigh. "Fine, hand it over."

He throws the weapon at me. I catch the hilt easily in my left hand. He twirls his sword in his right. "All right, Silent, do your worst."

I grin despite myself. "That wasn't smart of you to say."

"How so?"

"You'll see," I reply and then I lunge.

I dart to his right, throwing my weapon to my right hand as I step, but it was only a feint. He goes to block me, but I come at his left.

Smack.

The flat of my blade connects with his bicep. He hisses through his teeth and mutters a curse under his breath.

I go on the offensive, but he fights back hard, wary now that he's seen what I can do.

We struggle against each other. We dodge, duck, twirl, lunge, parry, and block. Back and forth.

I speed up then, switching my sword back to my left.

The sword smacks against his lower leg as I duck the blow he aims at my head.

"God," he cries out, hand going to his leg automatically.

I go in for the 'kill,' but then he does something unexpected; he grins.

"What?"

"Distraction!" he shouts and jabs his sword into my sternum as I straighten in surprise.

My hand goes to my chest. "Ow," I gasp. "What in the Guild?"

"I won," he says.

I swear.

How did he manage to beat me? How did I let myself get distracted? What is wrong with me?

"Ugh," I growl and chuck my weapon across the room. It hits the wall and snaps in half, wood pieces flying everywhere.

"Whoa!" Ajax exclaims. "*Chill.* It's okay."

"It is most certainly *not* okay," I snap. "I lost."

"That's going to happen sometimes. We're only human. It's not the end of the world."

"Yes, it is! If that sword had been real, I'd be dead. Dead! *I'm* supposed to do the killing and I was bested by *you.*" I jab a finger in his direction.

He scowls. "What's that supposed to mean?"

"Look," I say, "I'm not trying to insult you. I just... I expected better from myself, I guess. If... If I lost like that at the Guild..." I scrape my foot against the floor. "I would've been knocked down no less than five spots and given a thorough beating...." My whole body tenses at the memory. I can feel the ache in my bones, the bruises blossoming beneath my skin, the fingers tightening around my wrists so I can't fight back...

I shudder.

Ajax walks up to me and puts a hand on my arm.

I resist the urge to flinch.

"It's okay," Ajax says. "That's over now. You don't have to worry."

I shrug off his hand. "I don't need your sympathy."

"Too bad," he replies, "I want to give it. You're an amazing fighter, despite what you've done to get this far. I'm going to have significant bruises tomorrow and, if you really think about it, you *did* win this fight. You connected two blows. If your sword had been real, either of the blows would've distracted me long enough for you to kill me."

"True," I say, "but still."

"Look, Silent, don't be so hard on yourself."

I cross my arms. "I have to be, because no one else is now. I don't want to slack off just because my master isn't breathing down my neck anymore. It could be a fatal mistake. I have to stay in top condition. That's not me being hard on myself, that's me being realistic."

"All right, I get it, but remember, he's not your master anymore."

I nod. "Even still..."

"You want to try again?"

"Definitely," I reply. "Come at me."

He smiles and replies, "That wasn't smart of you to say."

• • •

We spar back and forth for the duration of the morning, taking ten minute breaks every half hour. We start with wooden swords and then move on to wooden knives, axes, and finally he lets me shoot blunted arrows at the targets. He commends me for everything I do right and doesn't criticize me for mistakes. It's a new and strange experience.

By lunchtime, we're both exhausted and we sit at the table alone, nearly dozing into our grilled cheese sandwiches. Bast and Blake are still out on their respective missions. Ajax tells me they won't be back until tonight.

"What do you guys do on your missions?" I ask him. "The three of you are on a team you've said, but they're out and you're here. Would you be with them if I wasn't in the picture?"

Jax puts down his sandwich. "We're a team because we're from the same initiation class and we were all born in the same month," he starts. "Some months have a lot of people, so they're divided into multiple teams. Being a team means taking turns on each job and supporting one another out of the field. This week, Blake is on train patrol, Bast is on city watch, and I would normally be scouting for the Guild, but that job is kind of obsolete now since you're here."

"But weren't you one of the guards at the entrance when I arrived?"

He nods. "When it's my week for city watch, I guard the Warehouse instead."

"I see. Well, it all sounds interesting. A lot more variety than killing every day. A change in scenery and mission must be nice."

"It is, but I'm often wishing for a vacation."

I sigh. "Aren't we all?"

We pause our conversation to take a few more bites of our meal. Never has grilled cheese tasted so good.

"So what are we doing after lunch?" I ask him after a moment. "Nothing too physical I hope?"

"No, I'm done torturing you for the day. Jenson wants me to educate you on the way we operate."

My eyes light up. "We're going on a mission?"

"No," he replies, "we're going to an initiation lecture."

My mood plummets to my toes. "I thought you said you were done torturing me?"

"Oh, come on, it's not that terrible. Everyone has to do it. I'm sure they had something similar at the Guild."

"I wouldn't know," I reply.

"How is that?" he asks, lifting his sandwich to his mouth for a bite.

"I grew up there, had all the rules and regulations ingrained into me from a young age."

He sets his sandwich down. "You grew up there? What do you mean?"

"I'm what they call a Guild Ward," I reply. "I was orphaned as a child, many kids are these days, and the Guild takes them in, in order to manufacture a new generation of loyal assassins. If that's all you know, you'll never have a reason to leave."

"Makes sense," he muses. "How... How old were you when..."

"My mom died?" I finish for him.

"Yeah."

"I was five. It seems young, but some lose everything before they can even speak up for themselves. They started with simple lessons first, teaching us how to read, write, and talk properly. Then they hit us with the weapon training. We began with knives and slowly worked our way up.

"If you made a mistake, you were punished, and if you lived to tell the tale, you made sure you learned from it. I wasn't the only Ward; I grew up surrounded by other orphans-turned-assassins. I was always one of the best though and always seemed to be favoured among the higher agents."

Until I took their place.

I sigh. "I killed my first victim when I was ten, was christened Silent Night at age twelve, and, by the time I was fifteen, had secured a spot in the top ten rankings of the Guild. I thought I was amazing. I thought I was doing the right thing. Now... Now I don't know what to think." I poke at the crust scraps left on my plate.

"I mean, it's not exactly your fault?" he tries. "Like you said: if it's all you know, it's all you know. What matters now is learning what you *didn't* know. I grew up in the Resistance; my mom was a top agent. This would be all I know, but the Resistance doesn't keep us in the dark. We believe in being aware of any information we can possibly get our hands on. We never know what we might need to do our job."

"Your mom *was* a top agent? What happened?"

He gives me a sad look. "She died. I was thirteen. Not as tragic as your loss, but..."

"Every loss is tragic," I interrupt him, "no matter your age. I may pretend I don't have a heart, but I do understand the pain of loss."

He smiles. "Thanks."

We sit in silence then, finishing our sandwiches.

Then he looks at me and says, "So, you ready for a lecture?"

"Ready as I'll ever be."

CHAPTER NINE

We continue like that for the next two weeks, training hard in the mornings, eating lunch together, and going to lectures in the afternoon. Bast and Blake join us for dinner each night and I find myself getting comfortable.

I have trouble building relationships with them at first. Ajax and I are on good terms, but it's hardly a friendship. Bast is all right, though his excessive questions regularly get on my nerves and Blake... Well, I find her kind of cold and unresponsive, but then again, that's probably how I come off as.

I notice Natalie lurking about more often than one would deem normal, but only in crowded halls where she could write an encounter off as coincidence, though she never gets close. I wonder if her father is still begging Jenson to get rid of me. I wonder if she'll ever have the guts to show her teeth.

At the end of my second week at the Resistance, Ajax says he has a surprise for me, but that it'll wait until the morning. I hope that I'm getting an audience with Jenson, but the real surprise is even better. When I wake to his knocking and go to the door, he looks at me with excited eyes and says, "We're going on a mission."

"What?" My eyes grow wide with disbelief. "Are you serious? You'll pay dearly for it if you're joking." I jab a finger into his sternum.

He holds his hands up in surrender. "Relax, I'm telling the truth. Jenson approved it. He says it's time you enter the field."

"It's only been two weeks; he trusts me?"

"He doesn't, but I do."

Silence descends between us. I don't know what to say to that. Something bubbles in the pit of my stomach. I push it down.

"Why would you trust me if your superior doesn't, and why would he trust your judgment?"

"I consider myself a good judge of character and I've spent enough time with you to get a good read. Jenson trusts me because he trusted my mother. He knows I would never do anything to intentionally harm this organization. If what you say about taking down the Guild is true, you could save all of our lives. So for now, I choose to trust you. God help us all."

"Fair enough," I reply. "I'll get dressed then."

I go to turn away, but then he says, "You'll need these." He hands me a pile of clothes.

"What's this?"

Then I see. It's a new uniform, and it's black.

106

"Assassins below," I breathe. A part of me wants to cry, but I hold it back. "Thank you," I say.

He shrugs. "It's not my choice; we never wear grey in the field, too conspicuous. You can wear your cloak too, if you'd like."

"Would I?" I smile then, a big goofy smile. Funny, I don't remember the last time I did so.

I go back into my room, closing the door behind me. Hurriedly, I pull off the grey suit I'm wearing and slip into the new sleek black apparel. In reality, it's no different from the grey uniform, but in my opinion, everything is three times nicer when it's black.

I notice the belt along the waist of the suit with several horizontal hoops. If I didn't know any better, I'd say they were weapon holders.

Do I dare to dream?

I grab my cloak from its hanger in the closet and rejoin Ajax in the hall. I realize now that he too is wearing black. How did I miss that earlier? It looks good on him.

Wait, what?

I shake off my thoughts and say, "Do I get to have a weapon for the mission?"

He raises an eyebrow at me. "What makes you ask that?"

I pull at my belt. "I know what these loops are for. I haven't lived under a rock my whole life."

"Yes," he sighs, "I've decided to test your loyalty by giving you a weapon. I've decided to trust you that far. Don't prove me wrong."

107

"I won't disappoint you," I assure him, though I can't promise anything.

"Better hope you don't," he replies, "or I'll have to skin you alive. It wouldn't be pretty." He smiles to let me know he's joking.

Still, I grimace as memories flash through my mind. I can feel the cold, can smell the iron. "No, it's not," I say.

He shoots me a look. "How would you know?"

"I've seen it done."

His eyebrows shoot up.

"Are you really that surprised?" I ask him. "I mean, according to you, assassins are nothing but animals. What's a little bit of torture?"

"I didn't think..." He rubs the back of his neck. "Well, I've been taught that you do, of course, but a lot of our lessons are based on speculation. In my head, you're merciless killers, sure, but I thought maybe you drew the line somewhere."

I laugh. "The Guild has no lines. I was eight years old when they started training me and my fellow Wards in the art of performing and withstanding torture. Skinning someone alive... That was one of the lessons."

Ajax looks like he's about to be sick. "That's... That's horrible," he chokes out.

"It was, but I suppose, after a while, you get used to the screams."

At least, that's what you tell yourself. Sometimes, I still hear them in my nightmares, clear as if I never left my spot against the wall in that cell...

I shiver. I have to move on to another topic before I take a long and terrible trip down memory lane.

"Anyway," I go on, "can I see the weapon then?"

"In a minute. We have to retrieve it first."

• • •

Ajax leads me to a part of the base he never showed me, to a door at the end of a dark hall. He types a code I don't catch into a panel beside the door and it slides open with a hiss. Inside, it's an assassin's paradise. I do my best not to drool. I thought the weapon collection in the training room was extensive...

The walls are covered and the room disappears into shadow, hiding its extent.

"Assassins below," I breathe.

He shakes his head. "You wait out here. I'll be back." He slips inside, closing me off from the wonders.

A few minutes later, he returns, holding something behind his back. He clicks the door back into place, locking the rest of the weapons away from my reach. I admire his effort, but his first mistake was showing me the location of the store. Now it's only a matter of cracking the code, if I decide to turn on them.

"Close your eyes," he tells me.

I hesitate a second before complying. I hear his footsteps coming closer.

"Hold out your hands." His voice comes from in front of me.

I do as he says and he places the weapon in my hand. My fingers curl around a familiar sword sheath.

I gasp, opening my eyes. I'm holding my own sword. "Are you serious? Do I... Do I get to keep it?"

He nods. "As long as there are no hiccups on this mission, it's yours. You've earned it."

"How?"

Is he insane?

He sighs. "Silent, you're one of the most notorious assassins in the history of Haven. You came to the base of your lifetime enemy and didn't start any fights. No one has been injured or killed. You've exercised self-control I honestly didn't think you possessed. In short, I'm impressed; I never would've been able to do the same."

"Thank you, I guess," I say, feeling a slight heat in my cheeks.

"I should be asking how you do it," Ajax continues.

"I don't know," I reply. "I just... Well, I haven't gotten angry at anyone. Not enough to act on it anyway. You're all so...nice. I'm in shock still. Also, it's hard to commit mass murder when you took all my weapons."

He gives me a look. "We both know you don't need a weapon to kill someone."

"Well..."

He smiles. "Save it, let's gear up and get going while there's still daylight."

"Fine by me." I slide my sword sheath into one of the belt loops on my uniform.

Then I watch, envious as Ajax goes back into the armoury to retrieve weapons for himself, but I know better than to ask for another. Giving me even a sword is an enormous act of faith; I don't want to test it.

"What's your favourite weapon?" I ask as we head away from the armoury.

The question catches him off guard and he says, "Does it matter?"

"No, I was just wondering. Trying to make small talk actually, but I don't know much about it."

He shakes his head. "I'll add that to your lessons," he jokes. "I guess, if I had to choose, I'd say the gun. I like the range and the power."

"Huh," I say.

"What?"

"It's my favourite too, though knives are a close second."

"Interesting choices," he says.

"I suppose," I reply. "They were the easiest to learn and the easiest to stay good at."

He nods. "That makes sense. Now, aren't you going to ask me where we're going?"

"Sure," I say. "Where are we going?"

He grins. "You'll see when we get there."

• • •

We leave the Resistance the same way I came in. It's hard to believe that was already two weeks ago. It doesn't seem like much has happened.

I'm kind of nervous to be leaving the base and venturing out into the open. The Charger will still be looking for me and if I'm seen with a Resistance member, it's game over. He'll seal all of the entrances I know of and place guards at the others day and night in case I find them. Not to mention the hunters he's sent after me. He'll have learned from his previous mistake after losing Three and possibly Anane. He might send One after me, and if he does, I'm screwed.

So, it is with much trepidation that I step out of the abandoned warehouse and into the street. We leave the field of pavement behind and start heading south towards the more populated parts of Haven.

I notice now how hollow the city is, the way both the buildings and people seem empty. It's a stark contrast to the Resistance. People shuffle by with their hoods down, clutching their parcels tightly. They don't seem to notice Ajax and I or care about the obvious weapons we carry.

The buildings around us droop, like flowers after a hard rain. Porches sag and lean, as if trying to escape the damage. Roofs are as tattered as the coats beggars pull tighter against the wind. Brick bungalows seem sunken under the weight of the past hundred years.

And here I was, thinking the Resistance was grey and dull. Haven is faded. What colour that manages to pop through the cracked sidewalks is out of place. Haven City is a graveyard just waiting for the rest of us to call it quits, and it won't hesitate to help us get there quicker.

My lectures have taught me that Haven was a grand city in its youth, that its buildings scraped the sky, but looking around now, it's hard to imagine that. Haven's past is but a memory that is slowly fading into its broken storefronts and barren streets.

As we walk west, the pavement beneath our feet becomes an ankle nightmare, one wrong step and you'd be hobbling for life. The asphalt isn't so much cracked as cratered. The Charger made us race each other through these streets at midnight when the other Guild Wards and I were seven. If you couldn't make it to the finish line on your own two feet or by dragging yourself if necessary, you were left to die.

We walk in silence until I say, "Why won't you tell me where we're going?"

"Because," he replies.

"Ugh, can't you at least give me a hint? Is it a secret or something?"

"In a manner of speaking... Look, all I can say is that it's a place you might recognize."

I narrow my eyes.

"Would you just wait until we get there?" he asks me. "You'll understand then."

"Fine," I say, crossing my arms, "but if it's something ridiculous, you'll be sorry."

"We'll see," he replies.

He leads me to Haven's east end, to where the houses thin out into fields. We pass the railway tracks and head out into the vast open space of the farming district. Ajax guides me down walking trails through the various crops spread around us. Cabbage patches make way for rows of carrots. Stalks of wheat brush our shoulders as they rustle in the wind.

"What are you expecting to find out here?" I ask him.

He sighs. "We're almost there. Can you keep your questions for five more minutes?"

"I'm not sure."

"Well, you better figure it out."

I scowl and stick my tongue out at him when he turns his back.

Finally, he comes to a stop on top of a small grassy hill.

"What is this place?"

"One *second*," he replies. He walks down to the base of the hill and into a ditch made by a long dried up stream. "Some Resistance members discovered this last week," he continues. "After years of searching, we think we might have finally found something and Jenson has sent the two of us to check it out."

"*What*? Spit it out already, would you?"

He hops into the ditch and pulls apart a clump of weeds to reveal a metal manhole cover.

"What the... What is it?"

He gives me a strange look. "I'm surprised you don't know. We believe this could be an entrance to the Guild."

114

I dissolve into a fit of laughter, but cut myself short when I notice the unamused expression on his face. "Wait," I say, "are you serious?"

He crosses his arms. "Why would I joke about this?"

"It's just..." I pause, trying to find the words. "It's preposterous," I go on. "Why in the Guild would we put an entrance in the middle of nowhere, in a ditch in the farming district?" I stick my nose up at the tall grass around us, at the barrenness of the land. This is not a place fit for assassins. The farming district is where the poor find refuge, where people toil away day in and day out to feed our crumbling city.

"Why *wouldn't* you?" Ajax argues. "The most unlikely places are always a good choice."

I snort at his logic. "Well, for starters, we reside in the *south* end of Haven."

He raises an eyebrow. "So the rumours are true then?"

I throw my hands in the air. "*Everyone* knows that! Why do you think no one lives there? The houses are in perfect condition."

"We couldn't be certain. It didn't make sense for your hiding place to be so well known. We figured you must have put out false rumours to shake us out. Besides, people *do* make up stories and though we concentrate most of our efforts there, we've yet to find a trace of you."

"That's because we don't want to be found." I stare at him with eyes of steel. "Look, Ajax, if you brought me here to trick me into giving you information, you're wasting your breath and my valuable time. I told Jenson I would tell him everything and I will, as soon as he has the presence of mind to listen. *This*," I gesture to the manhole, "is just insulting."

Silence descends. Ajax looks at me as if I've transformed into a horrifying monster. In a way, I have. He's never seen this side of me, the side I've been locking away for the past two weeks. The lock has broken.

"Silent, honestly," he says, running his fingers against his forehead, "that's not my intention. Calm down. You'll get an audience with Jenson as soon as we trust you."

My heart clenches, dropping like a stone into my stomach. "You said you *did*."

"I do," he assures me, "it's the rest of them that don't."

It's a quick response and I don't entirely believe it. Faith is an even trickier concept than trust.

"This mission is one of the steps in gaining the council's trust, in gaining Jenson's trust," Ajax goes on, ignoring my frown. "So just humour them and help me investigate this, even if you don't agree with our assumption. If we follow this lead and it turns out to be nothing, it'll be a sign to trust your judgment in the future. If it *is* an entrance to the Guild, you'll have helped us find an in. Either way, you win."

I sigh. "All right, I see your point. Let's check it out then, but I'm telling you, you're wrong."

It takes the two of us to lift the manhole cover up and drop it in the ditch, barely missing our toes. It rolls a few feet before settling in the dense weeds of the ditch. In the hole below, a metal ladder descends into the dark.

"Ladies first," Ajax says, bowing to me.

I roll my eyes. "If you insist." I adjust my sword on my belt and lower myself into the hole, making sure my boots won't slip before I descend into the gloom.

Ajax follows, about two feet above my head.

I get a strong sense of deja vu as I continue. I feel like I'm in the Guild again; similar ladders through the dark are not too distant memories. Even though I know this can't be an entrance, a part of me still feels it and I shiver.

We reach the bottom a couple of minutes later and find ourselves properly in the dark. I can feel a dirt floor beneath my boots and know, from experience, that there's a tunnel in front of me. It's about three feet wide and a foot taller than Ajax.

Lucky him.

"Let's go," I say.

"Wait," Ajax says, dropping to the ground behind me. I can't see him, but I hear the crunch of his boots against the earth. "How do you know where you're going? It's pitch black."

I give him a look. "My name is Silent Night, genius; I grew up in the dark. I learned long ago to navigate without the help of light."

"Well, would you care to *enlighten* me?"

I roll my eyes at his poor joke, glad he can't see. "There's a tunnel in front of us heading west," I tell him. "It's about three feet wide and tall enough for the both of us to walk without stooping. Is that good enough for you?"

"Perfect, thank you. How far do you think it goes?"

"No idea, but if this *is* an assassin entrance, we'll have to watch out for traps. Stick close to me and you'll be fine."

"As long as you know what you're doing."

• • •

We walk for what seems like forever, but is only about twenty minutes. We haven't spoken since Ajax insisted we light a torch and I snapped at him for being impractical. He's pouting now, but I'm not the least bit sorry. What happens if we *do* encounter assassins? We'll hardly be able to hide from them with a fire alerting them to our presence, but poor little Ajax can't handle the dark.

Weakling. Scared little boy.

"Hey, would it kill you to be louder?" he asks. "The silence is unnerving."

I turn around and glare at him.

He grimaces under the weight of my gaze. "I'll take that as a yes then," he says.

"Would it kill *you* to put out that forsaken light?" I retort, raising my volume. "No, but still you insist on keeping it. My name is *Silent Night. Silent.* The whole point is that I don't make any noise!"

He winces. "You're being pretty loud now."

"That's because you're infuriating me!" I clench my fists at my side to keep from lashing out and pause for breath. "I should've just killed you," I mutter, "still could."

He looks at me sharply. "*What?*"

"Back in the cell when I first met you, I should've killed you then, so I wouldn't have to deal with this."

"And how were you going to manage that? You were weaponless."

"Well, I'm not now, so shut up if you know what's good for you, and like you said, I didn't need a weapon to kill you."

Ajax's face is white and I bet if I raised a hand to his cheek, it would be cold to the touch.

Good. He should *be scared.* It would teach him not to mess with me.

"Look, Silent, can we just—"

I whirl on him, drawing my sword. He throws his hands in the air as I point the tip at his throat, barely an inch away from his skin. The torch clatters to the ground and rolls away, sputtering before going out. Darkness crashes in around us and I can feel the tension in the air, even as the darkness calms me. I can almost hear the frantic beating of Ajax's heart.

"You know, I don't have to kill you to shut you up," I croon in the silence, "cutting out your tongue is just as effective and three times as painful." It would be so easy to kill him, to lean forward and…

I hear his feet scrambling away, boots scuffing against the dirt, and a moment later the torch sparks to life again, illuminating him standing a few feet away from me.

He looks at me, eyes wide with…sadness.

What?

I lower my sword, the threat pointless now. "Why are you looking at me like that?" I ask him. "I was serious."

"I know," he says, "and I'm sorry. I'm sorry your life was so terrible it left an emotionless shell behind. I'm sorry

119

threatening people is one of the only things that brings you joy, but it doesn't have to be this way. You can change, Silent, but you have to want it." He walks around me then without another glance and heads down the tunnel, flame bobbing in the shadows.

I stand frozen by his words.

Is there nothing left of me? I wonder. Am I just an empty shell? And what if I am? Can I go back? Is there any redemption for someone like me?

No.

"Are you coming?" Ajax calls out.

"Yes," I reply. I turn around and follow him through the dark.

Ten minutes later, we come to another ladder. Ajax hands me the torch to hold and goes up first, returning a few seconds later.

"I need your help to push up the manhole cover," he says. "It's too heavy for me to lift on my own."

"Yeah, okay." I snuff out the torch and climb up the ladder with him.

We push both our hands against the metal cover to lift it up. Then we slide it over slowly and silently. Ajax pulls a gun out of his belt and pokes his head out of the hole.

"Anything?" I whisper.

He doesn't answer.

"Ajax? What's happening?"

"Silent, you have to see this." His voice is full of awe. It prompts me to take another step up the ladder and poke my own head out.

I don't believe my eyes.

We're in a warehouse, and it's full to the brim with boxes and crates of food: fresh fruit and vegetables, bread, crackers, pastas, bottles of water and juice... I recognize it all from the meal line in the Grand Cavern.

Is this...? It can't be.

Ajax jumps out of the hole and starts to walk around.

"What are you doing?" I snap. "There could be booby traps or assassins guarding the door."

He ignores me and keeps walking.

I sigh and jump up to trail behind him, drawing my sword as a precaution.

"So, you think this belongs to the assassins?" he asks as I catch up.

"Yes," I confess, "this is the kind of food we eat."

"Funny, 'cause these are the exact shipment contents of the trains that are raided. Guess we know where that disappears to and who takes it."

"I guess," I reply.

"We'll give the place a thorough search," he goes on, "and see where the front door leads."

"It won't be connected to the Guild," I say.

"And how do you know that?"

I put my hands on my hips. "I just do."

"All right," he says, shrugging.

I know he doesn't believe me, but that's okay. I wouldn't believe me either.

We scour the first and second floors, finding no assassins or traps. From the second story window, we confirm that there are no guards outside and that the warehouse leads to an empty city street in the south end. I was right.

"Where to now?" I ask.

"Home, I guess," Ajax replies. "We've done all we can. We'll leave the same way we came in, in case they have someone watching the place."

"I agree."

"Let's go then." He puts his gun back in his pocket and we go back downstairs.

We drop down into the tunnel, replacing the manhole cover after us, as if we were never there at all.

CHAPTER TEN

A couple of hours later, we stand in front of the door to my room.

I hold out my sword. "Here," I say, "you'll want this back, I suppose."

"Keep it," he replies.

"What? After everything I did today, after I threatened to kill you?"

"But you didn't go through with it," he says, "and I meant what I said before. I trust you. You're an assassin. I'd be more worried and even suspicious if you *hadn't* threatened me. It's a gut reaction for you; it's the way your entire life has worked. I can't expect you to change in two weeks, not even a month. None of us can."

I grimace. "So, what, you're saying there's no hope for me?"

He presses a hand into his forehead. "No, that's not what I'm saying. I'm saying you need more time to adjust. I'm saying I'm not angry at your actions today, though I want to be. I'm saying I still trust you." He takes a breath. "Keep the sword. I'll see you at one o'clock so we can give Jenson our report."

He walks away and I stare at him in disbelief until he's out of sight.

• • •

I'm sitting on my bed sharpening my sword when a knock comes on my door. The Resistance members never confiscated my whetstones and the butter knife under my mattress would cut through flesh quite nicely now. It's around twelve thirty in the afternoon and I just returned from lunch.

"It's not locked," I call out, "come in."

I hear the knob turn and the door open, but I don't look up.

"So this is the festering hole they cage you in," a girl's voice mutters.

Why if it isn't miss Priss Roseanne.

I raise my head and give her a look of absolute boredom. "Careful," I say, "I'm the one holding a sword."

She takes the tiniest unconscious step back and I smile.

"That's exactly why you shouldn't be here," she retorts. "You *should* be in a cage."

"Well, unluckily for you, they trust me."

"Hopefully not for much longer," she says, smiling. "They'll see the errors of their ways soon enough. Until then, we'll be seeing more of each other."

Joy.

"And why is that?" I ask.

"My father assigned me to a room in this hall."

Translation: daddy dearest wants her to keep an eye on me. Guess he *doesn't* want her to live to see her next birthday.

"Why should I care?" I ask, setting down my sword and crossing my arms.

"I thought you should know so you can stay the hell out of my way."

"That's a fine tongue for a princess."

"And this is a fine place for an assassin," she counters.

"Touché," I reply. I stand up and walk over to her. "Listen, Natalie, is it? I don't want conflict and trust me, neither do you. So, if you stay out of my way, I'll stay out of yours. Deal?"

"I make no promises," she says.

I shrug. "Then I can't promise your safety. Cross me, Natalie, and you'll regret it for the rest of your brief life."

"Touch me and you'll be sent back to the hellhole you came from faster than you can blink an eye."

"Is that so?"

"Neither my father nor Jenson will be so trusting if you harm a hair on my head or harm anyone in this base for that matter. You weren't stupid enough to think this freedom was a kindness, were you?" She nods to the sword and something in me shrinks back. "Leaving you unsupervised, unlocking your door, rearming you... It's all a test. I, for one, am itching to see you slip up. Then I can go back to my peace and quiet and you... Well, who knows what'll happen to you."

My skin crawls as I realize the truth in her words. Her father didn't just send her to watch me. He's hoping I'll try something and prove him right. I wonder if she recognizes that she's bait.

Well, I'm not going to bite today.

"Ajax is going to be back soon," I lie. "You should go. You wouldn't want him to start asking questions." Yet, something tells me that's exactly what she wants. Something tells me that behind that pretty face is a lethal player who might have a chance at winning the game.

"Oh, and that's another thing," she replies. "You can stay away from Ajax."

Oh, Guild. Here she goes.

"I don't think I can. He's obligated to escort me and if you really are testing me, I should keep him in my sights as much as possible."

Her eyes flare as she realizes her folly, but she doesn't waver. "I'm sure you of all people know how to bend the rules, know just how far you can push. I don't want you corrupting him. I don't want you putting him in constant danger simply by being near each other. I don't want you becoming friends. He's mine."

I want to tell her that you don't always get what you want, but I hold my tongue. Instead I say, "I don't give a damn about your stupid crush, Roseanne. You can have him for all I care, but I doubt he would want a girl like you."

She scowls at me. "And what's that supposed to mean?"

"You know what I meant," I tell her. "I haven't known him for long, but Ajax has taste and you are as bland as they come, princess."

Her face goes red. "Just stay away from him."

"Like I said, I don't want him. Knock yourself out or better yet, let me do it for you."

"Careful, that sounds awfully like a threat."

"And what exactly have you been doing since you walked in the door?" I counter.

"Whatever, Assassin," she replies. "I'd say it was a pleasure talking to you, but it wasn't, so I'll be going."

She saunters out of the room, leaving me thoroughly confused and concerned.

Assassins below. As if things aren't already bad enough.

• • •

At one o'clock, I meet Ajax outside the door to the council room, the same room where Jenson and the others discussed my fate when I first arrived. Ajax and I are there to give our report on what we found today. It's the first step of many to gain their trust and I'm as nervous as a Guild Ward holding his first knife.

Quit shaking, I tell myself, *everything will be fine.*

But what if they don't believe me? What if I say the wrong thing? What if Ajax gets punished for giving back my weapon? What if...

I trail off. Too many things could go wrong.

"How long is this going to take?" I ask Ajax.

"Not too long," he replies. "What, are you nervous?"

"Certainly not," I snap.

"Hey, it's nothing to be afraid of. Jenson doesn't bite."

"I know that but... What if this doesn't help them to trust me?"

"Don't be ridiculous. There is no way this report can hurt your case. Let me do most of the talking and you should be fine."

I don't like the idea of putting my fate in the hands of someone else, but I mutter an affirmative.

"Okay," Ajax says, placing a reassuring hand on my shoulder. "Take a deep breath and relax. You've got this."

I nod.

He opens the door and we walk into the room.

Jenson sits in the same spot he did the first time we met, two guards standing behind his chair. He asks us to sit across from each other at the opposite end of the table.

"I see you returned in one piece," Jenson begins. "There was no trouble then, I assume?"

Not from outside sources.

"We met no resistance," Ajax replies. Jenson laughs slightly and Ajax smiles at his own joke.

I roll my eyes.

"There was nobody in the tunnel or guarding its entrance and exit," Ajax goes on.

Jenson sits up straighter. "So you found an exit then?"

"Yes."

"Tell me."

128

"It led us to a warehouse in the south end, packed floor to ceiling with stolen food. There is no question now who the train raiders are and how they manage it."

"Was there no entrance to the Guild then?" Jenson asks.

"Sadly no, but Silent assured me it wouldn't be from the start. She proved to be right, but we decided to check it out anyway. At least the raider mystery can be put to rest and maybe we can prevent it from happening again."

"The bastards," Jenson says, "why would they have a separate building for their food?"

"Why wouldn't they?" I retort.

Ajax shoots me a look and I remember that I'm supposed to stay quiet.

"What's that, Assassin?" Jenson asks me.

I have no choice but to answer the question. "The assassins must've known you would discover that warehouse eventually," I reply, "so they didn't connect it to the base. Not every assassin knows about it either. I certainly didn't."

"Interesting," Jenson muses. "It seems the Guild likes to keep secrets from its members, doesn't it?"

"Yes, yes it does."

Jenson leans back in his chair. "Well, the two of you did well today, even if we didn't find an entrance. Ajax, take her scouting with you if you want and on any missions I assign you; she's earned that much. Oh, and make sure she's properly outfitted with weapons next time. That lone sword wouldn't have been enough if you ran into a gang of assassins."

My eyes gleam with excitement.

"Yes, sir," Ajax replies, "anything else?"

"I want you to take her to the Barn tomorrow."

"Are you sure?"

"We need his approval before we can take this much further."

"I suppose. Well, we'll see to it."

"Good, now run along. I have other business to attend to."

"Certainly," Ajax says and we leave the room.

I let out a huge sigh of relief. "Well, that was fun."

"I think it went well," Ajax replies. "You must have gained some trust or he would never recommend re-arming you."

"I guess," I reply, "what are we going to do now?"

"I propose another trip to the armoury and then we can do some scouting in town. What do you say?"

"I think it's a great idea."

"Then it's settled. Let's go."

CHAPTER ELEVEN

Later that night, around six o'clock, Ajax and I stroll into the cafeteria. We spent the afternoon traipsing around town, wreaking havoc with a group of new assassins and reacquainting ourselves with Haven City. I haven't had that much fun in months. The encounter in the tunnel has been forgotten and we are laughing as we make it to the front of the food line.

"The look on that kid's face though," I gasp out, half leaning on him to stay balanced through my laughter.

"Priceless," Ajax replies.

"Guild, that was fun."

"Yeah, but are you sure they won't go running back to your master to tell him they saw you?"

I straighten. "No, I frightened them good. They won't say anything unless he asks them personally, and he has no reason to think I would show myself to a bunch of Guild Wards."

"If you say so."

"I do."

"Then let's get eating."

We pile food onto our plates and join Bast and Blake at our table.

"Where have you two been?" Blake asks as we sit down.

"Oh, here and there," Ajax replies.

"I had my first mission today," I say, beaming.

"Congratulations," Bast exclaims. "I knew you'd do it. Someone with your talent couldn't stay in the dark for long."

"Right you are. It was wonderful to be in the field again, and Jenson says I can accompany Ajax whenever now."

"Sweet."

"You're telling me."

"What was it like?"

I tell Bast the tale of our adventures and Ajax offers his thoughts every once in a while. He's taking the spotlight again when I notice Blake grow quiet. Well, quieter than usual.

I reach across the table to poke her in the arm. "Hey, what's wrong?"

She doesn't say anything, just pulls at the end of her braid as she stares at something across the room.

I follow her gaze. There, standing at a table in the far corner, is none other than Ms. Natalie Sophia Roseanne.

Isn't that just wonderful.

Ajax and Bast notice something off with Blake too and stop their conversation. It takes them a few minutes to see who Blake and I are watching.

"Son of a..." Bast mutters. "What is *she* doing here?"

I cross my arms nonchalantly and reply in my best imitation of her insufferable voice. "Daddy has reassigned our dear friend Natalie to a room in my hall."

Blake laughs a little and so does Bast.

"Are you serious?" Ajax says. Clearly, he was listening more to *what* I said than *how* I said it.

"Deadly," I reply, "in fact, the little princess had the nerve to come to my room after lunch today just to tell me about it." I neglect to mention her threats. There's no need to get anyone else involved.

"You're kidding," Bast says.

"Not in the least," I reply. "She also warned me to stay away from her man."

Ajax raises an eyebrow. "What man?"

"You."

He groans and lays his head on the table. "I swear to God... I don't know why she can't give that up. I've been turning her down since I was twelve."

I snort. "I knew she was barking up the wrong tree."

"None of that explains what she's doing in the cafeteria," Blake points out.

"What, doesn't she eat here usually?" I ask.

"No," Ajax replies. "She never eats here. She and her father have dinner alone somewhere. It's the same with Jenson. It's odd to see her mingling with everyone."

"Well, if it's abnormal behaviour, I think I know the reason."

"What?" the three of them ask.

"Daddy dearest wants someone to keep an eye on me."

"That's undermining Jenson's authority," Ajax argues, "not to mention insinuating I'm not good enough at my job." He scowls into his soup.

"Who is this father of hers anyway?" I ask. "What gives him the authority to mess with us or question Jenson?"

The three of them share a look.

"What?" I ask.

Ajax sighs. "This father of hers is Nicholas Ross, Jenson's Second."

Well damn.

The last name tugs at me, as if I know it from somewhere. I wonder why it's different than Natalie's, but I can think on that later.

"Jenson's Second, eh?" I reply. "Why am I not surprised? Guess I'm stuck with that thorn in my side then, aren't I?"

They nod.

"Wonderful." I take a breath. "Well, it doesn't matter. Nicholas can do what he wants, but if he hasn't changed Jenson's mind yet, I doubt he will. As for Natalie, she's nothing but a moot point, but she's definitely cruising for a bruising."

"I'd pay good money to see that fight," Bast says.

"All I can say is that she better watch her back because one day, she'll turn around and I'll be waiting."

134

Blake shakes her head. "Spoken like a true assassin," she mutters, "but I hope you do."

I smile at her for once. "I'd be more than happy to oblige." I finger one of the knives in my belt. Ajax and I never bothered to change before coming to dinner. I just took off my cloak.

Bast notices my gesture and then eyes the weapons lining my body. "Jeez, Night," he says, "you think you've got enough steel? How can you carry it all?"

I shrug. "I could probably use a bit more, but I don't find it heavy. I've been trained so the weight doesn't bother me."

"How many are on you?"

"I have the two swords, at least ten knives, two guns, three packs of ammo, and various daggers."

Bast whistles. "I only ever carry a sword and bow, be it cross or long."

"Yeah, well, I've learned to never underestimate an enemy and to have whatever weapon necessary to end them on my person. You can't run home in the middle of a fight to grab a knife if you need one."

"I guess that's true," he replies. "Do you know how to use them all?"

I narrow my eyes. "Why in the Guild would I carry a weapon I couldn't use?"

He holds up his hands. "I was just asking."

I lean back in my seat. "You know, I could probably teach you guys a thing or two, if you wanted. I've noticed you stick to the same couple of weapons. You should broaden your horizons."

Bast and Blake share a look with Ajax.

He shrugs. "It couldn't hurt. You've definitely shown your skills and proven your trust. Besides, I could use a break from teaching."

"I suppose it could be fun," Blake allows.

"Of course it will, Blakey," Bast exclaims. "We'll be getting exclusive assassin-level training."

He's only half right. I don't think they could handle real assassin-level training. If anything, it would break Bast's spirit.

"We can get started as soon as you're done eating," I tell him.

Ajax smiles. "That could be a while."

"Hey!" Bast protests.

"It's the truth, man," Ajax argues. "You're slower than molasses."

• • •

An hour later, the four of us are still gathered in our usual training room. I've spent the better part of that time coaching the three in various forms of rare combat. Ajax is adept at most concepts I throw at him, which doesn't surprise me. Blake and Bast need a little more instruction, so by the end of the hour, Ajax is teaching alongside me. We go through knife throwing, sharp shooting, and I even made them do a couple laps before we got started. We end with hand to hand combat.

It's getting late, but Bast refuses to take a break until he can get a clear shot at me. I admire his resolve, but we might be going all night. Ajax and Blake are sitting on a bench against the wall, sipping water from plastic cups as they watch Bast and I spar.

"You have to keep moving," I tell him, bouncing around on my feet. "As soon as you're still, you're just asking to get hit."

He stops again as he takes aim at my head.

I reach through the hole in his defenses and tap his face with my fist as my other arm blocks his strike.

"See, you have to learn punch while moving."

He sighs and drops his hands. "Ugh, it's too much to remember."

I stop too and try to appear sympathetic. He would be disgraced at the Guild for giving up, would already be on the ground licking his wounds.

"It takes practice," I tell him. "I didn't get good at it overnight." The constant beatings had been an effective motivator to improve though, until I was strong enough to beat the shit out of my mentor instead.

"Yeah," he mutters, "I guess but..." And then he's swinging his left fist at me.

I duck and catch his right wrist with my hand as I straighten.

"Nice try," I tell him. "You're catching on to what I'm saying, but I saw that one coming."

"No fair," he groans.

"Oh, don't be a sore loser, Sebastian," Blake chides him.

Bast whirls on her. *"Don't* call me that!"

Blake gives Ajax a knowing look. "You're whining now, Seb."

Bast gives her a dark scowl I never thought I'd see him wear.

"Shut up," he snaps and I hear Ajax stifle a laugh. It turns into a coughing fit as he tries to choke it back.

I smile.

"What are *you* all happy about?" Bast asks me.

"Oh, come on, Bastian," I say, "chill out, man."

Ajax roars with laughter and Blake joins him this time. "Oh, man," Ajax chokes out. "That was priceless. You are definitely a part of this team."

Bast gives the three of us looks of utter contempt. "Idiots, the lot of you," he mutters.

"I think we should call it a night, Bast," I tell him.

"Fine, but I won't go so easy on you next time."

The two of us take a seat on the bench beside Ajax and Blake, and we all sit there in silence for a moment, Bast and I catching our breath.

Then Blake leans forward to look over at me. "So, Night, I noticed something missing from your weapon arsenal."

Did she now?

I do a mental check of my weapons. The only thing missing is a bow and…

Oh, please don't say it.

"You don't have an axe," she goes on and my heart drops. "I assume because they add a fair amount of weight, but I was wondering if you've used one before?"

138

"Of course I know how to use one," I retort, trying to keep my emotions in check.

"Would you be up for a duel? My preferred weapon is the battle axe, but these two are abysmal sparring partners. I haven't had a good fight with it in months."

"Hey," Bast retorts, "we're not that bad."

"Sure," Ajax replies, "says the guy who almost dropped the axe on his foot last time."

I smile at that as I consider my answer. I don't want to say no; it might ruin this sense of camaraderie we've got going on. On the other hand, I don't want to say yes either.

Why does it have to be a battle axe? Why couldn't it be something else, anything else?

I take a deep breath. "Sounds like a deal," I tell her. "When were you thinking?"

"Right now," she replies.

Great.

"Guess I'm ready for it; Bast didn't tire me too much." I grin at him and he scowls again.

Blake beams. "I'll go get us a pair of axes then."

She heads off to the weapons rack and I wait, stomach tying itself into knots.

This isn't going to end well.

I weigh the borrowed axe in my hand, swinging it back and forth to get a feel for it. I take a deep breath to keep myself from shaking. I don't know why I'm so nervous. It's not like this duel is a matter of life and death; it's a matter of social standing, but in this case, it's a battle of significantly more importance.

Blake paces the floor six feet across the mat from me. She holds the axe comfortably in her hand, like it's nothing more than an extension of her arm. I hold the double-bladed monstrosity like it's going to leap up and decapitate me at any second, though the blade is blunt. The extra weight of the padding Ajax made us put on isn't doing much to assure me either.

I've never much liked axes. They're too heavy and cumbersome, definitely not the ideal weapon to lug around town. I hate to say it, but I'm almost certain I'm going to lose this duel.

"All right, girls," Bast says, "take it easy on each other now."

I roll my eyes, but say nothing as I sink into a ready position.

Blake mirrors me, smiling a confident little grin.

Fire flares inside me. I will not let some Resistance agent best me.

It's game on, Blake. Game on.

We wait a few seconds more before Bast's voice punctures the silence. "Now!"

We charge.

Our weapons collide mid-strike as we both aim for the head. My heart beats wildly in my chest.

Focus.

I step back and twist as she swings at my waist. It takes considerable effort, but I manage to execute a counter strike at her unprotected left side.

She sees it coming a mile away. Dodging the blow with ease, she strikes out at my legs, forcing me to jump out of

140

the way. It knocks me off balance, costing me precious seconds and any advantage I might've had.

Guild.

My anger distracts me for a single second, but it's enough.

Crushing pain blooms through my chest and I fly across the mat, crashing to the ground several feet away. I lose my grip on the axe and it clatters to the floor.

Assassins below.

I might forget my plans and kill that girl.

Ajax runs over to me. "Silent! Are you okay?" He leans down and holds out a hand to help me up.

I swat it away. "I'm fine," I gasp. My head is spinning and my ribs are throbbing.

She will pay. Oh, she will pay.

"You don't look fine," he argues. "Come on, let me help you."

"I'm *fine*! Leave me alone!"

He jumps back, startled by my tone.

I struggle to my feet, ignoring the floor as it spins. Then I lock eyes with Blake. "What the *hell* was that?" I snap. "You could've killed me! I thought this was supposed to be a bit of fun competition?"

She winces. "I didn't mean to hurt you. I thought you'd block that."

Liar.

"Well I *didn't*."

141

Basl jumps in between the two of us. "Hey," he says. "Hey! Let's not get feisty. It was an accident. She's sorry. You're alive. Everything's good, right?"

"Wrong," I reply, and then I march out of the room. I've had enough of their stupid games.

• • •

I sit cross-legged on my bed, my throwing knives spread out beside me. I pick them up one by one and fling them at the door. Five hang quivering in it now and chunks of wood are missing from its face. Wood chips and sawdust litter the floor beneath it.

Blake.

I can see her dark silhouette in front of me.

She thinks she's all that, thinks she can get away with trying to kill me as if I wouldn't notice...

Thud!

My arm moved of its own volition, my thoughts propelling it forward. I check the door.

Damn.

It was only a shoulder shot. It wouldn't kill her.

Oh no, not precious Blake the axe wielder.

Cur-thump!

I smile wider.

That's much better.

I jump off of the bed and retrieve the knives. Some take more effort than others, having embedded themselves deep into the wood.

142

Once I have them all, I return to my bed and throw again—just as the door opens and Ajax steps in.

The weapon hits the edge of the door instead of the centre and ricochets off, clattering against the bed frame before coming to rest on the floor.

My eyes widen.

That was a close one.

Ajax glares at me. "What the *hell*, Silent? I know you're mad at Blake but that's no reason to—" That's when he sees the door. "What are you doing?"

"Taking out my anger," I reply.

"By drawing the outline of a person on your door and throwing knives at it?"

I cross my arms. "Would you rather I go out there and throw knives at a real person? Blake, perhaps?"

Ajax sighs. "You seriously wish her harm for what she did?"

"She tried to kill me."

"No, she didn't, Silent," he argues. "That was never her intention. After watching you fight all evening, she expected you to block that move."

"But I didn't!"

I swear if they say that one more time...

"Okay, you didn't," Ajax allows. "We see that. The point is, she misjudged and she's sorry."

"Why didn't *she* come tell me that?"

"She tried to in the training room, but you refused to listen, and to be fair, I don't think your room is a safe place for her right now. You know, what with you throwing knives at a door you're pretending is her."

143

"Yeah, I get that, but..." I sigh. "Can you blame me? I am who I am and I don't take well to near-death experiences. I'm used to doing the maiming, not being hurt myself."

"I understand that, but it doesn't condone violence. What you need to understand is that not everyone is out to get you."

"And isn't that a great way to be caught unaware."

"Oh, come on, Silent," he exclaims, throwing his arms up in exasperation. "You can't mean that."

"Yes I can, Ajax. You can't tell me how I feel. You didn't grow up the way I did, you haven't seen the sides of people I've seen. You can't understand. People would sooner take advantage of you than help you. They would sooner lie than tell the truth. And anybody who's faced with death or ending the life of another will choose to become a murderer. That's just how things are."

And aren't you a prime example?

"That's not true, Silent. Not everyone is like that. There are good people in this world."

"And you might be one of them, Ajax," I reply, "but I'm not and neither are most of the people in Haven. So I'm sorry for preserving myself by being paranoid and building siege walls around my emotions, but the world is a dangerous place and I intend to survive as long as I can. I'm not done with this life yet, not by half."

He gives me a sad look. "That's all well and good, Silent, but what good is surviving if you never really live? What good is life if you spend it constantly looking over your shoulder for the worst or locked up in a tower? You

144

have to let yourself experience the joys of life: fun, friendship, love. You're willing to give all that up so you can live longer, alone and unhappy?

"I... That's not exactly..." I fumble.

To tell the truth, I've never thought about it that way, the things I've missed out on by concentrating solely on survival. There hadn't been an alternative at the Guild, but now I have a choice. I can make friends and have fun. I can be happy without worrying about the consequences. I can be free.

But am I willing to let my guard down?

"Look," Ajax says, "just promise me you'll think about it, okay?"

"I will, thank you," I reply.

"Existence is great and all, but what's the point of life if you don't live it?"

I nod and he turns to go.

"Night, Silent, I'll see you tomorrow."

"Goodnight," I say and then he's gone.

I sigh. It pains me to say it, but he's right. He is so very right, but I can't help but wonder why he even cares. It's not like it'll change *his* life if I decide to start living. Maybe it's because he's a good guy and hates to see people unhappy. It's that big heart of his and his leadership. He wants to protect people I guess, but I'm sure that in my case, he chose the wrong person to save.

CHAPTER TWELVE

I wake to silence, which is strange, and it takes me a moment to figure out why that is. I wasn't woken by a knock on my door.

So why am I awake?

It can't be any kind of danger; my hair isn't standing on end.

I open one eye a sliver and scan the room by rolling over, as if I'm doing it while sleeping deeply. I find nothing out of the ordinary.

Huh.

I sit up and stretch. Then I hop out of bed and pad over to the door to look into the hall. Ajax stopped locking my door a few days ago.

There's still nothing amiss.

What's going on?

Maybe I'm early, simple as that, but why would I wake up early?

I go back into the room and check the clock: eight thirty-five. I'm not early; Ajax is late.

Where is he?

He usually arrives at eight o'clock on the nose, aside from the first day when he woke me at the ungodly hour of seven. Eight o'clock is the time now, not one second sooner or one second later.

Maybe something held him up. Maybe he slept in. Innocent enough reasons, but what if it's something worse? What if something happened to him?

What if Natalie got her wish and he's left me?

I have to find him.

I rush to get dressed, throwing on a grey suit and my cloak. Then I belt my throwing knives on and dart into the hall.

I try to keep a reasonable pace as I travel through the base, not wanting to look like I'm up to something, but it's killing me. I don't even know where to start looking. I have no idea where *his* room is.

After several moments of thought, I decide the cafeteria would be the best place. Blake or Bast might be there and they would know if he has a good reason for being late. Maybe he was called out on a last-minute mission or something.

It takes a great amount of effort not to break into a run as I make my way to the cafeteria.

Guild, is it always this far away? Did I take a wrong turn?

But then, there it is. I burst through the doors into a room of sleepy people. No one looks up as I enter. I scan the room for Bast or Blake and then...

Then I see him: Ajax, sitting at the squad table, laughing along with Bast.

He's okay.

I feel foolish. My reaction was stupid and completely out of character.

Since when do I care about the welfare of others? What is wrong with me?

Shaking off my panic, I get in line for food and quietly accept a bowl of cereal. Then I go over to our table.

"Morning," I say as I sit down across from Ajax.

"Hey," Ajax replies with a smile. "I see you finally decided to wake up."

I purse my lips. "You could say that, seeing as a certain person wasn't there to do so."

"You wake her up every morning?" Bast says, raising a suggestive eyebrow.

Ajax rolls his eyes. "That's not what she means, Bast, you dirty little..."

I try not to blush.

"I just knock on her door," Ajax finishes.

"*Right,*" Bast says.

Ajax scowls at him.

"You didn't knock today," I point out.

"I know," Ajax replies.

I know, as if it isn't a big deal.

"I... Where were you?" I fidget with my spoon, swirling it around the bowl.

"In my own room and then I came straight here, why?" He's giving me a strange look, but I'm not the only one acting weird here.

"Why weren't you there?" I ask him.

"Is it that big of a deal? I decided you don't need me to watch you every single second of the day. Surely you're capable of waking up on your own?"

I drop the spoon will a hollow ding against the rim of my bowl.

Is he really that stupid?

"That's not what this is about," I say, fighting to keep my volume under control.

"Okay," he relents. He looks over at Bast. "You think you could excuse us for a minute?"

Bast waves a hand. "Sure, go resolve your issues."

I glare at him before I follow Ajax out into the hall.

He leads me to a quiet, secluded corridor and then turns to face me. "What's wrong? I thought you'd be happy to have some freedom. It can't be all that great to have me breathing down your neck from sunrise to sunset every day."

"I appreciate the freedom, but..." I bite my lip. "Do you think it's wise to leave me by myself? I... I could do anything. I could go on a freak killing spree. I could leave and take the coordinates of your base to the Guild. I—"

He holds up a hand and I cut myself short. "The fact that you didn't do any of those things is exactly the reason why I decided this."

Funny, he's right again. My first thought when I woke up alone wasn't to escape or kill, it was to find him.

What does that say about me?

"I..."

"Relax, Silent. I told you: I trust you."

I can't accept that answer. "How *can* you? You've known me for what, two weeks? Ajax, that's crazy."

What does he see in me that I can't see in myself?

He puts his hands in his pockets. "Like I said before, I consider myself an excellent judge of character and I've deemed you trustworthy."

"But I'm not!" I protest, throwing out my hands. "I've been murdering people since I was ten. I'm a horrible person."

"No," he says, grabbing my wrists.

I don't shrink away from his touch.

"Don't say that. You're not a horrible person. The fact that you know killing is wrong immediately sets you apart from the rest of the assassins. Your old Master is the horrible person, Silent. He fashioned you into a weapon for killing, he *made* you the way you are. It's not your fault." He drops my arms, but not my gaze. His eyes burn into mine. "In a duel, is the sword the killer? No, the person wielding it is. You're not the person in the wrong; you never knew any better."

"So, what, you're saying I'm a sword?"

"No. I..." He scratches the back of his head. "It's a metaphor. I'm saying you have the capacity for change. You can step away from that horrible life and be the person you were meant to be before he came along and ruined everything. You still have hope, and that's why I trust you."

I don't know what to say to that. Somehow, he keeps managing to surprise me, to throw me off of my game. I never have an answer for his poetic speeches. His words make me think, make me consider things I wouldn't otherwise. Guild, I haven't even thought of my plan in days. Am I that good at pretending or is he getting to me? Getting inside my head, making me forget the real reason I'm here...

"Silent? You okay?"

I shake my head to clear it. "Yeah," I reply, "it's just that every time you say something like that, it catches me off guard."

I'm not used to being seen as anything other than an assassin, a killer.

He runs a hand through his hair. "Truth be told, Silent, you've caught me off guard too. You're constantly changing my mind of what a Guild assassin looks like. I'm finding you're more than the merciless killer you make yourself out to be. Maybe someday you'll be able to see it too."

"Maybe," I mumble.

"Are you going to come back to the cafeteria and finish your breakfast?"

"I might as well."

He smiles slightly at me. "Let's go then."

• • •

After breakfast, Ajax sends me back to my room alone, despite my protests. He says he'll come for me later. I still don't agree with the whole "let the assassin roam free" idea, but I don't have a choice.

I've been in my room for about twenty minutes when a knock comes on my door.

I let out a huge sigh of relief. "Thank the Guild, Ajax," I say as the door opens. "An assassin and free time is a horrible combination. I—" Then I realize the person standing in the open doorway is not Ajax. It's Blake.

Her dark hair is unbound for once and it makes her look younger somehow, kinder.

"Oh," I say, "hi. I thought you were—"

"Ajax?" she finishes for me. "I know, but sadly I don't fit the description."

She stands there awkwardly for a minute.

"What are you doing here?" I ask, doing my best to sound polite.

"Ajax sent me over with these," she replies, holding up a stack of clothes she has cradled in her arms.

"What are they for?"

"It's an entirely new wardrobe," she replies, "black outfits, dark blue and green, red."

"No," I gasp. "He didn't."

She smiles slightly. "He did. He says you deserve it."

"I don't deserve anything," I mutter, "especially after the way I treated you. I'm sorry."

"No, I'm the one who should be sorry; it was foolish of me to assume."

"Why don't we say it was equal fault and leave it at a draw?" I suggest, holding out a hand.

She nods her head to her load of clothes.

"Just put them on the bed," I tell her.

She sets them down gently and turns back to me.

"Is that a deal?" I ask.

She takes my hand. "Deal," she says and we shake.

"Now that's over with," I continue, "I suppose I should sort through these clothes."

"They're really good quality," Blake says, wincing. "I kind of looked through them. I hope you don't mind?"

I wave a hand. "Whatever, it's not like you would steal anything. No pretty dresses or baubles here."

She raises a thick eyebrow. "Dresses and baubles?"

"You know, the ridiculous outfits normal girls wear, girls that aren't me."

She gives me a look. "If that's what entitles being normal, then I'm certainly not either. I can't stand dresses."

It's my turn to raise an eyebrow. "You're kidding."

"I'm serious," she replies. "Cross my heart and hope to die. I wouldn't be caught dead in something you can't fight in."

"Wow, I thought... You know what, it doesn't matter. What matters is that I only want the red and black, so you can take your pick of the rest."

"Really?"

"Why not? Have a seat."

She sits down tentatively on the edge of the bed and we go through the pile of clothes together. I pull out a simply gorgeous black cloak with a fur collar.

"Oh my God," she breathes. "Is that what I think it is?"

"Yep, Georges Fleurner."

"That's where I buy my cloaks, when I can afford them."

"Me too. Guild, where did Ajax get these?"

"I don't know," she replies. "Hey, speaking of Fleurner, I've been wondering, where do you get your boots?"

And on the conversation goes.

We discuss cloaks, tunics, and boots, and then move on to weapons as soon as I mention how much I love the built-in belts the Resistance uniforms have. I learn that although the axe is her favourite weapon, she also likes swords and daggers.

We swap stories about our favourite blades and she tells me all about axes. I return the favour by educating her on firearms.

We've been sitting in my room for a solid forty minutes when a voice interrupts our babble.

"Oh, yeah, I simply adore that make and model, cuts through steel like it's pudding." Bast is leaning against the door frame, arms crossed and sporting a ridiculous smirk.

Without even thinking about it, Blake and I send him twin death glares, then look at each other and laugh.

The colour drains from Bast's face. He looks behind him and calls out, "Jax! You better come quickly! They're scheming, plotting to end me."

Ajax walks up behind him and stays standing in the hall. "Surely they aren't?" he says, smiling.

"Lock your bedroom door tonight, man," Bast continues, "I'm telling you. Not going to sleep a wink myself."

I smile and say, "Puny little lock won't keep me out, Sebastian."

His eyes grow to the size of saucers. "We're screwed, Jax," he breathes, "totally screwed."

Blake laughs and says, "Relax, Seb, we were only kidding, or at least, I was."

Bast bristles at the name.

"Oh, I was too," I agree readily. Then I grin at him and wink. I've never seen a more frightened face in my life.

"Anyway," I go on, "what brings the two of you to my humble abode?" I look at Ajax.

"We're all going out," he replies.

"Really? Where?"

"We call it the Barn. You'll see when we get there."

The Barn...

I recognize the name.

What...

Oh.

"Is that what you and Jenson were discussing yesterday? We have to seek someone's approval or something?"

"Yes, it was what we were discussing."

"Who is the him you guys were speaking of? And approval for what?"

"The him is the leader of our entire operation."

I frown. "But I thought that was Jenson?"

155

"Most people would, but Jenson is merely second in command. He runs the Warehouse, also known as the Resistance West. Our leader runs it all, of course, and he resides at the Barn, or the Resistance East. As for the approval we seek... Well, that would be for you."

"What?"

"Our leader is going to decide for certain whether or not you can stay with us, whether or not he thinks your inside information is worth the risk you may pose."

I swallow back my sudden terror.

Assassins below.

Blake puts a reassuring hand on my shoulder.

I shrug it off gently. "Why now?" I ask.

"We've put it off long enough as it is," Ajax says. "You've been here more than a fortnight. Don't worry about it, Silent. He's not ruthless. He won't kill you."

"How can you know that? I'm Silent Night. Lots of people want me dead."

"He's a reasonable guy, Silent. He'll see the potential in keeping you, what you and only you can help us accomplish. Honestly, if Jenson hasn't killed you yet, our leader won't either."

I sigh. "I hope you're right because I've just started living; it would be a shame if I died."

He smiles, but it doesn't reach his eyes.

"Well, we should probably get going if we want to get back before nightfall," Bast says. He inches into the hall and Blake joins him.

"Right," Ajax replies. Then he turns to me. "Grab all the weapons you think you'll need."

156

I frown. "Why?"

He takes a step closer to me and says, "Because if he *does* decide to kill you, Silent, I want you to have a fighting chance."

CHAPTER THIRTEEN

Half an hour later, the four of us have just crossed the North River and are heading in a north-easterly direction towards the middle of nowhere. The streets in this part of Haven are country lanes and hold about four houses each.

"This place is lifeless," I say, breaking the silence.

"It seems that way, but people *do* live here," Ajax replies.

"It's impossible to tell."

"Ever wonder if that's exactly what they want you to think?"

"I guess," I agree. "Are we there yet?"

"Not quite."

"It's okay, Night," Blake says, trying to be assuring.

I merely press my lips together and nod, not trusting my voice.

The houses thin out until we're walking through empty fields. Long grass wraps around our legs and sways in the breeze. Weeds and wildflowers alike claim the earth as their own. I get a strange feeling in my stomach, something I haven't felt in ages: fear.

"Almost there," Ajax says.

I let out a breath.

Thank the Guild.

We walk up a hill and I see an old barn in the valley on the other side. Well, old isn't the right word. The structure is ancient, red paint long peeled off to give it a pale pinkish look. Entire boards are missing and the roof has caved in. Wind rustles through the area and the wood creaks as the whole barn sways.

"What is this?" I ask.

Ajax looks at me and smiles. "Welcome to the Barn."

I choke on a laugh. "*This* is your Eastern operations? You've got to be kidding me. We're in the middle of nowhere and that thing looks like it'll collapse at any second."

"Appearances aren't everything, Silent," Ajax replies. "In fact, they're quite arbitrary. It's what's on the inside that counts."

I roll my eyes as he walks toward the barn, Blake and Bast close behind. I look on in disbelief. "What, you're serious? We're actually going in there?"

Ajax turns around. "Yeah. Are you coming or not?"

I look around, as if searching for a way out, and find no escape. "Assassin's below," I mutter. Then I march up to where they stand.

They take turns ducking under the sagging doorway and I bring up the rear of our little party. As I step into the darkness, I realize it's not actually dark. That's when I notice the ceiling and the little spotlights dangling from it.

What in the Guild?

Then I realize something else; the interior of the barn is not old or dilapidated at all. It's new and shiny, the walls made of metal.

"What *is* this?" I ask.

"Our most guarded secret," Ajax replies with a smile. "You want to see the rest of it?"

"Do I have a choice?"

He doesn't answer; instead, he walks over to the far wall and presses a button. A hatch opens up in the floor.

"Ladies first," Bast says, gesturing to me.

"Do you think I'm stupid?" I retort.

"Come on, Night, relax," Blake says. "It's just a staircase." She jumps down into the hole. "See?" she calls up. "No harm done."

I take a deep breath before dropping down beside her. Ajax and Bast join us.

"Down we go," Ajax says. He types a code into a wall panel and the hatch above us closes. I follow them down the steps, hoping with everything I am that this isn't how I die.

The descent is short, about the same time the elevator takes in my Guild entrance, but it's a hundred times more nerve-wracking. I feel like I'm descending into the belly of a beast. In a way, I am. The beast would be the Resistance, my enemy for life. The last two weeks or so were okay. I

160

handled it with ease, but something tells me this will be different. I don't know why.

My brooding thoughts are interrupted when the staircase ends and we step into the open. I look out and can't comprehend what I see.

We're at the end of a bright, tiled hallway with checkered marble floors and white walls. The hall is approximately fifty feet long. Floor to ceiling double doors stand at the end of it. Each door is flanked by a guard. They're dressed in grey uniforms much the same as ours, but their blue capes set them apart, not to mention the rifles they're cradling as they stare right at us.

My heart speeds up. "Ajax," I breathe, "I can't do this."

"Yes, you can," he replies, eyes ahead. "Don't worry. We'll get you through this."

I grab his sleeve. "No, you don't understand. I can't walk down there. I *can't*."

He whirls on me, ripping his sleeve from my grasp. "You *can*." He looks me straight in the eye. "Listen to me, Silent. You've spent *how* many years working for the Master Assassin and *this* is the time you decide to give into fear? I'm telling you: you'll get through this. *I'll* get you through this. I trust you, now you're going to have to trust me. Got it?"

I nod, his conviction silencing me.

"Then let's do this. You walk beside me. Blake and Bast will go behind. Keep your chin up. We're not escorting you to an execution."

The four of us set ourselves up how Ajax requested. I take a deep breath as we walk toward the doors and the two men with rifles.

Calm down, I tell myself, but it doesn't work. By the time we reach the end of the hall, I can barely breathe.

One of the men looks at Ajax and says, "Name and business?"

"I am Ajax Forrester, agent of the third level, here with Bast and Blake, agents of the second level." He nods his head at me. "This is Indigo. She's a new recruit and we're here to seek approval so she can continue her training."

"Sounds good," the man says. "I.D. chips please?"

Ajax reaches into his pocket and pulls out a piece of plastic the size of my thumb, hanging on a short chain. He hands it to the man, Blake and Bast following suit with their own.

The man takes a metal box out of his coat and inserts the chips one at a time into a slot on the bottom. They must hold information the box is able to read. The whole thing is beyond me; I never understood computers and they're scarce these days.

After a few moments, the man hands the chips back and says, "All right, you're clear."

The men step away from the door and Ajax opens it for us. We enter a hallway much like the ones at the Guild and my fear lessens the further we walk. We come to an intersection and turn right.

"What's with the key chains?" I ask.

"He has to make sure we're not lying about our identities," Ajax replies.

162

"Any good spy would be able to steal one of those."

"Maybe," he allows.

"You're all fools to think that's enough security," I argue.

"Shhh," he breathes, "we're coming into the base proper now. Someone might hear you. Do you want to be kicked out before we even see him?"

"That's another thing," I say, "this *him*, your leader. None of you have said his name yet. Is it a secret? He does have one, doesn't he?"

"Yes, he does," Ajax sighs, "but we can't tell anyone his name until they are approved. It's a rule. Do you tell anyone *your* master's true name?"

"No, we don't, but that's because none of us know it."

Ajax raises an eyebrow. "He doesn't tell you?"

"No," I say.

I may be the only assassin who knows, though the Charger isn't aware of this. It happened by accident. I was creeping around the Guild one night when I was about nine, practising my ability to blend in with the dark, when I stumbled upon his office. That was back when he didn't have two or three assassins guarding the door day and night.

I heard him muttering to himself in the office, boasting about his latest exploits. It was something along the lines of: he said I could never do it, that I couldn't take this city. "Sephtis Aeron," he said, "you're a fool." Well, I proved him wrong, didn't I?

I ran back to my room as fast as I could and barely spoke for the next week, fearing the Charger—or Sephtis, rather—would discover what I had heard, but he never came for me and here I am.

"Well," Ajax says, "is it that weird that our leader doesn't want you to know then?"

"I guess not," I relent, "but at least the Charger gave us something to call him so we didn't have to refer to him as *him* or the Leader all the time."

Ajax raises an eyebrow. "The Charger? You've never called him that before."

I realize that I haven't, not out loud.

"So?"

He narrows his eyes. "Isn't that the name of the black market leader?"

"Yeah, we borrow it sometimes, to throw you guys off." The lie is smooth; I don't even have to think about it.

He doesn't seem convinced, but Bast cuts off his protest.

"Would the two of you stick a sock in it?"

We look back at him in surprise.

"He's right," Blake agrees. "Argue about it later, we have bigger concerns right now."

Ajax sighs. "Okay. I hear you."

We continue in silence, following him through the base.

The Resistance East is much the same as the Resistance West. Hallways lead to a variety of rooms. People in grey uniforms watch our little procession as we walk past and I hear whispering in our wake. I notice the place is quieter than the Warehouse, cleaner too. It seems...empty somehow.

Ten minutes after we arrive, we head down a silent, dimly lit corridor. At its end, one person stands guarding the double doors—a woman with black hair, a black uniform, and a crimson cape. She intimidates with ease and I know without a doubt that the mysterious *him* resides in the room behind her.

We stroll up to her and stop a couple of feet away. Blake comes to stand at my other side, Bast doing the same with Ajax.

The woman looks at us and smiles. "Why if it isn't Ajax Forrester and his little band of misfits. How're you doing, kid?"

Kid? Who is she calling kid? She can't be two years older...

But, on second glance, I realize that kid was warranted. She's probably in her late twenties, early thirties. I hope I look that good if I make it to her age.

"Not bad, Trey, yourself?" Ajax answers.

She shrugs. "It could be worse. I see you've brought Sebastian."

He scowls.

"And Blake," the woman adds. Then she sees me. "Who is this, a new recruit? I suppose that's why you're here to see the big man. He..."

She trails off as she looks closer at me, real close, as if looking into my soul. She blinks her eyes in disbelief and I see a spark ignite in them.

"I know exactly who you are," she whispers.

Are those tears building up in her eyes?

"You're Silent Night," she breathes.

How?

"Yes," I say as she continues to stare at me. "How... How did you guess?"

She wipes her eyes—they *were* tears. "I'm sorry," she says, "forgive me. You... You remind me of someone I used to know."

"What happened?" I ask.

"I lost her."

"I'm sorry," I reply, and I am. She seemed broken as she looked at me.

"Well," Trey says, regaining her composure, "anyway, the reason I know your name is that I was once a part of the Guild and I try to keep tabs on the assassins. You, my dear, are renowned."

My eyes grow round. "What? You were in the Guild? You're an ex-assassin? A...a traitor?"

"Yes, I betrayed them, same as you did, I wager."

"How long ago was that?"

"Twelve years, give or take."

My jaw drops. "Twelve *years* and you're still alive? The Charger hasn't found you and tortured you until you were begging for death yet?"

"Guild, no," she says, using my favourite assassin curse. It's proof enough that what she says is true. "You think I'd let him get to me with the goal I have in mind?"

"And that goal is?"

"I wish to destroy him like he destroyed my life."

I grin. I could get to like this girl; we have the same endgame in mind.

"Hey, um, the rest of us are still here," Bast interrupts us.

"Yeah," Ajax jumps in. "I'd like to be home before nightfall, if you don't mind."

"Right," Trey says. "Sorry. Go right in. He's waiting for you."

What? Assassins below.

I forgot about the meeting we've yet to have.

Ajax turns to Bast and Blake. "You two stay here; we'll be out in a minute or so." They don't protest.

My nerves come back in full force.

Guild, I can't do this.

Ajax somehow senses my distress, for he puts a hand on my shoulder as Trey opens the door for us and we walk inside. I don't shake it off and a part of me whispers, *don't let go.*

We step into a large circular room with a long table. A single lamp illuminates the space. At the centre of the far side of the table, a man sits. He's tall, but of average build with dark hair and skin. He looks familiar.

"Ah, Mr. Forrester," the man says. "It's been a while. Have a seat."

I recognize the voice, but I can't place it.

Who is it?

I follow Ajax's example and sit down at the table beside him.

The man studies Ajax for a minute. Then his eyes fall on me and stay there. "Well, this certainly is an interesting turn of events. Unless my eyes deceive me, you are Silent Night."

It hits me then and it makes so much sense.

"Yes," I reply, "yes I am, and you're Avery."

He smiles. "Clever girl."

Ajax looks at me in awe. "How did you...?"

"I'd like to know the answer to that as well," Avery says.

"A little over two weeks ago, you had a meeting with a woman named Rachel at 1253 Charles Avenue. The two of you were not alone."

"You were following her, I presume?" Avery says.

"Yes. The Master Assassin suspected her and told me to find out what was going on. I reported back and..." I fumble with my words. I hate reliving the executions. I hate admitting I was a part of them. "She was executed," I finish.

Avery nods. "I expect nothing else from the Charger. Is that really what he calls himself these days?"

"I... What do you mean?"

"I'm not stupid, Assassin; I know that's not his true name. It's just one of the many monikers he's chosen. Master Assassin is another one of his favourites. The Charger is a cover-up name, so when we catch one of you, we'll write you off as black market lackeys, but I happen to know it's a ruse. Haven's black market and the Guild are one and the same."

I stare at him in utter disbelief.

How does he know these things?

I look over at Ajax, who is scowling at me. "You told me you borrow that name."

I did, but... Avery knows the truth. Why hasn't he shared it with his troops? Why let it slip now?

"What are you talking about?" Ajax asks Avery.

"Get your head out of the sand, boy," Avery says. "You should've seen this coming a mile away. He's been manipulating us for years. The black market is nothing more than a way for him to garner funds. If you don't believe me, ask her."

"Silent?" Ajax says, turning his eyes on me. "And tell me the truth this time."

"It's true what Avery is saying," I reply, "all of it. The black market is not a separate enemy."

"If the Charger is a cover-up name, then who is your real master?"

I go to answer, but Avery does it for me. "Tell me, boy, have you ever heard of Black Death?"

"No," Ajax breathes, colour draining from his face. "He's a myth, something mothers tell their children about to keep them in line. He doesn't exist."

"Oh, he does," Avery says leaning back in his chair, "and he's sitting at the Guild right now, bending everyone to his will."

Ajax looks like he's going to be sick.

"How do you know all of this?" I inquire. "Why haven't you told your agents?"

"If I told you the how, you'd figure out the why, but I'll keep my reasons to myself."

I scowl. "What in the Guild is that supposed to mean?"

"I'm sure you'll figure it out in time," he replies. "All I will tell you for now is that Avery Norin isn't my real name either, but it's in there."

I am so confused. "You're talking in circles. This isn't what we came for."

"Too right," Avery says. "You came seeking my approval and I give it."

I frown. "What? Just like that? Jenson interrogates me for an hour and you don't ask a single question?"

He shrugs. "I don't need to. Silent Night, you can give us something we haven't had in a long time: an edge. You are the key to the end of the Guild."

"How do you even know why I'm here?"

"Jenson contacted me the day you arrived at the Warehouse. He told me about your betrayal and your offer."

"And you agree with my plan?"

"Immensely," he says. "The *Charger* won't know what hit him."

Despite myself, I smile. "That is my plan, yes."

"I want you to move on to Stage One tomorrow and if Jenson gives you a hard time, well, just remind him who's in charge because it's not him."

I nod.

"Well, that's all I have for you. Think on what I've said, Silent Night. I promise it'll all be clear someday."

I stand up. Ajax follows.

"I'd say thank you for your time," I tell Avery, "but I'm not yet sure what the results of this meeting will be. You're hiding something and mark my words, I will find out what it is."

"I eagerly await the day that you do." He sounds oddly cheerful for a man who was just threatened.

I glare at him and march out of the room, Ajax trailing in my wake.

"So, how'd it go?" Blake asks as we rejoin her, Bast, and Trey in the hall.

"I'd wager they did well, seeing as she's still alive," Trey says.

"Yeah," I reply, "I've been approved and Avery wants me to move on with Stage One of my plan tomorrow."

"Really?" Blake says.

"Yep, the Charger's clock is ticking."

Ajax quivers at the mention of the name.

Bast gives him a funny look. "What's the matter with you?"

"Yeah, kid," Trey agrees, "you look awfully pale."

"I'm fine," he says, though he sounds anything but.

Blake frowns. "No, you're not, Ajax. What happened?"

"I said I'm fine."

She reaches for his arm. "Jax..."

He pulls away. "Leave me alone, Blake." He walks away then, nearly running.

I wonder what exactly he thinks he's running from, because the truth always catches up with you.

Blake goes after him, Bast trailing behind, and Trey puts a hand on my shoulder. I shrug it off.

"Hey," she says, "is he going to be okay?"

"I think so, he just had a bit of shock, is all."

"What kind of shock?"

"Apparently, the general populace doesn't take too well to the idea that Black Death doesn't only live in their nightmares."

She gasps. "Avery told him?"

"He told *you*?"

"You forget I once had to answer to Black Death, Silent, and aside from that, Avery trusts me."

"But you used to be an assassin, why would he trust you?" Why am I such an abomination if they already have an assassin in their ranks?

"He's my uncle," she replies, "and one of the few agents who knows my past."

"Well then," I mutter, "you must have a lot of willpower."

She scrunches a brow. "How do you mean?

"He's not exactly easy to talk to."

She laughs. "I suppose. You better go run after your friends. They need you."

I raise an eyebrow. "Friends? Who said they were...?"

She gives me a look. "One can only pretend for so long, Silent. Good day to you."

Feeling like my soul has been taken out and rifled through, I head down the hall after the others.

CHAPTER FOURTEEN

When we reach the Warehouse, the four of us disperse, heading our separate ways. Ajax doesn't even bid us goodbye. I suppose it's to my advantage; I have work to do. I head straight to my room to change my outfit. It's time to put my plan into action and I want to make an entrance.

I dress in the best clothes my limited wardrobe can give me: a deep crimson uniform with plenty of weapon loops, black boots, and my old cloak from the Guild. Then I load myself with weapons.

Nothing intimidates more than a fully-armoured assassin, especially Silent Night, and that's exactly who I'm going to play. It's time to show the Resistance who's boss or we'll never get anything done, certainly not a Guild invasion, and that won't do at all.

• • •

I burst into the council room, the door swinging open and slamming against the inside wall. The men gathered around the table jump up in surprise and then in fear. The eight guards draw their swords.

I laugh. "Put those wimpy things away. I'm not here to hurt anyone."

"Then why are you dressed for an assassination?" someone demands to know.

"Oh, I'm not dressed for an assassination," I drawl. "If I was, you wouldn't have seen or heard me coming." I grin wickedly. If they want an assassin, they'll get one.

"What is the meaning of this?" Jenson asks.

"I wanted to catch your attention, to remind you what I can do if you refuse to obey."

"Obey what?"

"My orders from here on out. Avery has approved of me and my plan. He wants Stage One to begin tomorrow. I'm in charge of the proceedings."

Jenson raises an eyebrow. "Did he now? And how do we know you're not lying?"

"You don't, but you can go ask Avery if it would make you feel better."

Jenson narrows his eyes. "Avery may trust you, Assassin, but I don't. Until we get word from him, nothing has changed. Good day."

It's my turn to narrow my eyes. "Jenson, let's not be unreasonable, we both know exactly how forgiving I can be..."

"I *said* good day."

174

"Call in Ajax then!" I snap. "He was in the meeting with me."

"Ha," Jenson huffs, "and how can we trust him now that you've had the chance to get into his head? *Good day, Ms. Night.*" He and his men go back to their discussion and I stand there, gaping like an idiot.

I lost them, just like that. They've dismissed me like I am nothing.

Well, I'm not nothing! I am Silent Night and I will not stand for this!

My hand goes to one of my throwing knives just as the door slams open again and Trey steps in.

What is she doing here?

Jenson and his men look up again and, from the looks on their faces, they're thinking the same thing.

"Morning, gentlemen," she says, "or afternoon, whichever it is. Hello, Jenson." She nods her head at him and he scowls.

"Trey," he says, "to what do we owe the pleasure?"

"Avery sent me over with the letter of approval for Silent Night here, so we can get Stage One on its way, but I see you're already in the middle of it. Avery will be pleased."

Jenson looks taken aback. Trey walks over to him and slaps a sheet of paper on the table, winking at me. I stand there, stunned. She just saved my butt.

Jenson reads the letter and then grinds his teeth. "I see. Well, we're certainly on it. Tell Avery that it's all under control and he needn't worry."

"I'm glad things are in order," Trey says, "you mind if I join in on the meeting? I'd like to hear for myself how Silent plans on getting us in."

"Not at all," Jenson mutters. "Why don't you have a seat?" He turns to me. "Well, let us have it then."

Trey gives me an encouraging look and I take a deep breath. "Certainly," I say. "So, to start, I'm going to need two black uniforms..."

• • •

The meeting is a success, the men listening intently and leaving their questions to the end. They agree to give me all the supplies I need and the title of leader on tomorrow's expedition. Ajax and I are going into the belly of the beast to see if my tunnels will prove to be a suitable entrance. If not, we're going to find more. Jenson is giving us three days and after that, we'll be considered lost if we're not back.

The meeting comes to a close and Trey asks me to wait for her outside. She has a few words for me. I heed her request and stand in the hall with much apprehension.

What if she doesn't like my plan? Does she have the authority to call it off? What is her position anyway?

A few minutes later, she joins me. "I just wanted to say that you did a good job in there."

"Thanks, I guess," I reply. "I... I didn't need your help, you know. I had it under control."

"Right," she says. "Silent, I'm not stupid. You were in deep shit before I showed up."

I sigh. "How did you know to come?"

"It might surprise you, but I was once in your shoes, the exact pair you're wearing right now. I came to the Resistance with a plan akin to yours. I was young and angry. I wanted the Guild turned to dust, but it wasn't meant to be."

"If you couldn't manage it, how can I hope to?"

"Simple," she says, "you're smarter than I was. I was seventeen and made my treachery obvious. I planned my escape a week in advance and told two people I 'trusted' exactly what I was going to do. I barely escaped with my life." She pulls up her right sleeve, revealing an ugly scar that runs the length of her arm from wrist to elbow. "I was ambushed that night by five assassins and received this before Kuen managed to come to my rescue."

I choke. "Excuse me, who?"

"My brother, apparently his soul wasn't as dark as it should've been."

My jaw drops. "You're related to Kuen? *The* Kuen? You're talking about the Charger's right hand man for years, the youngest Agent One in the history of Haven?"

She nods.

"Dude, that guy was a legend! Especially his disappearance; the stories say he just up and left one night, no reason. He just vanished, never to be seen again."

"Yes, like you did," she points out.

"What?"

"You disappeared just like my brother did and the Charger hasn't heard from you since. He has no proof or even suspicions that you're a traitor and is just hoping you'll come back, and the fact is, he'll let you.

"The Charger never closed up Kuen's entrances," she goes on. "He is free to go back and so are you. My entrances were completely demolished, but yours won't be. You're the only chance we have. You're our salvation. It will work this time. So that, Silent Night, is what you have that I don't: the Charger's trust."

Trust. Why does it always come down to that?

• • •

It's about two o'clock when I return to my room. I know I should feel good about what I accomplished, but it's bittersweet with the initial reaction I received. I appreciate Trey's assistance, but I feel like I can't do anything on my own anymore. I tell myself the only reason I'm bringing Ajax on the mission tomorrow is that Jenson would never let me go alone, but it's not the whole truth. I'm bringing Ajax because I need him.

I open the door to my room to find Ajax sitting on my bed. I jump back in surprise, hand going to my knife belt.

He puts his hands up in surrender and I relax my stance.

"Assassins below, Ajax," I breathe. "Don't scare me like that."

"Sorry," he says. "I was waiting outside but then I saw Natalie coming down the hall so I ducked inside to avoid her. I was also tired of standing and I didn't particularly feel like sitting on the floor."

"It's okay. Wait... How long have you been here?"

"An hour or so," he admits, "give or take a couple of minutes."

"Guild, Ajax, why on earth would you do that? You should've come found me."

"I didn't know where you were."

"That's a sad excuse..." I trail off as I finally notice the look on his face. "What's wrong?"

He gives me a look. "The same thing that was wrong at the Barn, what do you think?"

"No need to get snappy," I tell him. I sigh. "I'm sorry you had to find out that way. I know it must be hard." I shut the door and walk over to sit beside him on the bed. Our shoulders brush against each other, but neither one of us move away.

"It's just..." he tries, looking down at the hands he's wringing in his lap. "I can't wrap my head around it. We've been fighting the villain from every kid's nightmare, Haven's Black Death. We're protecting this city from the darkest assassin ever known. How... How can we win against him?"

"By not letting him get to us like this." I grab his hand in mine to still it and give it a light squeeze. His calluses rub against my own. "He rules by fear and Guild help me, he kept me under his thumb that way since I was a child."

179

His blue eyes gaze into my own. "How do you live with it? Knowing you worked for Black Death?"

"As you keep telling me, I didn't live with it, I merely survived it, and my mind was in a terrible place. I didn't care who he was, just that I could keep doing what I did and I could keep surviving."

"How could you betray him? Aren't you afraid?"

"No, Ajax. I'm terrified." I look at my feet. "Every time we step out of this base, every second we spend out in the open, I'm terrified. I keep expecting us to get attacked and keep seeing us all dying in new and horrifying ways, because of me, but I can live with it because life...life is better without him looming over me."

"But why did you betray him, if you knew death was so probable?"

I look up at the door in front of us. "I found out he had been lying to me, to all of the assassins. We don't just kill Resistance members. We kill innocent people too and that's not what I signed up for. Not that I actually signed up... That's another thing. I... I became a Guild Ward because my mother died; I told you that, right?"

I look over at him and he nods.

"She didn't die, Ajax," I sigh. "The Charger murdered her."

His eyes widen. "I'm sorry. I know it doesn't mean much, but I'm sorry." It's his turn to squeeze my hand.

"Thanks," I say, smiling slightly. "So that's why I left, because I discovered the truth, because he ruined my life and I didn't want to work for him anymore."

"But why did you come to us?"

"Because I want to kill him and I can't do it alone."

"I see," he breathes and we sit in silence for a moment.

In the silence, his hand in mine becomes a weight, something foreign. I've never come this close to anyone since my mom died, let alone comforted someone. I never would've thought I would hold the hand of my enemy.

Carefully, as if to avoid offending him, I slide my hand out of his grip and shift about an inch away, folding my hands in my lap.

He doesn't react and I'm relieved.

"What was her name?" he asks.

"What?" I didn't expect him to carry on the conversation.

"Your mother," he says. "What was her name?"

"Oh," I reply. "Ismae. Her name was Ismae Ballinger." I'm surprised at myself; I've never told anyone that before. It's something I've kept locked inside my heart.

"It's beautiful."

"Thank you."

"Sounds exotic," he muses. "Is yours exotic too?"

"What?"

"Your name, is it unusual? You *do* have a real name, don't you?" He pokes me in the arm.

"Of course I do, and no, I don't think it is. My mother always told me my father chose it. Why do you ask?"

"I'm just wondering. You wouldn't care to share it, would you?"

I scowl.

He holds up his hands in surrender. "No need to get testy. I was just asking."

181

He waits a moment and then asks, "You mind if I guess?"

I shrug. "Knock yourself out."

He grins. "It wouldn't by chance be Shirley or Bernadette?"

My scowl deepens.

"Kidding, kidding," he says. "Hmmmm..." He puts a hand on his chin and looks to be deep in thought for a minute. "Kate?"

"No."

"Lily?"

"Certainly not," I scoff.

"Oh, what about Elizabeth?"

"Do I look like an Elizabeth?"

He narrows his eyes. "On second thought, no. You're more of an Alexa or Taylor. What about Hunter?"

"No, but you're getting closer. Think on it for a while, but there is something I need to discuss with you."

He sighs. "Fine, what's up?"

"I had a meeting with Jenson and the others. Stage One is a go."

"Awesome," he says with a smile. "I'm glad they finally came around."

"It took a bit of convincing," I admit.

"I'll bet. So what's the plan?"

"You and I are heading to the Guild tomorrow."

Fear, cold and raw, flashes in his eyes. "We... We are?"

"Yes," I reply. "Does that bother you? I could take Bast or Blake instead."

"Don't be ridiculous, of course I'm coming. It's just... Are you sure it's a good idea?"

"It'll be fine. We just need to see if I can still access my entrances. If we do it right, we'll be in and out of there before breakfast, with none of them the wiser."

"I hope so."

"Someone will drop off a set of clothes for you tonight. Wear it tomorrow and fill all the weapon holders. That's crucial. We have to fit in."

"Okay, I got it."

"Good," I say. "I guess that's it then."

He smiles. "In that case... I'm thinking you're probably a Leah."

I wince. "You're getting colder, my friend."

"Claire?"

"No."

"Tia?"

"Nope."

"Laura?"

CHAPTER FIFTEEN

It's five o'clock and the four of us are sitting around our table, discussing our plans for the next few days. I tell them about my meeting and Ajax and I's mission. They wish us luck and Blake makes me promise to bring Ajax back in one piece.

She needn't worry. I won't let anything happen to him, which is strange of me to say, but it's the truth. I don't want to lose him.

"You want me to bring you back a souvenir, Bast?" I ask.

"Nah," he says, "we've already got one and she's this really bitchy assassin..." He looks up at me in mock horror. "Wait, did I say that last part out loud?"

"Shut up!" I exclaim and Blake defends me by nailing him in the arm with her fist.

"Ow!" he gasps. "What was that for?"

She shrugs. "Disrespect, immaturity, being an idiot... You take your pick."

He grins at her. "That's what you love about me."

She rolls her eyes. "Oh, sure."

"I know!" Ajax yells out. "It's Erin."

I smile and reply, "Wrong again. Sure you don't want to give up?"

"Positive."

"Wait, what?" Blake says.

"What are you going on about, man?" Bast asks.

"Ajax here," I reply, "has taken it upon himself to find out what my real name is."

"Interesting," Bast says. "Mind if I join?"

I cross my arms, smiling. "Not at all."

He turns to Ajax. "What have you tried so far?"

Ajax rhymes them all off.

Blake looks at them both with pity. "Good luck, boys," she says, "but if Night doesn't want you to know, I doubt you'll ever figure it out."

I smile at her.

How right she is.

"Quiet," Bast replies. "This table is positive talk only."

She smiles. "Fine, then I am *positive* this is a waste of your time."

Bast frowns and I laugh. "Nice one, Blake," I say.

"I try, Night. I try."

It's Ajax and Bast's turn to wield the twin death glares and it sends the four of us into a laughing fit. I kind of see what Ajax was talking about when he told me to live. I've never felt so free and never have I laughed so often. I smile fondly and vow to remember these moments forever.

Then I see someone out of the corner of my eye that makes my happy mood fizzle out into distaste.

"Don't look now, but her highness has arrived," I drawl.

The three of them immediately turn in the direction I'm facing.

I roll my eyes. "I said *don't* look now."

They whirl back to face me.

"Well, we've definitely caught her attention now," I complain. "You guys would make terrible assassins."

"Maybe," Bast says, "maybe not. For example... Did you see me do that?"

I narrow my eyes. "Do what?"

"Exactly," he replies, grinning.

I roll my eyes again.

Ajax smacks him in the arm. "That's for a ninja, you dimwit."

Our banter is interrupted by a honeyed voice. "Hello, darlings."

I can tell from the way my skin crawls that she is standing directly behind me. I scowl, but try to sound bored as I mutter, "Roseanne."

Beside me, Ajax shifts to face her and says, "What do you want, Natalie?"

"I just thought I'd check in," she replies, moving around Ajax into my line of vision, "see how things were going with you."

She gives him a smile that he doesn't return and I want to laugh at how oblivious she is. Ajax is not interested in anything she has to offer. The only thing I imagine that tight grey uniform is doing for her is cutting off her circulation.

Still, she places a hand on his shoulder and I bristle, until he shrugs it off by turning further in his seat.

I give her a smile in his stead, but it doesn't reach my fiery eyes. "Things were going great," I drawl, "that is, until you showed up."

Bast snickers.

Natalie gives me a severe look. "Excuse me?"

"You heard me," I say. "I don't appreciate your presence. In fact, I recall us discussing this. Didn't I tell you to stay out of my way? Didn't I say the results would be less than pretty if you refused?"

"As if *you* are fulfilling *your* end of the bargain," she retorts.

I roll my eyes. "I've done nothing; I can promise you that," I say, "and even if I had, what are *you* going to do about it?"

I glance across the table at Bast and Blake. They are looking thoroughly confused at the mention of a bargain.

"I have the power to make your life miserable," Natalie replies.

"I have the power to kill you without straining myself in the least."

"Please, Assassin," she says, waving me off. "I'm not afraid of you."

"You should be."

She walks back around Ajax to stand beside me. She leans down, bracing herself against the table with her right hand. She's trying to make it as if we're having our own private conversation, though I know the other three are hanging on our every word.

"I don't particularly care what you think, Assassin," she whispers. "You can't touch me."

Is that so?

My lips twitch into a smile for a second. Then, before either of us can blink, I whip a knife out of my belt and slam it down, point first, between her splayed fingers.

She screams and jumps back, bringing her hand up to her face for inspection.

Bast bursts into laughter and Ajax gives me a warning look, but I can tell he's forcing back a smile of his own.

Natalie looks at me like I'm a wild beast. "What is wrong with you?" she snaps. "You...you could've killed me. My daddy will hear of this and you'll go right back to the dark hole you came from!"

She's reminding me of her threats from yesterday, but I don't particularly care. I have witnesses here, allies.

"Oh, put a sock in it, Roseanne," I tell her. "It would hardly have killed you. You might've lost a finger, but death was not a possibility."

Sadly, I add in my head.

"Why you... I hope you're going to lock her in her room for the rest of the day after that stunt, Ajax," she says, turning her eyes on him.

"Not likely," he says.

She gives him a look of complete shock. "What do you mean? She needs to be punished."

"And you need to learn how to read people. She warned you. As far as I'm concerned, Natalie, you provoked her. Should I tell your father *that*?"

"What happened to the man who prided himself on absolving violence?"

"I'm still here, Natalie," he replies, "you're just too blind to see you caused this violence yourself."

"I don't understand why you would accuse me—"

"Save it, Natalie," he interrupts her. "You should go before this gets worse."

"Yeah," I agree. "Get out of here, princess, or the next knife will bury itself into your head."

She lingers a second more and then struts off, fuming.

I cross my arms and turn back to the others. Ajax is giving me a funny look.

"What?" I say.

He smiles. "You're something else, you know that right?"

"Well, I should hope so." I pull the knife out of the table top and tuck it back in my belt, grinning the whole time. "What about you? I didn't think you'd have the nerve to call her out like that."

"I probably wouldn't have, but *she* had the nerve to threaten one of my teammates and I don't tolerate that kind of behaviour." He smiles at me.

I smile back.

We all turn back to our dinner and peace has almost been restored when Bast says, "So, when's the wedding?"

I look up at him. "What wedding?"

"Jax and her highness," Bast replies with a huge grin.

Ajax chokes on whatever he was eating and drops his fork.

Bast erupts into a fit of laughter and after a second, I can't help but join.

"Man," Bast gasps. "The look on your face!"

Ajax scowls at him. "Four words: Over. My. Dead. Body."

I grin at him. "I can arrange that."

He looks at me. "If I ever consider Natalie as a mate, please do."

"Aw, come on, Jax, man." Bast says, "She's not that bad."

We all look at him for a second in silence and then the four of us let our laughter go.

• • •

I wake up the next morning around six o'clock to prepare myself. I haul my assassin clothes out of the closet and slip them on, wincing at the state of them, but they are more than necessary. If someone sees me, they'll ask questions if I'm wearing a shiny new outfit. I asked for a new one at the meeting so I'd have an extra in my wardrobe.

After I load the belts and sheaths with weapons, I drape my cloak over my outfit so I don't have to look at it. Then I slip on my old boots and sit down on my bed.

Ten minutes later finds me pacing the floor, cursing Ajax's name.

Where in the Guild is he?

I pause long enough to cross my arms and glare at the door, as if that will help my mood.

Well, you did wake up pretty early, I remind myself. *Did you even tell him what time to meet you?*

I scowl and tell myself to shut up. I'd go eat breakfast to kill some time, but I never eat before a mission, it's against my nature. I sigh and lie down on the bed.

Staring at the ceiling, I go through my plan one more time. We need to go through downtown to get to the south end so we won't attract attention and use my usual entrance so I don't look suspicious if someone is watching. Then I need to make sure Ajax doesn't die in the tunnel, get us to the Grand Cavern, and out through another tunnel.

Easy.

I sigh.

If only.

The door creaks open and I hear a familiar voice say, "Why the long face?"

I sigh again as I stare at the ceiling. "This is going to be way more difficult than it sounds. We have a fifty percent chance of survival."

"That sounds bleak," Ajax replies, "but maybe we should look at the bright side? You won't succeed if you don't believe you can."

I roll my eyes. "Stop lecturing me about that crap. It's my turn to lecture." I sit up. "Today is going to be hard enough. I need you to listen..." I trail off as I look at him.

It's as if I'm seeing him for the first time and I realize now that he is gorgeous. It takes putting him in assassin clothes for me to notice. Black is *definitely* his colour. The boots and pants are a perfect fit and the shirt has a comfortable tightness to it, showing off the chiseled ab muscles I didn't even know he had. He wears the matching cloak with the hood up, making him look dangerous, but completely irresistible. His blue eyes meet mine and a part of me doesn't want to look away.

Shit.

No. It can't be happening. I have a strict rule...

He smiles at me and I have to look away. I try to steady my heart before he can pick up on the change, before he notices the flush in my cheeks.

"You were saying, Silent?" he asks me.

"Oh, um..."

Assassins below! I completely lost my train of thought. *Damn him.*

"Um..." My mind is blank. All I can think of is his latent strength.

"You were saying that I need to listen?" he prompts and I silently curse him, though I'm thankful for the reminder.

I force myself to meet his gaze as I answer, struggling to keep my expression neutral. "Yes, I need you to listen to everything I say and obey without a second thought if you want to survive. The Guild is a dangerous place and you always have to be two steps ahead. If we somehow get separated, I want you to leave immediately. Do not come after me. I will find you."

"Listen to everything you say and leave you to die, got it."

I scowl at him.

"What?"

"Nothing," I reply. "Did you bring weapons like I told you to?"

"Of course; I'm stocked up like an arsenal." He eyes the weapons on his person as if he finds them offensive. I see even more beauty in the danger.

"Good, then let's go." I try not to look at him as I walk out the door.

As we head towards the Guild, I try to sort out my new revelation.

I like Ajax.

When did this even happen? The day I met him he was escorting me out of a dungeon at gunpoint and now the sight of him in black gives me butterflies, but I'm still the same person, aren't I?

Are you?

The truth is, I don't know. I've made friends and some new enemies, and I'm working towards the greater good for once, so I guess I *have* changed, but where does a crush on Ajax fit into all of that? When in the Guild did I fall?

Maybe it was during all those times he told me he trusted me, maybe it was because nobody has ever looked at me the way he does, as if I have a future, as if I'm not a soulless monster. Maybe It's the way his eyes sparkle when he laughs and how he makes me smile...

Maybe it was all those things and more, but the truth still remains; I have feelings for him and I don't know what in the hell I'm supposed to do with them.

Of course, I have to notice all of this *now*, as if I don't have enough to worry about with a trip to the Guild alongside a Resistance member. As if Ajax and I aren't in enough danger already without me distracted by something as trivial as feelings.

I shove the butterflies way down inside and vow to ignore their fluttering wings until we're back safe and sound at the Warehouse. I'm not going to jeopardize our mission because I've discovered my escort is hot.

The walk to the south end of Haven is quiet. I'm afraid of saying the wrong thing and I can tell Ajax is nervous, which is good. I'd be worried if he wasn't. No person in their right mind walks into enemy territory—especially the Guild—without being scared out of their wits, which proves I'm in the right mind and the right company.

As we near my entrance, my hands start to tremble and I clench my fists before Ajax can notice. I have to be confident for him or this will never work. I have to set the example, have to be courageous.

I sigh.

Why do I always get the hard job?

"Are we almost there?" Ajax asks.

"Nearly, but quiet, an actual assassin wouldn't ask that, they'd know."

"What does it matter? We're alone."

I shoot him a look.

His eyes widen. "You mean...? That's comforting." He looks cold and I wish I could put him at ease.

Instead, I cross my arms and say, "You think we'd let just anyone waltz into our part of the city? I told you, our security is *way* more extensive than yours."

"I guess," he says. "So, how much longer?"

I roll my eyes. "What are you, five?"

He stares at me.

"A few more minutes; hold onto your cloak."

We keep walking.

True to my word, we reach the right street five minutes later.

"Are we..." Ajax starts and I shush him.

I point down the street to a brick bungalow. "That's our destination there on the corner."

"The house?"

"Yes," I reply. "Surprised?"

"A little."

I pick up the pace. "Come on, I don't fancy being out in the open much longer."

He shivers. "Me neither."

We continue down the street and then up the front walk of the house.

I open the door a crack.

"It's unlocked?" Ajax asks.

"Yes, now be quiet." I angle my ear towards the inside of the house and listen: silence. "All clear," I say, "after you."

He sighs and enters the house. I follow and shut the door behind us.

It's still dark inside, seeing as it can't be later than seven thirty in the morning and the window curtains are all closed.

"What exactly are we doing here?" Ajax asks. "And how extensive can your security be if you leave the door unlocked?"

"The entrance is downstairs and the unlocked doors help the newer assassins identify where the entrance houses are. Besides, keys are easily misplaced."

"I suppose, and what do you mean by downstairs?"

"Come on," I sigh, "I'll show you."

I take the steps two at a time and head to the back bedroom.

"This place is eerie," Ajax complains, "like something out of a black and white movie."

I shrug. "You get used to it."

I walk over to the closet and open the door, beckoning to him as I step inside.

He looks at me funny. "You know, Silent, if you wanted some alone time with me, you could've just asked."

I can't see my face, but I know I'm blushing brighter than an apple. "You..." I try. "Idiot," I mutter. "That's not what I'm— just get in here." I am completely flustered.

He grins at me. "Relax; I'm just messing with you." He steps into the closet beside me and I shut the door. "Now what?" he asks.

"Now, you get over so I can get the door."

"Door?"

I nudge him aside and kick over the pile of clothes before crouching down to get a good grip on the trap door handle. Then I heave it open. It smacks down in the space Ajax just vacated.

"Whoa," Ajax breathes, "clever."

"Well, we try. Care to go first?"

He doesn't answer and I say, "You know what, I should probably go first actually, wouldn't want you to trip and fall down a hole. There's a ladder down the shaft here. As long as you stay close to me in the tunnel, you should be fine. Got it?"

"Crystal clear, captain."

I smile. "Then let's do this."

I drop in the hole and place my feet on the first rung. Then I descend. A few seconds later, I hear the metallic ring as Ajax follows me, his boots landing on the rung above my head.

It takes us a few minutes to climb down and a couple more for our eyes to adjust to the dark tunnel.

"Where are we?" Ajax asks.

"Underground," I reply, "and no, we're not there yet."

"How much further?"

"Not sure, haven't timed it before. On the bright side, we haven't encountered anyone yet and the tunnel is still accessible. It's a good sign."

"You mean your plan might actually work?"

"Shut up," I say, punching him in the arm.

"Ow, I was only kidding. I never doubted you."

"Sure, that's what you say now."

"Aren't we on a schedule?"

"Yeah, yeah, I'm going. Watch your step."

One hundred paces later, as usual, we come to the elevator.

Ajax winces at the sudden light and shields his eyes. "*Ah*, why didn't you warn me?"

"Sorry."

He looks over at the elevator then. "What is *that*?"

"An elevator," I reply.

"Great," he says, hugging his arms to his body.

"What's wrong with elevators?" I ask.

He looks at his feet. "I'm not too fond of them."

I raise an eyebrow. "The great Ajax is afraid of an elevator?"

"Don't laugh; I'm sure even *you* are afraid of something, something stupid."

"It's not stupid," I relent, "I was afraid of the thing the first time I used it too, but it's perfectly safe."

"So you say, but this could be the day the cable finally snaps and we plummet to our deaths."

"It could be, but you can't let that possibility ruin your life. Any day could be the day someone robs your house, but you don't refuse to leave it. Any day you could get food poisoning, but you don't refuse to eat. I'm telling you, Jax, it's going to be okay. We won't die and if we do, we'll do it together, all right?" I hold out my hand and he hesitates. "You say you trust me, here's the chance to prove it."

He steps forward and puts his hand in mine. I hope he can't hear how my heart speeds up.

Stop. It's not about you right now.

"You can do this," I tell him.

I lead him over to the door and type the code into the panel with my free hand. The doors slide open and he trembles.

I squeeze his hand. "You've got this; don't think about it, just focus on my hand. Okay?"

He nods.

We step into the elevator and the doors shut.

He tenses up, eyes closed.

"No," I tell him, "that'll make it worse. Look at me."

He does as I say and I can see the fear written in his blue eyes, but it dissipates as he focuses on me.

The elevator descends. His fingers crush mine, but I don't so much as flinch. I can be strong for him. His eyes don't leave mine for the whole ride and I know it is an experience I will never forget.

The elevator reaches the ground a few minutes later and Ajax rushes out the door as fast as his legs can take him. His hand rips out of mine in his haste. I walk out after him.

Ajax is panting, bent over with his hands on his knees. He looks up after a moment and says, "Thank you. I never thought I could do that."

I shrug. "What are friends for?"

He smiles and I try to keep from blushing. "Hey," I say, "if it would make you feel any better, I'll tell you about my 'stupid' fear, but you have to promise me you won't tell *anyone*."

"Sure."

"Do you *promise*?"

"Cross my heart and hope to die."

"Good," I reply, "because I will kill you if you let this spill. Now, try not to laugh, but I'm afraid of feathers and pillows."

CHAPTER SIXTEEN

I tremble as memories, unbidden, flash through my eyes.

No, I tell them. *Stop*.

"You're serious?" I hear Ajax say as if from afar. "The *great* Silent Night is afraid of feathers and pillows?"

The trembling worsens. The images won't stop.

"Hey, I'm not laughing. Silent?"

I fall to my knees, holding my head.

"Silent? Are you okay?"

His voice is fading...

"Silent! Look at me!"

I can't.

His fingers touch my chin then, pulling my head up to face him. His eyes pierce mine and my hands fall to my sides. His gaze shatters the reel of images spinning endlessly in my mind. All I can see now are his eyes. I could kiss him.

What?

SILENT NIGHT

Slowly, I come to my feet, not once taking my eyes from his. When the trembling finally stops and I'm breathing normally, Ajax takes me by surprise by pulling me towards him and wrapping his arms around me. I sink into his warm embrace.

"Don't ever scare me like that again," he breathes. His hand is around my head, his other against my back. My arms are around his torso, face buried in his chest. He's the one shaking now.

"I'm sorry," I say when I can manage to speak. I can't believe he's hugging me. He feels so safe. I could stay like this forever, but he pulls away a minute later.

"Care to tell me what happened there?" he asks. "I felt like I was losing you." He runs a hand through his hair.

"I... I have panic attacks, or something like them," I reply. "It's hard to explain without triggering another one. Um... Okay, so when I mention my fear, it usually brings back things I don't want to remember... Do we have to talk about it?"

He winces. "No, I can see it pains you. I'm sorry for asking."

"You deserve to know. It can't be easy watching me go through it."

"It's not," he assures me.

There's a silence between us, but it's not awkward.

"Is that why the pillows we gave you are under your bed?"

"You noticed that?"

"Well, most people keep them *on* the bed. I figured you had a good reason for it, so I didn't ask."

202

"Thank you."

"You're welcome. We should keep going, take our minds off of this whole experience here."

"Good idea," I say.

He holds out his hand for me to take it. Our touch gives each other strength as we continue.

• • •

"We have to be careful here," I tell Ajax. "Keep to my pace. I have to count my steps and I need to be accurate."

"Why?"

"Do you fancy walking off of a cliff and breaking to pieces on the jagged rocks below it?"

He winces. "No, not now that you mention it."

"I didn't think so. Let me do my thing here and we should be fine."

Twenty paces later, I come to a stop. "Now we head to the left. There's a ledge that goes around. Fifty paces of that and the tunnel will continue."

He follows me closely. "Well, Silent, you were definitely right. Your security is insane. How did you even figure out how to navigate this?"

"I took a lantern with me the first time and made sure to take precise measurements."

"I guess so," he replies. "Man, even if one of us managed to find the trapdoor in the basement, we'd never get past the elevator or these traps you've laid for us."

"Well, that's sort of the point."

"I know, I'm just saying that you're amazing. This never would've happened without you."

I'm suddenly rather aware of his hand in mine and I'm glad it's too dark for him to see the heat in my cheeks.

"Thanks," I reply, "it was nothing."

"Oh, I'm sure. How much farther?"

"About five minutes and then comes the hard part."

"Great."

Finally, we come to the part of the tunnel full of hanging light bulbs and I tell Ajax we're nearly there.

"But it's a dead end," he protests.

I smile. "That's why we're going up."

He follows me to the end of the tunnel and I point to the ladder carved into the wall.

"Clever," he says. "Ladies first?"

"It would probably be best," I agree.

"Lead on then."

The hardest thing about the whole endeavour is letting go of his hand. Then I climb up the ladder and push up the floor tile above.

I peer out into the hall. No one is coming. I listen closely, but hear nothing. I lower the tile and look down at Ajax. "The coast is clear but it won't be for long. You ready?"

"As I'll ever be."

I push the tile up all of the way and slide it carefully out of place without making a sound. Then I pull myself out of the hole and onto the floor above.

Ajax follows my lead and is soon standing beside me. I crouch down and slide the tile back in place. It disappears into the flooring.

"Whoa," Ajax breathes, "now *that* is genius."

"It is pretty cool," I agree, "but now is not the time to appreciate it; we've got things to do."

"Right," he says. "You going to give me the whole tour?"

"We'll see."

We head down the hall. Ajax fingers his gun and twitches at small noises.

"Act casual," I hiss at him under my breath. "You look exactly like what a suspicious person would look like."

"Sorry," he says and I watch him as he relaxes.

"That's it."

"Where are we going?"

"We'll visit the Grand Cavern first and then my old room."

"Sounds good."

We continue in silence and listen as the Guild noises grow louder.

"I hear sparring," Ajax says.

"Thanks, tips," I reply. "There are countless training rooms and armouries on this floor."

"Oh."

We pass by a couple in a few minutes and no one so much as glances at us. This might actually work.

"Almost there," I whisper.

"I think I can hear it," he says.

"I wouldn't be surprised."

"Is it always that loud?"

"Without exception, but I don't mind it."

"Really?" he says, crossing his arms. "You seemed to think our cafeteria was pretty loud."

"I *told* you, the two are not the same. There's a difference between background noise that is so loud you can't think and background noise that becomes a mild buzzing sound in your ears. Yours would be the former."

"Whatever."

"Quiet now, the doors are just around this corner. Remember, do what I do. Try to look intimidating without looking like you're trying to. Act like everyone is beneath your notice and feel free to finger a knife or two. Your height should be enough to intimidate a lot of them, but anything more can't hurt."

"My height?"

I look up at him. "Don't give me that, you're like a tree."

He frowns. "I'm only 6 foot 4."

I roll my eyes. *Only.*

"Avery's like 6 foot 5," he points out.

"So is the Charger, but my point is that a lot of people are shorter than you, so use that to your advantage."

"How tall are *you*?"

"5 foot 6 maybe? Look, it doesn't matter, just do what I said and you should be fine."

"All right, captain."

"Shut up," I say, smiling. Then I school my features into the guise of a cold-hearted killer and lead Ajax into the Grand Cavern.

The Cavern is exactly how I remember it: people everywhere, doing everything. Black market deals are being struck. Some guy is trying to sell a dead assassin's weapons. Food is being eaten, and thrown. Swords are being drawn. Fist fights are taking place in dark corners. Shots are fired. Insults, cursing, belching, and... Did that guy just get knifed?

"Assassin's below," I mutter.

It's eight o'clock in the morning and already this place has gone to hell. It likely never left it last night. Guild, this is something I do not miss.

"Stay close," I whisper under my breath, hoping Ajax hears me. Then I bundle my resolve and, with one hand on my best throwing knife, step into the crowd.

I head over to my spot in the far corner under the mezzanine. I duck knives, dodge brawls, and kick a few shins accidentally and purposely on my way.

We're almost there when I pass a table and trip over someone's outstretched foot. I hit the ground hard and swear loudly. I go to push myself to my feet, until I feel the cold press of metal against my neck.

Bastard.

He has *no* idea who he's dealing with. I'll skin him alive, but I can let him live out his fantasy for a second or two.

"What do you think you are doing?" I ask, my gaze on the floor in front of me.

"Securing myself an interesting afternoon," an older male voice replies. "You see, little lady, you're pretty and young and old Bruno here would like to have some fun. You catch my drift?"

"Oh, I catch it, but it's *not* happening. You can go to hell."

I slide to the left and kick at his leg with mine at the same time. It catches him off guard, but I still feel the sting as his knife grazes my skin. I roll over and draw my own knife.

We look at each other. He's an ugly little man, probably in his late forties.

Isn't that a little old for an assassin?

"So you want to do it the hard way?" he asks. "That's fine. Old Bruno likes a challenge."

Ugh, I'm going to be sick.

He lunges for me with his knife. I jump to my feet and then duck. His knife soars through empty air and he's knocked off balance. I aim my knife at his exposed back but...

Someone beats me to it.

A sword buries itself in his flesh up to the hilt and Old Bruno crashes to the ground, drowning in his own blood.

My saviour grabs me by the hair and pulls me to him. "Thanks, Bruno, old man," he says. "I haven't had such a fine catch in years."

Instinct has me driving my heel into his foot and he lets go, swearing.

I whirl around, ducking his fist and slamming my foot into his ribcage this time.

He groans, but pauses only briefly. Not a complete idiot then.

I pull a knife, but he still has his sword out and he favours it now over his knuckles.

We spar back and forth with minimal effort on my part. I'm toying with him at this point. It's been a while since I've taught a pervert a lesson.

Then our blades lock and I strain against him. He's stronger, but I'm smarter. I know just how to angle the blade to minimize the effort.

I'm about to give a final shove when I hear Ajax yelling for me.

"Indigo! Indigo!"

Oh, Guild. Is he hurt? I swear if he...

I hesitate for only a second, but it's enough.

My assailant shoves my blade to the side hard enough that I let go, leaving me exposed, and then his leg sweeps mine out from under me. I hit the floor of the Cavern for the second time in less than five minutes.

Shit.

The man drags me to my feet by my wrists, holding tight enough that struggle is futile. Before I can crush his other foot, he rests a long serrated blade against my throat.

"That's right, little lady," he croons, "the game is up." The fingers of his free hand stroke my cheek and I flinch. "We wouldn't want to harm your pretty face, now would we?"

My knees tremble. I want to reach for another knife, but I know it wouldn't be wise.

Assassins below. I don't know how I'm going to get out of this one.

The man holding me brings his mouth to my ear and a shiver goes down my spine as he whispers into it. It's not a pleasant one. "We're going to have lots of fun, you and me."

Oh, please. Please.

Then I hear the sound of a gun cocking, a loud click near my other ear.

What now?

"Let the lady go, you bastard, if you know what's good for you."

Ajax. It's *his* gun.

The man behind me flinches.

Oh Guild, oh Guild, oh Guild...

"Jax, no," I whisper softly.

"See," my captor says, "you hear what she said? She doesn't want you to shoot me. She wants to stay."

"No," Ajax replies, "she doesn't want *me* to get *hurt*. There's a difference." Then in a softer voice he adds, "It's okay, Silent. I've got this."

I try to focus on breathing in and out.

"Drop the knife," Ajax says, "or I *will* shoot."

"Shoot me and I'll slit her throat on the way out."

"You won't have the time or brains for that. I'm holding a gun to your head, so drop the knife before I blow it up!"

Ajax's voice is loud, angry, and underneath it all, I realize, scared. He doesn't want to kill this man. It's okay, because I'm not going to make him.

The guy, distracted by the gun to his head, never sees me coming.

I reach slowly for a dagger and then, quick as a lick, I bury the blade in the man's side and tear.

He cries out and drops his knife, hand going to the long gash I ripped open. "Bitch," he spits out as I jump away from him.

I sway a little and Ajax catches my arm, pulling me to him.

"You're dead, bitch. You hear me? Dead!"

"Whatever," I say, shrugging. "I'm not the one bleeding out on the floor." I turn to Ajax. "Come on, let's get out of here."

"Agreed," Ajax replies and we leave the Grand Cavern without a second glance at the two bodies we left behind. They'll be joined by more as the day progresses.

It takes everything in me to not full on sprint to my old room. I drag Ajax by the hand behind me. When we get there, I slam the door, grab the key from the bedpost, and lock it. Then I stand, half bent over, panting, in front of it.

Ajax flops down on the bed, launching a layer of dust into the air. "Holy Gods above," he breathes. "What happened back there? That guy... He was going to kill you or...or rape you. Or both. I was going to shoot him in the head. How did you...?" He looks over at me and fear flashes through his eyes. "You're bleeding."

I touch my neck. "It's nothing."

"No, it isn't. Sit down; let me see it."

"I don't..."

"*Now.*"

I sigh and drag my feet over to the bed. I sit down beside him and he tilts my chin up to look at my neck. I shiver at his touch.

This I like.

"It's not deep," he says, "you don't need stitches, but it's going to be tender for a while."

"I'm well aware," I reply. "You think this is the worst I've had?"

He gives me a tired look. "Not in the slightest, Silent, but I'm trying to be a gentleman here."

"Sorry," I say, "I'm still a bit shaken up. That…" I shudder. "That was a close call back there and I've never been worried about it before, but now… I'm not ready to die yet."

He smiles at me but then it fades. "Is it always like that in there?"

I nod. "It's like that throughout the base. We're bloodthirsty creatures. I've never been attacked like that before, but I don't think those men knew who I was. I wasn't about to tell them and ruin the mission either, though it might've been worth it to see the looks on their faces." I try to grin, but my heart isn't in it.

"Yeah." His voice changes and he looks down at his feet.

"What's wrong?" I ask him.

"Nothing."

I give him a look he doesn't see. "Jax…"

"Fine," he relents. "I'm ashamed of myself. How I let myself lose sight of you, how I managed to find a way to save you but couldn't pull the damn trigger." He wrings his hands to keep from making fists. "I failed you."

"No, you didn't," I say, taking his hand in mine. His body tenses. "You did everything you could. Your distraction was enough for me to slip through his fingers." I don't mention that he was the one who distracted *me* first. It's in the past now. I shouldn't have let myself be distracted. "Besides," I go on, "I don't expect you to become a killer to save me. I'm not worth it."

He looks up. "Don't say that. You are so worth it."

I raise an eyebrow. "How do you figure that?"

"Silent, every single person in this world is worth something. Not everybody can see that worth. Not everybody see yours, but I do. You're worth it to me."

I want so desperately to accept his answer, but I can't. Someone like me *is* worthless; someone like me would be hung out to dry if there were enough decent people left in this city. Instead, the monsters are left to run rampant and the Resistance is not enough to quell the darkness.

"Why though?" I demand to know. "Why am I so damn important to you?" My anger is sudden, fuelled by the lingering fear from my latest brush with death. "What did I ever do to deserve your trust, Ajax, your admiration, your *anything*? Less than a month ago, you were escorting one of Haven's most dangerous assassins out of a cell at gunpoint and now I'm worth something to you? It doesn't make sense. What changed?"

He laughs. "What changed? Huh, let me see." He ticks off the items on his fingers as he goes. "What changed was the way I saw you. What changed was the way you saw yourself, the way you looked at life. What changed was the fact that I started falling asleep with the image of your face firmly rooted in my mind. Silent," he pauses, "what changed is that I fell for you."

I stare at him, speechless.

Did he just...?

Assassins below.

It's not just me?

He's insane.

My heart wants to confess what I discovered this morning, but my brain forces me to hesitate.

What if he's lying?

It could all be a scheme to trick the assassin into letting her guard down. I don't want to think of Ajax like that, but I can't afford to be blindsided. I have to think of my safety, of every possibility. I can't bare my heart when I don't yet understand my own feelings.

I let go of his hand.

"Silent?" Ajax says. "Are you okay? Did you hear what I said?"

"I heard you," I reply, finding my voice. "I just... I don't understand how you could..."

"Fall in love with you?"

I wince at the word. "Ajax, you don't even *like* me." It's the truth. We've been at odds on and off since day one, finding me attractive doesn't change that.

He frowns. "How do *you* figure *that*? Do you really think I'd go on a mission like this with someone I don't even like?"

"Okay," I allow. "Maybe you like me, but how can you *love* me? We just met a few weeks ago. You *hated* me when we met. You're saying you did a complete one eighty? I don't think so. It doesn't make any sense." It's painful to do this, but I'm seeing now, necessary.

"Silent..." he tries, but I interrupt him.

"Let's say you do love me, okay? Why would you do that to yourself? I'm a monster."

"No, you're not."

"I am, Ajax," I insist, "just because you haven't seen it yet doesn't mean it isn't there, waiting, ready to pounce." Even now, I can feel it lurking in the corners of my mind, feeding off of my pain, my fear, my anxiety...my soul.

"I can help you fight it," he replies, "and this time, I won't hesitate to shoot." He gives me a small smile.

I realize then, in the silence, how dangerously close he is to me. If either of us lean in a little, our lips could touch. I'm sure that's what he's hoping for, but I can't let it happen. Tearing my eyes away from his, I stand up.

Ajax looks at me like I've slapped him.

I shift my gaze to the door so I don't lose my resolve.

This is for the best.

"I... I'm sorry," I breathe, "but I can't do this. Us. It'll end badly and it'll be my fault. I'll ruin you, I know I will, and you don't deserve that. You deserve so much more than I could ever give you. I *do* care about you Ajax, but that's why this can never happen; it will either end in heartbreak or bloodshed, and I don't feel like losing you to either."

SILENT NIGHT

"Silent..." Ajax starts again, but I ignore his attempts at reconciliation.

"We have to go," I tell him.

"So that's it then?" he says. "I don't even get to plead my case?" I can hear the annoyance in his voice.

Good.

It's better if he hates me. It'll make this so much easier.

At the same time, my heart clenches in my chest.

What if I'm making a mistake?

You live with the consequences, like you always do.

I look back over at him. "You can plead if you want, but I've made my decision. Besides, this isn't the time or place to discuss this. We need to *go*, before someone finds us and makes us their next victims."

Ajax swears under his breath. "Right," he says, "assassin's lair, imminent death. How could I forget?"

I roll my eyes. "Well, lucky for us, I have my mind on important things, like survival."

He doesn't say anything to that.

I can taste the tension in the air. I hate it.

"Come on," I say, "let's go. It should be easier to get out than it was to get in. There's a tunnel two halls over."

"Sounds good," he replies, "lead the way."

He doesn't call me captain this time and somehow, the absence of that single word hurts more than anything.

216

CHAPTER SEVENTEEN

It's ten o'clock in the morning when we arrive at the Warehouse. We didn't talk at all on the way back. Silence has never made me feel that uncomfortable. For once, I understand people's need for noise. I would've given anything for something to drown out my thoughts.

We exchange a few words with the guards as we pass by and then Ajax turns to me. "Is there anything else we need to do or am I free to go?"

"Don't say it like that," I reply. "I'm not keeping you here." His words sting. I didn't think he could be so cold.

He sighs, pinching the bridge of his nose, and says, "Gods, I didn't mean... I'm sorry. A lot happened today and that's no excuse, but... I just need to be alone." The pain in his eyes when he looks at me is almost too much to bear.

"I get it," I tell him, "go. I'm not going to stop you."

He doesn't reply, just heads off down the hall without me.

I stand frozen as I watch him go.

Guild, what have I done?

I head straight for the cafeteria, not even bothering to change out of my outfit or discard my weapons. People give me suspicious glares as I pass by, until I decide to take off my hood.

It's way past breakfast, but I get into the food line anyway. The cafeteria runs all day, thank the Guild. My heart doesn't feel like eating, but my brain knows I'll soon be starving if I don't.

I sit down at the squad's table alone and dig into my brunch. Once I start, my appetite returns and it's not long before I'm finishing off the last crumbs. I haven't eaten that fast in a long time.

After, I rest my head against the table and try to ignore the thoughts ricocheting off the walls of my brain.

You're an idiot.

What if he was telling the truth?

What if you made a mistake?

"Shut up," I tell the voices.

What's done is done. I made my choice.

"Shut up?" a voice asks. "I haven't even said anything yet."

I look up to see Trey sliding onto the bench across from me. "Sorry," I say. "I was talking to myself."

"That's always a good sign."

I scowl at her. "I've had a rough morning, okay? Not to mention a rough existence. I'm entitled to a little self-talk every once in a while."

She holds her hands up in defeat. "All right, don't get your cloak in a twist. I was just trying to make a joke."

I lower my head again. "Not in the mood."

"I can see that now. What happened?"

I sigh. "I'd appreciate it if you didn't ask; I don't want to discuss it."

"If that's what you want..." She's trying to lure me into saying more, but I'm not about to bite.

A long moment of silence passes before Trey speaks again. "Anyway, I came to ask about the mission. How'd it go?"

"Well enough," I reply, glad to change the subject. I sit up straight. "We were able to make it to the Grand Cavern."

"Were any suspicions raised? Did anyone recognize you?"

"No, it was a clean job," I lie.

"Well done, my young friend. I dare say you are exactly what I wasn't."

"And what is that?"

"Brave." She stands up.

"Wait, you're leaving already?"

"If you're not going to tell me why you look like you've made the worst mistake of your life, there's no point in me sticking around."

I wince at that; so much for being an expert at hiding my emotions.

"Besides," she goes on, "you look exhausted. Get some sleep, kid, you'll feel better after."

She leaves me sitting there alone and, after a moment of contemplation, I decide to heed her advice. I get up and head to my room. Maybe a good sleep will clear my mind. It's worth a shot anyway.

• • •

I wake up rejuvenated. My mind is less clouded; my emotions are muffled instead of suffocating me. I sleep much better here than I ever have, probably because I feel so much safer. The fact that I'm enjoying myself still continues to amaze me, but it's hard not to. I'm safe, I'm working towards a noble goal, eating good food, surrounded by friends and allies and...Ajax, though after this morning, whatever we had might be gone.

It's for the best, I remind myself. *We're in the middle of a war, have been for decades, will be for decades more. Anything can happen, anyone can die, and the worst thing you can do to yourself is get attached.*

Besides, my plan is to return to the Guild once the Charger is dead. I can't bring Ajax with me. I'm not even sure he would come, no matter how much he "loves" me. He and I are of different breeds, from different walks of life. Getting into a relationship is out of the question. It would be a death sentence when it goes wrong.

I sigh and roll out of bed. There are still things I have to get done today and I'll never do them if my thoughts keep distracting me. I decide to take some time in the training room. If a good fight won't do the trick, nothing will.

I walk over to the closet and pick out a plain black Resistance uniform. I decide only one sword is necessary

22121211101121100001

for the afternoon and strap it across my back. I look in the mirror before I go, for the first time since I arrived here.

A stranger's face stares back at me. There's a blush to my cheeks. I don't look as skinny, not as hollowed out. I've been eating a lot more lately. Then there's my hair. I used to describe it as black, like my soul, but now... It's more than that somehow. It's shiny, like ebony.

Bang.

A memory hits me.

I see my childhood room. I'm sitting beside my mother on the bed. She's reading me a story about a girl with ebony hair.

Snow White.

I close my eyes, blinking away tears as the memory fades. My eyes flick to my strand of blue hair.

I haven't forgotten mom. I will avenge you.

I sigh; I really do need a haircut.

• • •

The training room is empty when I arrive, which is a mercy. I walk to the middle of the space and take a deep breath.

It's going to be okay.

How? How do I fix this?

Maybe there's nothing to fix.

Like hell there isn't...

"Shut up!" I snap, but I'm talking to myself and I know from experience that the voices don't quiet easily.

221

I don't know why I'm so torn up over this boy, why I've let him shake me like this. Accepting his offer would've been a mistake. I would've been bamboozled. This is why trust is such a fragile concept. It can turn into a trap in the blink of an eye and by the time you notice, it's too late.

But what if it wasn't a trap?

Love *itself* is a trap. It chains you down and eventually, it ruins you because it's even more fragile than trust, though its grip on your heart is like iron long after it has turned to dust.

I should know. There's not a day that goes by that I don't think of my mother, but I had no choice but to get attached to her, to love her. I had no choice when she died either, and I have been a ruin ever since.

Bang.

I see her face in front of me: blue eyes and a soft smile, framed by long brown curls. All I can remember of her.

No. Not now.

I draw my sword and slice through the mirage in front of me, cutting my mother's face into ribbons until it dissolves into nothing.

Then I march over to one of the practice dummies and start swinging. There's nothing precise or fluid about my motions, that's not the point. The point is to exert myself until there's no energy left to form my wayward thoughts.

I lose track of time.

I lose myself in the pain of my arm muscles, in the sound of metal crashing against wood over and over and over again, until I start seeing the dummy as a person.

Until the wood becomes the flesh and bone of the man who destroyed everything I once loved, including myself.

I strike the Charger over and over again. I imagine the blood pooling on the floor. I imagine him begging for mercy. I give him none.

He wouldn't know mercy if it cornered him in a dark alley and shoved a broken piece of glass down his throat. He wouldn't know mercy if it sheared his head off of his arrogant shoulders...

I jolt back to reality when the head of the dummy flies off and ricochets across the room, knocking against the floor before rolling to a stop by the far wall.

I drop my sword and stare at the wooden head for a long while, panting. Then I walk over and retrieve it, setting it back on the shoulders as if nothing ever happened, to cover up the truth.

I pick up my sword and sheath it. I'm not sure how much time has passed, but it would probably be in my best interest to go see Jenson now. I feel better, better enough to face him at least. I've let out enough anger that I probably won't kill him. Maybe.

I smile a bit and head for the door.

I walk slowly and when I reach the exit, something makes me look back. There, suspended in the air, is my mother's face again.

I shake my head, but her image doesn't waver.

It's like she's trying to tell me something, but I don't know what.

Guild, I wish you were here.

I wish I knew what to do.

My thoughts turn back to the day's question. I don't know why I thought I could chase off the issue, though I'm not any closer to solving it either.

The truth is, love scares me. The only person who ever loved me is dead, but I wouldn't be here if it weren't for her. Love is dangerous, sure, but my love for my mother is the only thing keeping me going. Love is a killer, but sometimes, it also keeps you alive.

My mother's face fades into nothing and I head out the door without another glance.

CHAPTER EIGHTEEN

"Hello again," **I say** to the gathered men when I enter the council room.

"Assassin," Jenson replies, "we weren't expecting you back so soon." His tone implies he wasn't expecting me back at all.

I guess he doesn't take too well to being overruled. He's going to have to get used to it; I'm nowhere near done here.

"We left early," I tell him, "and I can be quick when I want to be."

"I see. I trust the mission was a success?"

"It was," I reply. "We were able to make it to the core of the base and back out again. There were no difficulties with my entrances."

"Wonderful, and were there any incidents?"

I shrug. "Nothing you should be worried about."

"What exactly does *that* mean?"

I roll my eyes. "It *means*, Jenson, that there wasn't anything that would interfere with the plan."

He slams the palms of his hands onto the table. "What happened?"

I sigh. "If you must know, two people tried to kill us."

Jenson's face turns red. "How exactly does that *not* interfere with the mission?"

"Because that happens all the time at the Guild. W-" I correct myself mid-word. "They don't trust each other, nor do they like each other. They're all fighting for the top spot and they kill each other on a daily basis to bring themselves closer to their goal."

"That's a terrible system," says the man sitting on Jenson's right. "How on earth is there anybody left to kill their targets?"

Something about his posture and attitude seems familiar. I mean, I've seen him before in these meetings, but he reminds me of someone else.

"It's a system based on strength," I tell him. "If you weed out all the weak ones, you'll be better moving forward. They recruit new agents all the time: criminals from outside of Haven, orphans, the children of their victims... But I didn't come here to discuss their methods. I came here to give my report."

"The assassin is right, Nicholas, stand down," Jenson tells the man, though I can see it pains him.

Nicholas.

This man is Nicholas Ross, Jenson's Second, the righteous father of Princess Natalie herself. Though their skin tones are different, they share the same face and the

226

same fire in their eyes when putting other people down. This is the man who has been trying to get rid of me since I arrived.

Again, something about that last name tugs at my memory, but I can't put my finger on it. I look at him closer, studying his dark eyes and short black hair.

"Can I ask why we're even listening to her?" Nicholas retorts. "She's the enemy, Jenson. We know the tunnels are safe; we don't need her anymore."

I stiffen at his words.

Jenson sighs. "I won't confirm nor deny if I agree with you at the present time, Nicholas, but it matters not what I think. Avery wants her here."

"That's right, boys," I say, grinning. "You're stuck with me."

Nicholas Ross whirls on me. "Excuse me, Assassin, but were we talking to you?"

I put on a condescending smile and reply, "Ross, is it? With all due respect, *we* weren't talking to *you*. *I* was merely telling Jenson how Ajax and I's near-death experience was not going to hurt the mission when you decided to disrespect us both by butting in. So really, Second, it was I who was interrupted, not you."

His eyes are like fire. "How dare you speak to me like that?"

"If you would excuse me," I reply, ignoring his comment, "I would like to continue my discussion with Jenson so we can make up for your delay."

He stares at me in disbelief and rage, but leans back in his chair and allows Jenson and me to continue.

I smile; I relish every victory.

"Now, Jenson," I go on, "Stage One has gone off without a hitch. The tunnels are usable and we have a sure-fire way into the Guild. I should like to move on to Stage Two, with your permission, of course."

"Of course," he replies, "and what would Stage Two entail? How soon until we attack?"

"Stage Two is paring down their numbers a bit and we'll attack during Stage Three."

He narrows his eyes. "How do you plan on accomplishing Stage Two, Assassin?"

"I will return to the Guild and convince the Master Assassin that a fair number of his assassins are traitors. He will then have them executed."

"Out of the question," he says. "I will not have you talking to your former Master. It's much too risky."

I scowl.

He ignores me and plunders on. "What about a bomb?"

"A bomb? You have bombs?" I raise a shocked eyebrow. It's a wonder they haven't yet used such a weapon, what with Jenson's patience.

Jenson regards me as if I'm an idiot. "We're fighting a war, Assassin," he reminds me, "have been since before either you or I were born. Of *course* we have bombs."

"Do you think a bomb is the best idea?" I ask, crossing my arms. "They'll know we're after them then. Lies and execution are a much more under the radar—"

"We've always been after them," Jenson argues, cutting me off. "What makes this any different?"

EMMA COUETTE

"If you go bombing the South End of the city, they're going to know they have a mole. They'll shut themselves inside their underground warren and you'll never find them again."

He shrugs. "Then we'll have to bomb the rest of Haven too. Make it seem like we have no idea where they are and are getting desperate."

I frown. "We can't bomb innocent civilians for our cause."

"Since when do you care about the civilians? I seem to recall you killed off quite a few of them."

I narrow my eyes at his audacity to bring up my past. "Since I had a change of heart," I reply. "The whole point of this entire endeavour, of your entire organization, is to save the civilians. We can't do that by hurting them in the process."

Jenson crosses his arms. "Then what else do you suggest, Assassin? I would be a complete fool to let you return to the Guild. Going with Ajax was one thing, but going alone is quite another. If I let you go prance around with your 'former' allies, who knows what secrets you might spill. You've already betrayed one organization. Who's to say you won't do it again?"

I do my best to ignore the fire his words ignite in me and think on his original question for a second, going over everything I've done since my arrival, all the new information I've received, and it comes to me.

I sit up straighter. "What if we bomb the food warehouse?"

He gives me a confused look. "What food warehouse?"

"The one Ajax and I found the other day, after we followed that tunnel you guys discovered in the fields by the train tracks."

"Oh, right..." He looks at me and a slow, cat-like grin begins to spread across his face.

I stare at him, unable to believe his sudden change.

"That's a brilliant idea, Assassin," he says. "We can take out their food storage and their way of getting more at the same time. We can turn this war into an old fashioned siege by starving them out."

"We must be ready for retaliation though," I warn him. "I suggest extra guards in the train. The assassins will be angry. The Master will be outraged. We will have to set Stage Three in motion shortly after, if we wish to keep our momentum going."

"Your opinion is noted, Assassin. Thank you for your time."

I raise an eyebrow. "Are you dismissing me?"

"Yes, you've given us a plan. We will take it from here."

"But—" I try to protest, but Jenson holds up a hand.

"There is nothing of value that you can add to this discussion, Assassin," he says. "You have done your part; now give us the peace and quiet to finish what you started."

His tone makes it sound more like they're cleaning up the mess I made than finishing what I started, but I press my lips together and say nothing.

Beside Jenson, Nicholas Ross is grinning at my dismissal. It's a familiar expression, but not one I've seen

Natalie wear. No, it had belonged to someone else, someone else with dark skin and hair…

And then it clicks.

Oh.

I knew three fellow assassins with that same smile, though one had been a blond—Luke, Jeremy, and Ashton Ross. I wonder if they know they have a sister.

What a secret you've been keeping, Ross, what a great shame it must be to have your children betray you…

My answering grin makes his disappear.

Oh, I can't wait to use my new weapon.

I take my leave and find Bast leaning against the wall beside the doorway, arms crossed and his usual grin taking up residence on his face.

I narrow my eyes. "What are you doing here?"

"Waiting for you." He stands up straight and his grin disappears. "Uh, Blake and I had a run-in with Jax this morning and he may have told us what happened between you guys." He scrapes his foot across the floor.

I roll my eyes. "Wonderful."

I wince at the curtness in my tone. I don't want to push Bast away too. Guild, I'm rebuilding my walls and I don't know if that's what's best for me.

"Don't worry," he says, "I don't want to know any of the details. Blake had to leave for a mission, but I'm here for support, if you need me."

"Blake told you to babysit me, didn't she." It's hardly a question.

His face reddens and he shifts his weight from foot to foot. "Well, uh...those weren't her exact words..."

I raise an eyebrow and give him my best assassin stare.

He shifts his eyes to anywhere but me and after a few more seconds of silence, he cracks. "Yeah, basically that's what she said, but she means well by it."

I roll my eyes again. "Oh, I'm sure, but we're going to have a few words the next time I see her."

"Fine by me," he replies. "So how'd the meeting go?"

"It went well. I didn't kill anybody and Stage Two is currently in development."

"Nice job," he says, smiling. "What's Stage Two?"

"We're going to bomb that food warehouse Ajax and I found, cut off the Guild's food supply to weaken them from the outside in. I expect swift retaliation though."

"That's actually not a bad plan. All your idea, I'm guessing?"

"Of course, but Jenson won't let me help any further."

Bast frowns. "I don't know what he has against you."

I look away from him as I answer, towards the door to the council room. Behind it, Jenson and the others carry on without me, as if I was never there. "In his eyes, I'm still the enemy," I reply, "and I doubt that'll ever change."

"Maybe, but don't worry about it. You're not here to impress him or be his friend. Hey, speaking of friends, what do you say we go have some fun?"

"Like what?"

"It's a surprise."

I narrow my eyes. "Should I be worried?"

He grins. "Terrified. You go back to your room and get changed into something less... oh, I don't know, doom and gloom."

I scowl at that, but he doesn't seem to notice.

"Oh, and do us all a favour," he adds. "Try to resist the urge to bring any weapons. I'll meet you outside your room in a minute."

"Where are you going?"

"I have to get changed too; I can't go to this place with my mission clothes still on."

"Can't you tell me anything about where we're going and what we're going to be doing there?"

"Not a chance, Night," he says, "a little bit of a surprise will do you good."

He disappears down the hall, leaving me standing there utterly bewildered. With nothing better to do, I head back to my room as he suggested.

• • •

I rifle through the clothes in my closet with no idea what to wear. Not knowing the destination or atmosphere makes it difficult to decide, but since Bast told me not to bring weapons, I judge it to be a non-hostile environment. So I grab an outfit that's a darker shade of grey than the usual and pair it with my black boots. I brush my hair out of my eyes, desperately wishing for a pair of scissors.

Then I stuff a large dagger in my left boot. I don't care what Bast said about that. I never go into an unknown situation without a weapon. That's an accident waiting to happen.

I go back into the hall and Bast shows up a minute later wearing the most casual clothes I've ever seen. "What are you wearing?" I ask.

He looks at me funny. "What, you've never seen jeans and a t-shirt?"

Is that what those weird blue pants are called? Jeans?

"I've seen t-shirts," I reply, "I just don't wear them. Jeans on the other hand..."

"You need to get out more," he says. "Everybody in the city wears jeans, Night. *Everybody*."

"I'm sorry I've never bothered to pay attention to civilian fashion."

"Do they upset you?"

"No, I just wanted to know what they were. Carry on."

"Okay, so you're going to love this place. It's one of my favourites."

He starts down the hall, but I can't resist asking. "What do you call those shoes?"

He gives me a look of complete shock. "Oh, please tell me you've heard of sneakers?"

• • •

I follow Bast down hall after hall for what seems like forever.

Finally, I have to say, "Are we there yet?"

"Nearly," he assures me. "Just down this hall here..."

We round the corner and a short, wooden door stands before us. It's set in an arch about a foot into the wall.

"What is this?" I ask him.

"We call it the Den." He pulls a key ring on a chain out of his shirt and unlocks the door. Muted sound escapes through the darkened doorway. "Just down the stairs, through one more door, and we'll be there."

"Lead on."

I trail him through the dark, down a spiral staircase and a short passage until we come to a metal door. The sound is louder now. Is that...music?

"Are you ready for the time of your life?" Bast says, reaching in front of me to put a hand on the door handle.

"It all depends on what that entails," I reply.

He smiles. "Always so cautious, but now is the time to loosen up." He opens the door and we step into a bright room. "Welcome to the party!"

CHAPTER NINETEEN

I don't believe my eyes. We're at the entrance of an enormous room. The ceilings are low, but the length and width of the room make up for it. Coloured lights spill onto a glass floor. Dozens of people dance in the centre, moving to the beat of the music that seems to be coming out of the walls. A bar stands to our left and its wooden counter spans the length of the room. Patrons sit on stools, sipping various drinks from fancy glasses.

I stand in the doorway, mouth open and gaping. There is an underground club in the Resistance. I never saw this coming.

"We're in a club," I say.

"Yeah," Bast replies, "not what you were expecting, is it?"

"Not really. I thought you guys were more formal. If anything, I would expect a ballroom."

"Well, everybody has their wild side, Night, and this is where we let it all go."

No sooner does he say it than a man stumbles by, sloshing his drink all over the floor just inches from our feet.

"That was a close one," I mutter.

"Terribly sorry, ma'am," the man slurs, "didn't see you there."

I gape again as I recognize one of the men from the council, who clearly is too drunk to recognize me.

Assassins below. So much for being sophisticated.

The man shuffles off, spilling more of his drink as he goes and I avert my gaze. I notice three red doors on the wall opposite the bar.

"Where do those doors lead?" I ask Bast.

"There's a game room, a lounge, and a tattoo parlour," he replies. "Why?"

My eyes light up. "A tattoo parlour? You're kidding."

"Nope, one hundred percent serious. You look excited."

"I am. Would you... Do you think you could excuse me for a moment? I need to um...touch up my ink."

That sounds believable, right?

He raises an eyebrow. "Now? And wait, you have tattoos?"

I give him a sly smirk as I walk away. "There's a lot you guys don't know about me. I'll be right back."

I lose sight of him as I enter the dance floor, shoving my way through the throng of swaying bodies. I try not to think about what happened the last time I was in a crowd like this, try not to think about what that led to.

Finally I emerge and steal into the parlour, guessing the right door on the first try. The room is decorated in gray wallpaper with white flowers instead of skulls.

The tattoo artist looks up as I walk in. "How may I help you?"

"I need something quick," I tell her. "A name. I want it just above my ankle. Can you do that quickly? I don't want it fancy or anything, just normal letters."

Slightly bewildered she replies, "I'll see what I can do. Have a seat." She gestures to the chair and I flop down onto it. "What colour?" she asks.

"Black," I answer.

When she asks for the name, I whisper it. I sit there silent as a statue, feeling every prick of pain as she inks the thirteen letters into my skin.

I re-enter the main club area twenty minutes later, after sitting through a lecture on the proper care of a tattoo. As if I don't already know.

Ugh, tattoo artists.

I spend a few gut-wrenching moments scouring the club for Bast, fearing he got bored and left. Then I see him leaning against the bar talking to another familiar face.

Guild, what is he doing here?

I duck through the crowds of people and walk over to the pair. When I reach them, I stand on Bast's other side, not wanting to get too close to Ajax. He notices me right away, and while he doesn't exactly scowl, he doesn't smile at me either.

"I didn't think you knew about this place," he says. The dullness of his voice pains me.

"I didn't," I reply. "Bast brought me down. I didn't think you'd be here."

Bast looks uncomfortable caught between the two of us and scrapes his foot across the floor. "Come on guys, can we *try* to get along?"

"Bast," Jax says, hunching his shoulders, "please don't." He swirls the drink in front of him, half a glass of amber liquid. I never would've pegged him as a drinker.

"Dude," Bast replies, "it's not the end of the world. We're still the same people we were yesterday."

"But it's not yesterday anymore, Seb. Things have...changed."

I swear I can feel his gaze burning into the side of my face, as if his eyes are tattooed on my cheek. I turn my head slightly to catch them. The contact lasts a second before he averts his gaze to the countertop, but it was enough to see the resentment and sorrow and somehow hope, all burning beneath the blue. I wrap my arms around my chest.

Beside me, Bast is bristling at the name. "Don't call me that," he growls.

"Then stop being so damn optimistic," Ajax retorts. He slides his glass down the counter, sloshing the contents on the wood, and turns to go. "I'll be around, if you decide to start talking sense." He stalks off without sparing me another glance and I can feel my heart crumbling in my chest.

Assassins below, my damn walls will be the death of me.

239

Bast watches Ajax go and then turns back to me. "So that went well."

"Are you kidding? That was a disaster. I know I broke his heart, but that doesn't give him the right to be an asshole to you."

"I was being sarcastic," Bast replies. "He still cares, you know."

"What?"

"He still cares about you, and I don't think he's given up yet."

"Wonderful," I sigh. "Look, Bast, I don't want to talk about him. Can you drop it?"

"Fine, but you can't blame me for trying."

We fall silent for a moment, and I survey the club. There are so many people.

"What's the occasion?" I ask Bast.

He shrugs, back to his normal self. "There isn't one," he replies. "The place is always like this."

"So it's like a regular club?"

"Yeah, we can't go into the city to have fun, not with the threat of an assassin attack looming over our heads."

I wince. "Sorry about that."

"Nah, it's not your fault. Besides, this is way more fun." He pauses. "Did you guys have anything like this?"

"Not exactly," I reply. "We had drunken parties in the Grand Cavern every once in a while, but they turned into drunken brawls pretty quickly. The last one was a couple of years ago."

"Then it's high time you had some fun... some real fun," Bast says. "Speaking of which..." He trails off and heads to the other end of the bar. He returns with a couple of glasses in hand, half-filled with what can only be alcohol.

Warning bells go off in my head.

He grins at me. "Care for a drink?"

"Not at the moment," I reply, heeding the orders my mind is giving me.

"You sure?"

"Positive, maybe later."

He shrugs. "Your loss," he says and then he downs one glass in a single go.

I narrow my eyes. "Aren't you a little young to be drinking?"

As if *I* have the right to ask that question.

Bast smiles. "According to the laws of the past, yes, but I live by the laws of the present, which are non-existent. I'm a free person and I do what I want."

Something in his voice makes me want to agree with him. Why *can't* I have a drink? What harm will one do? What happened before won't happen here. I'm safe and I can trust my friend to protect me. Besides, I could use the mild distraction. Guild knows I've dealt with a lot today.

Before I can say anything, I notice Bast's face go pale, his eyes fixed on something behind me. "Oh shit," he says.

"What?" I spin around and it doesn't take me long to figure out what I'm supposed to be looking at. A familiar blonde is making her way through the crowd on the dance floor. She's wearing a pale blue summer dress that sways around her as she walks.

"She followed us down here," I say to Bast, eyes still tracking her motions.

"You think so?"

"Of course. She's been watching me for weeks. I swear if she…"

I don't finish the sentence because…because she finds him then. Ajax is facing away from her, but I'd recognize that stance and brown hair anywhere. She rises on tiptoes and kisses him on the cheek.

He turns, but so do I.

My skin is burning, along with my eyes as I furiously blink back wretched tears.

It's all your fault, what happens.

My blood pounds in my ears, drowning out the music, drowning out the screams of protest in the back of my mind as I say, "On second thought, Bast, I think I will."

He turns to me. "What?"

"I'll have that drink you offered."

He gives me a funny look. "Are you sure?"

"Why not? This is a party isn't it?" I fight to keep my tone neutral, to not give into the rage building in my bones.

"Are you sure it's not because of…you know?" He jerks his head in her direction.

"Just give me the damn drink," I snap.

When he hesitates again, I reach out and rip the glass from his hand. Following his example, I down it all at once. I feel fiery.

Bast laughs nervously. "That's the spirit, I guess. What do you think of it?"

"I think I'll need another to give a solid opinion."

His laugh is more genuine as he heads off to get us some more.

I keep my gaze fixed on the bar in front of me.

We down our seconds in unison and my brain's protest dies out as the song in the club changes to something I recognize. "I love this song," I exclaim.

Bast raises an eyebrow at me. "You like *Skrillex*?" he says.

"Of course," I reply. "They might be old, but they sure know how to have fun. Come on, let's go dance."

He shakes his head at me. "I wouldn't have marked you as a dubstep kind of person."

Ignoring his words, I grab his arm and pull him onto the dance floor.

• • •

We dance and talk and laugh for what seems like hours. I've never felt so alive and free. I lose track of the number of drinks I have after my third and it isn't long before my swaying isn't in any way related to the music.

Ajax rejoins us sometime later in the afternoon, alone somehow, but I mostly ignore him and chat with Bast instead. We play this game he likes to call Who Would They Be? It's where you pick a person and based on their appearance and body language, you decide who they'd be if Haven wasn't the way it is, if war hadn't torn us apart for almost a hundred years.

I'm actually managing to enjoy myself, until a random girl comes around and drags Bast back onto the dance floor.

A memory tugs at my mind, but it feels...negative, so I ignore it.

Ajax speaks as soon as he leaves. It's the first thing he's said in hours. "We should go, Silent," he suggests. "Don't you think this is enough party for one day?"

"Oh, come on, it's never enough party. Don't be such a Debbie Downer." I finish my current glass of alcohol and leave my spot on the dance floor just long enough to order another.

It takes me a bit longer to reach the bar this time. I don't seem to be walking straight.

The bartender slides the glass over to me.

I reach for it, but a hand grabs my wrist. I jump.

"Don't," Ajax says, his voice coming from behind me. He must have followed me over. "You've had quite enough."

I turn to him, pouting. "Can't a girl have some fun?"

"Fun? You call *this* fun? Silent, I doubt you even remember where you are right now. We need to *go*."

"Don't be like that. Look, I'm sorry. Let me make it up to you." I rise onto my tiptoes and try to kiss him, but he pulls away, clearly pained. I vaguely remember a similar situation, but the details are faded.

"No, Silent," Ajax says. "You're drunk."

"What does it matter? I love you and I want you forever. Don't you want me?" I'm not even aware of what I'm saying now. My head feels all fuzzy.

"Not like this. This isn't real." He pushes me away gently, but I can't find my balance. He catches me before I hit the ground.

A wave of nausea wracks through me. Ajax's face is blurred and the music is fading.

Who is doing that? Turn it up, this is a party!

I hear Ajax's voice as if I'm underwater. He's saying something about silence and killing a bast. I'm tired though and don't want to focus on it.

When my feet leave the floor and the music fades away to nothing, I'm too far gone to notice.

CHAPTER TWENTY

When I wake, it hurts to open my eyes. Lights blind me and it feels like someone is jabbing a knife into my temple repeatedly. I wince against the pain, but that makes it worse.

My stomach roils and I groan at the nausea that surfaces in the waves.

Guild, what did I do to myself?

I sit up, despite my body's protests, and immediately lean over the side of what I assume to be the bed. I've closed my eyes again against the glare.

I heave for a few minutes, but nothing is forthcoming, despite my stomach telling me that everything needs to *go*.

"Easy, Night," someone says, "don't move so fast. The world will wait."

A hand touches my shoulder and I realize how much I'm shaking.

Guild, what did I do?

Why am I hung-over…?

And then it hits me.

Assassins below, I am such an idiot. Have I forgotten what happened the last time I gave in to drink?

Cursing my stupidity, I lean back in the bed and open my eyes.

My stomach rumbles under my clammy skin and I shudder at the discomfort.

Blake's brown eyes stare back at me. "You're okay," she says, "just breathe, and stay still. It'll help with the dizziness. Here, try to drink this." She hands me a bottle of water and I reach for it slowly. "Take sips only. It's not going to taste all that great at first, but it'll help. If you keep that down, you can have some of the toast." She nods to the plate on my bedside table.

It takes me forever to unscrew the lid on the damn bottle and the water tastes like chemicals on my tongue when I finally take a sip.

My stomach protests wildly and I squeeze my eyes shut as I wait for it to pass.

"I'm glad to see you're awake. Jax can stop pacing the halls now in his brooding silence."

I cringe and take another swig of water. "I'm sorry. Did he...send you here to look after me?"

"Yeah," she sighs, "he thought it would be best if he wasn't here when you woke up."

"I didn't think he still cared."

"Oh, he cares, Night," Blake says, "make no mistake. He probably cares more than he'd like to admit. He'll come around in time and then you'll have your friend back. We all will."

But what if I don't want to be friends?

I shut that thought down quick and say, "Is he mad at me?"

"A bit," she replies, "but it's mostly Bast he's angry with. He's not talking to him and if Bast comes in here, don't ask about his black eye. He's really sorry."

My eyes widen. "Ajax and Bast fought?"

Blake shrugs. "It was a spur of the moment thing. Jax was angry and sent a right hook into Bast's face. Jax blames him for what happened, but I think he also blames himself."

I want to sink under the sheets. "Was it really that bad?"

She nods. "You were mumbling apparently, couldn't even walk straight. You were trying to have your eighth glass when you passed out and Ajax had to carry you here."

"Sadly," I sigh, "that wasn't the first time, but we won't talk about my past with alcohol."

I look down at my hands and that's when I see what I'm wearing.

"Whose clothes are these?" I ask, frowning at the yellow fleece.

Blake tries to hide a smile. "They're mine. Don't judge them."

"But why am I -"

She gives me a look.

"Oh. Well, that's great. How many people saw me? Wait. Don't answer that. At least I didn't ruin one of my better outfits…"

248

She laughs. "Relax, Night. I'm sure your blood pressure is already high enough. How's that water sitting?"

I shrug. "Okay, I guess?"

"Let's try some food then. It'll get the alcohol out of your system faster."

"If I can keep it down."

She rolls her eyes. "Just trust me, would you?" She hands me the plate and I grab a piece of toast. I nibble on it as we continue our conversation.

"What time is it?"

"Around nine p.m.," she replies. "Ajax dragged you out of the Den around four this afternoon and I got back around eight."

Well, it could've been worse.

"Have I missed anything?"

"Not really. You missed what I wish I could've been away for. I came back from my shift to find a frantic Ajax sitting at the end of your bed and a drunken Bast trying to reason with him." She shakes her head. "But that's enough of that. The point is you're fine, the plan hasn't changed, and you'll be back to normal in no time, and don't worry about Jax, Night. What will be will be. Focus on yourself and let things happen as they will. If Jax loves you as he says he does, he'll understand." She smiles at me.

I smile back; I like her ability to forget the past and focus on the present.

"Thank you," I tell her.

"For what?"

"For everything, I guess. For being a friend. I haven't had many in my life and I appreciate it."

She laughs. "Night, you don't have to thank someone for being your friend. It happens naturally, and I'm glad to be yours. If you need anything, just ask. I need to go get some rest now though, if you think you're going to be okay. The worst of it should be over. Finish that toast and have some more water. You should try to sleep after. It'll be better in the morning. I'll let Jax know you're okay."

"That's fine and I guess I can try to sleep." I don't feel as shaky now. Sustenance seems to be helping.

She stands up.

"Wait, Blake," I say. "There *is* something I've been wondering if you could do for me."

"Shoot," she replies.

"Do you think you could teach me how to wield an axe better?"

She looks confused. "The great Silent Night needs me to teach her how to wield an axe?"

I grimace. "I've never been any good at it. Axes are one of my few weaknesses and I want to change that. You're talented and I trust you to be honest with me and my progress."

She brightens up. "I can certainly help you. We can do it in the mornings, starting the day after tomorrow, if you're up for it."

"Great, thank you."

"Anytime, Night. I'll see you later." She heads out the door.

I take another bite of toast and close my eyes.

• • •

When I wake the next morning, I feel a bit better, but I still decide to wallow in self-pity instead of facing the world. I don't know how much time passes before the knock comes on my door. I'm sitting in my bed, knees curled to my chest.

"Who is it?" I call out, not willing to open the door to just anyone in my current state.

"It's me, Ajax," he answers. "Can I come in?"

I groan. Do I want him to see me like this? We need to talk, but that badly?

"If this isn't a good time, I can come back later," he goes on.

I study myself. I'm still wearing Blake's yellow pajamas. I should have a shower or something.

"Silent?"

"Um, yeah, later might be better actually. I'm not really...fit to see anybody right now. Do you think you could come back in an hour?" That should be enough time for me to shake off my melancholy and put myself back together.

"Uh, sure," he replies.

"Great," I say. "See you then."

I listen to his footsteps walking away before I get to my feet.

The floor sways a little underneath me, but I ignore it.

You're fine. Don't be a wuss.

I grab a new outfit from my closet, the first one I touch, and then I head down the hall to the bathroom. The hall is empty, thank the Guild. I don't need any more rumours circling.

Did you hear what Silent Night did?

Yeah, she made a fool of herself.

Hardly intimidating now, is she?

I frown and shake my head to clear the voices.

My feet pad silently down the halls and then my boots click as the floor transitions from grey cement to white tile. I wince in the harsh white light of the bathroom and my head swims for a second before I get used to the change.

The world is punishing me today it seems.

You deserve it.

Whatever.

I grab a clean towel off the rack and go to the end shower stall, avoiding my gaze in the long mirror as I pass by. I do not want to see the extent of the wreck I am.

I hang up my fresh clothes and towel on the hook outside the shower and strip, leaving Blake's pajamas in a pile on the floor; I'm not sure if she wants them back. Then I step into the shower, slide the grey plastic curtain across, and turn the water on.

The cold stream is a shock to the system and goose bumps bristle on my skin upon contact. I don't flinch away as I turn the knob up and up. The water goes from frigid to boiling and I sigh as it singes my skin, hoping it burns away everything that is making me unclean. Burn away the doubt, the self-loathing, the spite…

I reach for the bar of soap and help the water cleanse me, rubbing it in as best as I can. Suds wash down the drain and I stand in the stream long after every inch of me has been scrubbed raw.

I think about last night. I think about how stupid I was. I could've stopped at one, at three, but I didn't. I made the decision to keep going and now I'm living with the consequences.

I think about Blake's face last night. It wasn't fair to her to have to come back from her shift and take care of me. I hope she got some sleep.

I think about Ajax. I wonder if I had disgusted him. I wonder if I care.

Of course you do.

Shut up.

I turn the water up even higher, as if I can drown out my thoughts, as if I can burn them away. I grit my teeth against the pain of the heat for a few moments before I turn it back down.

A memory surfaces then, despite my attempts.

I see Jax through a fog, remember him telling me I should leave.

I see myself, reaching up on tiptoe...

I love you, I told him.

My heart clenches.

Guild, why am I always so cruel? That must've been a knife to the gut after everything that happened yesterday. Can I do nothing right?

I don't even deserve love—much less his—and he deserves so much more than me.

That's when I remember what else happened last night, who really drove me to drink.

Natalie.

I bristle at the thought of what might have happened after I turned away. I wonder if she had fun with Ajax. I wonder if he finally gave in and indulged her...

Maybe he wanted to talk earlier to tell me the two of them are together.

A single tear runs down my face and is washed away almost as quick.

You had your chance.

He won't give up on you.

You will get better, will be better.

And what if I don't? What if I can't?

What if things just keep getting worse?

I shut the tap off quick before the cold can seep in again and I stand there in the absence, letting the stray water droplets run off. I listen to them drip one by one against the tile. Then I squeeze out my hair, creating a splattering of drops.

After a minute, I take a deep breath and reach out of the curtain for the towel. I wrap it around my shivering body, shocked by the abrupt change in temperature once again. I soak in the warmth for a few minutes and then towel myself off. I step out of the shower and trade my towel for my clean outfit.

Once dressed, I throw my towel in the wash bin along with Blake's pajamas and hope my outfit from yesterday found its way to a garbage bin.

I stand in front of the mirror then and am relieved to see that I don't look like shit. I run my fingers through my damp locks. The blue is still showing through, for now. I keep meaning to take care of that.

I sigh.

You're prolonging the inevitable, I chide myself.

"Yeah, yeah," I mutter to the empty room.

I can't hide from Ajax forever, as much as I'd like to. It would definitely be easier.

I sigh again and leave my reflection behind, heading back to my room. Ajax will be there soon. I guess I'll twiddle my thumbs until then.

• • •

It's an hour on the dot when someone knocks on my door.

"If that's you, Ajax, you can come in," I call out, fighting to keep the nerves out of my voice.

The door opens and Ajax steps in. He's back to his usual grey uniform, but he isn't any less attractive. It makes staying away from him so difficult.

His blue eyes land on me and he runs a nervous hand through his scraggly hair. "Hey," he says. It feels like there are a thousand miles between us. "How are you feeling?"

"Okay," I reply. "I've been worse, but I've certainly been better too."

"Yeah," he says.

He looks so lost standing there in the doorway so I say, "Have a seat. I mean, if you want to."

He crosses the room in a few steps and sits down on the edge of the bed, as far away from me as he can get. I swing my legs over the side of the bed so we're facing the same direction, several feet between us.

"Look, Silent, I'm sorry," he says softly.

"For what?" I ask.

"For being an asshole, to both you and Bast. I shouldn't have expected anything from you. Maybe if I'd been more courteous, the events of last night wouldn't have happened."

"I don't know what game you're trying to play, but last night was not your fault, and neither was it Bast's. You're right about being an asshole though."

I look over at him to catch him grimacing.

"I'm just telling it like it is," I say. "The only one at fault was me. I know what alcohol does to me, but I chose to drink anyway. I let Bast's carefree attitude persuade me; he didn't actively beg me to drink." Not strictly true; Bast had little to do with it.

He sighs. "I guess I don't blame him for that. He just...he doesn't think."

"To be fair, I wasn't thinking either, but I guess that's kind of what I wanted."

"Why?"

"Why?" I laugh. "Do you think I enjoyed breaking your heart? I may be cold-hearted, but I understand how much that hurts. I felt like shit and then…" I hesitate, but he deserves to know the truth. "Then I saw Natalie. So when Bast offered an escape, I took it and it didn't take much to render me incompetent."

"Natalie?"

"Don't pretend you don't know what I'm talking about. I understand that I turned you down, that you're hurting. You have every right to move on, but Natalie…that's a low blow."

"Oh," he says, eyes wide. "We didn't… We're not together."

"What?"

"Yeah, she got one kiss through my defenses, but I told her off for it. I half dragged her out of the club and told her to stay the hell away from the both of us. I told her that if I ever caught her spying, I'd make sure she *never* gets a boyfriend."

I can't help but laugh. "You what?"

"I told her we could never work. I told her to give up. It was a long overdue discussion. She reported me to her father on grounds of emotional abuse. They're taking my weapons away for a week."

"They're so stupid," I mutter. "What will that accomplish?"

He looks at his feet. "I think they're punishing me for defending you."

Silence.

"You seriously turned Natalie down?" I ask him.

"Of course," he replies. "I'm still hurting. I can't let myself make reckless decisions."

As if deciding to like me isn't reckless.

"But why do you care?" he asks, looking over at me.

"Because...because it's Natalie, because I'm selfish." I hold my head in my hands. "It crushed me when I saw her kiss you."

"You're pretty good at playing indifference."

"I have to be. We never would've left that bloody Guild if I couldn't convince you that I couldn't care less about your feelings."

He gives me a look. "Wait, does that mean...?"

"Yeah," I reply. "I care Ajax, more than I'd like to admit, but it doesn't change who I am. I can't be who you want me to be."

He nods. "I'm sorry I pressured you. I can't expect you to commit to this, whatever we have, right now. That would be too much to ask. Your life has been turned upside down these past few weeks and I'm just making it more complicated. Maybe, when this is all over, we can revisit this."

"There might not be an after," I reply, especially with the plan I have in mind. A plan I forgot about until yesterday.

Can I leave Jax and my other friends at the Resistance, to become the queen of assassins? Can I go back to the person I was two weeks ago? Do I want to?

Well, I can't go back to the person I was *before* the assassin. Can't go back to that cute little girl who helped her mother plant tulips...

Because my mother is dead.

A single tear escapes my eye and trickles down my face.

"Hey," Ajax says. "It's okay. I'm sorry. Forget I even brought it up. I..."

I raise my head. "No, it's not you. It's not your fault. The mission with you was awesome, these weeks with you and the others have been amazing. I haven't had this much fun in years, not since my mom died. And Guild... You make me question everything."

"Then why?"

"Because everything is tainted now," I tell him. "Tainted by the Charger, tainted by what I've become, by what he made me. I'm afraid, Jax, terribly afraid I'll try to love you and end up impaling your heart on a sword instead."

He regards me with sorrow, but also with encouragement, as if he knows something about me that I don't. "Silent, I don't particularly care that you might kill me; I'd rather die happy and in love than never experience this at all."

"You don't understand what you're saying," I reply.

"I do," he says. "You're not that person anymore. You don't have to be."

He's right. I deserve to be happy, to defy the Charger by showing him that he didn't break me, that my mother's precious daughter is still in here, struggling to get out, that I'm trying to set her free, but not yet. I trust Ajax, but I don't trust myself. Until then, this can't go any further.

"I don't know why you're bothering to give me another chance. You should get Jenson to give me a new escort and try to forget about me."

He shakes his head. "I can't do that, not only because Jenson wouldn't allow the change, but because I can't bear to watch that unfold. I can't imagine anyone else would treat you well. Not all of us are as accepting. I mean, imagine what your experience would've been like if I never stopped threatening you with that gun or if you were still locked in your room at night."

"I wouldn't be happy," I admit. "Somebody might be dead by now."

"Exactly," he says.

"But wouldn't you be happier with me out of sight and out of mind?"

"No, I wouldn't. I'm not going to give up on you, Silent. I know you wish I would and I know my chances are slim, but I can't help it. I'm willing to wait for you. You've made your choice; I've made mine."

"If that's what you want…"

"It is."

"Even after last night?" I ask him, bringing the conversation back to the original issue. "Am I worth the heart attack I gave everyone?"

"Maybe," he allows. "Maybe if you promise us you'll never do it again. There's only room for one drunkard in this squad, and Bast already fills that spot."

"I wouldn't dream of stealing Bast's glory," I assure him. "I feel like I was run over by a train."

"Good," he says. "I'm glad you learned your lesson."

"I should've known better," I reply. "I've heard enough horror stories from the Guild… I was lucky I was surrounded by friends this time."

"We would never let anyone hurt you," he assures me.

Maybe not, Ajax, maybe not, but you might be the death of me.

CHAPTER TWENTY-ONE

We sit together on my bed for a while and just chat, mending the tears in our friendship. I'm glad we can address the issues like adults and move on for now. Guild knows we have much bigger things to worry about.

Around noon, Ajax leaves for a meeting. I let him go, knowing some space will be good for us.

Ten minutes later, Bast comes in and, after he apologizes profusely for what happened, he joins me in the cafeteria for a small lunch. After, we walk around the base playing Who Would They Be until I feel back to normal.

We return to my room to find Ajax leaning against the wall outside. I tell them we aren't going to dinner until they make up. They exchange some words and less than friendly expressions, but finally they clasp hands and clap each other on the back, not best buds once again, but well on their way. I smile, glad I can fix the damage I caused.

Dinner is a quiet affair since I'm still not feeling one hundred percent, but I manage to have some fun. Ajax walks me to my room after and we talk for a few minutes before he leaves me be. My thoughts keep me awake for a while before I fall asleep.

• • •

The next morning, I'm back to my old self or rather, my new old self. I hum a happy tune as I get dressed and run a hand through my unruly hair. It's nearly to my shoulders and it's driving me crazy.

I *have* to find a hairdresser. Surely they have one here. I mean, they have a tattoo parlour for Guild's sake. Sadly, I don't have time to go searching for one now. I have to meet Blake in the training room at nine. It's eight twenty; I have just enough time to grab breakfast and head over.

I'm the only one at our table when I arrive. Bast is working his shift and Ajax must still be in bed. Blake, having to work the night shift, probably ate breakfast early. I don't mind eating alone, I did it for years, but I've grown to enjoy the company of my friends.

Friends.

It's a foreign concept. A part of me still balks at the idea, but nobody has stabbed me in the back, yet. Maybe nobody will. Comfort can be dangerous, but right now I am content.

I eat alone in the quiet din of the cafeteria I've grown used to and then I make my way to the training room, thanking whoever is listening that Roseanne didn't show up for a chat when my friends were gone. I don't think I can behave myself anymore when it comes to her. She is such a nuisance.

• • •

Blake is alone in the training room and her voice sounds awfully loud as she calls to me. "Night, glad you didn't chicken out on me."

I walk up to her, crossing my arms. "I wouldn't dream of it."

"Sure you're up for this?"

I snort. "A little hangover isn't going to pin me down. Teach away."

"If you say so, but I won't go easy on you."

"I'd be hurt if you tried."

She smiles. "Let's get you an axe then."

I follow her over to the weapon wall and she studies the axes for a minute.

"Let's see..." she mutters. "What hand are you?"

"Right, I think?"

"You don't know?" she says, raising a thick eyebrow.

"I was born right, but I'm ambidextrous now," I explain. "All assassins are made that way."

"Do you write with both hands?"

"Yep."

"Wow. Well, okay then. Do you know your weight by any chance?"

"Why does it matter?"

264

"You need to get the weight ratio exactly right when choosing an axe for a person."

"I suppose you would know," I reply. "Last time I checked, I was one hundred and forty pounds."

"All right, that would mean you would need..." She scours the racks and pulls down a small double-bladed weapon. "This should do."

She holds it out to me and I take it in my right hand, swinging it a couple times to get a feel for it.

"Seems good," I say. "What now?"

She grins. "Now the real fun begins." She whips her dark hair into a quick ponytail and faces me. "Fighting stance," she barks.

I spread my feet apart and crouch.

"Axe on an angle, like this."

She draws her own weapon and I mirror her.

"Now go!"

She flies at me and I dodge and block her blows, not landing a single thing before she disarms me.

"Tsk tsk," she mutters. "We have a lot of work to do."

She gives me a few pointers before she comes at me again.

The next hour is a blur of shouted words, metal, and bruises. Blake is a force to be reckoned with, whirling her axe around her like Mother Nature wielding a tornado. I try to stay out of her way, but I still feel the sting of her blade through the armour she makes us wear. She's a good teacher though and by the end of the lesson, I've landed a couple of blows myself. I walk out of the training room with the promise that tomorrow will be easier, knowing that means it will be leagues more difficult.

● ● ●

Ajax is standing outside my room when I arrive. I try not to think much of it. This is a normal occurrence. He's here because he's *supposed* to be watching me, not because he likes me.

"Jax," I say. "What are you doing here?"

"I thought I should see how your lesson with Blake went. She might have told me about it."

"I see. The lesson was good. I can hazard to guess I learned a thing or two. Blake gave me this." I hold up the axe I'd been sparring with. "It's a simple training one, but she says it'll be good to carry around so I can get used to it while they make me my own, whoever *they* are."

Ajax laughs. "*They* are the Resistance agents who fashion all of our weapons, highly-trained individuals. Did you order anything special? They like a challenge."

I shrug. "Just a black handle so it'll match the rest of my collection."

"Nice," he says and then, "What do you say we go for a walk?"

I narrow my eyes. "What for?"

"No reason; it's just something to do."

"All right then," I reply. "Just let me get changed."

He nods and I head inside, changing into a clean grey uniform, before joining him in the hall.

"So, are we going anywhere in particular?" I ask as we start walking.

"Nope," he replies, "we're just walking."

"That's kind of boring."

"Well, I was thinking we could walk and talk, nothing too serious. I realized the other day that we don't really know much about each other, and since you won't tell me your name, I thought we could start with favourite colours."

"Okay," I say, not expecting this at all. "Um..."

It's actually a hard question. I've never thought about it before. Automatically, I want to say black, but then I realize that isn't right.

What is *my favourite colour?*

And then I have it.

"Blue," I say, "but not a light blue, a deep blue, like the sky just before dark."

He smiles. "I like that. Is that why you dyed part of your hair blue? I've been meaning to ask you about it for a while now, but never got around to it."

I touch my hand to it. "No, it's actually in remembrance of my mother. It's her favourite colour too, light though, like a baby blue. I tell myself that as long as I never let the dye fade away into nothing, my memories of her won't fade either."

He smiles. "That's a great way to honour someone. She must have been an amazing woman."

I allow myself a small smile in return. "She was, from what I can remember anyway." I shake my head to clear my thoughts before I can slip into nostalgia. "How about you? What's your favourite colour? Your mom's too, if you'd like."

"Mine is green, like a forest green. Mom's was any shade of purple. She was a typical girl when it came to that."

"What was she like...your mom?" I don't know why I ask, but for some reason I want to know more about the person who gave Ajax life.

Ajax sighs. "My mom was Superwoman or at least, that's how I saw her. She was an agent of the highest level, one rank below Ross. She doted on me, called me her greatest achievement." He smiles. "She loved to sing and she would dance around our house as she did the chores. She was so vibrant, full of life. I guess that's why it was a while before I could believe she was dead."

I go against my instinct and place a hand on his shoulder. The two of us come to a stop.

"I'm sorry," I tell him.

He turns his head to look at me. "Why? It wasn't your fault."

"I know, but it was the Guild's fault and I apologize for them, since they never will."

"Thank you," he says and we start walking again. "What about *your* mom?"

"What about her?"

"What was she like?"

"Oh, um... She was a gardener. We grew every type of flower imaginable in our backyard. Tulips were reserved for the front yard though. She was quiet and beautiful. She always said I had her eyes..." I break off, a single tear running down my cheek. "I miss her."

"I don't blame you," he sighs. "What I wouldn't give to have my mom back... But they're gone and there's nothing we can do to change it. We just have to remember them like you said and make their killers pay."

"Oh, I intend to," I assure him.

"What are you going to do when this is all over, when you've made the Charger pay and avenged your mother, what then?"

I sigh. "The truth?"

He nods.

"I don't really know," I admit. "I thought I did. I had all these plans but now... I'm torn. I'll have to get back to you on that, if I ever get my life figured out."

He laughs. "Fair enough. I tend to look at the small steps and right now, my future looks like lunch."

I laugh at that. "I guess our walk has a destination now."

"Funny how that happens, isn't it?"

CHAPTER TWENTY-TWO

We spend the next week and a half doing much the same. I wake up at eight, have lessons with Blake from nine to ten, and then I spend the rest of the morning with Ajax. We talk and laugh and just get to know each other better. He doesn't bring up the L word again and I find myself getting comfortable.

I like it a lot better when we're on speaking terms. I wouldn't want to lose our friendship over something as silly as love. I don't know what that says about me.

The two of us have lunch with Bast every day and then I spend the afternoon back in my Resistance lectures. The number of times I contemplate putting a knife through the teacher's throat is appalling.

After dinner is free time, which I spend with either Ajax or Bast. We play our game while Ajax goes to meetings. He's helping the council finalize the plan to bomb the food warehouse.

On the day before the appointed date, Blake, Bast, and I are sitting at lunch, waiting for Ajax to come back from yet another council meeting.

"I can't believe the second stage of your plan is happening tomorrow," Blake says. "I can't believe we're blowing up a warehouse. We're declaring war."

I cross my arms. "We've been at war for decades," I point out. "We're simply stepping out of the shadows we've hidden in for far too long. We're showing them we're not afraid and that they shouldn't underestimate us, not that they would. We're also taking their food. That'll weaken them, but I know their retaliation will be swift and brutal. We are not in the clear, far from it. We're stepping into a field of open cannons and daring them to fire."

"Lovely," Bast mutters.

Blake's eyes reflect a hint of fear.

Good. She should *be afraid. I* am.

"What comes after this then?" Bast asks.

"We wait to see what they do and react to it. Everything we do from here on out depends on them."

"What do you think will happen?" Blake asks.

I sigh. "No idea," I reply, "but I know we'll never see it coming."

"A bit like her royal highness?" Bast wonders aloud. He turns halfway in his seat to face the entrance to the cafeteria.

I follow his gaze and swear under my breath. We haven't seen her at all since the Den incident. Ajax scared her good, but she must've heard he wasn't here today.

"If she comes over here..." I growl.

"As your friend, I will fight her off for you," Bast assures me.

I smile. "Thanks, but I think I can handle her. I'd just rather not have to knock some sense into her every time I see her. It's getting tiresome."

"She better sit somewhere far away," Blake mutters, putting her head on her arms on the table.

"Now, Blake," Bast chides her, "we have to be nice to the royalty."

She sends him a look that could melt steel and he shuts right up. I feel like I'm missing something.

Is Blake...shaking?

Before I can ask, Natalie walks up to our table. "Hello Bast, Blake darling, *Assassin*," she purrs.

I'm not crazy; Blake is definitely shaking.

What is wrong?

"Roseanne," I mutter. "To what do we owe the utter displeasure of your presence?"

"I just wanted to give you an update on my accomplishments."

I roll my eyes.

Why does she insist on pushing me?

She is gaining nothing that I can see. I can't wrap my head around it. Maybe she *is* stupid.

I start to tell her that I don't particularly care, when she starts talking.

"Me and my team," she says—*my team and I,* I correct her in my head, "went scouting in the farming district and caught a couple people stealing food from the stores. We suspect they are assassins so we brought them straight here. I disarmed them so fast. You should've seen me. I'm practically running this place." She beams, head held high.

I lean over towards Bast and whisper in his ear. "The only thing she's running is her big fat mouth."

He sniggers and Natalie stops her story. "What's so funny, Assassin?"

"The fact that you think I'm interested in your bedtime story. You couldn't catch one assassin, let alone two."

"What are you implying?"

"That you're lying to yourself and bragging about something you didn't even accomplish. Those two 'assassins' are probably farmers who you took to the barn cells. They'll stay there for a few days before they're let out again. That's it. It's not worth a pat on the back."

"How dare you...accuse me of..." she scoffs.

"Oh, shut up and listen for once, princess," I snap. "You are nothing special. You're actually terrible at being a Resistance member. Your daddy probably sends you on all the easy missions and assigned you to a team to get you out of his hair. I'm not impressed by you. I don't *like* you. No one at this *table* likes you, least of all Ajax Forrester."

She flinches at the mention of his name and stands frozen for a second before she replies with, "You aren't anything special either. You're not really a Resistance member. I bet Jenson's just keeping you alive long enough to see this plan through and then he'll have you executed. It's no less than you deserve, you despicable human being."

I smile, my wicked little 'I would like nothing more than to kill you' smile. "You think I haven't considered that possibility, Roseanne? Make no mistake, I'll be the one doing the killing if it comes down to it and you'll be on the top of my list."

She swallows hard and I know I have her.

Move in for the kill, Night.

I lean back in my seat. "I met your father last week, Nicholas Ross I believe his name is? He's quite the character. He tried to get rid of me again, but I put him in his place. Answer me this, princess, why do you have a different last name?"

She crosses her arms in an attempt at defiance. "I don't have to tell you that."

"Then, I would be right in assuming you're adopted?"

"I am *not*. My father gave me my mother's maiden name to remember her by, after she died in childbirth."

"How sweet," I drawl.

"At least I'm not an orphan," she retorts. "You probably did it to yourself; slit your parents' throats while they slept."

She says it so casually, as if she is talking about what colour to paint her room, but in that moment, all I can see is red.

I stand up, slamming my hand against the table. "Shut up!" I snap at her. "Just shut up!"

Bast puts a hand on my arm and I shake it off.

There is a wicked gleam in Natalie's eyes as she looks at me and says, "I don't think I will."

"Leave her alone," Blake says softly, speaking for the first time in the conversation.

"Or what?" Natalie demands. "What will *you* do?"

Blake looks properly chastised and Natalie turns back to me. I look at her darkly, daring her to dig her own grave.

"As I was saying... You murdered your family. You put them out of their misery though, because they never actually liked you. They hated you because your heart was and still is black as pitch." I don't disagree completely with the last sentence. "Yet, the apple didn't fall too far from the tree," she goes on. "Your father was a liar and a drunkard, and your mother, well..."

I start to tremble as I brace myself for what she will say next.

"Let's just say that she was often seen in the loving company of less than reputable men."

All the resolve I've been holding against her, the walls I've built to keep my killing desire inside all these days, shatters and scatters in the wind like shreds of paper. With a scream, I lunge across the table at her—

Or at least, that's what I mean to do, but as I start, I look over at Blake.

The look on her face is a familiar one, though not one I have seen in a long time. My mother was the last one to wear it, and now, as I look, I see her in Blake. The resemblance is uncanny, but there and gone in an instant. In its absence, I forget how to breathe. My walls snap back in place and the storm within me dies.

Mom.

Why must you haunt me?

A memory surfaces.

We're in the garden.

I'm chasing a butterfly.

It heads toward the fence.

It's getting away.

I jump and clap my hands up to catch it…

My mom yells at me, scaring it away and my fingers brush a wing before gravity pulls me back down.

"We don't kill the butterflies. It is not up to us to judge."

She gives me that look—that Guild-forsaken look….

I squeeze my eyes shut as I return to the present. Blake is just Blake now, but she is right. Natalie is far from a butterfly, but it's not up to me to judge. Now is not the time to let everything I've gained go to waste, not over her. Now is the time to hold my head high and use my words to wound instead of my fists.

I take a deep breath, pushing away the image of my mother. This is the second time I've seen her in two weeks; I hope it will be the last.

"Excuse me, Assassin, did you hear me or have I finally managed to shut you up?"

My eyes fly open in annoyance, but most of the wind has fled from my sails.

"Oh, I heard you, Natalie," I say, "and as far as I know, you might be right about my father, but it could be worse." I walk around the table to stand right in front of her as I say the rest so only she can hear. "At least *my* family didn't leave me to become assassins."

Her eyes go round like big white orbs and her mouth opens into an o of shock. "How did you…?"

I smile. "Oh, princess, it wasn't that hard to figure out, not once I got your daddy's last name; they look so much like him."

"You can't tell anyone," she breathes.

"How do you know I haven't already?"

She goes paler than a sheet of paper.

I laugh. "Scared you, didn't I? But no, I haven't said a word and I won't, as long as you stay away from me. You hear? Show up at this table again and all bets are off. Oh, and stay away from Ajax too. He has enough to worry about without your harassment."

She has nothing to say to that and let me just say, I've never seen a person walk away from me so fast without running in all of my life.

I shake off the nasty feeling that settled on me and return to my seat. "So," I ask Bast, "if Haven wasn't the way it is, who would Roseanne be?"

He laughs awkwardly for a moment, still shaken up by what I almost did and the final exchange he didn't hear. Then he replies, "Oh, she'd be Ms. Priss in her designer dresses, four-inch stilettos, and genuine diamond earrings her daddy gave her."

"Right," I agree, "and she would be the queen of her prestigious boarding school because her daddy can't stand to have her at home."

That sends Bast into a fit of laughter. "Oh man, that's good. And she would own a horse."

"A horse?" I repeat with a giggle.

"Yeah, you know, she'd parade around on it. It would be a pure white stallion, named Rufus."

I clamp a hand over my mouth in an attempt to contain myself, but to no avail. Bast and I get weird looks from everyone until we settle down and are able to breathe again.

I lean back in my seat, sighing. "I love this game."

"See? I keep telling you: it's great for the mood."

"I think it's stupid," Blake says, crossing her arms.

"That's because you have no vision," Bast replies.

"Whatever."

"What's up with you?" I ask her. "You always get super touchy after an encounter with her highness."

"It's nothing."

"No, it's not. I've seen your eyes when she's around: eyes of fear, like you're her prey, as if she's holding a knife over your head, daring you to say something."

Her eyes grow round at my words before they shut down in anger. "I *said* it's nothing," she snaps, standing up and stalking off.

I smile ruefully. For once, I hate being right, but I'm going to find out what Roseanne has on Blake and then I'm going to put a stop to it.

Bast and I are getting ready to leave the cafeteria when Ajax walks in. He looks a bit down, but his face brightens into a smile when he sees us.

"Afternoon," he says, sliding onto the bench beside me.

"Hey," I reply.

"What's going on?"

"We were about to leave actually," I say.

"So soon?" Ajax says. "You sure Sebastian's had enough to eat?"

Bast scowls. "Watch it, man," he says.

"Sorry," Ajax replies.

"How come you hate your full name so much?" I ask Bast.

"How come you won't tell us yours?" he counters.

"*Oh...*" Ajax says lowly with a smirk tugging at the edge of his lips.

I give Bast a look. "Well played, Bast," I say, "well played."

He smiles but it fades quickly. "I'm serious though, Night," he replies. "What are you afraid of?"

I don't say anything for a moment.

Nothing. Everything.

The fears are impossible to explain, but they're there, chaining me to the darkness.

"You wouldn't understand," I reply.

"That's because you won't give us the chance, Night."

"Look," I tell him, "I don't want to argue. Can we drop it?"

He sighs. "Fine." He looks at Ajax. "Any news then?"

Ajax nods. "Everything is finalized. All units are to be inside the base by midnight tonight and the bombs will be dropped promptly at eight tomorrow morning. Jenson wants our team with him in the control room at seven."

"Why do we need to be there?" I ask.

"Maybe because it was your plan?" Bast suggests.

"Yeah, but you and Blake don't need to be there. Not that I don't *want* you there, I'm just saying."

"I know what you mean," Bast replies, "but we're your team and we have your back for everything."

"Thanks."

"Where did Blake go?" Ajax asks, just now noticing her absence.

"She stormed off after I confronted her about her Natalie problem," I reply. "You know anything about that?"

"No, I don't. What happened?"

"Her highness paid another visit and Blake just wasn't... Well, I've noticed she's never herself when Natalie's around. I asked her about it and she got all angry. I have a feeling Blake did something she isn't proud of and Natalie knows about it."

"What makes you say that?"

"Just a girl instinct I guess. I also came *this* close to strangling her highness today." I hold my thumb and pointer finger a millimetre apart.

Ajax tenses. "What did she do this time?"

I take a deep breath. "She basically called my father a drunkard and my mother a whore."

"That little witch..." Ajax mutters, his fingers curling into fists. "If she wasn't a girl, I'd beat her up myself. What stopped you?"

I pause for a moment and in the silence, I see the butterfly. I blink and it fades from sight. I decide to give him half of the truth.

"The look on Blake's face," I tell him, "the look that said she wasn't worth it."

CHAPTER TWENTY-THREE

Later, Ajax bids me goodnight at my bedroom door.

"Are you sure you don't want to go do something?" I ask him. I don't want him to go; I don't want to be left alone with my thoughts.

He shakes his head. "It's late, Silent, we should both get some rest."

"I just... Guild, I'm scared, Ajax." There, I finally said it.

He raises an eyebrow. "I thought Silent Night was only afraid of feathers?"

"And pillows," I add, "but this too. I'm terrified something will go wrong and I'll lose everything I've gained here and grown to love or that I'll go back to the person I was. I don't want to go back. I want to stay the way I am."

"Don't be afraid," he replies, "we're all here for you and I'm not going to let you do a one-eighty. We've worked too hard for that."

I look up at him, crossing my arms. "That's not what I mean. I'm afraid I won't *let* you guys be here for me, that I'll push you away. I'm afraid of myself, Jax. How can you protect me from me? How can anyone?" I hold myself tighter and set my gaze on the floor.

"We just have to try." He sighs. "We'll work something out, Silent, don't worry."

I meet his eyes. "Will we?" I challenge.

"We will," he replies, determination in his gaze. "I can't promise you there won't be more bumps in the road, but I *can* promise you we'll all navigate them together, and I will not stand back and watch if you decide to reject us. You've come so far, Silent. You're stronger than anything holding you back. You're stronger than the voice in your head."

"You think so?"

He smiles. "I know so. I've seen it. Now get some sleep. We have a big day tomorrow."

"I'll try," I reply, placing my hand on the doorknob to my room.

"Night, Silent," he says.

I smile; it's so weird to hear him say that. "Night, Jax," I reply.

He heads down the hall and I disappear into my room, hoping sleep will come tonight.

I wake up tense and tired the next morning, sleep having evaded me for the most part. I'm groggy and sore as I peel myself out of bed and dress in the blackest clothes I can find. I feel dark this morning. I don't know if that should scare me.

The only weapons I grab are my guns as I leave my room.

I sweep into the control room at seven o'clock on the dot. Over three dozen people look up from what they are discussing to stare at me.

"Ah, Assassin," Jenson drawls, "nice of you to join us."

"I wouldn't miss it for the world."

"Have a seat."

I walk around the table and take the empty chair on Ajax's right. Bast sits on Ajax's left with Blake on his other side. I give the two of them a little wave. Bast waves back and Blake gives me a small smile. They join back into the conversation as I turn to Ajax.

"Hey," I say.

"Morning," he replies, "you were cutting it a bit close there, don't you think?"

"What are you, my mother?"

"No, I'm just trying to save you from Jenson's wrath."

"I can handle him."

"I know; I'm just saying."

"Assassin, Ajax, listen up," Jenson barks.

I jump.

Ajax shoots me a look, *I told you so* written across his face.

I roll my eyes.

"Yes, Jenson?" I ask with a yawn.

"I was just wondering, Assassin, what our next move is?"

"Maybe if you hadn't kicked me out of our last meeting, you would know," I reply.

"Enough with the games," he says, his bravado dying, if only for a second.

I sigh. "Fine. We see what they do and then, when appropriate, we attack."

"And when will that be?"

"When I see fit. Am I in charge of this assault or not?"

"As far as Avery is concerned, yes, but I don't agree with his choices and therefore I am inclined to bend the rules. I do not deal well with surprises. So I ask again, when do we attack?"

"I don't know," I retort, "and I *won't* know until well after that bomb is dropped, tomorrow at the earliest. You need to exercise patience I'm not sure you possess."

"You watch your tongue. I can easily throw your carcass out of this base."

"And I can easily walk away and never come back. Face it, Jenson, you need me."

I pause and it gives me enough time to notice the stares we're being given. There's more here than our usual crowd and the newcomers can't believe the way we're talking to each other. I suppose I could've toned it down for appearances sake, but I often forget we have an audience. Once we start our arguments, it's just me and him; nothing else matters but who is going to be the victor.

I turn my gaze back to Jenson and say, "Now, are we going to drop the bomb or what?"

"It's not yet eight o'clock," he replies. "We have many preparations to go through and last-minute checks to make. The four of you can sit there and be quiet. Think you can do that?"

"I suppose, but why were we called here if we're not going to do anything?"

"I wanted you in my sight and your teammates will keep you here. Sit tight, Assassin."

I shrug. I didn't plan on going anywhere.

We watch as the men bustle around the room, hooking up all the systems, including the viewing screen that will show us the bomb when it drops and the communications to the planes.

Finally, at five to eight, Jenson gives the order for the planes to take off.

The remaining minutes drag on. I resort to biting my nails to deal with the nerves.

Then, the planes appear on the screen, showing the food warehouse beneath them.

This is it. No turning back. Ever.

The number ten shows up on the screen in green digital letters. I hold my breath as the clock counts down to zero and the warehouse goes up in a column of black smoke and rings of bright red fire. A few moments later, a tremor shakes my seat and I shudder to think how far the energy went, how far the repercussions will spread.

The warehouse is nothing but a pile of debris and ashes ten minutes later. I regard it with a mixture of excitement, fear, and guilt. A part of me still feels like I've hurt my allies, but then I chide myself. They are nothing but the enemy now. I feel no sympathy for them. I mustn't feel sympathy for them. They lied to me and they deserve nothing less than a slow death by starvation, especially the man behind it all.

I am coming for you, Charger. Make no mistake.

"Well, that's that then," Jenson says. "I'll have our crew survey the damage and we'll get back to you. How soon before they make a counter strike do you think, Assassin?"

"As soon as they feel like it," I reply, "and there will be no way to prepare. We will not see it coming. I'd suggest no one leave the base, but I have a feeling you won't listen."

"I will not cower in my own base," Jenson replies. "We cannot afford to halt our other operations. Now, if the four of you would run along... We have work to do."

"Very well," I say, standing. "Don't come crying to me when countless Resistance agents lay dead at your feet."

He says nothing, just watches me go with an expression of complete contempt. The feeling is mutual.

The others join me in the hall a few moments later.

"You okay?" Ajax asks.

"Peachy," I mutter.

"You don't sound it."

I sigh. "It's just... Jenson is so... *Ugh*. I want to strangle him sometimes for his utter stupidity." I pause. "Don't tell him that."

Ajax laughs. "I won't."

SILENT NIGHT

Bast smiles. "Don't worry, Night, you're not the only one. He drives us all crazy, including the big man."

"Good to know I'm not alone."

"Nah, sometimes I want to put a crossbow bolt through his head just to put us all out of our misery."

I laugh and the others join me.

"*Bast*," Blake gasps after a second. "That's awful."

He shrugs. "I won't apologize for it."

I laugh again. "And that's why I like you people. Sometimes, I feel like I'm not the only soulless one."

Bast and Blake start down the hall, but Ajax and I linger behind. Guild, he's like a magnet that won't let me stray too far. I'm not sure how much longer I can ignore the pull.

"You're not soulless, Silent," he says after a moment.

I look away from Bast and Blake's retreating figures to him. "And how do you figure that?" I ask.

"I can see it. It's in your eyes, the spark in them when you smile or laugh. It radiates from your core, from your entire being. Make no mistake, Silent; you have a soul and it's breathtaking."

I wince. "Jax..."

"I know, I know. I'm not trying to— Bast or Blake would say the same. Well, not exactly the same but..." He looks at his feet.

I sigh. "It's okay. I know what you mean. I appreciate it."

And I do, truly. It can't be easy to find light and hope in a black heart like mine. It's not easy to let his light in either, which is why I've been holding back. I'm afraid my heart won't be able to take it.

"Hey!" Bast calls out. "Are you guys coming or not? I'm starving."

"You can't wait for more than two seconds?" I call back as Ajax and I start walking towards him and Blake.

"Not really," Bast replies. "Look at me. I'm wasting away."

We catch up to them and I nail Bast's shoulders with mine as I pass him. "More like wasting my time with your whining," I say.

"Ow!"

"Oh, go on, that didn't hurt."

"Yeah, but... It wasn't necessary," he points out.

I grin at him. "No, but it felt good.

He shakes his head. "You're crazy."

"I know. Isn't it wonderful?"

"Children, please," Blake says, "let's not argue."

Bast and I roll our eyes at her.

"Blake's right," Ajax says, "why don't you two drop it so we can all go get some food?"

"Sounds good to me," I say. "Shall we call it a draw?"

Bast grins. "For now."

"Great," Ajax says, "because, as Bast said, I'm starving. Let's go."

"Right behind you," Bast says.

• • •

After breakfast, Bast and Ajax tag along for my latest axe training session. I beg them to go do something else, but they won't hear of it. In the words of Bast, they want to see how much I suck.

I stop by my room first to drop off my guns and grab my axe.

Bast studies me for a second and says, "I don't think an axe becomes you."

"Thank you for your wise words, Sebastian," I reply, "but I don't give a damn."

He holds his hands up in surrender. "I was just saying."

"Well, maybe you should keep your mouth shut then."

Bast gives me an indignant look, but says nothing more.

Point: Silent Night.

The four of us head to the training room and Blake and I take our places in the centre of the mat. We crouch down and circle each other slowly.

"Beat her, Silent," Jax calls from the sidelines.

"Carve her into minuscule pieces, Night," Bast adds.

Blake whirls to look at him and slices him with a death glare.

Bast swallows and says, "I mean, *go Blake go.*"

I laugh. "All right, Blake, let's give them a good show."

"Agreed," she says and we lunge for each other, axe blades flashing.

We move almost too quickly to see as we strike and counter strike, dodge and duck. I work with the weight of the weapon, instead of letting it work against me. I swing it around me, deflecting her blows as if I've been doing it all my life.

Yet, she does the same.

Our feet are like lightning, our weapons like thunder when they clash against each other. Our battle storm echoes in the open space of the training room.

I've definitely improved. Never have I lasted so long. I smile and push harder. Blake matches me and we go on like that for another few minutes before I make a mistake.

She lunges at me, axe swinging for my head and I duck, but it was only a feint. Her axe comes at my legs and it's too late to jump.

The weapon hits me square in the thighs, denting my armour, and I collapse onto the floor, head banging against the cement. For a moment, I see stars.

I hear Jax's voice. "Silent, are you okay?" This is the second time I've been in this situation in front of him and Bast. "Talk to me, Silent." His voice is close and worried; he must be kneeling beside me.

I lift my head up and moan at the wave of nausea that crashes into me.

"Thank God," I hear him breathe.

I try to get into a sitting position at least, but I am much too dizzy. "Assassins below," I mutter.

"Take it easy, Night," Bast says.

"I am so sorry," Blake gasps.

"It's okay," I tell her, squeezing my eyes shut against the pain, praying the room will stop spinning. "I'm just a little disoriented from slamming my head against the floor. It's not your fault."

I give sitting another attempt and this time I manage it, but I bring my knees to my chest and put my head down. I open my eyes again to see Jax kneeling in front of me, spinning slowly.

A few moments later, he comes into focus and I know the worst of it has passed.

"Well, that was fun," I say, looking up at Blake. "Let's do it again."

Blake shakes her head. "I think that's enough for today."

"If you insist," I sigh, "but I'm fine now. I can handle it."

"I know you can," she replies, "but Jax looks like he'll take my head off with my own axe if I let you continue."

I turn and glare at him.

He scratches the back of his head. "I just thought... You did well. Maybe that's enough for one day."

"Ajax, I suck at this, still. She disarms me in five minutes flat. I've improved, sure, but not enough. I need more practice."

"You need to rest after what just happened."

"You need to back off," I snap.

"What?"

"You don't get to tell me what to do."

"I wasn't..." he tries. "Look, I'm trying to help."

"Well, you're not. If you really knew me, if you really loved me like you claim you do, you'd know that. You wouldn't have said that."

His eyes darken. "Would you just listen for a second?"

"No," I retort. "I'm busy. I decide my fate. You don't own me."

I grab my axe and stand up, turning my back on him to face Blake. "Again," I tell her.

She hesitates.

"Blake, he doesn't own you either. Come at me."

She sighs, but lowers into a crouch and begins circling.

"Silent..." I hear Ajax say.

"Not listening," I mutter.

He sighs as Blake and I lunge at each other.

We fight for another seven minutes before she sends me crashing to the ground again. This time it's only her and Bast's voices that I hear. Ajax is nowhere to be seen.

Immediately, I regret my words and the abruptness with which I said them. I know I need to fix the seam I tore; I just hope it didn't fray.

• • •

The problem with Ajax is that I don't know where to find him. Yet, it doesn't matter because in the end, he finds me. I'm just coming back from checking the cafeteria when I see him leaning against my door.

I guess it says something in that he always comes back. I haven't screwed up too badly. Yet.

"Hey," I say as I walk up to him. "I've been looking for you."

"Have you now," he says, not as lighthearted as usual.

I grimace. "Jax," I start, "I'm sorry for what I said earlier. I didn't mean to sound so..."

"Cold?" he offers. "Aggressive? Mean? Bratty? Like Natalie?"

I flinch at each one.

I want to lash back, but I am tired of ignoring the truth.

"Right," I say. "Look, I didn't mean..."

Ugh. Why is this so hard?

I can't meet his gaze as I blunder on, can't bear to see his disappointment.

"Mentioning how you feel...that was a low blow, even for me. I shouldn't have brought that up, especially after I made my opinion in the matter so perfectly clear. I've done nothing but ignore this...thing between us."

Assassin's below. It sounds like a sad excuse even to my ears. I'd rather pull out my own eyes than continue to have this conversation, but I've learned all too well that your mistakes will haunt you if you don't set the record straight, if you don't make things right. I have enough ghosts, too many mistakes I didn't give a damn about.

Not this time.

I look up at him, taking control.

"I'm sorry I snapped at you," I tell him. "I know you meant well, but I don't appreciate taking orders, especially after having escaped the Master Assassin. I don't take too well to people thinking they know what's best for me better than I do."

"Maybe I was trying to save you from yourself, like you asked me to."

I scowl. "That's not what I meant."

294

He throws up his hands. "So what, I'm supposed to be able to tell the difference?" His eyes are fiery. "I'm sorry if I was trying to stop you from getting a concussion."

I cross my arms. "If I got a concussion, I would've learned my lesson."

"Oh, yeah, and you'd be in a great frame of mind to help us when the assassins attack then, wouldn't you?"

"I..."

Guild, he's got me there.

He runs a hand through his hair. "Silent, being a part of a team means thinking about more than just yourself. I was trying to stop you from getting hurt because I know we need you."

I narrow my eyes. "You're sure it's not just because of your feelings?"

"Yes," he replies. "Of course I don't want to see you hurt, but it's not just about us."

"So what exactly are you saying?"

"I'm saying that I know you are a strong, independent person. I realize I don't have a say in what you do, that no one does, but I'm just asking you to try to see the whole picture. I bet you never thought I'd say this, but the Resistance needs you. I'm not trying to stop you from learning, Silent; I'm trying to teach you. There will be more moments to train, but not if you're in too rough a shape to survive the next battle."

I hate his words, but only because I know he's right. I'm too brazen for my own good and Jax is too kind for his. He keeps giving me chances; I wonder how many I have left before his rope grows too thin to hold our fragile bond.

"I'm sorry for how I reacted," I tell him. "I will try to be more...open-minded."

"I forgive you," he replies, "and that's all I'm asking."

In the silence that follows, the magnetic pull is stronger than ever. Again, there is that small gap between us, a gap that would be so easy to close. A part of me wants to close it, wants to explore this avenue and see where it leads. I want to let myself be vulnerable.

Remember who you are, what you've done.

Don't give in to temptation.

He's lying.

I clench my fists and pull away before he can notice the short distance I leaned in.

The pull remains, but I resist.

He's lying.

As he faces me with a smile and I look into those blue eyes of his, I can't help but wonder if I'm lying to myself.

CHAPTER TWENTY-FOUR

It's three o'clock in the afternoon when we get the call from Jenson. The four of us are hanging out in the cafeteria, waiting for news, when his voice comes over the P.A. System.

"Would Ajax Forrester, Blake Solarin, Sebastian Foster, and Silent Night please come to the council room immediately. I repeat: Ajax Forrester, Blake Solarin, Sebastian Foster, and Silent Night, report to the council room at once. Thank you." The P.A. System clicks off.

I give Bast a quizzical look. "Foster?"

"What?" he says.

"It doesn't seem to go with Sebastian. I would've thought you'd be more of a Luciano or something."

He laughs. "Probably; it's not my real last name. All the orphans of the Resistance are given the last name Foster unless they happen to know their own. I wasn't so lucky."

"Hey, could the two of you stay on topic?" Ajax asks.

"Hmmm?" I ask, looking over at him.

He sighs. "Jenson's summons."

Oh, right.

"What do you suppose that's about?" Bast asks.

"What do you think?" I reply. "The repercussions have started and Jenson has forgotten that I told him not to come crying to me."

Fear flashes in Blake's brown eyes. "What do you think happened?"

I shrug. "How should I know?"

Ajax stands up. "We better go find out," he says, and the rest of us follow him out of the cafeteria.

• • •

Jenson is pacing the length of the room when we enter, hands clasped behind his back, an anxious expression plastered on his face. He is alone. Something drastic has definitely occurred. I resist the urge to start our conversation with a smug *I told you so*. Barely.

"You called us, Jenson?" I ask. "What's the problem now?"

He stops pacing and turns to face us. "Assassin," he sneers. "So good to see you haven't fallen down a well."

"Likewise," I growl. "Now cut to the chase. We don't have all day."

"Our problem is this: Haven's main supply train has stalled halfway down the track with this month's complete food shipment from the farms. We have no way of knowing if it is in any way related to the assassins, but it cannot be allowed to sit there unprotected until the problem can be fixed. Otherwise, the assassins will find an opportunity to use this to their advantage."

"I see, so it looks like you do need me after all. Imagine that."

He scowls at me. "I'm not going to beg, Assassin. Either you help us or you don't. It's your choice."

"Nice to see I have options," I mutter, tracing a pattern on the table with my finger, "but your tone of voice seems to suggest I should agree to help or be shunned for all eternity." I look up at him. "So where is this train and what would you have me do?"

"I have already sent my best troops to the location; you are to join them in protecting the train and its cargo from all threats. I expect you to follow through with these orders, even if you come up against your former assassin allies."

"With all due respect, Jenson, they were never allies. I have the Resistance's back and I will be using *my* knife to slit the *assassins'* throats. Clear?"

"As crystal. Now move out. The coordinates should already have loaded to Ajax's GPS."

"We'll see you around then and just know I am going to do everything in my power to survive, if only to spite you."

"I look forward to it," he replies. "Good day."

We leave the room and Ajax turns to us. "Okay, team. You know what to do. Suit up and we'll meet by the exit in," he checks his watch, "ten minutes."

We all nod.

"All right, move out."

We head to our rooms. I change into a simple grey Resistance uniform and go about arming myself. Five minutes later, I'm laden with two swords, a dozen throwing knives, four daggers, my two guns, and my new axe just in case.

Five minutes after that, I join the other three at the entrance.

Bast has a crossbow, two quivers, and a sword at each hip. Blake has an axe in her right hand, a long sword across her back, and a second axe on her left hip. Ajax has a sword at one hip, a glock at the other, dagger hilts sticking out of his boots, and a string of spare bullets adorning his shoulder. He cradles a heavy-duty rifle in his hands.

Ajax sees me and says, "Everyone's here, let's go."

The guards wave us through the doors and we enter the streets. We walk through Resistance territory only, to keep from attracting unwanted attention.

• • •

It takes us forty minutes to reach the train. It's four o'clock now and the sun is beginning its slow descent. The world is eerie; the sky heavy and laden with moisture. Either it's going to rain soon or we're going to be invaded by fields of fog.

"We're here," I say to Ajax. "What do we do now?"

"We check in with the agent in charge, get our assignment, and wait."

"Sounds like fun."

He smiles ruefully. "You have no idea."

Blake, Bast, and I follow him to the engine car where he says our superior should be.

We're greeted by a tall, middle-aged man with black hair and suspicious brown eyes. He regards me with disgust and speaks to Ajax alone, as if the rest of us are invisible. This does nothing for my patience and I cross my arms as I tap my foot. I despise men like him.

When the encounter is over, Ajax leads us back outside to give us our instructions.

"Garrett says we are to guard the last car; everything else has been taken care of."

"Great," I say, "of course we get the hardest job. Guarding the rear is hell. We'll have to do the brunt of the fighting."

"If it comes to that," he replies.

"Oh, trust me, it will. I feel it in my bones."

I can see the others trying to shake off their unease as we make our way to the last car in the line. We arrive to find that Garrett was pulling our legs. The train car we've been assigned to protect is empty.

Finally losing my patience, I pull out a knife and fling it at the side of the car. It penetrates the steel, going in a good inch.

The others stare at me.

"What?" I ask them. "I am so sick of being treated like I'm worthless because of where I came from. At least I'm honest; I know plenty of people that play at being good."

Thunk goes the second knife. An inch and a half this time.

Nice.

"We feel you, Night," Bast says, "but there's nothing we can do about it at the moment."

I sigh and walk over to pry my knives out of the side of the train car. "I guess we can still do our part in guarding the train, even if it's just a metal shell." I look over at Ajax. "Where do you want us?"

"You tell me," he says. "Where do you think they'll attack from?"

I'm surprised he asked for my input, but then I switch to defence mode.

"They'll come at us from all sides. We should open the doors and have one person at each. Bast, you can go up to the roof so you can pick them off with your bow."

He nods.

"Blake, you can guard the north side. Ajax and I will both take the south because they'll be more likely to send more of their troops there."

"Got it," she replies.

I look at Ajax. "Thoughts?"

"I like it," he says. "Everyone take your places and get comfortable. We could be a while."

Blake opens the car doors and heads to the other side, sitting down and hanging her feet over the edge. Bast climbs onto the roof and settles in for the long wait ahead. Ajax clambers inside and sits down, leaning against an empty crate. I stand against the wall.

"Why don't you have a seat?" he asks after a moment. He pats the spot beside him.

I sigh and walk over, lowering myself to the floor. I sit with my knees up, arms wrapped around them.

"Care to tell me what's wrong?" he says.

In a moment of weakness, I let the pull take me enough for me to lean slightly against him before I answer.

"It's just all these people," I sigh. "Garret, Jenson, Ross, Natalie... They treat me like I'm dirt and I'm tired of it. Can't they see I'm trying to help them? Can't they see I've changed?"

"Some people see what they want to see. They knew you as a ruthless assassin and they refuse to imagine you as anything else, anything more, but you don't have to worry about them. The rest of us believe in you. You have me, Bast, Blake, and even Trey. You're not alone."

"I know. I just feel outnumbered. It's stupid."

He looks over at me. "It's not stupid, Silent. Lighten up a bit. You're difficult to talk to sometimes, you know that, right?"

I hang my head. "Sorry."

"No, see that's the problem. You don't have to apologize for it. You're stubborn, but I admire that. You're determined. It's what makes you... you."

I smile, leaning closer. "Thanks, I guess."

"Forget about all the people who don't care about you and keep doing what you do best because people who are bothered by it aren't important and people who are important aren't bothered, or something like that. I can never remember it correctly."

My heart skips a beat and I sit up straighter so I can turn and look at him properly. "Where did you hear that?"

"My mom used to say it. Why?"

"*My* mom used to say it too. Did she read you those books...?"

"'The Cat in the Hat' and 'The Lorax'?"

"Yes, that's it! I used to love those. My mom would do voices sometimes or read the rhymes really fast until I was a mess of giggles." I look at the floor. "Guild, I miss her. It's hard when you lose all those who matter and are left with all those who mind."

"Yeah," he agrees, "but that's why you have to regain the people who matter, to find those with whom you can let yourself run free."

We sit quietly for a minute after and I lean my head against his shoulder. He doesn't react, but his senses must be on fire. Mine are.

This isn't so bad, I tell myself.

Is there any harm in needing comfort from a friend?

Friend. As if that's all this is, as if I can keep ignoring the truth, delaying the inevitable. The magnet keeps getting stronger and my resolve is weakening.

I sit there and listen to the steady rhythm of his breath.

He's so warm.

"So," he says suddenly, nearly making me jump, "which one was your favourite?"

"What?" I ask, pulling my head away with an inward sigh.

"Which of those books was your favourite?"

"Oh, um... Probably 'Green Eggs and Ham'."

"Yeah, that was a good one. I liked 'Horton Hears a Who'."

So we talk about Dr. Seuss and the blissful innocence of childhood until the sun starts to sink below the horizon and the fog rolls in.

CHAPTER TWENTY-FIVE

It's twilight, the time of day where it's difficult to see, where you're not sure if something is a shadow or a figment of your imagination. The wall of fog certainly does nothing to aid the situation. We can't see the enemy, but I know they are coming.

As soon as the fog falls and the eeriness strikes, I feel it in the pit of my stomach, the undeniable truth that we are about to be ambushed.

I jump to my feet and unsheathe my swords. "They're coming," I tell Ajax. I yell the message to the other two as well.

Ajax stands up and loads his rifle. "Are you sure? How can you tell?"

"I feel it in my gut and trust me; I know what it feels like to have an assassin stalking you."

"I trust you," he says and then louder, "Bast, Blake. Hold your positions. Weapons ready."

They don't answer, not wanting to give away their whereabouts. We need to have some kind of advantage. I suspect the assassins aren't expecting someone to be on the roof, so they won't guard their heads. I tell Jax as much and we stand side by side as we wait for the assassins to emerge from the mist.

It doesn't take long before I see shadows moving in the murk.

"Show yourselves," I call out. "Let us know if you're friend or foe, or we *will* attack."

No reply comes, which is answer enough.

"It's them," I whisper.

Jax nods.

I sheath my swords in favour of my guns and sink into a crouch.

"Now!" Ajax yells.

I take a step forward and start shooting, collapsing several shadows. I hear the sound of gunfire echoing down the length of the train.

Good, the others have seen the threat.

The assassins continue to advance as Jax joins me in using them as target practice. There are no screams, only gunshots and dull thuds as bodies hit the ground.

I don't understand why they're not returning fire.

Then the shadows start running.

"They're coming in fast!" I yell. I return my guns to my belt and pull out my swords again. This is going to get messy. I don't mind messy. It's more fun than clean, but don't get me wrong; I'm not a violent person.

In moments, they are upon us and there's no time for regular thought; all instincts change to kill or be killed. Survive. I slip into attack mode and nothing can touch me.

Ajax shoots at our assailants with his rifle and whoever gets past him gets to meet my blades. They cut through the fog like knives through warm butter, and their results on flesh are even better. Hardly any of the assassins last longer than thirty seconds as I come at them, blades singing.

Lunge, parry, dodge, and thrust. One down.

Slash, block, duck, and lunge. Two down.

Jab, dodge, parry, backslash, and stab. Three.

A pile of bodies lay at my feet and Jax's bullets have created a line of shadows further out, but they keep coming.

Then I hear a click when Jax goes to fire.

"Empty," he says.

"You don't have any extra?" I ask without taking my eyes off of the enemy.

"Used them all. I'll have to rely on the sword now."

"What about your glock?"

"Not enough range."

"Great. I'll watch your back."

"Same here."

The next wave rolls in and we jump back into the fray.

The second wave of assassins are more skilled and I have to duel with them for several minutes before my blades find a way into a vital organ or main artery. I'm breathing heavy and starting to tire, but I don't let it get to me.

Other than that, I feel great. I'm in my element, doing what I've been trained to do since childhood, but this time, I'm doing it for the greater good. I smile as I plunge my sword through my next victim's chest.

Ajax is a whirl of motion beside me, never slowing, never stopping. He's pretty good, but I'm still better. I can't see Blake or Bast, and I don't have time to look. I can only pray they're holding the line. I hear the occasional battle cry from Blake that tells me she's still alive.

Ten minutes into the second wave, a skilled assassin manages to knock away one of my swords and I face them with a single blade. I step away from the body moments later, covered in their blood.

Five minutes after, I hear Ajax scream beside me.

For a second, I freeze, but then I whirl to face the direction the scream came from and my heart drops to my toes.

Ajax is lying on the ground, his sword gone and an assassin looming over him. His glock lies just out of reach and the assassin has a sword of his own, ready to plunge it into Ajax's chest.

I can't breathe, but I have to call out to him.

Wait...

Now!

"Jax!" I scream. "Catch!" I throw the sword before I say the words.

He catches the hilt in his left hand and rears up, blocking the blow that was seconds away from piercing his heart.

I breathe again.

Something stings my arm and I turn to face it. A woman in her late twenties faces me. She's grinning, holding a knife. My arm is wet.

She cut me.

I pull my gun and shoot her.

Then I jump into the battle once more.

My guns drop assassins like stalks of wheat, until I too run out of bullets and I throw the weapons to the ground in frustration. I pull out my daggers and barely manage to block the blow an elder assassin aims at me with his mace.

The battle is total chaos and I can't tell who has the advantage, if anyone does. The only thing I *do* know is that I can't keep this up much longer.

I wonder how Blake and Bast are faring. If I'm tired, they must be exhausted. I think back to our little competitions. Blake was able to best me and that girl is like a rock. She will be fine, though I imagine her arms will be burning from swinging that hefty axe around. I worry about Bast. Sure, he's a sharp shooter, but what happens if someone gets in close? I didn't get to see his sword skills.

Relax, he's on the roof. He'll be fine.

I hope so.

I sustain several more injuries: cuts to my leg, cheek, and shoulder. None of them are lethal, but they hurt like hell. I have to restrain myself to keep from using my daggers to carve up whoever inflicted the wounds.

That is, until I lose the daggers too.

310

I fall back to the train, using my throwing knives to lower their numbers a bit more as Ajax follows me. Surprisingly, he still has my sword.

"There's so many of them," he pants as he comes up beside me.

"I know. I don't see a way out of this."

"Don't say that."

"Why? It's the truth."

"Doesn't make it any better."

"Neither does denying it."

He looks over at me, glaring. "Do we have to argue about it now?"

"I guess not."

His answer is interrupted by the crackle of a radio: "All units, this is Jenson in the control room. Hold your ground. Backup is coming. I repeat: hold your ground for five minutes longer. We are coming."

"All right," I say, releasing my last knife. It buries itself to the hilt in an assailant's throat. "If he's lying and I survive this somehow, I will skin him alive."

"I'll let you," Ajax replies.

I pull out my axe, my last resort. "Let's do this," I say and we advance forward, back to back.

In the next few minutes, I'm so grateful for my training with Blake; without it, I don't know how I would've survived.

The assassins keep coming and it feels like forever, and I'm sure Jenson and his reinforcements aren't coming, but it's barely been a minute and I'm tired of holding on.

Losing my will is my fatal mistake.

The next man who comes to challenge me is wielding a double-bladed battle axe and that's when I know I'm screwed. The first blow he deals me reverberates up the length of my arm when I block it. Barely. The strength of the blow makes me dizzy.

As if the man sees my weakness, he smiles wickedly and whirls his blade at me.

I duck and watch as chunks of hair flutter to the ground.

The monster.

I have to move faster in order to avoid his blows, but I am exhausted and he is a fresh soldier.

Thirty seconds into the fight, I begin to panic. It's something I have been trained to avoid at all costs because nine times out of ten, it will cost you the fight, but it's the one rule I'm not focused on remembering.

He swings his axe at me and I jump back.

He slashes at my head again and I duck but...

It was only a feint.

His axe rushes toward me.

Time slows.

The man grins and my heart skips a beat.

No. I'm not ready.

The blade slams into my shin, slicing through my Resistance uniform and into my leg with ease. My skin severs and the cold shock of the metal zaps through my exposed nerves as if I was doused with ice water.

I collapse to the ground with a shriek unlike anything I have ever heard.

The pain hits me a second later. It's blinding, debilitating, earth-shattering agony, which increases tenfold when the man rips the blade out of my flesh with a sickening squelch.

I scream again and try to focus on breathing in and out as blood runs down my leg, little rivulets of life leaking out.

I can smell the iron.

Oh Guild. Oh Guild, I'm going to die.

I don't want to die.

I look up at the man looming above me, raising his axe, but I have no strength left to stop him.

I close my eyes.

At least make it quick.

Then a familiar voice fills my ears. "Silent!" It's a piercing plea and it's followed by the unmistakable sound of a gun being fired.

I hear a thud beside me and open my eyes to see Ajax standing over me instead, glock in hand. I let out a breath but the relief is short-lived. My body tenses in pain, every muscle clenched as if that will distract me. My leg is on fire, every inch itching and burning. A constant stabbing pain beats out a rhythm in the wound.

Breathe.

In and out. In and out.

"Jax," I gasp.

"Shhh," he says, kneeling down beside me, "don't talk. The reinforcements will only be a few minutes longer. You can hold on. You have to hold on."

"I can try."

A fresh wave of pain hits me and I hiss.

"Assassins below."

My shin is damp and I can't feel my toes. He dabs at the deluge with his shirt sleeve, but it won't be enough.

"Jax, I'm losing too much blood."

He turns to shoot a few assassins who are getting too close. "Bast! Blake!" he calls out. "Silent's hurt; watch my back!"

Their replies sound muffled.

Ajax rips a huge strip off of his shirt, exposing his skin. I feel the urge to blush, but it fades quickly, overshadowed by the pain and the beat of my heart, pumping my blood out, more and more by the second as it races, faster and faster...

I close my eyes and shudder.

"Steady, Silent," he says. "I'm going to tie this around your leg, okay?"

I nod.

He lifts my leg up gently to get the strip of cloth under it, but I can't choke back my scream. My eyes fly open, teeth clenching as he knots the fabric and pulls it tight. A gasp escapes me. I look over Jax's shoulder...and see the enemy coming close.

"Be-behind you."

He turns and shoots, and then he grabs me by the arm.

"We have to get to the train. It's a few yards away. Can you make it?"

"I think so."

"Good. Let's go."

He pulls me to my feet and we turn and run. He covers our retreat with gunfire. Each step for me is like shoving a molten piece of iron through my leg. There is fire in my veins.

I reach the train and can't find the strength to clamber in. My limbs are so heavy.

Jax grabs me by the waist and hauls me up before turning and sending more bullets into the mist.

I collapse against the floor of the car, shaking. I can't breathe.

I can't breathe.

"I'm going to die," I gasp. "I don't want to die." Tears stream down my blood spattered cheeks. I close my eyes and suddenly, all I want to do is sleep. I can barely feel the cold sting of the metal cradling my face.

I hear footsteps approach, followed by Bast's voice. "She doesn't look too good, man."

"Damn," Ajax snaps, "the tourniquet came off. You got something I can use?"

The sound of ripping fabric.

Then cool hands against my leg.

Searing pain.

I scream and my eyes fly open. Ajax kneels over me.

"Sorry," he gasps. "I'm so sorry." He's crying and I can see the terror written in his eyes. I'm going to die and he can see it too.

"No," I whisper, "*I'm* sorry. Sorry I...couldn't stay."

"No. Don't say that. Don't you dare—" He stops. Then he takes my hand in his. I never noticed how well they fit together. "Silent, you're not allowed to give up. You

315

haven't done what you set out to do. The Charger is still out there."

I barely register his words, but I try to hold onto his voice.

"I can't. It hurts. Sleep."

My vision is blurry and I can't feel my legs. Sounds are muted. Gunfire rings against my eardrums as if miles away.

"You *can*."

A moment of silence and then, "Bast, I need you to go help Blake guard our backs."

"What are you going to do?"

"What does it look like?"

Jax's hand slips out of mine and I can feel myself fading out of focus, until his hand moves to my leg and presses....

Fire rages and I scream and I scream...

"I'm sorry, I'm sorry..."

There is nothing but the pain. Nothing but the fire. Nothing but the edge of a cliff, beckoning me to fall...

I feel myself slipping.

"Stay with me...Bast...watch the...Silent..."

For a second, I'm falling...but no!

My eyes flutter open and I see Jax bent over me, covered in blood, sobbing.

"Please," he whispers. "Oh God, please don't take her from me."

I'm too far gone to recognize his pleas as a prayer.

"I'm sorry," I breathe. "I wish...we had a chance."

I close my eyes again and drop into the sleep that beckons. It promises freedom from the pain and the things that haunt me. I go willingly.

A weight settles on my chest and the voice ceases.

My last memory is a flash of light beyond my lids and the whispered words of, "Come back to me. I'll wait for you."

CHAPTER TWENTY-SIX

The first thing I notice is that I can feel my toes. I take a breath, and then another. A slow methodical rhythm starts again. Silence echoes in my ears instead of the ringing from before.

"Quiet now. She's stirring."

"Oh my God." The second voice is a familiar one.

"Maybe it's not a good idea to have the boy in here."

"No. I have to be here when she wakes up. She'll want to see me. Besides, she'll be reluctant to trust you. She might cooperate if I stay. Please. Don't make me wait outside."

"Okay, I'll allow it for now, but we'll need space to do our job. You can sit in the chair next to the bed while we check her over. Clear?"

"Perfectly."

"Good."

I hear footsteps coming toward me and feel a presence settle down in a chair I assume is beside me.

Something touches my hand.

I flinch.

"What did I do?" the familiar voice asks of the other.

"It's okay. She's responding to your touch. Talk to her; she can probably hear you."

"Okay. Um..." The voice pauses before going on. "Silent, it's me. It's Ajax. I... You gave us quite a scare there. We thought we were going to lose you...but you survived. The Resistance nurses fixed you up right good. You might have a limp in your right leg for a bit, but they say you should be good as new within the month. I... I feel kind of stupid talking to you like this. I'm still waiting."

Those three words send electricity jolting through me.

It's time to wake up.

It's time to tell him the truth.

I reach deep within myself and open my eyes to reveal Jax's deep blue ones staring back at me.

"Oh my God," he breathes. "She's awake. She's awake!"

People bustle all over the room at the news and I just stare at him, unable to peel my eyes away, lest I fade once more. Jax is my anchor, tethering me to this world.

"Hey," he says, "did you hear everything I said?"

I nod, not trusting myself to speak.

"Good." He pauses. "You think you could do me a favour and never scare me like that again?"

I smile. I'm so happy to be alive. I'm so happy I get a second chance, that *we* get a second chance. Almost dying taught me that he was right. I don't want to die without at

319

least exploring the bond we have. I can't die happy without ever experiencing love at all.

"I'm sorry," I say softly in answer to his question.

A single tear escapes his eye. "You don't have to apologize just... God, try to be more careful."

"I wasn't finished," I chide him. "I'm sorry I tried to leave without telling you."

He frowns. "Telling me what?"

"Jax, I've been lying to you about how I feel, lying to myself. I said before that you're the only thing that makes sense and instead, I gave you excuses because I was afraid. Guild, I was so stupid..."

"Hey," he interrupts me, "we don't have to talk about it right now. I said I will wait for you, and I will. You should save your energy. There will be lots of time to..."

I reach a hand up and cover his mouth. "I'm tired of waiting, Jax," I tell him.

His eyes go wide the moment he finally wraps his head around what I'm saying. "You mean...? You want to...? Are you sure?"

"Yes, now shut up and kiss me," I snap.

He does what he's told.

Our lips meet and an electric current zaps through my body, setting me on fire. I kiss him back, urgent, breathless, like I can't get enough.

Now *this* is something worth dying for.

His hands tangle in my short hair and I reach up to wrap mine around his back.

More. More. More. My mind repeats the words over and over, in tune to my beating heart. And then...

My heart monitor screeches.

We jolt away from each other as if shocked, remembering our surroundings, remembering we have an audience.

"All right, that's enough of that," the one nurse says. She's wearing a baggy blue outfit with owls printed on it, her dark brown hair pulled up in a tight bun. The laugh lines on her face suggest she's older than Jenson. "As you said yourself Mr. Forrester, there will be lots of time later. Right now, I need to check your girl over to make sure she's going to stay alive."

I blush and she shoos Ajax back to his seat beside the bed.

The nurse checks my vitals and, judging from her facial expression, everything seems to be in order. She continues her work in silence.

"How long have I been out?" I ask Ajax after a minute, turning my head to face him. I fight to keep a goofy smile from creeping onto my face.

I just kissed him. We did that. It was real.

"A couple of days; they've kept you sedated," he replies. "Don't worry though, you haven't missed much. The city's been rather quiet actually."

"Strange," I remark. "The assassins are definitely up to something."

"Probably," the nurse says, "but it's not your job to worry about it. You need to rest. I'm not going to let all my hard work go to waste. Close your eyes. You need to sleep this off. Trust me."

I roll my eyes. What does she know? Injury or no, I can't just relax. The Charger is still out there, planning, killing... The train battle was the first of many. This war is far from over. Yet, I do as she says, sinking back into the pillows...

Pillows.
There are pillows on my bed.
Oh Guild. I am lying on a pillow.
I'm going to die.
They're coming.
They're going to shoot me.
Oh Guild...

A beeping sound goes off in the room as I sit bolt upright in bed, eyes flying open. "Jax! Get them away! They're coming for my mother! Help me!"

I'm not seeing the hospital room anymore with its faded pink wallpaper. I'm seeing the blue painted bedroom from my nightmares, blood everywhere and my mother lying lifeless, me unable to do anything but scream...

I rip the pillows from the bed, throwing them like they are hand grenades that will blow off my fingers at any second.

I hear Jax's voice. "Oh God," he whispers, "the pillows."

Then the nurse, "Somebody sedate her!"

I'm seeing two places at once. My mom's dead face stares up at me as the nurse comes forward and plunges a needle into my neck.

The world fades again and this time, I wonder if I'll wake up. I wonder if I care.

CHAPTER TWENTY-SEVEN

The room is dark this time and I'm lying on my side. Either there are no voices or I've lost my hearing. I crack open my eyes and look to my left. Jax is in the chair again, slouched over as if sleeping.

I let out a sigh of relief. "Jax?"

He jumps in his seat and then scoots it closer, taking his hand in mine. "How much do you remember?" he asks me.

"You were there. The nurses were there. We...we kissed and then... Then there were pillows..." I shut my eyes tight. "How bad was it?"

"Not too bad," he replies, squeezing my hand. "I'm so sorry. I never even thought..."

"It's okay. It's hard to remember a fear that's so stupid."

"No," he argues, "it's not stupid."

"You know," I sigh, "I should tell you why it scares me. Maybe talking about it will help."

"If that's what you want to do, then I'm all ears."

I take a deep breath.

This isn't going to be easy.

Are you sure you want to tell him?

Do you really think this is a good idea?

I do, I tell myself.

I have to tell somebody and he's the only one I trust enough to be vulnerable, if only for a little while. I need to get this off my chest before it crushes me.

You need to let her go.

I wince.

"Silent?"

"Yes," I reply, "I'm getting to it. This isn't...easy."

He squeezes my hand. "It's okay. Take your time. You can do this."

He's right. You can do this.

I can do this.

I take another deep breath before I plunge in. "One morning when I was young and still lived with my mother, I woke up to a silent house. Sunlight was streaming through my bedroom window and I wondered why my mother hadn't woken me yet. It had to be nine o'clock in the morning, if not later. I thought it was strange, but I was five years old. I didn't consider the gory possibilities; I just hopped out of bed and walked the short distance down the hall to my mother's bedroom."

I take a shaky breath. I can see myself walking down that wallpapered hall. I can hear my feet making the hardwood floors creak...

"My heart was full of light and laughter as I padded down the hall," I go on, "the floorboards squeaking under my weight in the old house."

Mommy slept in, I thought. *She'll feel awfully silly when I wake her up instead. Maybe I can be mother today.*

"I planned to surprise her by waking her up instead," I tell Jax. "I was giggling when I stopped in front of her door and I clamped my hands around my mouth to silence the sound. The door was ajar, but I thought nothing of it."

I can feel myself shaking, feel the silence of the house pressing in on me, but still, my younger self did not notice the strangeness, could not tell the difference.

Don't wake her up yet. It's a surprise. It's not like the surprise of blue tulips from her garden. She won't be upset this time. This is a good surprise.

I continue talking to Jax, continue to relay the story, but my mind loses itself to the memory. I'm standing outside that door on that fateful day, with no idea that I'm in for the kind of "surprise" that will make me hate surprises for the rest of my life.

I stifle another giggle and push the door open the rest of the way. It swings without a sound, playing along with my game.

Wait for it…

I step into the room.

Now!

"Rise and shine, Mommy!" I call out. "It's time for another day!" I raise my hands in the air and grin, but both my arms and smile fall when there comes no response.

325

"Mama?" I say.

I look across the room to the bed.

Maybe I wasn't loud enough?

But then, I notice. The room is covered in white...stuff.

There are some by my feet and I pick one up.

A feather?

My happy mood fizzles out.

What happened to the birdy?

I look around the room and realize the feathers are everywhere. Mommy's beautiful blue masterpiece has turned into a snow globe.

"Mama! Mama! What happened? What happened to the birdy?" I exclaim.

I'm crying as I run to her bedside, stray feathers tickling my bare feet.

I skid to a stop a few feet away, nearly losing my balance in my urgency to halt.

I feel cold suddenly and start to tremble as I look at my mother in bed. I curl my arms around myself as more tears build up behind my eyes.

Mommy isn't sleeping.

No, she has to be! The birdy...

But it isn't a bird, I realize now.

The feathers came from the pillow...a once-white pillow that is now very, very red.

Blood is splattered across the headboard, pooling on the pillowcase, and dripping onto the floor a few inches in front of where I stand, shaking.

"Mama..." I whisper, crying now. "Mama!"

But she won't hear me.

She's dead.

"No!" I scream. "No, Mommy, come back!"

The feathers are covering her, sticking to her pale face, and my screams turn louder as I lift my feet to scrape off the ones attached to me.

"Get off, get off!"

Standing on one foot, I'm unbalanced, and a second later I slip.

I hit the ground hard and my movement stirs up the feathers around me. They swirl in the air and land on my face, arms, legs...

"No! Get off! You can't have me!"

I claw at them, nearly tearing my yellow pajamas.

I scream and I scream and I scream....

"Silent!"

The voice pierces through my skull, tries to drown out the screams still ringing out.

Mother is dead. Mother is dead.

"Silent, can you hear me?"

Someone is shaking me, but that isn't right. That's not what happened.

Rough hands grasp the side of my arms and hold tight. It shocks me and the image of my mother's bedroom flickers.

Flickers?

Oh.

"That's it, Silent. Breathe. I'm here. Look at me."

Ajax.

My mother's blue room fades into Jax's blue eyes as I listen to his voice.

Oh Guild...

His eyes bring me back.

"Are you okay?" Jax says. He's standing over the bed, hands still around my arms, but loose now.

"I... I think so." I take a shuddering breath. "Damn. It felt so real... I could see myself there. It was horrible."

"I could feel it too and I am so sorry..." He leans down and holds me close, as much of a hug as we can manage given my state and the IVs still stuck in me. I savour his warmth, his presence, his reality. He is alive. I am alive. We're okay.

"Did I get the whole story out? I kind of lost track of time and place." I mumble the words into his chest, careful not to mention any details. My body is still quivering.

"Enough of it, I think," he replies. He squeezes me tighter. "You should rest."

He pulls away and I look up at him. "No, I need to tell you the rest."

He grimaces. "Are you sure that's wise? I don't think I can watch that unfold again."

"The worst of it is over. All I have to do now is fill in the gaps."

"Okay," he sighs. "Go on, but if you start shaking again, I'm calling it a night, deal?"

I nod. "Deal. So, I learned much later that she'd been shot in the head with a pistol. My young mind didn't know enough to put together the cause of death, only that she was gone." I shudder.

He grabs my hand and squeezes it. "It's okay. I'm here. You're not alone. God, I feel like I've lost her too, listening to you talk about her. She didn't deserve to die, but her death made you stronger."

I try to smile. "Maybe," I allow, "but before it made me stronger, Jax, it destroyed me."

"Yes, loss always does, but look at you now. You could've given up lying on that floor, you could've gone through the rest of your life like a zombie, but you didn't. That's a lot for a five-year-old to go through, to witness, and yet, here you are. You're a little rough around the edges and the past will never disappear, but don't think for a second it destroyed you."

How does he always know what to say?

I don't know what to say to him, as usual, so I continue on with the story instead. Maybe the words will come. "So anyway, I screamed and cried for what felt like hours after I found her. Eventually, I left the carnage and returned to my room where I crawled into bed and stayed there for the longest time. They came for me in the afternoon."

Jax looks at me sharply. "Who?"

"The assassins," I reply. "They told me that Resistance members had killed my mother and that I should go with them if I didn't want to be next. That's how I became a Guild Ward, how most become Guild Wards I imagine, and that's how I developed a deep hatred for your organization and a fear of pillows and feathers."

I take another deep breath.

"I had nightmares for the first six months after and panic attacks regularly for the first year. It's a wonder I survived, given how distracted and exhausted I was daily. I'd wake up every night freaking out, terrified that someone was going to come shoot me because of the pillow I was sleeping on. I learned soon enough though, and refused to use them at all. It was better once I got my own room and could let go of the fear of waking to other people's last screams, simply because they slept with pillows.

"That's another thing too," I muse. "I never heard my mother scream that night or the gun go off and I've always felt so guilty because of it. If only I had heard something, I might have been able to save her. She could still be alive, but then...I might never have met you." I look up at him.

He smiles slightly and says, "I'm sorry that was how you lost her. I'm sorry you *had* to lose her, but I'm not sorry I met you and I never will be. No matter what happens, I will always hold onto these memories, the new memories we will make together."

I'm tearing up and all I can choke out is a feeble thank you.

He smiles wider. "You're welcome. You'll probably think me crazy for mentioning this, but you should get some sleep now."

I reach out and grab his hand. "Don't go."

"Silent, I..."

I squeeze his hand tighter and lock eyes with him. "Stay. I just need to know you're there. I need someone to keep the nightmares at bay."

He nods. "Okay."

I shuffle over and pat the now empty space beside me. "Here," I say.

He smiles. "You sure we're both going to fit?"

I shrug. "There's no harm in trying."

He sighs. "Fine, try not to fall off the other side, eh?"

I laugh and grab hold of the bed frame as he eases himself down beside me and lies down over the covers. We fit perfectly and I relax, laying my head on his shoulder. I close my eyes.

He runs his hand through my hair. I listen to his heartbeat and the sound of his steady breathing. Soon, it lulls me to sleep.

The nightmares stay away.

CHAPTER TWENTY-EIGHT

Jax is still there when I wake up and I've never been happier. He's so warm and comfortable. My head rests on his chest, rising and falling with each breath he takes, each breath that tells me we're both still alive.

I sigh, happy, and Jax groans. His eyes flutter open. He looks confused for a second, but then he sees me and smiles. I smile back.

"Morning," he yawns. "Sleep well?" He closes his eyes again and I almost faint. Sleepy Jax is the most adorable thing ever.

"Actually," I say, "I had the best sleep I've had in a long time. Thank you...for staying."

"You're welcome," he replies. "I slept pretty well too." He opens one eye and grins at me. "We should do this more often."

My heart stutters. Butterflies dance in my stomach and I blush.

He looks at me curiously. "I meant sleep, Silent. Calm down. What did you think I meant?"

I slap him on the wrist. "That is not what you were implying, Jax! Don't lie to me." I try to sound stern, but I can't stop smiling at him. Guild, this whole love thing isn't so bad.

"All right," he sighs, "I give in. You're right; that's not what I meant, but do you blame me?"

"Sadly, no."

He laughs. "You know me so well, it's dangerous."

"What's dangerous is the fact that you slept with an assassin."

"Reformed assassin," he reminds me, "and what do you mean by slept with? Did I miss something last night?"

"What? No! I... I meant sleep and you know it!"

He laughs harder. "Relax, I'm just teasing you."

I cross my arms. "Well, I don't like it."

"Oh, don't give me that look. Where's that dangerous assassin you spoke of?"

I scowl at him.

"There she is," he says.

I smile. "You're something else, eh?"

"Well, I should hope so," he replies, grinning. It's the same answer I gave when he asked *me* that question weeks ago.

"Get out of here," I say.

"Never," he replies. He kisses me on the top of the head.

I lean forward involuntarily, hoping for something more, but then the door bangs open and I hear a stern voice say, "And just what is going on here?"

We jump apart like scalded cats and sit up straight, facing the intruder. The same nurse that scolded us the day before is standing in the doorway, studying us with her cold "I will not take any crap" face, her hands on her ample hips. She's wearing a black outfit with red flowers this time, hair still up.

"What do you think you are doing, boy?" she asks Jax.

"I..." he stammers, face red and I almost laugh as I realize he's embarrassed, and intimidated by this old lady. "I was keeping Ms. Night warm. It, uh...gets pretty cold in here. Don't know if you've, um...noticed."

I do laugh now. "Nice cover story, genius."

The nurse scowls at the both of us. "I don't know what you're playing at, Mr. Forrester, but this is not going to help her recover. So get out and let me and the other nurses see to our jobs."

"No," I protest. "Don't make him leave. Can't he sit in the chair again?"

"And have him screw up your heart monitor results? I don't think so, young lady. He goes."

I sigh. "Fine," I give in, but I give the woman my best glare to let her know who she's pissed off.

The lady just rolls her eyes and looks at Jax. "Well?"

He sighs too. "All right, all right, I'm going. Just give me a second." He leans down and kisses me quick on the lips. The heart monitor screeches again and I flinch a bit at the noise.

I look at the nurse when he pulls away; she is giving us a death stare that could level buildings.

Jax is leaving me alone, with her?

Jax jumps off of the bed and smiles at the nurse. "Good luck, Shirley. This one won't be nearly as cooperative now that she's awake."

I clamp my hands over my mouth to keep from giggling. The nurse's name is Shirley.

Jax winks at me. "Don't worry, Silent. I'll be right outside if you need me."

"Enough already," Shirley says. "Get out."

"I'm going," Jax replies and he heads out the door, closing it behind him.

I smile to myself. He really is something else.

I have to deal with the nurses poking and prodding at me for a good hour. I don't get a moment's peace. They check my blood pressure, heartbeat, temperature, and reflexes. They shine flashlights in my eyes—with great pleasure, I might add—and cut off my pain medication. That's when I realize how close I came to dying, as soon as my lower leg starts throbbing. Then, the nurses pull up my gown to check the wound.

It takes a lot of effort to hold back my gasp. A line of thick stitches closes up the angry red gash on my leg.

Shirley feels the skin around it and I flinch. "How deep...?" I gasp through the pain.

It hit the bone," she replies. "You have a hairline fracture you'll have to be careful with, but no permanent damage. You're lucky the axe hit your shin and not your thigh or you never would've lasted long enough for us to get to you. We were nearly too late as it was. You're a fortunate girl, Ms. Night, and you can thank your boy for making that tourniquet. It saved your life."

"Will I be able to walk?" I wonder.

"To a certain extent, yes. We're giving you a leg brace for the fracture and we ask that you stay away from strenuous action for at least a week. Do you think you can handle that?"

"I don't know," I reply. "It all depends on when we decide to initiate Stage Three of the battle. I will be there, broken leg or no." Jenson and I need to discuss that as soon as possible. The thought of waiting much longer makes me nervous.

"That's what I was afraid of," Shirley says, "just please, be careful. I don't fancy seeing you in here again anytime soon."

"When do I lose the brace?"

"When I see fit," she replies, "but we'll see you back here in two days to remove the stitches. They'll have been in for a week by then."

I nod. "If I must."

"You will," she says.

I sigh. "When are you going to put the brace on?"

"I'm going to call the other nurses in a moment and we'll do it then. You're going to have to lie back down and if you don't lie perfectly still, we'll sedate you again."

I roll my eyes. "Whatever, just get on with it."

"If you think you're ready..." She walks over to the door and calls out.

I take a deep breath and lie down, staring at the ceiling. I imagine Jax's face as the nurses surround me. I close my eyes.

One of them touches my leg and I flinch.

"Just do it," I hear them mutter.

I feel a sting in my arm and then nothing.

• • •

When I open my eyes, it's dark again and I can feel a presence beside me. Immediately, I fear the worst and tense up.

I hear a groan and someone speaks. "Hey... It's okay, Silent. It's just me."

I sigh and relax; Jax. "What are you doing?" I ask. "If the nurses find you..." I yawn. "Shirley will tan your hide."

He laughs. "We don't have to worry about that. They moved you while you were out. We're in your room."

I tense up again, senses on hyper drive. Jax is lying in my bed.

Assassins below. This is seriously testing my self-control.

Jax notices my distress and says, "I can leave if this makes you uncomfortable. I just thought you might want someone here when you woke up and you don't have a chair in your room and I was tired..."

I put a hand on his arm. "Jax. It's fine. Don't get so worked up about it." It's a reminder to myself too.

"You're okay then?" he asks.

I sigh. "I've never been better, but I'm going to go back to sleep now."

"You do that. I'll be right here."

So I fall asleep, once again nestled in his arms, listening to the beat of his heart in sync with mine.

CHAPTER TWENTY-NINE

The next morning, when I wake, I'm alone, but the bed beside me is still warm. Jax must have left recently, maybe a few minutes ago. I smile, closing my eyes again and envisioning his face. I rub my thumb across my bottom lip. I can't believe he kissed me. I can't believe I kissed him back.

Who am I?

I have no idea, but I like the new me, my new life, and above all, my Ajax. I laugh. It sounds ridiculous to call him mine, but the alternative is boyfriend and I don't think I'm ready for that yet.

I sigh and sit up. Only then do I realize a detail I missed last night when I was half asleep. My right leg is held tight by the brace the nurses must've snapped on after they knocked me out again.

Damn nurses.

I haven't been awake for more than an hour in, well... It has to be at least five days. I should probably find out what day it is, how much time I've lost, how much time the Charger has had to prepare a counter-attack.

I slide over to the edge of the bed and swing both legs over, careful not to bang the brace against the bed frame. Tensing up, I place both feet on the floor and stand. There's a dull ache in my leg, but I can take it. I was expecting a lot more pain.

I relax my stance and begin a slow hobble to my closet. It's more like a waddle.

Guild, it's going to take me a while to get used to this.

I reach the closet and search through it for something to wear, breathing a lot heavier than necessary.

I hate this.

I decide on a black uniform shirt and cloak. I'll have to tackle changing my pants later, maybe ask Blake for help. I have no idea how to navigate around this damn brace. I never should've let that axe man get to me.

What was I doing? I never should have let that one guy separate me from my sword.

Speaking of which, where in the Guild did all my weapons go? I hope someone recovered them. I've had that sword since I was ten years old. I earned that blade through blood, sweat, and tears. Mostly blood though.

I get dressed and waddle over to the mirror to check out my latest look. I laugh when I see my reflection. I look like shit.

My hair is in complete disarray and I run my fingers through it in an attempt to tame it. It doesn't help that the axe man got away with several strands of it, but I don't think that's the main issue. Dark circles linger under my eyes and a red line runs across my right cheek, courtesy of a man with a hunting knife. I let him get a bit too close. Then I let him get personal with one of my daggers; they didn't get along. The cut doesn't look deep, so hopefully it won't scar.

I check my other injuries: the shallow cut on my left leg and the slice on my shoulder. The nurses must've found them because they're healing nicely.

Finally, I decide to quit delaying the inevitable. I'll have to face the world eventually, might as well do it now.

Sighing, I make my way over to the door and into the hall. The hall is empty, but I won't be alone for long. It's always busy near the cafeteria.

Well, if anybody laughs at me they'll soon see just how incapacitated I am as I decapitate them. I don't need a knife to pry their heads off of their shoulders. That's what most people don't realize.

It takes twice as long as it should for me to get to the cafeteria. No one makes fun of me as I waddle down the halls. A solid glare is enough to keep the snickers and name-calling at bay. However, I don't doubt that someone will run along to her highness to let her know how stupid I look.

I swear, if she shows up at our table, I will skin her alive with my fingernails. I'd rather screw up my other leg than see her ugly face.

I shove my way through the crowds in the cafeteria and plop down on the bench beside Bast at our table. Blake sits across from us. They both jump at the sight of me.

"Night!" Bast exclaims. "Jax didn't tell us they released you from the infirmary yet. How are ya? We would've come to visit you, but the rules are family only and they almost refused to make an exception for Jax."

"That's okay," I reply, "I understand, and Jax probably didn't tell you because I was released late last night." I don't tell them he slept with me. That would be an awkward conversation, especially since I'm pretty sure they don't know about our new relationship status.

"Right," Bast says, "but how are you?"

"I feel okay. I'm a little rough around the edges, but what do you expect? The real problem is trying to deal with *this*." I stand up and show off the leg brace.

Bast whistles. "Nice, man. That looks fun."

I roll my eyes. "Oh, yeah, fun is definitely the word I would use to describe this monkey suit."

He shrugs. "It's for your own good."

I scowl.

Blake looks at Bast and says, "Zip it, the poor woman's already been through enough, she doesn't need you poking fun at her."

"What are you," he counters, "my mother?"

"I don't like your tone, Sebastian," she scolds him.

He glares at her.

Blake and I laugh. "You brought that one upon yourself, Seb," I gasp through my giggles.

"Aw," a voice says from behind me, "what did I miss?"

We all turn to face Jax and he squishes onto the bench beside Bast and I.

"Just a Bast joke," I tell him.

"Damn. Was it a good one?"

"Oh, lay off of it," Bast whines.

"It's not as if you don't tease the rest of us," Blake chides him.

"I'm not going to apologize for it if that's what you're implying, Blake."

"Okay, okay," Jax says, "let's everybody calm down. There's something we need to talk about."

Bast's face loses its cheer. "What is it? What happened?"

Jax laughs. "Oh, don't look so serious; nobody died. I just want to tell the two of you that Silent and I are—"

"—together now," I finish for him before he can use the word "dating." It seems like such a juvenile term. This isn't a fling. This is something I've invested in, something I've put my trust in.

Bast raises a fist in the air. "Yes! I knew that ten bucks was mine!"

"What?" I ask.

He runs a hand through his curls. "Um... Trey and I might've had a bet going..."

"On our relationship status?" I ask.

"Yeah."

I scowl. "Are the two of you five years old? Do you have nothing better to do?"

"Yes and no," he replies.

I roll my eyes and shake my head. Beside me, Jax is frowning.

"But, uh, congrats," Bast goes on. "I was rooting for you either way."

SILENT NIGHT

"Uh huh," I say.

Blake smiles at Jax and me from across the table. "I'm glad to hear it," she says. "This will be a nice change."

I smile back. "I hope so."

"Thanks, Blake," Jax says, "good to see *someone* cares about us."

"Hey, I said congrats didn't I?" Bast complains. "It's only a little bit of money."

"You gambled on your friends, Bast," Jax retorts.

"Yeah, those are the easiest bets to win; I know you guys."

Jax shakes his head. "All that aside, Silent and I are together, but that doesn't change how this team operates and I still regard all of us as equals. Now, there are a few more important things we need to go over."

"Like filling me in on everything I missed since the train?" I suggest. "What day is it, for starters?"

"It's June eleventh," Jax replies.

Ugh. So I did lose five days. Great.

"How did any of us even survive that battle?" I ask.

"The reinforcements arrived shortly after you lost consciousness," he tells me, "and they bombed the remaining assassins so we would all have time to evacuate."

I wince. "That should make the Charger *real* happy."

"There haven't been any repercussions yet. I think we're both just watching and waiting."

"Lovely. Has Jenson come up with our next move?"

344

"No," Jax replies. "He wanted to, believe me, but Avery told him to wait for you to recover, because you're the leader of the mission."

"Avery came here to talk to Jenson about *me*?" I'm astounded. I know Avery trusts me more than Jenson does, but I didn't think he would postpone the entire operation because I was out of commission.

"Well, actually," Jax answers, "he came here to *see* you."

"Me?"

"Yeah. Jenson sent him a message, telling him what happened, and an hour later he showed up with two bodyguards and demanded to be escorted to the infirmary."

"You're kidding."

"No. It was the weirdest thing. Oh and that reminds me, we should probably go see Trey sometime today. She's been in hysterics ever since she heard what happened."

"Why?" I didn't think she cared.

"No idea."

"Probably a girl thing," Bast pipes up.

Blake scowls at him.

"Don't give me that look, Blake." He leans back in his seat. "Hey, you know, we should do something to celebrate Night's recovery."

"Like what?" I ask.

"I was thinking about a trip to the Den and a way cool party..." He trails off; the glare Ajax is shooting his way silences him. "What? Come on, man, it would be fun. I won't do anything this time, I swear."

Jax takes a deep breath. "I don't like it at all, but it's not up to me. Silent?"

I swivel my head, gazing from him to Bast and back again. "Well, this is a fun decision." I sigh. "I agree with Bast; it could be fun. It'll take everyone's minds off of what's been happening and Jax, I promise you I won't drink anything unless I'm positive it's a glass of water."

"You swear?"

"On my life and my mother's grave."

"Even with your injury?"

"I can still walk; I'm not incompetent."

"All right, I guess it's a go then, but if you feel any strain, let me know and we'll get you to bed. Oh, and that reminds me: I'm supposed to give you these." He pulls a bottle of pills out of his coat pocket and sits them on the table. "You need to take two to start and then one at every meal and before bed until they're gone."

"Ugh. Must I?"

"If you don't, Shirley will kill the both of us."

I laugh and take the bottle.

I down two pills as Jax turns to Bast. "So, when were you thinking for the party?"

"Tonight?" Bast suggests. "Eight o'clock should do it. I'll get the word out. Sound good?"

I nod and reply, "As long as Natalie doesn't find out, I'm okay with whomever."

"Yeah, no. Her highness is *not* invited. Over my dead body."

"Which can be arranged," I reply, grinning at him.

"Oh, I know, believe me."

"Good."

"Well, Silent," Jax says, "are you going to eat something or can we go and get this meeting with Jenson over with?"

I raise an eyebrow. "Meeting? What meeting?"

"Right, I forgot to tell you. Jenson wanted to meet with you as soon as you were released. Like I said earlier, he wants to move on with the planning, but we can eat first if you want."

"Oh, I intend to, and I think I'll go see Trey too before I bend to his will."

He shrugs. "Go right ahead; I'm not going to stop you, and if Jenson wants to punish you, he'll have to go through me first."

I smile. "You know, I'm mighty hungry. This might take a while."

He laughs and Bast says, "What do you guys want on your tombstones? Flowers? Adjacent graves?"

"Lay off it, Bast," I say, standing up.

He shrugs. "I'm just saying."

I snort and hobble over to the counter to get some food. Jenson has been waiting for five days. He can wait a couple more hours.

CHAPTER THIRTY

After I eat, Jax and I walk to Trey's room. I still don't understand why she was so upset over my injury. I didn't think she thought that much of me. I didn't even think we were friends. I mean, she's obviously connected enough to bother placing bets with Bast, but I didn't think she liked me.

The cafeteria is a few halls behind us when Jax speaks. "Hey, I just want to let you know that so far, Bast and Blake are the only people that know about us. Well, other than the nurses, I guess."

"Yeah," I reply. "So?" My hand brushes his as we walk and our fingers intertwine, almost without thought.

"Well, I was thinking we might want to keep our relationship on the down low for a bit."

I stop walking, dragging him to a stop beside me. "Why, are you ashamed of me?" I'm hurt by his words, but he looks horrified at mine.

"No! That's not it at all," he assures me. "I just don't think our leaders would approve, seeing as we come from two different worlds, so to speak. They might forbid us from—"

"Screw them," I snap, "we're both human. I will not let anyone tell me what to do or who to love."

"Are you sure..."

I cut off his sentence with a quick kiss. "Positive."

He kisses me then, deeper but just as quick. I moan when he pulls away, wanting more.

"If that's what you want," he says, "then that's what we'll do, but don't say I didn't warn you."

"Danger is my middle name, Jax; warnings don't scare me."

"Hey, speaking of that," he says as we start walking again, arms swinging between us. "Now that we're together, can you tell me your real name?"

I grin. "Not a chance."

"Rylie?"

"No."

"Blair?"

I snort at that.

"Dallas?"

I laugh. "Now you're just being ridiculous. Don't you like not knowing? Doesn't it add to my mystique?"

"Quite, but I'm still curious."

"Well then, you'll just have to keep guessing."

He sighs, but does just that all the way to Trey's room. He doesn't get anywhere close.

Trey is staying in a guest room and we reach the guest hall five minutes later. It's a dead end corridor with five rooms on each side, but it looks friendlier than the usual square corners and grey palettes of the rest of the base. The ceiling is arched, the walls painted a dull green.

Trey's room is at the end and Ajax knocks on the door. We hear footsteps from within and then the door opens a crack. Trey peeks out.

She sees us and smiles. "Jax, Night, nice to see you. Come in." She opens the door wider and we follow her inside.

I find myself jealous of her room. It's painted a deep purple and it has a couch, an armchair, a small kitchen table set, and a bed. Jax and I sit down on the couch side by side while Trey leans on the chair arm.

"You're looking good, Night," Trey says. "You certainly gave us a scare a few days ago. How're you feeling?"

"Better than I was. I'm still a bit sore, but I guess that's to be expected seeing as I escaped death by a hair. The nurses say I'm really lucky."

"That you are. How do you like that leg brace?"

I snort. "I hate it. It's a ridiculous get-up. I can't even walk properly."

She laughs. "I know what you mean."

"How is that?"

"I received a similar injury some years back. It was a sword though instead of an axe. Came about as close to dying as you did and had to wear that stupid brace for weeks. I hated every second of it. You can't do half of the things you want to do and you can't stay on your feet for long without excruciating pain running up your nerves." She pauses and smiles at me. "It's a great time. You'll love it."

I roll my eyes. "Oh, I'm sure, but did you say *weeks*?"

"Yeah, I wanted it off sooner, but the nurses wouldn't allow it. They said I would end up breaking it again if I didn't let it heal completely. I listened to them, seeing as I broke my foot the year before and ended up screwing it up even worse when I took the cast off early."

I wince. "Ouch. That must've been rough."

"Well, I learned my lesson, that's all I can say."

"I suppose you did."

We're all quiet for a minute and Trey slides off of the chair arm so she's actually sitting in the chair.

"What brings you guys here then?" she asks. "Now that we've got all that out of the way."

"Nothing much," Jax says, answering for me. "We just wanted to let you know how Silent was doing. You were pretty distraught the other night when you heard the news."

Trey rubs the back of her neck. "Yeah, well," she looks over at me, "I didn't think you deserved to die, Silent. Coming here, I know it's changed you for the better, and I was afraid it would all be for naught, that the Guild would end up taking that away from you again."

"Again?"

"Well, they killed your mother and took away your innocence. They were trying to finish what they started if you ask me."

"Right, yeah," I reply. Something about her answer bothers me, but I can't put my finger on it.

"Well," Jax says, "I guess we should be going then. Jenson is expecting us. We have a meeting; the man's so impatient."

Trey laughs. "Thanks for coming and have fun. Good luck with the old man."

I snort. "Luck will get us nowhere with him." I go to stand up and Jax reaches for my arm to help me. I shrug it off. "It's okay, I can do it."

He sighs. "Fine, I was just trying to be a gentleman."

I get up fine on my own and we head for the door when I remember something. I turn back to Trey. "Oh and by the way, I should let you know that you lost your bet with Bast."

Her eyes are blank with confusion for a second and then her face distorts into a grimace. "Damn, I thought I had him. The two of you are really together?" She points to Jax and me.

I smile. "Yeah. It's a relatively new concept, but something I've been ignoring for a while. We'll see where it takes us."

Jax wraps an arm around my waist and pulls me close. I smile wider.

Trey shakes her head. "Young love... You, my friend, just cost me ten bucks."

I shrug. "What can I say?"

"You can say goodbye and leave me to mourn my losses," she jokes. "Nah, in all honesty, I'm happy for you

352

guys, just don't go ignoring your duties or anything. Remember what's at stake."

I nod. "We will."

"You don't have to worry about that," Jax agrees. "We've got our eyes on the goal. We're not going to let anything stop us."

Trey nods. "Good. Now you better get going, Jenson is waiting."

We say our goodbyes and head out.

Once we're alone, I turn to Jax and say, "If you were a real gentleman, you'd do more than help me to my feet; you'd carry me in my time of need."

He smiles. "All you need to do is ask," he replies and then he scoops me up, throwing me over his shoulder in a split second. He's walking down the hall before I have time to react.

"Assassins below, Jax!" I screech. "Put me down!" My chest is against his back and I now have a wonderful view of the floor.

"Sorry," he replies, "no can do."

I beat my fists against the backs of his thighs, but when that doesn't shake him, I resign myself to the journey as he heads to the council room.

When we reach the right hall, Jax puts me back down on my feet and I say, "Never do that again."

"Why not?"

"Because... Because..."

He raises an eyebrow. "Does it scare you?"

"No."

"Then what's the problem?"

"Nothing, I guess."

He smiles at me. "That's what I thought."

I can't help but smile back. "All right," I say, "you're a total genius. There, I said it."

He grins. "I know."

I roll my eyes. "Come on, wise guy; let's get this meeting over with."

He sighs and takes my hand, making my heart skip a beat, and we continue down the hall to the door at the end. We don't bother knocking; we just walk in like we own the place, or at least, that's how I do it.

"Jenson, my friend," I say, getting the ball rolling, "how have you been?"

"Splendid," he replies. I get the impression he would've rather I kicked the bucket. I also sense exhaustion lingering behind that ever-present scowl of his. The battle must've taken a mental toll on him.

"Great." I take a seat at the table across from Jenson and Jax follows my cue, grabbing the seat beside me.

"Anyway," I go on, "I heard you wanted to see me as soon as I was able, so here I am. What did I miss and what do you wish so desperately to discuss with me?"

He scowls. "Cut the bullshit, Assassin. I am pleased you recovered so quickly, but I would like to get on with the mission."

"What has the enemy been up to?" I ask him. I'm all business now, the better to get this over with. The pills Jax made me take this morning definitely took the edge off. I can feel the pain creeping back in.

"Not much," Jenson replies, "which I find strange. They've been rather quiet and I would like to silence them for good before they get their heads together enough to execute another counterstrike."

"What do you think we should do?"

"You tell me, Assassin; both you and Avery keep reminding me that this is *your* plan."

And rightly so.

"In that case, we should start planning Stage Three."

"And what will that entail?"

"It's the assault on the Guild. I think we're ready."

"I beg to differ. Our manpower has been stretched thin. How can we hope to wage a final battle?"

He must be tired indeed to let slip even a kernel of doubt.

"With the element of surprise, Jenson. They still don't know I am with you, that I can lead you straight into the centre of the Guild and unleash hell. They will never expect to fight in their own territory. We are bringing the battle to them for once.

I clear my throat and prepare to lay out the plan I've been drawing up in my head ever since I kissed the Guild goodbye. It leaves no room for error.

"Here's what we're going to do," I say. "We need to split your forces—all you are willing to send out—into twenty equal platoons. I have twenty entrances which I will mark out on a map after our discussion. Each platoon will use a different entrance and each will have their own exit. There is one emergency exit."

"How did you come up with those numbers?" Jenson asks me.

"As Agent Two of the Guild, I had access to twenty entrances and exits. The emergency one is that of the double agent, Rachel, that I took down the last couple days I was there. I followed her through one of her exits and the Charger won't think of checking there. He'll forget I know about that tunnel.

"Now, each entrance and exit comes with specific instructions which must be followed to the letter, else your men and women wish to perish. If they follow the directions, they should be fine. From there, we'll hit the assassins with our surprise attack and take them down before they know what hit them. The Charger, of course, is mine."

"I think not," Jenson argues. "Whoever catches him will bring him back here for questioning."

I snort. "Good luck with that."

"Excuse me?" Jenson says.

"You'll never get a word out of him," I reply, "even if you do somehow manage to catch him and get him all the way back here. He's not the Master of all assassins for nothing you know."

"What exactly are you saying, Assassin?"

"I'm saying he's dangerous and you shouldn't underestimate him. Jenson, do you know why no one has ever done this before, why Trey and I as traitors are exceptions, not the rule?"

"Why, Assassin?"

356

"Because we're all too afraid," I admit. "Any captured assassin won't talk for anything. They'd rather die than let the Charger find them. They know that if they talk and you set them free, there will be consequences. They know the Charger won't die until he doles out his punishment and that the odds of you finding and killing him are slim to none. They'd rather die of Resistance torture than have to endure the kind of agony the Master Assassin's wrath can bring upon you. So, Jenson, if you think you can capture the Charger, by all means, be my guest, but you might want to finalize your last will and testament first, and decide if you'd rather be starved to death and skinned or made to bleed out while you're burnt alive."

Jenson looks at me in horror and Jax shivers beside me.

"It's the truth," I sigh, "and the sooner you realize it, the better. The Charger should not be dealt with lightly. I'm your only chance at getting him, alive or dead, and even then, my chances are low. I will do my best to end him, but it might not be enough."

"If you are speaking the truth about his prowess," Jenson says, "how do you expect to stand a chance given your current condition?" He nods to my leg. "If you thought I wouldn't notice that detail, you are sadly mistaken. How do you hope to fight with a broken leg?"

"It's only a fracture and unlike the rest of you, I know how to work through the pain. I've dealt with broken limbs before and if you couldn't learn to fight with them, you didn't survive. The assassins sniff out all weaknesses, so you had to be sure to turn each one into a strength before they found you. My leg is only a hindrance if you see it as such. I'm still your best bet at beating him. Even injured, I am better than any soldier you could throw at him."

"Why do you want him dead?"

I blink. "What?"

"Why do you want to kill the Master Assassin so badly? I am not stupid enough to believe you turned your back on the Guild simply because you learned you were killing innocents, Assassin. I have seen the bloodlust in your eyes, the anger when you say his name. That does not come with mourning strangers."

"I..." I don't think I've ever heard him say this much outside of our arguments, never thought he was that observant.

"Who did he kill, Assassin?" he asks me. "Answer that one question and I'll grant your request."

He's caught me off guard and for some reason I don't hesitate. "My mother," I reply. "He killed my mother." And he killed me, every day after that, piece by piece.

For once, Jenson doesn't scowl at me. There is something like understanding in his eyes as he nods and says, "Very well, Assassin, you can have the Charger. You better hope you are telling the truth about your skill and make sure he suffers long and hard for his transgressions."

I wonder what the Charger did to him, who died. I wonder if that is why he is so cold now.

"Oh, believe me," I tell him, "he'll be begging for his death long before I'm through with him. I won't grant his wish until I'm satisfied he has paid for my mother's death and the deaths of everyone else twice over, in blood."

"See to it that you do," Jenson mutters. "Now, about that map and directions..."

I spend the next forty minutes marking the entrances and exits on an old city map and writing out the specific instructions for each, from the number of steps to take, to elevator codes, steps to avoid on staircases, and booby traps to duck. Every motion the men will make is written out in detail.

"Lose these instructions, Jenson," I remind him, "and the lives of all of your men will be forfeit. They'll die long before they even get near an assassin."

"I get it, Assassin," he says. "You don't have to keep telling me."

"Yes, I do. I will repeat myself until the knowledge is burned into your brain cells. This is not a game. There are no retries. This is it."

"When do we march?"

"As soon as everything is in order; three days from now should do it."

"I will make it happen. Go prepare yourself; I have important work to do."

He shoos Jax and I out of the door and I mutter a goodbye under my breath.

It was a pleasure, Jenson. I can't wait until we meet again.

"So," Jax says, "that was fun, right?"

"Wrong. Does he think I'm not smart enough to catch his idle threats?"

"Hmmmm," Jax mutters "Do you know the definition of hypocrisy, Silent? Because, oddly enough, that sounds exactly like someone else I know." He gives me a look.

I scowl. "Shut up. I am not like that."

He raises an eyebrow. "Oh, really? The 'you should decide if you'd rather be starved to death or skinned' was simple conversation?"

"That wasn't a threat. That was merely a promise of what will happen if he doesn't take the Charger seriously. Black Death is not an assassin to be trifled with; he makes my deeds look like child's play."

Jax winces at the mention of the name.

"Sorry," I say softly, "but it's the truth."

"So is what Jenson said about your leg," he argues. "The nurses told you to lay low and now you're planning battle in three days? Couldn't you have postponed it so you could recover more?"

"We don't have time for that. If we don't strike now, the assassins will do it for us. We've already risked enough time as it is and I'm not going to sit back at the base while others fight my war for me."

He sighs. "You're impossible."

"I know, but we shouldn't worry about what will go wrong. There will be plenty of time for that later. Can we just enjoy ourselves for now?"

"Sure," he says, "what do you want to do?"

"How about we go back to my room and enjoy the peace and quiet while we still can. You got any funny stories?"

"Oh, I've got plenty," he replies with a grin. "Did I tell you about the time Bast accidentally set the Den on fire?"

I laugh. "Oh Guild, how did he manage that?"

"It took some talent, I'll tell you that much..." He goes on, weaving the threads of his story together as we head to my room, content in each other's company.

CHAPTER THIRTY-ONE

The day drags by. It seems like eight o'clock will never roll around. Jax and I sit in my room talking and stealing the occasional kiss until dinner. I still can't believe I waited so long to tell him how I feel.

He waits until six o'clock to tell me that I have to go to a therapy session for my leg. It's a gigantic pain in the ass. The nurse tells me I'm doing fine, but to remember to rest it as much as I can. I assure her I will and head back to my room to get dressed for the party. Blake is there when I arrive and I graciously accept her help.

"How about blue? I bet you look great in it."

I am sitting on the bed, watching her as she pulls one outfit after another out of the closet.

"No, too...bright," I reply.

She puts her hands on her hips. "How is blue bright?"

"It just is," I argue. "I prefer black, red, grey, and the occasional dark green."

EMMA COUETTE

Her eyes light up. "Oh, well in that case, I have just the thing. I'll be right back. Don't move."

She runs out of the door and I can hear her footsteps echoing down the hall until she turns a corner. I wonder what she has in mind and if I'll even remotely like it.

Ten minutes later, she returns with a bundle of clothes. She pulls out a pair of tight black pants and black boots.

"Oh," I breathe. "I like those."

She smiles. "I thought you might, and this will finish off the look." She holds out the shirt with a flourish. It's a deep green cloth, with a v neck and a slight shimmer when it moves. It's simple and beautiful.

"I love it."

"Wonderful," she says, "let's try it all on."

She helps me with the pants, which take a fair bit of work, but waits in the hall while I change my top. Eventually, the outfit is complete, and I call her back in.

Blake looks at me in awe. "You're gorgeous, girl. Have a look." She pushes me over to the mirror.

I hardly recognize the girl staring back at me.

There's one word for the way I look: amazing. The dark green goes great with my hair and eyes, and the black pants diminish the bulk of the stupid brace. The boots look pretty sexy too.

I smile and say, "I love it."

"Of course you do," Blake replies. "Poor Jax won't be able to take his eyes off of you."

I laugh and surprise myself by saying, "I don't plan on taking my eyes off of him either." I intend to enjoy this time

363

with him. It's our first chance to do something together that doesn't involve fighting for our lives or sparring verbally with Jenson. I mean, there will be other people there, so we won't be alone, but he's the only person I plan to focus on tonight.

It's Blake's turn to laugh. "Honestly, I can't tell if you two are adorable or sickening."

"Gee, thanks."

"I'm glad Ajax found somebody though and I'm glad you're that somebody. The two of you fit together somehow. You make sense. And God knows life's too short to spend it alone."

"Yeah," I reply. "Hey, I bet you'll find someone soon, unless there's already somebody you fancy?"

Her dark cheeks lose their colour. "No, not really," she says.

"Liar!" I exclaim with a laugh. "I saw your face. You almost went white. There's something you're not telling me. Who is it?"

She sighs. "I paled because I hate getting flashbacks of things I don't want to remember. There was someone once, Night, but he's gone now. I don't think I want to love again. I don't think I trust myself to do the right thing this time."

She's dead serious. Bitterness, fear, and regret coat her words, and I know I shouldn't push her any further, but I just got an idea. I think I might know why she hates Natalie.

"Blake," I say softly, "what happened between you and Natalie... Did she break your relationship apart?"

Blake laughs. "Hardly," she snorts. "She's been infatuated with Jax since any of us can remember." Her eyes grow even darker than usual. "No," she sighs, her whole body seeming to heave with the motion. "The story is much more tragic than that."

In that moment, she sounds so much older than I am, so much wiser, as if she's seen and done things I couldn't begin to imagine. It's the first time I notice the age difference between us. Even though it's only a year, it seems like dozens.

"I'm sure there is nothing you can say that will scare me off," I tell her. "You don't have to share with me right now, if you don't want to, but I'm here for you regardless."

She gives me a grim smile. "Thank you, but I think..." She pauses, eyes tight. I can feel her pain from here, can feel the tension in her bones like a live wire. Her hand reaches up to clutch her braid. "I think you of all people should know, if...if you are to continue being my friend. You have been honest with me about your past and I have kept secrets."

I put a hand on her arm, but she doesn't react. It's like I'm not there. "You had no reason to trust me in the beginning, Blake, and if I told you everything from my past, you'd probably be physically ill. Some things are better left alone, but if you want to tell me now, I'm listening."

"It was two years ago," she says finally. "I was seventeen and..." She takes a deep breath.

I smile to encourage her.

"I was pregnant, Night," she says, "pregnant and happy."

I can barely hold back my shock. This is not at all what I expected.

Blake was pregnant? Who was the father? What happened to the child?

I'm still reeling when Blake goes on.

"I was with the love of my life," she says with a tight smile, "or so I thought at the time. I'm not going to mention his name. We had made a mistake, but he said he would marry me and we'd be a family and everything would be okay, but then... A month before our child was due, he left me. He said he couldn't take that kind of commitment, didn't know how to be a father. The baby... She didn't make it. I wanted her so bad, and I wanted him to want the both of us." She stops, silent tears streaming down her face.

I put a hand on her shoulder. "I'm so sorry. You don't... You don't have to continue."

"I do. I need to finish the story."

"Okay." I understand; the same way I needed to tell Jax about how my mother died. Some stories can't be left untold once you start or else they hang about the corners of your mind, waiting to pounce on you.

"I broke a couple of days after I lost my daughter," Blake goes on. "I shattered, completely lost my senses. I rushed to my ex's room as soon as I was physically able and broke down the door with my axe. We fought brutally with words and weapons, and the next thing I knew, he had a knife in his gut and I was covered in his blood. I killed him, Night, and when I turned around, Natalie was

366

standing in the doorway. She saw it all, but she kept her mouth shut and has dragged me around on a leash ever since.

"My guilt was punishment enough. Even after what he put me through, he was still my first love and I couldn't believe he was gone, couldn't believe I had taken his life from him. It was not up to me to pass judgment, but I got away with my horrific deed. His murder was blamed on a rogue assassin who had escaped our dungeons. I didn't talk to anyone for a month and it took Jax and Bast several more to coax me back into going on missions and eating lunch with them again."

We don't talk for a minute. We just stand there. Her heart is pouring out and I'm breathing in her pain. No wonder she was reluctant to let me in at first.

"Do..." I start softly after a while. "Do the boys know?"

"That I killed him or that I was pregnant?"

"Both."

"Natalie is the only one who knows about the murder," she replies. "Everyone in the base knows about the pregnancy, but I chose to forget and everyone honours that, especially Jax and Bast."

"So you pretend it never happened?"

"For the most part," she says. "For me, it never disappears. Sometimes, like today, the pain hits me like a fresh stab to the heart." She sighs. "I was going to be a mother, Night. I felt her growing inside me like a ball of fire for nine months and then the light was extinguished, as easily as someone blowing out a candle."

"What happened to her?" I ask.

"She was sick, born with a rare disease whose cure has been lost during the wars. The nurses tried their best to save her, but in the end, it was no use. She died in my arms..." A single tear runs down her cheek, but she takes a deep breath and stands up straighter. "But that was a long time ago and crying won't bring her back; nothing will. There's no use bemoaning what happened. You have to move on."

I understand now her fondness for those children my first morning here and why her eyes had been so sad to let them go. They were a glimpse of what she could've had, what she still wants by the sound of it.

She looks at me then, as if remembering I'm there. "Sorry I piled that on you right before your party and everything," she says. "You must be feeling pretty depressed now."

"It's okay," I tell her. "I understand the need to get things off your chest."

"Thank you, Night," she says, smiling, "you're a true friend, you know that, right?"

It's strange to hear someone say it. It's even stranger to believe it. "I'll be there for you whenever you need me and if Natalie ever tries...anything, I'll knock her down a few pegs. Perhaps a few legs."

Blake laughs. "Now *that* I'd like to see, but we better get going or we'll be late." She heads over to the door, wiping her eyes with her hand.

"Fine," I sigh, hobbling after her. "I'll deal with her highness later. Oh, and for the record, Blake?"

"Yeah?"

"I think you're going to get that happy ending you dreamed about, you just don't know it yet."

She smiles at me, fresh tears glistening in her eyes and says, "Thank you."

We take each other's elbow and walk arm in arm down the hall, supporting each other, and somehow I know she will always be a pillar in my life, holding me up.

CHAPTER THIRTY-TWO

It's chaos in the Den. People are everywhere, dancing, laughing, and singing to the music blasting from the speakers. I can't hear myself think and I don't see anyone I know. I hold tighter to Blake's arm.

"Do you see the boys?" she asks me.

"No," I reply, raising my voice to be heard over the music.

"We better have a look around then. They're here somewhere."

She drags me into the crowd, which would be hard enough to navigate without a leg brace strapped to my shin. I almost trip a couple of people who slur swears at me as I pass by.

"Looks like most people don't even know who this party is for," I mutter.

Then Blake says, "There's your man." She points and I see him, lounging against the wall beside the door to the tattoo parlour. "I'll get you over there," she goes on, "and then I'll try to find Bast. Knowing him, he's probably hanging out by the bar, horribly drunk already."

I laugh. "Good luck with that."

She rolls her eyes and parts the crowd for me. We close the distance between Jax and us, and when we're about a metre away, he finally looks up and sees us. His eyes go wide and his mouth gapes open.

Blake laughs. "Well, would you look at that; you've rendered him speechless. Go on. You two enjoy yourselves. I'll be around, and remember who gave you that outfit in the first place. Don't forget to thank me later." She lets go of my arm and disappears.

I gather up my courage, feeling suddenly shy, and walk the last few steps to Jax's side.

He takes my hand in his, eyes still wide, drinking me in. "Silent," he breathes, "you look...gorgeous."

I blush. "You don't look too shabby yourself." It's a bit of an understatement. With his black suit and pants, polished shoes, and sparkling blue eyes, he is the picture of beauty, but I don't know how to tell him that.

"Thank you," he says, smiling. "Where did you get that outfit?"

"Blake lent it to me. I'm supposed to remember that and thank her later."

"Oh, I'll be thanking her too," he says, pulling me closer.

I lean into him, resting my head against his chest and breathing him in. He smells so good, like home.

His lips brush my ear as he whispers into it, "I *love* the shirt."

I pull away from him a foot and say, "Behave yourself. We're in a public setting,"

He laughs. "Relax. I'm just messing with you. Or am I?"

I roll my eyes. "You're impossible."

He grins. "I know, it's part of my charm."

I try to scowl at him, but end up smiling. Now that I've let my guard down, he's just so damn impossible to stay mad at.

I sigh. "What exactly do you want from me?" It's an innocent question.

"How about this dance?" he replies, holding out a hand.

I look at him. "You can't be serious."

"Deadly."

"But my leg..."

"I have a solution for that, just say yes."

After a moment's hesitation, I place my hand in his. "I trust you," I say.

"Good, then you might want to hold on."

"What—" I start, but then his hands are around my waist and he's lifting me. I'm so surprised that I forget the rest of my words.

He sets me down after a second, placing my feet on his. "There," he says, "perfect." He takes one of my hands in his and drapes the other over his shoulder; his other hand stays around my waist.

He starts swaying side to side, moving around in slow circles. I smile and close my eyes, content to stay in this moment forever.

"This isn't so bad, eh?" he says after a minute.

I open my eyes and reply, "Not at all." I lay my head against his shoulder as we continue to sway, totally out of sync with the horrid rap music that's beating out its disjointed rhythm, but we couldn't care less.

He rests his head on mine. "I love you," he whispers. A shiver runs down my spine and my heart stutters.

I should've seen this coming, but I didn't think it would be this soon.

Is it real?

Does he know what he's saying?

Love is a very weighty word to be throwing around.

"I..." I try, but I'm not sure what to say.

"Hey," he says, pulling back to look at me. "It's okay. It's okay if you're not ready to say it back. This relationship got off to a rough start and I'm not going to force you into something you're not ready for, but I love you and that's the truth. I'll wait until you're ready to say it back, however long it takes, even if it's never. I'm not going to rush you; I'd wait forever for you."

Something wet drips down my cheek. I try to wipe it away before Jax sees, but he takes one look at me and says, "Are you crying?"

"No," I snap as another tear trickles down my face, "don't be ridiculous."

He reaches out and wipes the tear away with his thumb. "Hey, I didn't mean to upset you."

"No, I'm not upset. I'm..." I sniff and wipe at my own eyes, brushing his hand away. "You're beautiful, you know that? No one has ever...treated me the way you do, as if I'm actually important, as if I'm special. You've shown me so much love, though I don't know what I did to deserve it. I'm afraid I won't be able to give you all you've given me, that I haven't changed enough to be able to love you in the way you deserve."

"Oh, Silent," he says, looking into my eyes, "never think that. I fell in love with you, with all of you, and that means the assassin too. I love you for you and whatever you can give me is enough because it's what's real."

I can't stand it anymore. I close the inches between us and kiss him.

He kisses me back, slow and sensual, making me dizzy. His hands tangle in my hair and my fingers fist against his shirt, pulling him closer, always closer. I need him and, somehow, that doesn't scare me anymore.

He pulls back long enough to plant kisses along the length of my jaw. I shiver and run a hand through his hair. He sighs and presses his lips against mine again.

We're lost to the world until someone bumps into me from behind and Ajax staggers, struggling to grab hold of me before I fall. We break apart and Jax sets me on my feet as we face the perpetrator.

Somehow, I'm not surprised by who stands before us, nor does his condition alarm me.

Bast grins at us, leaning precariously to one side. He has a drink in one hand and the other hand in his pocket. "Hey there...guys," he slurs. "You know, you should...get a room. There *is* such a...thing as too much...information. Watching you two suck face...is enough to make a guy...nauseous."

I blush and look at my feet.

"You know what else makes a guy nauseous, Sebastian?" Jax asks.

Bast doesn't even flinch at the use of his full name. "What, man?" he asks.

"Drinking too much," Jax says. "Seriously, Seb, how many have you had?"

"Who's counting?" Bast replies, grinning madly.

"Somebody should be," Jax argues. "You look on the brink of passing out."

"Where's Blake?" I ask Bast. "She was going to find you."

"The lovely lady with the...brown skin and chocolate hair? Yeah, I saw her, but she wouldn't give me a kiss so I..." He sways. "I moved on."

"*You* tried to kiss *Blake*?" I say.

"Don't give it much thought, Silent," Jax tells me. "He's so past drunk I doubt he remembers our names."

"Is this...what I looked like?"

"With you, it was scarier because I didn't know what to expect. This is typical Bast, but someone should take him to his room. Do you mind if I...?"

"I'll go with you."

"You don't have to. It's your party after all."

I shrug. "As if anybody knows or cares. It's just an excuse to get drunk and make out with people. I couldn't care less if we come back or not, but I'm going wherever you're going. Don't leave me alone."

"Never," he says. "Are you okay to walk on your own though? I have to focus on supporting him."

"Yeah, I got this."

He walks over to Bast and slips his arm around him. Bast falls against him immediately, eyelids half-closed, still swaying.

"Come on, big guy," Jax mutters, "let's get you to your room so you can sleep it off." And with that, he starts walking towards the exit, half-dragging Bast beside him.

When we reach Bast's room, I wait in the hall while Jax heaves an already-asleep Bast into bed.

A few minutes later, Jax comes back out and leans against the wall beside me.

"Will he be horribly hung-over tomorrow?" I ask.

"Not really," Jax replies, "he has a tolerance for the stuff, which only makes him drink more. He rarely has to endure the consequences."

I sigh. "I wish I could be so lucky."

He laughs. "You know I wouldn't let that happen, right?"

"Yeah, I know you'd take care of me."

"Forever and always," he replies.

I look over at him and smile.

He moves his arm closer to mine and our fingers brush together, instantly intertwining. He smiles at me. "So where were we when Bast so rudely interrupted us?"

I grin and step in front of him. "It looked something like this, if I recall correctly," I say, wrapping my hands around his waist and pulling him closer.

"Right," he replies and I can feel his heartbeat pick up through his shirt.

I smile wider. "Making you nervous, am I, Jax?"

"Not in the slightest," he breathes.

"Liar," I laugh. I kiss him quick on the forehead. "How about now?"

"No."

I run a slow hand through his hair. "Now?"

He shivers. "No."

My lips brush his ear. "What about now?" I whisper.

"Dammit, Silent," he says. Then he turns his head and catches my lips with his.

Our hearts beat wildly as we kiss with fervour, never wanting to be separated. I want to melt into him, to become one, to...

I pull back long enough to say, "Bast said something about getting a room..."

I hear his intake of breath and feel his heart as it stutters before picking up again. He looks down at me. "Are you sure?"

"I've never been more sure of anything in my life," I tell him.

Then, I let him see the desire in my eyes, how much I love him, even though I'm too afraid to say it.

His eyes sparkle with the same desire and he kisses me quick before saying, "Come on then."

He grabs my hand and together we race through the dark halls, as fast as my leg will allow. We skid around corners and laugh when we accidentally run into a wall. He takes me to a part of the base I've never been to before and we stop in front of a blue door.

"Where are we?" I ask as he pulls out a key and unlocks the door.

He smiles as he pushes it open. "Welcome to my humble abode."

His room is beautiful. A chest of drawers stands against one wall, a weapon rack hangs on another, but my eyes are inevitably drawn to his four-poster bed. His bed, in *his* room.

I'm standing in his room, alone, with him.

Suddenly, I'm nervous, but then he takes my arm and I look at him and it all falls away. He's beautiful and I want this more than anything. It's the first time I think the assassin might be gone.

I smile at him and it seems to be all the invitation he needs. He leads us over to the bed, but slowly, giving me time to change my mind if I want. This is why he's so amazing.

We reach the edge of the bed and he stops, wrapping his arms around me. "If... If you want to stop, just say the word. I would never force you into..."

"Jax," I breathe, "all I want is you." Then, I kiss him and push him lightly so we both fall back on the bed.

"Silent..." He warns.

"I trust you," I say and I do and it doesn't scare me.
Then he's kissing me and nothing else matters but him and this and us.

CHAPTER THIRTY-THREE

His hands run through my hair and my head spins.

I kiss him harder and reach for his shirt.

He doesn't flinch, just holds me tighter.

I help him out of it and my heart skips several beats as I separate from him long enough to stare at his muscled chest.

He kisses my forehead and I brush my fingers across his abs. The thin hairs on his chest stand on end at my touch and I run my hand across the goose bumps that arise.

Then I slide my hand around his bare back, feeling every muscle as I go.

"You're..." I start, but he presses a finger to my lips.

"No talking," he mumbles.

I close my eyes as he kisses me again, faster, stronger...

I forget what life was like before this, before him, before a love so amazing I don't know what to do with it. I just know I need more.

SILENT NIGHT

Then his fingers brush my stomach as he reaches for my shirt and starts to lift it up.

Only then do I snap to my senses.

I try to grab his arms, but it's too late; he's already seen a hint of black.

Before I can protest, he pulls my shirt off the rest of the way.

He doesn't look at my body—I mean, he does, but not the way a guy usually would—he just stares at the countless names inking my chest, back, and arms.

"What the hell, Silent?" He reads a couple of them, tracing his finger along the letters and I shiver.

I want to curl up in a little ball and die of shame.

"Are these..." he says. "Oh God, are these the names of the people you've killed?"

I hang my head down as I reply, "Every last one."

"God, Silent, there are so many."

I nod, tears running down my cheeks. "I ran out of room. The latest one had to go on my leg." I pull up my pant leg to reveal the name "Lincoln McColl" scrawled in black just above my ankle bone.

He's quiet a minute before he says, "Why?"

"Why?" I repeat. "Because I didn't want to kill any of them. I didn't *want* to be a killer, I hated it. I regretted everything I did, but I knew I could never take it back."

"If you hated it so much, why didn't you leave?"

I laugh sadly. "You don't just leave the Assassin's Guild, not unless you have a death wish. I couldn't refuse to kill, but I could remember the people whose lives I'd

380

ended. I could remember the horrible deeds I'd done. I could become the bearer of all that pain."

"I'm sorry," he whispers.

"For what? It's not your fault."

"I'm sorry you had to become a killer to survive, I'm sorry your life sucked."

I laugh again. "Thanks, I guess."

He wipes a tear off of my cheek. "You don't have to be ashamed. We all do what we must to survive."

I give him a small smile he returns.

"So this is why you always wear a long sleeve shirt," he says.

I nod. "I couldn't show any of the other assassins my true nature, and when I came here... Well, I didn't think you people would appreciate me walking around tattooed with some of your members' names."

I look at him, but he is still, his finger frozen on my shoulder.

"What is it?"

"This Molly," he says, his voice wavering. "What... What was her last name? The lettering is smudged."

I don't wonder at his voice or ask myself why he wants to know, I just answer immediately with, "Forrester. Her name was Molly Forrester."

His hand falls down into his lap and he closes his eyes in apparent pain.

"What's wrong?" I ask, alarmed. It doesn't occur to me that I will not want to know the answer.

He takes a deep breath and says, "She was my mother."

My heart shatters into a million pieces.

Forrester, Molly Forrester...

"Oh God," I whisper.

My thoughts race as I comb back through my memories to see how she died. Had it been quick and painless, or had I been ordered to make her suffer? I hope it is the former. I hope to give Jax some peace of mind, but what can I say to fix this?

I killed his mother.

Then the memories of that night come back to me. I had climbed through her bedroom window around three in the morning and slit her throat while she slept. Quick and nearly painless then.

I start to tell Jax that, but then I remember something else: the squeak of a floorboard behind me as I tried to escape back through the window. I turned, and there in the doorway stood a boy about my age.

"It was you," I breathe. "You saw me that night. Why didn't you say anything?"

He looks up at me. "I didn't report you because you looked so scared when you saw me. I told the Resistance agents the next day that I hadn't heard a thing."

It's the same reason I didn't tell the Charger about being seen. The boy, Jax, had looked terrified.

"The agents said it was Silent Night, but I didn't believe them. Silent Night would never get caught."

That was the first time I did. Lincoln McColl was the second.

"So...so you knew," I say.

"Knew what?"

EMMA COUETTE

"You knew it was me that killed your mother. They told you it was me. Why didn't you say anything when I first came here? Why..." I'm blinking back tears.

"Even the Resistance makes mistakes," he replies. "There was a chance they were wrong, so I tried to give you the benefit of the doubt, tried to be a good person."

"But you saw me that night."

"That was a long time ago, Silent. It was dark and your hair was longer back then. How was I supposed to match the face of a child to the woman I met last month? You think I wanted to believe it was you?" He pauses. "Maybe at first I did. That was why I was so cold, but then I got to know you, started falling for those blue eyes and that fiery personality and I... I kept praying it wasn't you, that you hadn't done it, but now..." He's crying and a single tear falls down my face.

"I'm so sorry," I whisper, though I know it is inadequate.

"Sorry doesn't cut it, Silent," he snaps. "You killed my mother!"

His tone stabs me. "Well, what else do you want me to say? I killed a lot of mothers, fathers too. What do you want me to do? I can't bring them back."

He doesn't say anything to that and we sit in silence.

Then he says, "I think you should go."

"With pleasure," I reply, standing up and stalking to the door.

"Take your shirt." He throws it at me.

I catch it and say, "Whatever."

I leave the room and storm down the halls, not bothering to put my shirt back on. What do I care if someone sees me now? They judge me for a second and I'll slit their throats.

When I finally get to my room, I slam the door behind me so hard, the walls shake. I grab a blanket off of my bed, crumple it into a ball, and scream into it. I was so stupid, so stupid to think our relationship was a good idea.

I throw the blanket at the wall, but it doesn't satisfy, so I throw a pair of boots instead. They leave gouges in their wake. Then I pick up the blanket and rip it in half; fabric flies everywhere, but it isn't enough, isn't nearly enough to numb the pain.

I go to the closet and grab one of the bottles of alcohol Bast asked me to hide for him a week ago. I pop the cork with a knife and take a long drink.

Not enough. Not enough.

I take another sip and then throw more things at the walls, counting the fresh dents as I go.

Three. Four... Seven. Eight. Nine...

I keep drinking as I tear through my room like a hurricane. When I finish the first bottle, I chuck it at the wall as well and reach for another. I wait for it to take me away from the pain.

Finally, the room starts to get hazy and I stumble as I walk.

A few more swigs and then the current bottle slips from my hand. It smashes on the floor, glass flying in all directions.

I make it a few more steps before I collapse.

What are you trying to forget? I ask myself before the darkness takes over.

I don't know, I reply.

Then I think I smile.

CHAPTER THIRTY-FOUR

"Well, I have to say, Night; this is low, even for you."

I groan, but don't look up. "What time is it?"

She answers with another question. "What did you do to your room, or more importantly, why?"

I shrug and grab for the shirt beside my hand. I hadn't managed to put it on last night after what happened. "I was angry," I reply, "and slightly drunk."

Blake raises an eyebrow. "You don't say?"

I pull on my shirt and stand up. The room sways a little, but I can take it.

"What happened, Night?" She sounds genuinely worried.

I sigh. "It's over between Jax and I. The Assassin's Guild always ruins everything." There is an edge to my voice and I want to throw something again.

Her eyes are wide. "What? Why?"

"We found out that I killed his mother."

Blake's expression goes from shock to sorrow.

I put my face in my hands. "God, I killed his mother. Why did it have to be his mother? Why did I think for a second that I could have a normal relationship with normal people without the Guild getting in my way?"

I kick the bed frame in my fury with my good leg and pain shoots through my foot, but I don't care. The one person I care enough about to want a future doesn't want me anymore.

I want to cry again, but I am done being weak.

I walk toward the door. "Let's go do something."

"Like what?"

"Anything. Anything to help forget the pain."

"How about breakfast to start," she suggests, "because I'm sure that hangover is going to hit you any minute now. How much did you drink?"

"I don't remember."

She shakes her head and says, "You're worse than Bast. Come on, let's get you fed." She grabs me by the elbow. I don't protest as she drags me out of the door and down the hall towards the cafeteria. I don't look back.

Sure enough, Blake is right. I've only just sat down when a wave of nausea crashes through me. I put a hand to my mouth and lean forward in my seat, my other hand clutching my stomach.

I will not puke in front of all of these people. I will not.

My head starts to pound and I groan, despite myself. Drinking had been a terrible idea and I know I won't do it again for a long time, if ever.

I take a few sips of water from the glass in front of me and grimace.

From his spot across the table, Bast says, "A little hungover, are we?"

How does he notice these things?

I shoot him a glare. "Wipe that smirk off your face, Bast, or I'll do it for you, with a switchblade."

He laughs. "Oooooo feisty!"

I don't reply. The nausea has pulled me under again. I start rocking slowly back and forth in my seat. My head feels like someone is beating it with a cinder block. I can still feel Bast watching me, Blake too.

"Man, you look awful, Night," he says, his voice concerned this time. He eyes my dishevelled hair and swollen, red eyes. "What happened?"

"None of your business," I snap.

He looks at Blake.

She holds up her hands. "Don't look at me. It's not my story to tell." She turns to me. "You should eat something."

I don't look up as I say, "I'm not hungry."

"It'll help."

"I don't want to eat!" I snap.

She flinches at my tone, but says nothing, striking up a conversation with Bast instead. I don't listen.

She is right. I should eat. It will get rid of the headache, but it isn't that pain I am worried about, it's everything else.

I am awakened from my brooding a few minutes later when Bast exclaims, "There he is, the man, the legend himself!"

I look up and follow his gaze, though I know who he is talking about. Ajax has entered the room. Fresh pain pierces my heart at the sight of him. He looks the same as he always does, so either he feels nothing at all after what happened or he is great at masking the pain. I don't want to know the answer.

"Jax!" Bast calls out to him.

I shift in my seat.

Blake shoots Bast a warning look he doesn't catch.

"Jax, over here!"

I have to leave before Jax hears, before he comes over to the table. I can't face him right now, not like this. Maybe not ever again.

I stand abruptly and sway a little on my feet as the blood rushes to my head. I almost vomit, but hold it back as I say, "I'll see you guys later." I turn my back on the table and begin stalking away.

"Night! Wait!" Bast calls after me. "Where are you going?"

I ignore him and walk faster. When I am safely outside the cafeteria walls, I begin to run. Fast as possible, I put as much distance between myself and Jax as I can. My headache and injured leg protest wildly.

I vomit in the garbage can as soon as I reach my room and then I finally allow myself to cry again.

I'm still lying on my bed forty minutes later, bemoaning my Guild-forsaken life. I need to do something to get my mind off of him. He who shall not be named. I need...

Guild, I need a good fight. I need to feel the blood and adrenaline rushing through my veins. I need the thrill of the hunt to take my mind far away, but I can't kill anybody in this moral-friendly place. I'll have to settle for a plain old sword drill or knife throwing.

Not entirely sure what I'm doing, I peel myself off of my bed and march out of the door, ignoring the nausea that's still trying to pull me under its sickening waves.

I go to a training room I've never been to before, not wanting to run the risk of *him* being there or anybody looking there for me. I stalk over to the weapons rack and grab a sword fit for a king. I give it a few experimental flourishes and grin wickedly. It should do nicely.

I dance through my usual sword drills, getting faster and more aggressive as I go. My feet pound against the floor, arm and sword flying everywhere at once.

It doesn't take long for my shin to start protesting. It throbs like a beating heart, but I ignore it.

Let the pain come. I am numb. I am ice. I couldn't care less.

But the sword isn't enough. It doesn't give me the rush I need. My thoughts are still circling around me, watching and waiting like vultures. I need to get rid of them before they swoop in for the kill.

I go back to the weapons rack and pick out a mean looking crossbow and its matching bolts. It takes me a few minutes to load the bow with my stupid leg brace and my anger is a living thing by the time I raise the weapon, facing the target on the far wall.

I fill the target with the image of Jax's face and fire.

390

Slam!

Direct hit.

Again.

Thump!

Again...

I pull the trigger in a steady rhythm until all the bolts are quivering in the target, Jax's 'face' riddled with holes.

His beautiful face...

Assassins below. It isn't enough, isn't nearly enough...

I throw the crossbow down in my rage and march to the rack for a belt of throwing knives. If they won't do it, nothing will, short of going on a killing spree, which I might have to resort to. Screw the Resistance and their peace. I need blood.

I grab a knife and fling it at the far wall. It thuds, point first, into the centre of the target beside the one full of crossbow bolts.

The other nine follow it in quick succession.

As I feared, there is no rush, no wave of adrenaline to drown out my emotions. I sink to the floor, burrowing my face against my knees. My breathing is ragged and my heart is shuddering, but my thoughts are still beating against my skull.

The pain is too much, the memories are too much. I have to get rid of them both before they destroy me, before all that is left is a lifeless husk.

A tear runs down my cheek and something inside me breaks, splintering in half like a tree struck by lightning.

I will not be weak again, I will not. I am done crying and I will not allow my emotions to turn me into a wreck.

I stand up and march out of the door, down the hall toward the Resistance's exit. I'm going out there into the city and I'm going to hunt and I don't care if I come back. One way or another, the pain will stop.

I speed up as I go, until I'm sprinting through the halls, skidding around corners. My leg pleads with me to stop, but I ignore it. Soon, all the pain will be gone.

I don't bother returning to my room to get more weapons. I enjoy a good challenge.

I'm almost to the exit, almost to freedom and fresh air and the glorious hunt when I round a corner and smash into someone. We both go sprawling and my head bangs against the floor. I don't pass out, but for a moment, I see stars.

Who in the Guild did I run into? What do they think they are doing? I will punish them dearly for their transgression.

I smile as I drag myself to my feet. It looks like I'm not going to have to leave the base to get the fight I'm looking for after all.

Across the hall from me, the other person is just getting to their feet. Groaning, they turn to face me. My smile widens, turning into a wicked grin.

Why, if it isn't Ms. Natalie Sophia Roseanne.

CHAPTER THIRTY-FIVE

"Hello, Roseanne," I purr. "What brings you here?"

She stares at me as she brushes herself off. "I could ask you the same thing, Assassin. I was just walking down the hall minding my own business when you barrelled into me. You should watch where you're going."

"And you should watch your tongue," I snap. "See, princess, you have just so happened to come across me at the exact wrong time."

"Oh, I heard," she says, smiling. "Ajax finally saw you for what you really are: a monster."

I flinch, unable to stop myself. "Yes, well," I reply, "these things do happen, but they woke me up. It reminded me that I *am* a monster and that I love it. I love the thrill of the hunt, the feeling of adrenaline and blood rushing through my veins, love watching my prey struggle futilely while I end their miserable existence. Unluckily for you, you've become my next victim."

Fear flashes in her eyes, cold and wonderful. She's not so confident now that the two of us are alone.

"You can't hurt me," she says, "and you certainly can't kill me. My father—"

"Screw your father," I snap. "I don't see him coming to save you. In fact, I don't see anyone. Face it, princess, no one cares about you. *You are alone.*"

"That's a lie!"

"Well, if it is, it's a damn good one."

She swallows. "What are you going to do to me?" It's amazing that she hasn't turned tail and ran yet.

"I don't know," I reply. "Not sure yet. Oh..."

This should hurt.

"What were your brothers' names again, princess?"

She goes white. "Leave them out of this!"

I ignore her and answer my own question. "Oh right: Luke, Jeremy, and Ashton. I remember them. Jeremy's the blond-ish one, right? He acted like everyone was beneath him too, but he bled just as easily as all of the others. Oh, don't worry, it was but a scratch—if you'd call a missing arm a scratch." I smile.

She puts her hands on her hips, but that doesn't stop them from shaking. "If you think you can hurt me by using my brothers, you're wrong. They left father and me. They're dead to me."

"That's the excuse everyone gives, but deep down, it bothers you that I'm the reason Jeremy's arm was amputated. It bothers you that I'm the one who put Luke's leg in a cast. It bothers you that the scar up the side of

394

EMMA COUETTE

Ashton's head was caused by my switchblade. Don't deny it, Roseanne. I know."

She looks like she's about to be sick. "You're a monster," she repeats, voice wavering.

"I am, thank you, and so are you, we're just different kinds. I cut people down with swords and you... Well, you cut people down with words and pretty lies."

"How dare you? I'll..."

"Tell daddy on me? Save it. You're just too weak to stand up for yourself."

"That's a lie."

"Oh, really? Why do you think he sends you on the easiest missions? Because you'd have been dead long ago if he didn't, that's why."

"You... You know nothing." Her face is full of pain and I love it.

"Don't I?"

"You're a heartless...bitch and...And I hope you burn in hell with all the other soulless monsters of this world. You don't deserve Ajax and I'm glad he saw sense before it was too late."

"As if he'd rather have you," I spit. "He thinks you're a nightmare."

She ignores my comment and continues on. "He fell for you and you tore him apart. You were toying with him all that time, waiting to kill him, just like you did his mother." Her face is red with her fury, but it nowhere near matches mine.

"Say that again, princess," I hiss through clenched teeth, "Say that again, bitch, I dare you!"

395

I see crimson and I hope to Guild she takes the bait. Regardless, she's done for.

"You tried to kill Ajax. You hated him. You never wanted him. It was all just a game!"

Yeah, well, the game's over now.

Before she can say another damning word, I lunge.

She shrieks like a banshee and turns to run.

Too late for that, princess.

I grab her around the waist and tackle her to the ground. She hits the floor hard. I hear her bones as they bang against it.

She rolls around so she's looking at me and reaches her fingers toward my face. I dodge and her fingernails claw the side of my throat instead.

Bitch! She'll pay dearly for that one.

I grab hold of her wrist and twist, feeling her bones move under my fingers.

She screams and goes limp enough for me to sit up and punch her in the face.

Let's see how she likes having ugly bruises marring her skin. Maybe next time, she'll learn to keep her mouth shut. If I let her live.

"G-get off me you lunatic!" she yells. It's a feeble attempt.

"Oh shut up!" I slam my fist into the side of her jaw again and she flinches, curling in on herself. "Fight back you useless little girl!"

She doesn't move.

I get to my feet and kick her in the ribs.

She moans.

"If you have even an ounce of courage in you, fight back!" I spit.

"L-leave me alone," she whimpers.

I shake my head in disgust. "You're a pathetic waste of space. Your father might thank me for ending your miserable existence."

She jumps at that and scrambles to all fours. She tries to drag herself away, but I walk over and step on her calf, just behind the knee. She freezes.

"Any last words?" I croon.

"You can't!" she gasps. "You won't."

"Won't I?" I take my foot off of her leg and walk around in front of her. Before she can make another move to escape, I grab her by the wrists and yank her to her feet. I wrench her left arm up behind her back as I hold her against me.

She whimpers.

I use my free hand to push my left sleeve up past my elbow. Then I switch hands, draw a long knife, and shove my left arm in front of her face, blade gleaming in the artificial light above us. My tattoos are beacons. "See these?" I whisper into her ear. "These are the names of all of the people I've killed. I can make room for you. My arms, back, and chest are full, but I still have plenty of leg left."

She shakes as I raise the knife to her throat and touch it against her perfect skin.

Then she's crying, tears streaming down her face and sliding across the blade before continuing down. "Please don't kill me," she gasps "Please... If you have an ounce of un-blackened soul left in you..."

"And what's in it for me, princess?" I ask her, pulling the knife away a hair. "What will you sacrifice for your life? I'm not going to spare you just because you asked nicely. You have been nothing but a nuisance since I met you."

She trembles and for a moment, I don't think she's going to answer. For a moment, I think I'm going to kill her, but then she says, "I'll stay away from you. I'll return to my original room. I promise, you...you'll never see me again."

Her body tenses, wondering if it will be enough.

It isn't, at least, it shouldn't be, but I am suddenly exhausted and I don't want to spend another moment with her.

I drag my knife quick against the skin of her throat, barely more than a whisper.

She hisses in pain and blood drops to the floor, but the cut is shallow.

"This is a warning," I tell her. "Next time I won't be so careful. If you renege on your promise, your death will not be so quick."

I shove her away from me, letting go of her arm and she staggers. She doesn't get far before I knock her legs out from underneath her again with one swipe of my good leg.

My sword is out before she hits the floor and I slam my pommel into her head before she can raise it again.

"Sweet dreams, princess," I mutter.

I leave her unconscious on the floor and head back to my room.

CHAPTER THIRTY-SIX

I slam the door shut and strip out of the ridiculous clothes I'm wearing. The real me wouldn't be caught dead in green. I tear through my closet for proper assassin attire and finally find what I am looking for.

It takes me a good five minutes to pull on the pants over the brace and I have half a mind to tear the thing off of my leg before I'm done.

Next comes black leather boots, the tallest I can find, and then my shirt. I choose a midnight black sleeveless piece with a zipper up the front. Let them see my arms; I'm not ashamed anymore.

There's only one more thing to do. I grab my best dagger and stand in front of the mirror. It's about time I cut my hair.

Ten minutes later, I'm ready. The old me slips back on effortlessly. It fits like a glove. Silent Night is back and she's better than ever. I don't know why I tried to change, why I thought it would be a good idea.

Why had I been so stupid? Why did I let another person have my heart, let them have the power to crush it?

It won't happen again; my heart is made of ice now. You can shatter it, but I won't feel a thing. Never again will I let emotions get in my way.

Oh, it feels glorious to be back.

Now, it's time to pay Jenson a visit. I can't wait to see the look on his face when he realizes what kind of monster is loose in his base.

• • •

I burst into the council room with a satisfying crash as the door slams against the inside wall, nearly coming off of its hinges. The men around the table jump and Jenson looks up sharply.

"Afternoon, gentlemen," I purr.

"Assassin," Jenson growls.

I draw my sword and point it at him. "That's Silent Night to you or so help me, I will slit your throat."

"Oho," Jenson says, smiling. "So the assassin is back is she? I was terribly afraid you were going soft."

"Yes, well, as it turns out, you can take the girl out of the Guild, but you can't take the Guild out of the girl."

"Very well put."

"Of course, but I shall cut to the chase." I slash my sword through the air and start walking towards his end of

400

the table. "I'm here about our mission, particularly a certain Stage Three."

"Go on, Assass— I mean, Silent Night."

I smile.

That's right, Jenson, you will obey me.

"There has been a little change of plans," I tell him.

"How so?"

"I've realized we need to try something a bit more...drastic, so to speak."

His eyes darken. "What exactly do you have in mind? Spit it out."

I reach out and touch my sword to his throat. "Shhhh... Patience, my dear Jenson. Patience."

He doesn't say another word, nor does he make a single move.

"At ease, my good man," I tell him and he relaxes, but only slightly. "I was thinking, for Stage Three to be most effective, we need to bomb a certain south end. What do you think?"

I look at him and he eyes the sword.

"Oh, right," I say, as if I forgot. "Terribly sorry." I pull the sword away. "Go on."

He rubs his chin before he speaks. "I think it is a s-splendid idea. When do you want to act?"

"Tonight, and tomorrow morning, while smoke and the screams of dying assassins still fill the air, we shall march."

"Tomorrow? The invasion was planned for two days from now."

"Yes, well, it has just been moved up."

He swallows and stares at me with wide eyes before hanging his head. "Very well, Silent Night, it shall be done."

"See to it that it is." I sheath my sword and head for the still-open door, pausing in the frame. I turn around. "Oh and Jenson?"

He looks up.

"Try not to bomb the tunnels we'll be using or we'll have even bigger problems, now won't we?"

I smile sweetly at him and whirl around, leaving the council room in a flourish of black. Then I head to the cafeteria, my high-heeled boots echoing up and down the halls.

• • •

All eyes turn to me as I enter the cafeteria. People stare at my tattoos and my outfit with wide eyes. Soon, the whispers start, but I could care less. Let them talk about me, they are insignificant.

I march up to the food counter and fill my tray. Then I head over to the table beside the one I used to share with my so-called friends. I can't wait to see the looks on their faces when they realize the monster I truly am.

Let Ajax come too. He can't hurt me anymore. I no longer care what he thinks. He had been a weakness, nothing more, and I rectified that. I care no more for him now than I care for a bug on the street. He is merely a boy, a tool I used to get where I am. A tool I will use again if I have to, but never in the same way. I won't fall into his trap, will never again fall prey to that deadly four letter word. Love.

Ugh. It makes me sick.

I don't have to wait long before my "friends" show up. Sebastian and Blake come first.

They stop by my table and Sebastian says, "What are you doing over here, Night? You do realize you're at the wrong table, right?" He grins at me and I smile wickedly.

"Oh, I'm well aware, Sebastian, but I don't intend to join the two of you at *your* table."

He looks at me with utter bewilderment and then, running a hand through his mop of hair, he says, "Listen, Blake told me what happened and I'm sorry, but I won't let it come between our friendship."

I shrug. "Whatever, what's done is done. What Ajax and I had, whatever it was, it wasn't real and I'm glad it was short-lived."

Blake gasps. "How can you say that?"

"Because it's the truth. Ajax was merely a distraction, one that led me astray, but I'm back on the right path now. I suppose I should thank him, though it was entirely his fault in the first place."

Blake looks at me like I've killed her best friend and I guess I have, in a way.

"What happened to you, Night?" she asks softly.

"I woke up," I snap. "Everything—friendship, changing my ways, Ajax—it was all just a horrible nightmare. Thankfully, I managed to find my way back to reality before it was too late."

"Don't say that, Night. It wasn't a nightmare. It was real. Please, don't leave us. This isn't you."

"Oh, yes it is. This is the real me. The person I paraded around in for months was a disguise, a crutch my wounded, betrayed heart could lean on, but I'm healed now and it's time to focus on what I really want: revenge."

She says nothing to that, only stares at me with her sad, pitiful eyes. Her caring heart will get her killed someday. Maybe I'll still be around to see it.

Ignoring their presence, I turn to eat, but then Sebastian's voice interrupts. "What's with all the ink?"

I flinch at first, but then smile, remembering something he asked me way back when. "You wanted to know how many people I've killed. That's only a small portion of them."

He and Blake both blanch.

I laugh. "Who knows, "friends," *your* mothers' names might be on there too. Still think I'm worth saving, Blake?"

She doesn't say a word at first, just shakes her head in disbelief. Then, "I don't care what horrible deeds you've done, Night. You'll always be worth saving because you are my friend. I don't care if it was a lie for you. For me, it was the truth. I won't stop fighting for you. I don't leave my friends alone in the dark. I promise you that."

"Then you're going to end up breaking that promise," I tell her, "because I'm doomed."

I stand up and walk away, leaving my food untouched. I don't have time to play knight in shining armour with the enemy. I have an assassin kingdom to overthrow.

• • •

I'm sitting on my bed later, sharpening my sword, when a knock comes at my door.

"Who is it?" I call out, daring it to be Blake or Sebastian.

"It's Trey, Night."

Lovely.

"What do you want?"

"Just to talk. Can I... Can I come in?"

I sigh and get up, stomping over to the door. I unlock it and swing it open. "There," I say, "talk."

Trey stares at me with grief written in her eyes.

So, she's heard the news, eh?

"If you're here to ask me what's wrong or to try to talk me out of who I am, save it," I tell her. "I don't want to hear it."

"That's not what I was going to say."

"Then what?"

"Jenson sent me for you." She looks pained.

"What's the old fool want now, more time? He's not going to get it."

"No, Night, they... They found Natalie. She was attacked and she says it was you. Unless you can prove otherwise, they're going to punish you."

I laugh. "Oh, they finally found her did they? How long did she lie on the floor, bloody and broken?"

"Night..." she warns.

405

"Save it, Trey. I won't try to prove it otherwise because I admit to doing it. I broke Roseanne's spirit, almost slit her throat, and enjoyed every second of it."

She gives me a grim look as the light in her eyes dims. She looks deadened, defeated. "So what Blake and Bast said is true. You've gone back to the assassin."

I shrug. "It was suicide to have ever changed."

"If that's the way you see it, but that's not the current issue. Are you going to come with me willingly or will I have to use force? I'd rather not, but I will."

"What do you think?" I ask.

I rush at her, but she's fast.

Her hands wrap around the back of my neck and something cold and metallic pricks my throat. My eyelids droop.

Somewhere, I can hear Trey crying.

"I'm sorry, Night; so sorry I failed you again. The first time by running and now by hiding, but I won't give up on you yet. Keep fighting."

CHAPTER THIRTY-SEVEN

I wake to a buzzing silence, one that presses in on me, one that strikes fear into my heart, but I soon shake that off. Silent Night is not afraid of anything. I open my eyes and it seems that someone is trying incredibly hard to prove me wrong.

I'm sitting in a vast circular room, my hands tied to the arms of the wooden chair they've propped me up in. At least forty pairs of eyes are watching me. I try not to crumble under their unforgiving gazes. I recognize the two men at the front: Jenson, and Nicholas Ross.

Then it comes back to me. I'm here because of what I did to Natalie. They want to punish me for breaking the poor princess' spirit, and nearly slitting her throat.

They can try, but I've been trained to withstand torture.

"Ah, Assassin," Jenson drawls, taking great pleasure in calling me that now that I'm tied up and can't kill him for it. For the moment, at least. "Good of you to finally join us."

"Was the drugging necessary, Jenson?" I ask him.

"Ah, ah, ah," he says, "*I* will do the talking."

Oh, I do believe someone just secured themselves a spot on the top of my kill list, after the Charger, of course.

"So you thought you could get away with violence in my base, did you?" he asks me. There is a fire in his eyes I have not seen before.

"Excuse me?"

"Don't act like you don't know what I'm talking about, Assassin. Trey says you admitted to assaulting Natalie, there's no use trying to deny it now."

"Oh, that..." I mutter.

"Yes, that. What do you have to say for yourself, Assassin?"

"Nothing, except that the little bitch deserved it."

Ross stands up and yells at me. "Take that back, you insufferable monster!"

I smile at him. "Not a chance, your majesty."

Jenson gives the both of us a look and tells Ross to stand down.

Point: Silent Night.

"Fine," Jenson says, "you don't regret it and it wasn't an accident. We can take that. In fact, I might actually get to enjoy this now."

He wants me to suffer for what I've done. I can see that desire in his eyes, but I can also see a hint of sorrow, though not for me.

"So, what exactly is the punishment here for assaulting someone?" I ask. "You know, at the Guild, I would've been rewarded for teaching the brat a lesson. At the Guild, I probably would've finished the job instead of toying with her. I could've done *so* much worse."

"Which does nothing to excuse your behaviour. At the *Resistance,* we don't condone such violence, we protect those under our watch or we die trying." That sorrow surfaces again, but he seals it away with a scowl. "You're in my base, Assassin, so you play by my rules or you can go."

"So you're saying I don't get to plead my case?"

"No, you have done enough damage already," he snaps.

"Am I to be executed for my crimes or will your soft hearts take the easy way out and simply imprison me?"

His fire seems to flicker when I mention execution.

I knew he wouldn't have the guts.

"Did you know that was my job at the Guild, to bring traitors to their executions? I dragged Rachel to her death, after I caught her talking with Avery, and then my fellow assassins tore her apart piece by piece. Is that what you'll do to me? I'll warn you, I won't go down without a fight."

I grin, showing my teeth and Jenson doesn't say anything. The room is hushed at my confession, horrified by the Guild, horrified by me.

"Oh, don't spare me now, Jenson," I spit. "Don't give me sympathy. I did what I had to do and so will you, but you better decide soon. I'm not a patient person."

"You're playing with fire," Jenson says finally, face unreadable.

"No, I'm simply deciding my own fate," and with that, I stand up, receiving gasps of shock from those gathered.

While they had been distracted by my attitude and threats, I had been focused on removing my bonds. My wrists are chafed and bleeding now, but it's worth it.

"So, while I'd love to stay and watch you all hem and haw, Jenson," I go on, "there are places I need to be." I grin. "See you around."

I run for the door, hearing Jenson's yells behind me as he comes to his senses. "Somebody stop her!"

Catch me if you can.

I hang a left out the door and break into a sprint. Then I wind my way through the halls, going this way and that, until any pursuer would be hopelessly lost. I know I've succeeded when the only footsteps I hear echoing are my own.

I slow to a walk. No need to run now and raise suspicion; though I'm sure my black attire is a dead giveaway of who I am, I don't need to add anything else to the list. I'm in enough trouble as it is. I have no idea what kind of punishment Jenson and Ross have in mind, but I'm not going to wait around and find out.

Ten minutes after fleeing the trial room—as I decide to call it—I reach room 2413 again. It's time to pack up and head out.

I tear through my closet, pulling out random items of clothing and shoving them into my rucksack that's lain in the corner since my arrival. Then I suit up. I grab my two swords, throwing knives, daggers, and then my guns. Thankfully, all of my weapons were recovered from the train battlefield.

I toss a case of spare bullets into my sack.

That should do it.

Goodbye, room 2413, I hope we don't meet again.

I head out the door and come face to face with Blake and Ajax.

"What do you want?" I growl.

"We..." Blake starts. "We wanted to talk."

"Well, I don't want to so..."

I try to walk past them, but Ajax pushes me back towards the door. "Shut up and listen for once, would you?"

The nerve.

"You watch it, Forrester," I spit, "or I'll slit your throat like I did your mother."

My words elicit the exact reaction I was going for.

"Shut up, Assassin!" he snarls.

I laugh. "You hate me so fully now, don't you? Funny, just yesterday, you were telling me how much you loved me. Tell me, Ajax, was it a lie then?"

His face softens a bit. "No, of course it wasn't a lie, but you're not the person I fell in love with, not anymore. Besides, this...this isn't about what happened to us. You've slipped back into your old ways and we... It hurts to look at you." I can see the pain in his eyes and I relish it.

Serves him right.

"We..." he goes on. "We just came back from seeing Natalie. Why did you do that to her?"

"Why?" I scoff. "Because she's a heartless bitch that needed to be taught a lesson."

"And you're a heartless assassin," he retorts. "God, Silent, what happened to you? I don't even know who you are anymore."

"And maybe that's exactly how I want it."

"You..." he starts, but Blake cuts him off.

"Leave her alone, Jax," she says. "You're not helping."

"Not helping... Look at her, Blake." He throws his arm out towards me. "She's beyond help."

Blake puts her hands on her hips as she faces him. "Yeah, and you want to know whose fault that is? Ours. We call ourselves her friends and yet we weren't there when she needed us the most. We left her alone to cope and she did what she does best. She rebuilt her walls. She returned to the version of herself that can't be hurt by anything. It's our fault she's like this. We failed her in every way that matters."

"How can you side with her?" Ajax snaps. "You saw what she did to Natalie!"

"You know Natalie, Jax. I'm sure she isn't entirely innocent."

"It doesn't matter, Blake. No one deserves to be treated like that, no one."

I decide to step in. "I'm sorry you don't approve of my choices," I say, "but this is who I am—take it or leave it. Judging from the look on your face, you're going to leave it, and guess what, Ajax? I don't care. I gave it a try, but I'm done caring now. It's pointless and stupid and everyone gets hurt in the end because we're all going to die eventually.

"So goodbye. It was nice knowing you, but I'll be going now. I'd say I'll see you in the afterlife, but, well, you're all going to heaven and we all know I'm headed in the opposite direction."

Blake steps forward, tears in her eyes. "No, don't say that, Night."

"Why? You see these names on my arms; I'm a monster. You think they're going to let me through the pearly gates? I'll tarnish the air just by breathing. You guys enjoy it though; I hear it's nice up there."

And with that, I turn and walk away.

CHAPTER THIRTY-EIGHT

It doesn't take me long to reach the exit, meeting no resistance on my way. I slip past the guards at the door and into the night, sighing as the cool breeze hits my face. I missed this, the great outdoors, roaming the streets at all hours of the night. I missed the freedom.

I run through the city, past office buildings and sleeping houses. Everything is dark, save for the homeless fires that pop up here and there. I have no idea where I'm going, but that doesn't matter. I just need to be gone. I need to put as much distance between me and the Warehouse as I can without stepping foot into assassin territory. I need to feel the wind fly through my hair.

There is nothing better than this: this feeling of complete liberation.

I run until my leg starts to protest. Then I slow to a walk and look for a place to rest.

Eventually, I come to a familiar red brick house. It doesn't surprise me that my feet brought me here. This is where it all began. It makes sense that this is where it should end.

I sigh and walk up Lincoln McColl's front steps.

The front door is unlocked, so I step right in, closing it quietly behind me. The house is cold and dead, silent as a tomb.

I can't believe it's been months since I was last here, that it's been months since the Charger's betrayal, since everything I knew was turned upside down. It's been months since my life changed forever, but it will soon be over. Tomorrow, the Resistance will attack the Guild, and I will enact my revenge. The Charger will die for his crimes and I will rise up as the new Master Assassin, defied by no one, ruler of all. Someday, the Resistance will bow before me too.

I stand in the cluttered kitchen a minute more before heading up the stairs. Unconsciously, I skip the fifth step, some part of me remembering that it creaks.

At the top of the stairs, I stop for a moment. I'm unsure of where I'm going exactly, but some part of me knows.

I open the door to the storage room and peer inside. It's empty—of humans at least. The Resistance removed Lincoln's body long ago, yet all of the boxes are still here. I step inside and rifle through a couple of them, not the same ones as before.

The first box I open is full of pens, blank paper, and shredded documents. Nothing is readable. The second box holds something much more promising: an old faded yellow photo album. I open it up to the first page and almost faint when I see the picture, when I see my mom's blue eyes staring back at me.

For a moment, I'm frozen, suspended in time, trapped in the memories of days gone by. My mother... She looks exactly like I remember her: long wavy brown hair frames her honey-coloured skin and her sparkling blue eyes smile back at me.

Mom...

A single tear escapes my eyes, splattering against the laminated page.

Oh Guild, how I miss her.

Then time crashes forward again and I'm hit by an enormous question. Why the hell did Lincoln McColl have a picture of my mother?

I turn the page to find another photo, masterfully preserved by the lens. I flip again and again...

Soon the pages are flying through my fingers as countless pictures of my mother turn into blurs before my eyes.

Mother as an adult, a child, a teenager...

Wait.

Mother as a teenager, her arm around a teenage boy with matching hair and eyes, and a face I recognize from the picture on the mantel downstairs. Lincoln.

Were they...involved?

I pull the photo out of its sleeve, nearly ripping it in my haste, and turn it over. In the bottom left hand corner, a note is written in a neat, curly script.

I read it once. Twice.

Assassins below.

It's not hard to understand, I just don't want to believe it.

Ismae and Jean Ballinger, 16.

Lincoln and my mother had been siblings—twins.

I killed my uncle.

Lincoln's final words come back to me.

What happened to that cute little girl who used to help her mother plant tulips in the front garden?

He knew.

He knew because he was there. He probably planted some of them with us. He sacrificed himself so I could learn the truth...

Tears stream down my face.

I... I have to go.

I get up and leave the room, but I don't make it far.

I head into the spare room, the room I scoffed at when I first came here.

I suppose this is the room Lincoln would have offered to his "niece." Too bad she isn't real. My own voice echoes in my head.

Oh, she's real all right. She is far too real.

I collapse on the bed and pull my weapons off. One by one, they clatter to the floor. Then I lay back and close my eyes, waiting for sleep to take me away from the horror of reality, the horror of what I've done.

Memory and regret tug at my heart until sleep drags me under. It is a welcome relief.

• • •

Colours swirl together and separate again. Dust motes decorate the air, floating in the sunlight streaming through my open curtains. I recognize the faded flower pattern.

Am I...?

I sit up in the bed, a bed that's far too small, and look around.

I am.

I'm in my childhood room. Everything is covered in a layer of dust and colours are muted, as if asleep, as if...empty. It would be haunting if not for the sunlight, but it reminds me of a tragic morning. It's the same scene, but different. I'm not five years old anymore.

I get to my feet.

As I walk to the door, I realize my feet don't leave footprints in the dust.

I exit the room and a door that always creaked doesn't make a sound.

The floorboards don't squeak beneath my tired feet as I take the familiar route to my mother's room, down a hall I've trodden countless times in my nightmares.

It's too early to tell if this is yet another one.

The silence around me is not unnerving though. It's almost...soothing.

I reach my mother's door and I don't hesitate. I push it open quick and avert my gaze for a moment, afraid of what I might see.

"Honey? Why aren't you asleep?"

Tears stream down my face as I look up at my mother, sitting on the edge of her bed with a frown on her face.

The pillows are intact, crisp and white.

Sunbeams dance all around her.

"What's wrong?" she asks me.

I wipe my eyes. "Nothing," I whisper. "Nothing at all. Not anymore."

She stands and almost floats as she walks over to me.

"You're such a beautiful young lady," she says, brushing the hair out of my face, "but this blue does not become you." She tugs at the blue strands, almost faded down to nothing now.

"I'm proud of you, my girl," she whispers.

"You are?" I ask.

"I am."

"Even after everything I've done? Mama, I'm not the innocent girl I once was. I don't deserve your pride; how could I have possibly earned it?"

She smiles. "And yet, I see the shame in your eyes, the guilt. You do not pride yourself on the horrors you have committed, and that is why I can be proud of you. Look how far you've come, my girl. You are not the child I remember, but neither are you the woman you were a couple of months ago. You've survived, you've grown, and you have not been defeated."

My tears fall faster. "But what if I slip again?"

"You will get back up," she says. "You always do. You are strong, my flower, so strong. Never underestimate that."

She takes a step back and I reach out to take her arm, but it passes right through her and for a moment I see the windows instead of her face.

"No. Don't go," I gasp.

"I am already gone," she whispers. "You don't need me anymore. It's okay to let me go."

A butterfly flits across the room and lands on my arm.

I blink at it once before turning my gaze back to the half-faded presence of my mother.

"You are strong," she says. "You will do the right thing," she nods at the butterfly, "but it's not up to me to judge. It's up to you."

She smiles and then fades away completely. The curtains sway in her absence and the butterfly follows the pull of the breeze, out the open window.

"I love you mom," I whisper to the empty room. "I will do the right thing."

Then the room fades too.

CHAPTER THIRTY-NINE

I am awakened by a great booming sound and the shaking of the bed. I sit up and reach for my sword, only to come up empty.

Where…?

Then I recognize the grey walls and remember where I am. I'm in Lincoln's house, in his guest bedroom. Lincoln, who is actually Jean, Jean who is my uncle. I remember last night, remember dumping all my blades on the floor before collapsing into the bed.

Another boom sounds and I almost fall off the bed. It takes a few more minutes and a couple more near falls to realize what the sound is. The Resistance is bombing the south end, just like they said they would.

Huh.

I guess they decided to go through with the plan I fashioned for them, even though they think I've turned on them. Well, they won't have to worry about that.

I realized something last night, something I've been hiding for a long time. Everything I've done in my life has been for survival. Silent Night was a disguise I threw over myself to keep me safe when I entered the Guild, but it wasn't who I was. It isn't who I am. For a long time, I fell prey to that disguise; I lost myself in it. My time at the Resistance hadn't been a nightmare, it had been a glorious reality, but the assassin in me tried to drag me back under.

No more.

The assassin was a survival tactic, but I no longer need it. I can survive just fine on my own, the way I am. The Resistance taught me that.

I stand up and start picking my weapons up off of the floor. I rearm myself as I come to terms with my decision. The heavier I get with weapons, the lighter the burden on my heart feels. This is right, I know it is.

My time at the Resistance was happy. I laughed, loved, and did things I haven't done since my mother died. I returned to the old me and she isn't weak. No, the old me is strong, an ever-burning light within my heart all these years. Against all odds, she survived and the assassin can never fully extinguish her spark. I coax those flames now and smile.

I look to the bed for a second, silently thanking Lincoln—I mean Jean—for everything. That's when I realize something. I never took the pillows off the bed last night before I slept. It's a miracle. I haven't slept with a pillow since... Well, since my mother died, what, thirteen years ago?

Wow. Has it really been that long?

422

I look at the pillows, and for the first time in thirteen years, I don't see my mother lying there, blood spattered across the pillowcase. I've finally managed to let her go, and my fear went along with her.

"I love you, mom," I whisper to the empty room. "I love you and I miss you and it all ends today. Either I kill the Charger or I join you in whatever comes after. I hope... I hope I can be forgiven for all I've done."

Another boom sounds like a rumble of thunder and the house shakes. I head downstairs, grabbing the banister to keep from falling. I pause in the doorway, taking one last look around, before I step out onto the porch and close the door behind me.

"Goodbye, mom," I whisper. "Goodbye, Uncle Jean."

I wonder for a second if I have the right to call him that, but somehow it feels right. I still can't believe he was my uncle, hiding in plain sight all this time.

What if I opened the box with the album the first time I visited his house? Would I still be where I am today or would everything be different?

I look down the street. Dawn will be here soon. It's time to move. Hopefully Jenson's forces are already on their way to the tunnels. I need to join them.

I leave my uncle's house and start walking, toward the Guild and hopefully toward a better future.

• • •

The sun has just risen when I come upon the old barn leaning in the field. It seems like forever ago that I followed Rachel here. I wonder if I'll meet the same fate, torn apart by the people I once considered allies.

I won't let it come to that, I'll kill myself first.

My fingers hover over the spot on my abdomen where Rachel's name is etched into my skin.

"I'm sorry," I whisper.

I can't take back what I've done, the people I've killed, the lives I've destroyed, but I can become something better and never perform those despicable deeds again. I will change, will leave Silent Night far behind, but first, I must become her one last time.

Silently, I approach the barn, wary of enemy forces within, though logic says it should be empty. Rachel died two months ago, her tunnels should be forgotten.

I creep up to the door and listen. Hearing nothing, I push it open an inch and peer inside. A yawning darkness beckons me and I take an involuntary step back.

It's okay, I tell myself. *The darkness will not claim you again.*

Resolved, I push the door open the rest of the way and step inside, leaving it ajar. My eyes soon adjust to the lack of light, my time in the Resistance not hindering my basic skills. I locate the trapdoor easily and enter the tunnels beneath.

An earth-shattering boom interrupts the silence of the morning once again and soil rains down on me from the ceiling above. I close my eyes and keep walking, hoping none of Jenson's bombs land on this tunnel, trapping me forever.

Twelve minutes later, after navigating through the treacherous pitfalls and traps of this particular tunnel, I turn a corner and find myself in the section lit with bulbs every few feet.

Almost there.

I walk to the end of the tunnel and climb up the ladder to the Guild above. Easing the trapdoor open, I watch and listen.

No one passes by the tunnel entrance and I hear no footsteps on the stairs above, though I can make out the sounds of a distant battle. I guess the fighting has already begun.

Well, I'm of no use here. Let's get moving. I have a certain Master Assassin to take out and it will not be easy.

Quiet as...well, as me, I exit the tunnel and crouch under the stairs. I stop and listen again before creeping out and making my way up. I pause at every landing, slowly making my way into the Guild proper.

I duck into a doorway as I enter the first hall and reassess the situation. The sounds of fighting are louder now, closer, but I still appear to be alone. I say appear because I'm in the assassin palace where things are never how they seem.

When I'm as sure as I can be that I'm safe, I step out of my hiding spot and continue down the hall. I stay close to the wall so I can hide if someone comes.

The fighting gets louder the further I go on—the closer I get to the centre. Most of the fighting will be down in the Grand Cavern and the halls surrounding it. I need to get to the Charger's office, where I know he'll be waiting, leaving the fighting to his agents and letting them die for him.

Selfish bastard, destroyer of lives.

It is *his* turn to feel the sting of betrayal and loss and pain, before he feels nothing ever again. I will end him, but first he will suffer retribution for the hundreds of souls he ended through torment. I am going to his office, but first I will have to get past the Grand Cavern and past the fighting. It isn't going to be easy.

True to my word, I meet my first enemy agent in the next hall I turn down.

At first the assassin, a younger one, looks at me in relief thinking I am an ally. Then I draw my gun and point it at his face.

He raises his arms in surrender, fear jumping in his eyes like a scalded cat. "Hey now," he says, "we're on the same side."

I laugh. "No, we're not."

"Please..." he says.

My finger brushes the trigger.

Wait. What are you doing? I ask myself. He's surrendering.

Kill him. He deserves to die for showing such weakness as to beg for his life. My old voice echoes in my skull. Kill him.

He's innocent, I tell myself.

He's weak.

Yeah, well, I'm strong, stronger than the darkness.

426

My hand shakes, but I lower the gun.

"Go," I tell the boy. "Leave the Guild and don't come back."

"I... What?"

"You heard me." I raise my voice. "Go! Get out of here before I change my mind, and if you breathe a word to anyone...you'll be sorry."

With one last glance at me, he turns and scampers away like a scared rabbit.

I keep going.

Soon, I start walking over dead bodies, through halls spattered in blood, Resistance agents and assassins alike having left nothing but carnage in their wake. I don't look down at the faces, afraid to see someone I know. My stomach flips at the thought of seeing Blake, Bast, or Ajax lying there unmoving, glassy eyes staring up at the ceiling, lost to me forever. I never even said a proper goodbye.

I shudder and then freeze as I hear the scrape of a sword being drawn behind me.

"Turn around, little lady," a rough voice orders.

I obey and come face to face with a line of six male assassins, all of them armed to the teeth. I recognize one face in the crowd, the boy I spared not five minutes ago.

Bastard.

Well, his life is forfeit now. I will not spare him a second time, not after he led all of these men here to kill me.

"What do we have here?" the tallest one says and I know from his voice that he's the man who first spoke. "A pretty little lady. All alone. You lost, girl?"

"Not in the slightest," I purr, smiling.

"Is that so? Tell me, how did you find this place? You one of them resistors?"

"Not in the slightest," I repeat, seeing frustration flare in the man's eyes. "I'm one of you."

"You? An assassin?" He laughs and his men join in.

I stare them all down with cold, dead eyes and their laughter cuts out.

They stay silent and I say, "Now, boys, shall we do this the hard way or the easy way? I'll give you one chance to get lost."

The men don't hesitate for a second. They draw their weapons and sink into ready stances.

I sigh. "Have it your way then," I reply.

I shoot two of them in the head before they even know what's happening. Then I trade my gun for my sword, wanting to get a little more personal with the remaining men. They recover quickly, realizing I'm not going to be an easy target, and take up the defensive.

They could surround me easily, but they hesitate, standing back as they study me for weaknesses.

Well, I don't have all day.

I lunge into their midst, slashing and swiping, forcing them to fight back, reminding them with every stroke of my sword that they chose this. The boy could've walked away, but he didn't.

428

I pivot, fending off a sudden fiery attack from one of them, leaving my right side open for a second.

I regret it as soon as one of their swords slams into my shin.

I go to scream until I realize that it didn't puncture me. I look down and laugh despite everything. The poor fool's sword is stuck in the brace. Guess the stupid thing is good for something.

Shaking off the blade, I run the man through with my sword.

Three down. Three to go.

The remaining men surround me, circling slowly.

I smile at them, daring them to come closer.

Finally, the boy rushes me.

I snap my good foot against his knee while my sword parries the blow aimed at my back from the man behind me.

The boy collapses to the floor, screaming, and I turn my attention to the two men left standing, drawing a second sword.

My dual blades flash, zipping this way and that, blocking, thrusting, parrying, slashing...

I miss a beat and cold steel burns against my arm, tearing through my sleeve.

I hiss, but don't let the injury slow me down, not when my leg is pulsing beneath me, urging me to sit down, to take a minute. The stinging in my arm is a mere inconvenience.

My retaliation is swift and brutal. Blood splashes on the floor and two more bodies join the other three.

I rip some cloth from one of their shirts to tie around my arm. It's only fair. I kneel down beside the boy as I cinch it tight. He's gasping for breath, fighting to stay conscious against the pain.

"Who...are you?" he manages to get out.

"I have many names," I tell him, "but you would know me as Silent Night."

His eyes go wide for a second before I put him out of his misery, sword burying itself in his heart.

I resist the urge to scream.

Wiping my swords off on my coat, I continue on.

CHAPTER FORTY

I'm nearly to the Charger's office when I realize I'm being followed. I've run into many assassin parties since the first, killing them all and sustaining nothing but the occasional scratch or bruise. I'm just a few halls away from my goal when I realize something isn't right.

Everything has gone silent, way too silent, and I haven't seen anybody in a long time. This close to the Master Assassin, I suspect some kind of guard.

My suspicions are confirmed when the hairs on the back of my neck stand up and a chill runs down my spine.

I am not alone.

Still walking, I turn my head slightly, barely catching a black form as it darts behind a pillar.

How long have they been following me? *How* have they been following me?

I stalk people, not the other way around.

Who has the capability to...?

And suddenly I know.

Agent One.

I really should've killed him before I left the Guild.

I stop and turn around. "Show yourself, Assassin," I say. "I know you're out there."

I hear a deep, bone-chilling chuckle and a man steps out from behind a pillar, not the same one I watched him disappear behind just moments ago.

His spiked blond hair is flecked with blood and so is his black leather jacket. He puts his hands in the pockets of his ripped jeans as his eyes study me, dancing with glee.

"It's great to be noticed finally," he says. "You're losing your touch, Silent Night."

I roll my eyes. "Hello, Hai," I reply.

He smiles. "So you know who I am. Excellent."

"What do you want?"

"Well, ever since you disappeared, someone had to do your job. I became the one to sniff out the traitors and I tell you, you reek of treachery."

"Is that so? Maybe that's because *I'm* the one who was betrayed."

He laughs. "And how is that?"

"I found a document, a record of all our kills. We're not just killing Resistance members, Hai, we're killing innocent civilians and that's not the worst..." I trail off as Hai laughs again, longer and harder than before.

"Of course we kill innocent civilians," he says. "We're assassins. The innocent ones are more fun, snuffing out their bright lights. It makes the blood rush, don't you think?"

I feel sick. I guess I wasn't the only monster.

as.

"As I was saying," I go on, "that wasn't the worst part. The Charger killed my mother."

He smiles. "Aw... Poor Silent Night thought the Resistance killed her mommy. How do you think we get our Guild Wards?"

I try to keep my stomach inside me. "So you knew," I choke out.

"Of course I knew," he scoffs. He starts to circle me. "He killed my mother too, but I suppose the old man neglected to tell you. I wonder why? But then again, there are lots of things he's neglected to tell you."

"Like what?"

"Oh, it's not mine to tell. Don't want to risk his wrath."

My temper is dangerously close to snapping so I decide to throw a wrench in his plans. "Well, did you know he wanted to kill *you*?"

He freezes and I smile.

Checkmate.

"Who?" he asks.

"Oh, you know who," I reply. "The Charger. Your beloved master."

His eyes go dark. "When? Why? Tell me!"

I cross my arms. "Anger issues much? It was the day before I left. He called me into his office and we had a cryptic yet interesting conversation. He didn't tell me straightforward to kill you, but he mentioned how you were the only one standing in my way and that he wouldn't be upset if you were found dead the next morning."

Hai's face is red. "Bastard! Why would he want me dead? I am his favourite!"

I snort. "Hardly. He said he had grown tired of you and that you don't have what it takes. Not so sure of yourself now, are you?"

"You... You bitch," he spits. "You don't deserve to be Agent One. You don't deserve anything, not the way you've been taking everything from me all this time."

"Me? I haven't stolen anything."

"Oh, you are so oblivious. I never understood why he would want to give you..." He stops himself. "But again, it's not my story to tell. Unlike you, I will stay loyal until the end. I won't betray my people. I'm not stupid, Silent Night. I know it was you who led the Resistance here and for that, you shall die."

He draws his sword and I draw my two.

"Is that so?" I ask him. "Well then, we'd better get on with it. I have places to be, Master Assassins to kill." I grin, sinking into a crouch.

"Traitor," he spits out. "The Charger would give you everything and you're going to throw it all away because he killed your mother?"

"Yes," I say, "and that's the difference between me and you. I still have a heart."

"Then you'll bleed just like anyone else," he says, and then he lunges.

I block his thrust with one blade and push back, sending him staggering.

He laughs. "You know, you're strong for your age."

434

"I'm young. You're old and decidedly more breakable."

I go for him this time, sending one blade arcing toward his head, the other to his feet.

He blocks the one blow and jumps over the second.

My blade comes back and he sidesteps it, slashing at my face.

I dodge and stab.

He parries it with ease.

Faster and faster we dance.

Block, parry, and jab.

Slash, stab, and dodge.

Our feet and swords are mere blurs across the floor and through the air. Never before have I fought like this, never have I been so challenged.

My fractured leg is starting to feel it.

No. Dammit. I don't feel anything. Just another brawl. Keep going.

Then I hear a thump as his sword meets my brace.

Shit.

"What in the hell is this?" he yells out, trying to free his sword from the brace. "What is this bloody contraption?" He pauses and then, "Oh."

I see him smile before he slams his foot into my shin.

I let out a shriek like the sound of breaking glass as something shifts in my leg and I go flying. The force of the blow throws me into a pillar and I collapse at its foot, unbidden tears streaming down my cheeks.

His dark chuckle fills the hall. "Oh, Silent Night, how's that broken leg feeling? Better now?" He cocks his head. "No?"

His laughter takes him for a minute.

"You know better than to fight someone openly when you have such a weakness they can exploit," he chides me. "I doubt you can walk now, but you know what that's like, breaking someone's leg. It's almost your signature move."

I shudder and say, "No."

"Don't agree? Well, that's okay, I know people who do." He paces back and forth in front of me. "Take Anane for example. Pour bastard hasn't been walking properly since the incident on the iron bridge, after you led him out there, hoping he'd slip and fall to his death."

I raise my head. "Do you blame me for that?"

"No, but he does. He would've become the new Agent Three if it weren't for that leg. He didn't take too kindly to being demoted to Sixth.

I wince. "Ouch."

"Yeah, and you're not too terribly sorry, are you?"

"No. Anane was and still is an idiot. He can fall off a bridge and break his leg anytime."

"Says the girl who's about to die."

It's my turn to laugh. "Maybe soon, Hai, but not by your hand. You know, you shouldn't give your victims time to chat and distract you."

His eyes go wide, but I'm already pulling the trigger of my gun.

His whole body jumps and he claws at his chest as he collapses, slamming against the concrete and convulsing in pain.

Oh, the throes of death.

I take my time getting up. He won't be coming after me dead and I don't want to screw my leg up even more. What was it the nurse said about vigorous movement? Well, it doesn't matter now. I have to keep going, though a part of me wants to make sure Hai is dead first.

I limp over to where I dropped my swords and sheath them, just as footsteps come up to the hall. I look up to see another line of assassins facing me.

Guess I'll just have to hope he's truly dead.

Shots ring out and I turn and run, pulling out my gun and aiming it behind me, my finger a constant motion on the trigger.

I round a corner and once safe, I put my gun back and break into a sprint, or as much of a sprint as I can manage with my leg. Every motion sends a searing line of fire through my nerves and I can feel something wet and sticky under the brace, but I ignore it and keep going.

• • •

Only when I finally enter the dark hall that leads to the Charger's office do I stop. The usual guards aren't standing at attention in front of the doors. In fact, the hall is empty and eerily quiet, but I know he is there, in the office, waiting for me.

I take a deep breath and open the door, slipping silently inside.

The chair behind the Charger's desk is empty.

My eyes scan the room, terrified, but it only takes a moment to deduce that he isn't hiding in a dark corner. I am alone, but at the same time, I am not. I can feel him, a dark presence not too far away, but where?

There has to be something...

I search the room, the walls and floor, finding nothing until I trip over something in the dark.

I land on the floor with a bang, barely containing my cries of agony.

That damned leg...

What in the Guild did I trip over?

I crawl across the carpet, feeling for anything out of place. I touch something cold and my fingers close around a metal rod.

A lever?

I brace myself and pull. The floor begins to shake.

Then, as suddenly as it began, it stops and I get to my feet, noticeably leaning on my good leg. I turn toward the desk and behold a doorway standing ominously behind it, nothing but black beyond its arch. A shudder runs through me and I know this is it. The Charger waits beyond the door.

Refusing to fear, I walk through the door. I can tell I'm in a bigger chamber from the way the air changes. I keep walking, slowly, until my foot bumps into something, something short and long.

It's a step. I don't wonder how far the staircase goes. I just step up and ascend, higher and higher, toward the belly of the beast.

It gets lighter the further I go up and eventually I come to the top of the stairs, stepping into a huge torch-lit cavern. In the centre, on a throne of what appears to be solid gold, the Charger sits. His dark eyes look up as I enter and stare into mine a long while before he speaks.

"Hello, Silent Night," he says. "I've been expecting you."

I tremble. "You have?"

"Of course, ever since you disappeared, love. I've always expected you to come back home."

I bristle at the word love and shake my head. "Home? This isn't home."

"Of course it is," he argues. "You grew up here. I—"

"Silence," I snap. "I had a home once, a home I shared with my mother. A home where I was happy, but you tore that all away when you killed her. You shot her in her sleep, you bloody coward!"

The Charger winces. "So you found out then. That's why you left. I thought it was because I asked you to kill Hai."

"Oh, I found out all right and then I wondered to myself, *why* exactly would I kill Hai for you? Why exactly would I do *anything* for you anymore?"

"You have every right to be angry, Silent Night. I won't hold that against you."

"You... Wait. What?" I cock my head at him.

"I said you have every right to be angry."

"Excuse me?"

"I shouldn't have killed your mother and I wouldn't have, if she had upheld her part of the bargain."

"Bargain," I repeat. "What bargain?"

He smiles. "The bargain we made the night you were conceived. I got the child or her life. Yet the foolish woman tried to protect you, tried to keep you from me. In the end, I got both you and her life."

My mind is spinning.

"The night I was conceived?"

Conceived.

The child or her life.

Oh.

Oh God.

"You're lying!" I scream.

"Am I, Silent Night? Why do you think all of the assassins feared you from the time you could hold a blade? Why do you think Anane hates you? Who do you think you get your black hair and sinister tendencies from? It's certainly not from your mother."

Every bone in my body aches as the horrible weight of the truth settles on my shoulders.

The Charger is my father.

CHAPTER FORTY-ONE

My world is crumbling.

I never asked about my father as a child, never cared to know. My mother only told me that he gave me my name and dark hair. That was all she offered and I never asked for more.

Why did it have to be him? Haven't I suffered enough?

"Why?" I demand to know. "Why did you need me so badly? Why couldn't you leave us alone?" My voice drops to a whisper as I try to hold back tears. I think about my mother. I wonder what she ever saw in this monster standing before me.

"Because I needed a successor," he replies, "and my other children, though they had grown, were not up to the task."

The word successor echoes in my head, but I decide to ask something else.

"Other children? I have siblings?"

"Half," he replies, "and we're not talking about them. We're talking about you, my perfect child."

"You—you have no right to call me that!"

"Of course I do. You are my daughter through and through, by blood and by personality. You are the perfect assassin, the perfect one to inherit the Guild."

"I don't want your stupid Guild!" I scream. "I came here to kill you. Don't you understand?"

He laughs. "Oh, I understand perfectly well, daughter, and you're welcome to try, but we both know you can't defeat me, especially with that leg of yours."

I glare at him, drawing my sword defiantly.

I freeze when a new voice intrudes on the silence.

"Maybe she can't defeat you, but she's not alone. Two heads are better than one, I was always told."

The voice sends a piercing stab of pain through my heart.

No. Not him. Not here. Not now.

I never wanted you anywhere near the Charger. You stupid, arrogant...

The Charger's booming laughter interrupts my thoughts. "What's this? A challenge from a Resistance worm? Do you know him, Silent Night? He seems to know you."

I nod my head grimly and turn to face the newcomer.

Armed to the teeth, with his sword drawn, Ajax smiles at me. His blue eyes stare into my soul.

"What the hell are you doing here?" I snap at him, my eyes saying everything I cannot.

I thought you hated me.

442

I don't want you to die.

Don't leave me alone.

"Saving your butt apparently," he replies.

"Well, isn't this lovely," the Charger says. "A friend come to save you, but you won't need saving if you give up your ridiculous vengeance and accept who you are."

My resolve is like steel. "*Never.*"

The Charger sighs. "Very well then." His eyes flick to the corners of the room and his hand flies forward. "Kill them," he snarls.

Assassins stream out of the darkness, at least a dozen of them, and converge on us.

I look at the Charger for a second—*arrogant, dishonourable bastard*—before throwing myself into battle.

Chaos descends quickly. Ajax and I draw our weapons and stand back to back, so as not to get flanked. I sink to a crouch, my injured leg protesting wildly, and face off against the first assassin.

He comes at me with a whirl of daggers. I deflect all that he throws at me and slam my sword against his short, toothpick-like blade. The handle snaps off and he throws it aside in disgust, grabbing for another, but I send my other sword through his chest and he crumples before me.

I hear Ajax fighting behind me and resist the urge to glance in his direction. There are still assassins coming at me.

One jabs his sword at my head while another aims for my heart. I parry both blows with my swords and begin duelling with the two of them, one blade per enemy.

My blades flash and my blood sings.

This is easy.

I run them both through.

Three more wait.

Eager to put this to an end, I sheath my sword and draw my gun.

Three shots ring out; three bodies hit the floor.

Thump, thump, thump.

I turn to help Ajax, but he is surrounded by bodies as well. We face the Charger together.

"Is that all you have?" I ask him.

He smiles wickedly. "Hardly," he snorts. "Who do you take me for? I was just testing."

I sigh. I should have known...

Another wave of enemy soldiers steps out of the dark.

"It's okay," I tell Ajax. "We can do this."

I raise my gun and open fire. Beside me, Ajax does the same. We cut them down like stalks of wheat, but they keep coming.

My mind reminds me of a similar situation, involving a train and enemies for miles...

I shake my head.

No time now.

When I'm down to one bullet, I put my guns back and draw my swords again. Then I carve a path through our enemies.

Stab, block, duck, parry, and slash.

Dodge, jab, and behead.

Blood flies and body after body hits the ground.

Their numbers are waning, but so is my strength. I can't keep this up much longer, not with my leg the way it is.

Damn Hai. I still don't understand how he snuck up on me...

That's it.

I don't know why I didn't do it from the start. I need to pull my vanishing act, disappear into the shadows. I need to be the silent assassin. I need to defeat the Charger with cunning and throw his "perfect assassin" line in his face. I'll sneak up behind him and bury my dagger in his neck, but how can I disappear? He'll notice.

Damn it all. I am Silent Night.

If I can't vanish from plain sight, I don't deserve that title.

Focus.

I keep doing what I'm doing, fighting, cutting down the enemy, but slowly, I move closer and closer to the edge of the room, closer to the shadows. Then, using their bodies as a shield, I step into the dark.

Ah darkness, my old friend.

I shall be a child of darkness once more before I abolish that side of me once and for all.

I slip silent as a wraith through the shadows, creeping ever closer to the Charger's throne.

In the centre of the room, Ajax is still dancing with the enemy, unaware he is now facing them alone. I wonder how long it will take the Charger to notice my absence or if he already has. Regardless, it matters not. I am closing in for the kill and soon he will *notice* cold steel against his skin.

I reach the final stretch and pause in the shadows directly behind the throne. This will be the difficult part. I have to step into the open in order to reach the throne. I'll have to rely on all of my training for this.

Go slow. No sudden movements.

Keep your eyes on the target. If you do nothing out of the ordinary, you should appear almost invisible to most casual observers.

Above all, make not a sound, but I mastered that by the time I was six years old.

Silent as the grave, I creep ever closer to the Charger, who remains unaware of his imminent death. I resist the urge to smile.

One more step.

I draw my dagger and lay it against his throat.

"Surprise, *father,*" I growl.

He doesn't even flinch, but I hear him mouth the words, one and two and...

When he gets to three, I feel the sharp press of metal against my own throat.

"Surprise, *sister,*" a familiar voice coos.

CHAPTER FORTY-TWO

I freeze.

I try to slide my dagger across the Charger's throat, but Hai drags me away, kicking and screaming.

"Let me go, you bastard!" My neck moves dangerously close to his sword with each word.

"*I'm* the bastard?" he scoffs. "You're the one who was trying to stab our dear father in the back." He pries my dagger from my hand.

"It was the throat actually," I retort.

"And I was talking about a figure of speech, sister."

I kick at him. "*Don't* call me that!"

"Why? It's the truth."

I've had enough truths for one day.

"If you were a real brother Hai, you wouldn't have tried to kill me." I stop. "Wait. You're supposed to be dead."

"Not yet, I'm afraid." He taps his chest. "It's a thing called armour. I'd suggest you try it, but sadly, you won't be around for much longer. Now, if you don't mind, I have a Resistance agent to deal with."

My heart skips a beat.

"*No.*"

I kick and scream and claw at him, cursing that he was able to take my dagger. "Leave him *alone*," I snarl.

"Aw... How touching. Our dear Silent Night, fallen in love with the enemy." He grins.

My eyes burn with hatred. "You touch him Hai and so help me..."

"Oh, shut up," he says, throwing me to the floor.

My head bangs against the cement and my ears ring. Despite that, I try to get to my feet, but he places a boot on my leg.

"Get down and stay down," he snaps. Then he presses down until my leg starts to give.

The brace snaps and I feel the fracture grow.

My leg holds on for longer than I thought it would, but then the strain becomes too much. It breaks with a crack and I shriek, tears running down my face as I watch Hai stalk over to Ajax.

I can't think through the pain, but I know I have to because Ajax is in danger and I won't be able to live with myself if he dies.

Get up, I tell myself, but my body won't respond.

Dammit, Night, I scream at myself. *Get the hell up!*

Somehow, I manage to get to all fours, putting absolutely no weight on my now completely broken leg. Still, the pain forces me to take sharp breaths through clenched teeth.

Now get to your feet.

My whole body shakes.

Come on. Ignore the pain. You can do this. For him.

Then a screams tears through the silence.

I'm on my feet faster than you can blink. I whirl in the direction the sound came from, pain blurring my vision.

In the centre of the room, surrounded by bodies, Hai and Ajax stand. Hai is holding Ajax captive, pressing Ajax's arm against his back. Any farther and the arm will snap. I can't let him.

I pull my gun and aim it at Hai. "Let him go, Hai, or breaking his arm will be the last thing you do."

My voice shakes, but I can't help it. My leg pulses like a beating heart. Blood oozes down it, but I can't stop to think of myself. For the first time in a long while, my own life doesn't come first. Ajax's life means more to me. He's done so much for me, brought me out of the dark, the least I can do is keep Hai from extinguishing his light.

Hai looks at me sadly and shakes his head. "We both know you won't do it, sister."

"Shut up!" I snap. "Blood means nothing. Loyalty is determined by whether or not you can trust a person and I don't trust you one bit. I don't care that you're my brother. I don't care that the Charger is my father." I risk a glance in his direction. He still lounges on his throne, watching the three of us with a bemused expression.

"I will kill you both," I go on, "to ensure my freedom and Ajax's freedom and the freedom of the people you've been terrorizing for years. I will put it all to a stop, even if I have to sacrifice myself. That's true loyalty, something the two of you will never be able to understand. The fact that some people in this world come first, before yourself, and that's okay."

I can see tears streaming down Ajax's face.

I'm proud of you, his eyes tell me through the pain.

Hai just laughs. "Well, sister, I do believe you've gone off the deep end. Hardly a perfect assassin, are you?"

"I never was!" I explode, throwing my arms out and exposing my tattoos. They seem to flicker in the torchlight. "See these names, Hai? These are the names of every single person I've assassinated, and they're not trophies. They're scars, reminders of the pain I've caused, the lives I've destroyed. I regret every single one. I only killed to survive, in the hopes that one day it would all be better, that Haven would change from the dark place it's always been. So when I learned how my mother really died, I went straight to the Resistance. I betrayed all of you. I told them where to find the Guild. I coordinated everything. I made sure I would be the one to come and find the Charger. Do you still want me as your successor, father, traitor that I am?"

I whip my head in the direction of the throne, but he is no longer there.

A cold hand settles on my shoulder.

"Oh, Silent Night," the Charger says from behind me, his breath tickling my ear. I shudder at his touch. "Of *course* you betrayed us. I knew where you were all along. I knew who you had gone to, what you were planning. I knew you would come back. It was all part of *my* plan. Everything can be forgiven, daughter, if you would but perform one simple task."

450

I do not want to be forgiven by this man, but I still wonder.

"And what might that be?" I ask.

"Well," he whispers, so Ajax and Hai can no longer hear him, "originally, I thought it would be fun to watch you kill your brother, but since that lovely Resistance agent showed up..." He trails off, letting me fill in the rest.

No.

"It's a small request, Silent Night," he goes on, "kill the Resistance agent and I will forgive your transgressions. You will return to your rightful place as my successor. I'll even promote you to Agent One. Isn't that what you've always wanted?"

Once. Once that had been my goal, but not anymore.

"Kill him, daughter," the Charger says, "and I'll let you live."

Ah, there it is.

I'd been waiting for him to throw that, to let loose the demon writhing behind his cool, calm facade.

Even still, my answer is the same. I won't sacrifice Ajax to save my own skin.

"Father, I..."

"Go on."

"Father, I'm sorry, but I can't be the person you want me to be."

He stiffens.

I raise my gun again and shoot Hai in the head. He crumples to the floor and Ajax falls free, landing on his knees beside the body.

The Charger's hand closes around my throat.

"Insolent child," he hisses. "I would've given you the world. You would've been respected by all, challenged by none, and you throw it all away for what, a boy? Foolish girl."

"No," I gasp as his fingers close tighter. "That life would've given me nothing but despair. I threw it away in favour of happiness, and love, and freedom, three things you could *never* give me."

His fingers cinch even tighter.

I can't breathe.

"It's a pity your mother died in vain," he spits at me, but she didn't.

She died trying to keep me safe, the me she loved, and I'm still here. I survived. Even as my lungs strain for oxygen and my vision blurs, I smile.

Somehow, I've won.

CHAPTER FORTY-THREE

I don't know how long I'm out, but eventually I feel myself waking up. Though there's a slight pain in my chest with each intake, my breathing seems normal.

Then the pain in my leg comes back and my eyes fly open.

I'm sitting on a metal grate in an inch of water, my clothes already sopping wet. My back rests against a solid wall and across from me, leaning against the glass of our small prison is Ajax.

Despite our circumstances, he smiles at me. "Hey," he says, "I was afraid you weren't going to wake up."

I don't smile back.

"Jax," I breathe, "what happened to your face?" Huge purple and black bruises mar his once-perfect skin and my heart aches to see him in such a state.

He shrugs. "The Charger roughed me up a bit after you passed out and then he threw us both in here."

"I'm going to kill him," I hiss.

"Good luck with that," he sighs. "We can't get out."

"It's a glass tank," I reply, standing shakily, "surely there's a way."

"There isn't, Silent," he assures me, "I already tried." Slowly, he holds out his left hand. It's a broken, bloody mess. His knuckles are shattered, fingers lying limp.

It doesn't take me long to find where his blood spatters the glass.

"Jax," I whisper. "You shouldn't have..."

He trembles. "I was just trying to get us out. I don't want either of us to die like this. We have so much life left to live..." His voice breaks into a sob and he turns away from me.

I put a hand on his shoulder. "Jax, why did you come after me? I thought you hated me."

"I thought I hated you too," he admits. "Maybe it was the pain talking, maybe it wasn't. I don't know what I think now, but I knew I couldn't let you die after what we said to each other before you left." He turns around and looks me in the eye. "It's not all forgiven, Silent, I'd be lying if I said that, but there's hope. I came here to tell you that and to fight by your side. To save you or to go down with you. Am I crazy? Probably, but there's still a part of me in there that doesn't want to let you out of my sight again."

It's my turn to cry, silent tears running down my cheeks. "You're beautiful, you know that, right?" I whisper.

He says nothing, but he wipes away my tears with his thumb.

I lean into him and he wraps his arms around my waist, resting his chin on my head.

In the silence that follows, I hear water trickling. Startled, I look down and gasp. Jax and I are now standing in water up to our calves and it's still rising.

"Jax," I say, "look."

"Oh God," he gasps.

We break apart and frantically begin beating at the glass walls. We ignore the pain in our tired limbs as we slam them against the glass over and over again. Bruises blossom on my skin, but I keep going, desperate to escape, to live, to not die this way. The water rises faster and faster and the glass shows no sign of weakness. I'd sink to my knees if that wouldn't put me up to my shoulders in water.

"Jax," I gasp, tears blurring my vision. "What are we going to do? I don't want t-to die. I don't want you to die because of me. This is all my fault." Horrible sobs wrack my body.

"Hey," he says, "it's okay. Don't cry. I... I wouldn't have wanted it any other way, than to die by your side, to die fighting."

My tears fall faster.

We stand in silence for a moment as the water continues to rise. It's up to our waists now. I splay my hand across the glass, wishing it wasn't real, that it is just a horrible nightmare and we will soon wake up safe in our beds, but I know I am wishing for the impossible.

This is real and we're going to drown in a glass tank. There's no hope left for us.

I make a decision. I have to tell him. I owe him at least that much after everything we've gone through.

"Quinn," I gasp as the water reaches my elbows.

"What?" Jax asks.

"My name is Quinn," I reply. "I figure you might as well know now, since neither of us are going to live to tell this tale."

"Don't say that." He's quiet for a minute and then he says, "Quinn. I like it. It suits you."

"Thanks."

He smiles and says, "I love you, Quinn."

I don't hesitate this time. "I love you too, Ajax."

All of a sudden, it's like a wall has been smashed between us and we can't get to each other fast enough. He kisses my purple lips with his and I kiss him back harder, even as our teeth chatter and our whole bodies shake. We pull ourselves as close as we can get.

The water rises around us, but we don't care. We may be dying, but we have each other and that's all we need to know. I'm content knowing I won't die as Silent Night, but as Quinn, the innocent girl I knew was inside me all along.

To be continued in...

Sacred Ruse

THANK YOU

Thank you so much for reading! I hope you enjoyed the first book of my Guild Trilogy and that you are looking forward to the next installment. Please consider leaving a review on Amazon and/or Goodreads. I look forward to hearing your thoughts!

ACKNOWLEDGEMENTS

First, I want to say thank you to my significant other, Allan, who hasn't been with me through the whole journey of this book, but who never once doubted that I could publish it and be an author.

Second, to my sister, who listened to all my rants.

Third to my parents for nurturing my imagination.

Fourth to my IRL writing buddy, Coyote Newell who is my sounding board for any and all ideas. You will forever be an asset my dude.

I also want to thank Koral Lambert, William McGinn, and Claire Allore, three friends who read this book in its first draft and gave invaluable feedback. Thank you so much for reading Silent Night when it was a rubbish pile and finding the diamond tucked inside it.

Thank you to my amazing Critique Partner, Taylor, who seriously took Silent Night to the next level and has given me so much support over the endless months of revision, editing, beta readers, and so much more. You rock.

Speaking of Beta Readers, thank you to Rachel Cole, Paige Engling, Stevie Hayden, James Matthews, Mickey Miles, and Emily Weisenburger. For those of you who were only able to read part of it: your feedback was still used and much appreciated :) .

Eternal gratitude for my cover designer, Rena Hoberman over at coverquill.com. I still can't get over how gorgeous this cover is!

Big thanks to Nicki Richards who edited my book. Thank God I had her to fix all my em-dashes and to point out that my one character rips the sleeves off what was already a sleeveless top. *face palms* Check her out at Richard's Corrections.

Shoutout to the writing community over on Instagram. I would've lost my sanity as a writer a long time ago if not for my writer friends there. I wish I could name everyone, but I do want to mention Amie Mcnee @inspiredtowrite for her endless motivational posts, Bethany Atazadeh for her well of self-publishing knowledge, Rebecca K. Sampson for always believing in everyone, and Bruna Reis, for the Pondering Writer Retreat.

Last, but not least, thank you to *you*, my readers. I know you read this in every book, but you're the reason I do this. I write stories to get them out of my head, but also to be read by others. I hope that I can help someone with my words, that I can empower people with the unique worlds and characters I create. I can't wait to see where this journey goes, and I hope you come along for the ride.

ASSASSINS BELOW

Guess what? I have a present for you. As a thank you for reading the whole book – and perusing the end matter – I would like to invite you to the Guild Trilogy page on my website. This page gives you access to aesthetics, character art, deleted scenes, and much more to come soon. Normally, you have to sign up for my newsletter to receive the password, but here it is: AssassinsBelow.

Interested in that Newsletter? You can sign up via my website which I will put below. I send monthly updates on writing, releases, my own reads, and more! Membership gives you access to my Members page which has my Writing Advice Column and list of favourite writerly resources. (Hint: it's the same password as above)

emmacouetteauthor.com

ABOUT THE AUTHOR

Emma Couette **is a** Canadian wordsmith whose second passion is wood working. She has written a few award-winning short stories and dabbles in poetry when the inspiration strikes her. Her dreams include travelling the world, being a mom, and owning a small library. *Silent Night* is her debut novel, the first of many adventures.

Made in the USA
Middletown, DE
23 August 2021

45938965R00279